# Praise for
# *Lauraine Snelling*

## Heaven Sent Rain

"Snelling's story has the potential to be a big hit...The alternating narrators make the tale diverse and well-rounded. The premise of the story is interesting and the prose is very moving."

**—RT Book Reviews**

## Wake the Dawn

"Snelling (*One Perfect Day*) continues to draw fans with her stellar storytelling skills. This time she offers a look at small-town medical care in a tale that blends healing, love, and a town's recovery...Snelling's description of events at the small clinic during the storm is not to be missed."

**—Publishers Weekly**

"Snelling's fast-paced novel has characters who seek help in the wrong places. It takes a raging storm for them to see that the help they needed was right in front of them the whole time. This is a strong, believable story."

**—RT Book Reviews**

"Lauraine Snelling's newest novel will keep you turning pages and not wanting to put the book down...*Wake the Dawn* is a guaranteed good read for any fiction lover."
**—Cristel Phelps, *Retailers and Resources Magazine***

# Reunion

"Inspired by events in Snelling's own life, *Reunion* is a beautiful story about characters discovering themselves as the foundation of their family comes apart at the seams. Readers may recognize themselves or someone they know within the pages of this book, which belongs on everyone's keeper shelf."
**—*RT Book Reviews***

"*Reunion* is a captivating tale that will hook you from the very start...Fans of Christian fiction will love this touching story."
**—FreshFiction.com**

"Snelling's previous novels (*One Perfect Day*) have been popular with readers, and this one, loosely based on her own life, will be no exception."
**—*Publishers Weekly***

# On Hummingbird Wings

"Snelling can certainly charm."
**—*Publishers Weekly***

# One Perfect Day

"Snelling writes about the foibles of human nature with keen insight and sweet honesty."

**—National Church Library Association**

"Snelling's captivating tale will immediately draw readers in. The grief process is accurately portrayed, and readers will be enthralled by the raw emotion of Jenna's and Nora's accounts."

**—*RT Book Reviews***

"[A] spiritually challenging and emotionally taut story. Fans of Christian women's fiction will enjoy this winning novel."

**—*Publishers Weekly***

# Someday Home

*A Novel*

## Lauraine Snelling

New York • Boston • Nashville

FaithWords
Hachette Book Group
1290 Avenue of the Americas
New York, NY 10104

www.faithwords.com

Printed in the United States of America

RRD-C

First Edition: July 2015
10 9 8 7 6 5 4 3 2 1

FaithWords is a division of Hachette Book Group, Inc.
The FaithWords name and logo are trademarks of Hachette Book Group, Inc.

The Hachette Speakers Bureau provides a wide range of authors for speaking events. To find out more, go to www.hachettespeakersbureau.com or call (866) 376-6591.

Library of Congress Cataloging-in-Publication Data
Snelling, Lauraine.
  Someday home : a novel / Lauraine Snelling. -- First edition.
    pages ; cm
  ISBN 978-1-4555-8620-2 (softcover) -- ISBN 978-1-4789-0418-2 (audio download) -- ISBN 978-1-4789-3406-6 (audio book) 1. Older women--Fiction. 2. Female friendship--Fiction. I. Title.
PS3569.N39S65 2015
813'.54--dc23
                                                    2015010925

*To Ellie and Pippa, who shared stories with me of their history and how they came to share their home. I see them as true Renaissance women and I love to visit them.*

# Someday Home

# Chapter One

M om, I think you should sell this house, this place, make life easier for yourself."

Marlynn Lundberg, simply Lynn to those around her, stared at her elder son, Phillip. He looked so much like his father sometimes she had to jerk herself back to reality. Well, like his father twenty years ago and less one slight paunch that had crept on over the years. "Why would I do that?"

"Well, with Dad gone and money tight as it is, if you sold this you'd have some money to invest and provide for yourself. We could build you a smaller place next to our house. We have plenty enough land to subdivide, you know, like you and Dad talked about doing someday."

"Wait. What do you mean, 'next to'? The only thing separating your house and this one is a cow pasture, and it's less than ten acres."

"Well, yeah. Tom and I were talking about it; we're thinking right beside. And we could build a breezeway between them. Then you and the kids could visit without going out in the weather." He scrubbed his chin with two fingers, another trait of Paul's.

Paul, who had gone to work on plumbing a new house for a change, not just repairing older plumbing, which was most of their bread and butter. And dropped dead before noon.

Just keeled over; the doc said an aneurysm blew. They'd never known he'd even had an aneurysm. He'd been the picture of a healthy, robust man who loved his family, his Lord, and his work, the order depending on the day. Paul, whom she had loved since she was sixteen in high school and he returned on leave from his four-year stint in the army. He'd been a good friend of her older brother Swen, so not a stranger, but four years' difference was a big one when you were sixteen and your father said you could not date anyone in the military.

The thought of selling the place made her teeth gnash and grind. But she did the books for both personal and the plumbing business. Between Phillip, the eldest, and Tom, the middle child, the business was outwardly successful, but supporting three families took a lot of pipes and toilets and sinks. Just like it always had.

Lynn wagged her head. "There must be some other way."

"I sure hope so, but I think we need to be realistic here." Arms crossed over his chest, butt against the island counter-top, and his third cup of coffee in one hand, he studied his mother.

Lynn hated to be studied by anyone but especially by one of her kids, of which there were three, all adults, and two of which had already provided grandchildren. Paul totally believed the old adage, *Had I known grandchildren would be so much fun, I'da had them first.* Paul and Lynn had been good grandparents. They'd been good parents, too, thank the good Lord, one of Paul's favorite sayings.

Their mostly perfect life ended the day he dropped dead.

"Mom, you're woolgathering again. You aware how much you do that?" Phillip took a sip of his coffee, made a face, dumped the remainder in the sink, and refilled from the carafe that kept coffee hot.

Maybe yes, maybe no, her awareness, that is. At times grief did strange things to one's mental stability. "I do know one thing for sure—well, other than God is in His heaven and…" She had to stop. She used to finish that line with "and all is right with the world." But that wasn't so true any longer or at least those times that missing Paul broadsided her like an eighteen-wheeler. In a skid. On ice.

She sucked in a breath and blew it out, rounding her cheeks to make it blow better, a trick she had learned through the grieving. Her shoulders dropped but at least her legs kept sturdy. She swallowed and started again. "Your dad and I promised each other we would keep this place for our kids and our grandkids. No matter what happens in this messed-up world, you would all always have a place to come back to, a place that could at least provide food and haven no matter what else was going on."

She watched him sigh and wag his head. "Phillip, we are not in arrears on anything; there is money in the bank, albeit not a great deal; the business, while not growing like we'd appreciate, is still keeping us all busy; we are healthy, and I don't ever want to have this discussion again. Not with you, not with your brother." She kept her voice even, in spite of the trembling that seized her mind and body. She did not leap across the counter and shake him until his teeth rattled or bang her head against one of the log walls. Or run screaming down to the dock and throw herself in the calm waters of Lake Barnett. Had any of those things worked or she became seriously demented, the latter of which was the most possible, she might have given them a try. Especially in the dark nights when the empty bed, the empty closet, or her empty arms overwhelmed her.

Those nights when God seemed an impossible dream, and alone was the only sound she heard.

She asked, "Does Travis have baseball today?" She loved the way Phillip's older son took everything so earnestly.

"No, but he and Davey are playing catch in the backyard, practicing." Phillip shrugged and set his coffee mug in the sink. "You realize, if you lived right next door over there, you'd already know that. I'll tell Tom we're not selling the heavy equipment after all." The grin he sent her over his shoulder made her pick up a dish towel and throw it at him.

She missed Phillip, who ducked aside and left, but almost got Miss Minerva, who was just padding into the kitchen. The cinnamon tiger with fluffy fur leaped up onto the counter and stared at her.

"Sorry, Minerva. I didn't mean you." She stroked Minerva from ears to tail a couple times, currying forgiveness. Tom and Phillip seemed to be in agreement. What about their little sister, Lillian, who seemed to love her career—teaching—that she had embarked on just before her father died? Lillian, the apple of her father's eye. And Lynn's. And now her father would not be there to walk his daughter down the aisle, if and when she got around to marrying.

*Stop it! Just stop it!* Lynn slammed her coffee cup on the counter. The cup shattered, coffee with cream flew up and out, raining on counters, sink, cupboards, the floor, and the front of her white T-shirt. Her new white T-shirt with the HAPPY BIRTHDAY, GRANDMA and their signatures on the front. The one given to her by her grandkids, who had painted the front with their handprints in various bright colors of paint. And now coffee spotted.

Tears not only rained down her cheeks, but also spurted from her eyes like a spring in full spate. Sobs drove her into the laundry room, where she pulled the shirt over her head, sprayed it with stain remover, and ran cold water into the machine to let it soak. "Please, Lord, don't let my shirt be ruined. Please! Please!" She slammed the lid of the machine and sank down on the bench in the combination laundry and mudroom, where everyone sat to pull off their boots before tramping on her kitchen floor. Collapsing forward, she hugged her knees, the sobs ripping her apart.

A cold, wet nose and a warm tongue took care of her ear, her neck, and bare shoulder since she cowered in her bra and jeans. *Stop this, you old fool.* Calling herself names did nothing to stem the onslaught. One would think in the year of many tears she'd have learned she could not stop it with cruel words to herself or anyone else, God included. The only way was through.

Orson, the rapidly aging yellow Lab who had been Paul's hunting dog and constant companion, had grieved right along with her. But in his doggy wisdom, he had accepted the inevitable and sort of switched his allegiance to Lynn. She thought she had accepted the inevitable as well, until some little thing happened, usually something stupid, and she melted into a puddle of pity. Self-pity—the disgusting kind.

One year. One year and nine months ago. She should be over this by now. The shaking abated, but instantly, she was drenching wet and not from the tears. With nothing left but her bra, she should be shivering. But no—she was on fire. What was wrong now? Instinctively she started toward her favorite chair in front of the wall of windows overlooking the lake, but then sat back down on the floor. Out on the deck was cooler. She got up again and went out there.

*In your bra?* This time her mind screamed at her. Good heavens, who cared? Well, anyone boating or canoeing by on the lake, anyone who came around to the deck or the front door on the south side of the house. Wrapping her arms around the gray-muzzled, arthritic dog, she dried another wave of tears on his soft ears and let him lick whatever he felt needed fixing. But cold April showers hit about as fast as her own drenching. She went back inside to the mudroom.

A knock at the door ten feet from her and "Mom?" announced her daughter-in-law Margaret Marie, trained nurse and mother of three of her grandchildren. Lynn grabbed for any shirt that peopled the line of wooden pegs on the wall, above the cubbyholes for boots, garden shoes, and whatever, that had been a godsend when they put them in. All three of the children had given up and kept boots and schoolbooks in the assigned cubbies. She crammed her arms into the sleeves of a denim shirt and with her back to the door, buttoning as Maggie closed the door behind her.

"You're crying."

"How do you know?" One button refused to slide into the hole. The urge to rip the entire shirt off and fling it against the wall made her sniff.

"The ceiling is raining?"

Lynn left the button at her chest undone and, finger combing the sides of her hair back so they were no longer tear glued to her cheeks, shrugged. "You are too perceptive for your own good." She cleared her throat and felt a tender hand on her shoulder. "Please don't do that." The tears blinded her again.

"That bad, eh?" The hand left and two arms came around her and gathered her close to a tall, slim shoulder that had absorbed tears before. She just held Lynn and let her cry, then pulled a tissue from a box on top of the cubbies. Lynn had learned to keep tissues everywhere. "Here. How about a cup of tea?"

"The kitchen is a mess."

"Your kitchen is never a mess."

"Then you better grab a broom and a mop, because that stupid mug shattered instead of just breaking the handle."

"I see. Mug of what?"

"Coffee with cream. And if it permanently stains my new T-shirt..." She sniffed and blew her nose again.

"We'll make you a new one, Mom, no big deal." They moved into the kitchen and Maggie burst into laughter that bounced around the pine cabinets and off the tongue-and-groove pine ceiling. Miss Minerva was up on the counter, daintily licking at the spilled coffee. At least she was nowhere near broken crockery.

"Shoo!" Maggie tipped Minerva off the counter and the cat darted away. "You weren't kidding, Mom. What set this off?"

Lynn grabbed the broom. "Let me get the glass swept up before we grind it into the floor."

"I reiterate, what happened?"

"Nothing, at least nothing big or worthy of the onslaught, but..."

"But...?" Nearly as tall as Phillip at six feet, Maggie leaned her rear against the counter and watched Lynn sweep. Finding the dustpan, she looked into the sink. "I'll get the glass out of there before we mop." She grabbed several paper towels off the roll hanging under the cabinet, and after picking up the bigger pieces, she used the wet towels to catch the smaller shards. "There's some on the counter, too."

Between them, they cleaned up the mess. "Good thing Orson didn't come over here."

"I know. But he was out on the deck and came through his doggy door when he heard me crying." Lynn stood back and studied the floor against the light to see if anything glittered. "There's coffee in the carafe."

"Tea sounds better." Maggie filled the royal-blue teakettle and set it on the gas stove. With the burner lit, she fetched the china teapot from the cupboard and two teacups with saucers. "Today you need some extra beauty in your life." She smiled at the two dainty teacups, one with lavender pansies, the other with violets. "I'm so glad you have kept these out to use instead of sticking them in the china cabinet like Grandma did."

"She was keeping them for a special occasion."

"So, what made an occasion special enough? A visit from the Queen of England?"

"No, Norway."

When the two sat down to tea, cleaning out the cookie jar of ginger and molasses cookies, Maggie watched her good friend, let alone relative, closely.

Lynn poured the orange and spice tea into the cups and set the pot down. "You're giving me the nurse look."

"I know. I think it's time you went and saw Dr. Eleanor. You are right, you're not yourself."

"I have too much to do to be sick."

"Or ailing at all. Your life has been turned upside down, you know."

*And sometimes I feel stomped right into the ground,* but how did one explain that to a doctor, who was more percep- tive than many. She had switched to a female doctor sev- eral years earlier, after Dr. Gregson retired and she wasn't thrilled with the younger man who had bought the practice.

"Are you sleeping all right?"

"Most of the time." But not the night before. Both night- mares and a wet bed, not an accident in the bed, but a sweaty body, woke her up. The two often seemed to go hand in hand. And she woke in the morning, dragging herself out of bed. Maybe that was why she was so weepy.

"So have the kids told you they're counting the weeks until school is out?"

The change of subject caught her by surprise. "Not yet. But I'm getting all the details about baseball. Not Miss Priss, of course."

"Of course not." Maggie stirred sugar into her tea. "She has no interest in sports, as you well know. She told me today that she wants to be a ballerina."

Lynn smiled. When they had prayed for a girl, God gave them one who had no intentions of copying her brothers. She let them know it in no uncertain terms. With two brothers and two boy cousins, she went outside the family for a best friend. Good thing Beth lived right across Lower Lake Road. Since they lived out in the country, two miles from the almost town of Barnett and ten from Detroit Lakes, there were not a lot of other kids close by.

"You will call Dr. Eleanor, right? You tell Mrs. Teller that you need to see her sooner rather than later."

"Yes, ma'am."

Maggie could be such a bossy daughter-in-law. And infinitely loving.

After Maggie left, Lynn scheduled an appointment in two days. Then recovered from her jag, she sat down in her home office with a cup of tea and attacked the books for the plumbing business.

Here again, Paul came back to mind and strongly. He knew that a plumbing business takes up lots of space, so he bought enough acreage for his house and the plumbing business and land for the future, as well. True, the plumber does not bring work into a shop; they work on the customer's site. Still, the company needed a pipe yard for keeping long lengths of PVC pipe, septic tanks, terra-cotta pipe for septic systems, enough room to park trucks and heavy equipment, and somewhere to house the office and inventory.

First, right on the shore of Barnett Lake, he built the lovely two-story farmhouse with long verandas and plenty of yard to play in; his family needed a home. At the other end of the large property he erected a galvanized building larger than he needed and soon filled it anyway. The pipe and equipment yards were screened off with dense shrubs; that was Lynn's idea. The office that had been partitioned off inside the huge shed became too small for all the paper and files, so now they lay about in stacks and baskets. But Annie, their part-time helper, and Lynn both knew exactly where everything was and could find any document needed.

The business was truly a family affair. Often Lynn was the voice on the phone when people called for help, making the appointments and running down one or the other of the boys when an emergency arose. Annie often had to deal with family emergencies, and she knew Lynn would step in.

Sometimes it seemed that running the business herself was easier than dealing with employees, but Phillip and Tom insisted she not spend all her days at the office in the metal building. Now computers could make working out of her home much easier; her home computer and those in the work office were linked. So was the phone line. It was all so smooth, until it decided on its own to give her fits; that is when she wanted to discipline the infernally opinionated machines with a baseball bat.

She pondered all this a few moments as she turned her back on the wall of bushes and trees hiding their livelihood from view and gazed out over the peaceful lake. Then she buried herself in the accounting for the last two months. She hated getting behind.

At two she took the bag of frozen cookie dough out of the

freezer and set the cookies on sheets to thaw so she could bake them just before the grands got home from school. They had an unerring radar that told them when G'ma had baked cookies for them. That sense saved her the job of running a flag up a pole or something.

Hearing a strange sound, she glanced around her office. Orson was not in either of his usual places, right by her chair or asleep on the dog bed. He'd had to give up sleeping in the recliner because his back legs just didn't lift him that high any longer.

"Orson?"

Another noise, a whimper, *what?* She found him in the mudroom, lying on his side right in front of the door. A puddle on the floor was her first clue something was very wrong.

"Oh, Orson." Only the tip of his tail moved. "Oh no." The tears broke through immediately. She dropped to her knees beside him. He tried to lift his head but even that effort was too much. The whimper again.

"How do I get you to the car?" She leaned closer and spoke into his ear, petting him all the while. His breathing was slow and shallow. His legs twitched, but would not obey, or could not.

Where were the guys? Off on a job. She hit speed dial for the office. "Annie, can you come help me carry Orson to the car. He can't get up."

"I'll be right there."

Lynn grabbed a blanket out of the cupboard and rolled it up beside Orson's back. When Annie burst in the door, together they lifted the dog up enough to roll out the blanket under him; then Lynn threw her purse over her shoulder, and together they lifted him and carried him to the van.

"You want me to go with you?"

"No, someone needs to be here when the kids get off

the bus. I saw Maggie leave for her shift at the hospital, so no one is there. Turn off the oven, please. I didn't get the cookies baked. Call Dr. Knight's office and tell him I'm on my way."

At least the vet was in Barnett, not clear in Detroit Lakes. Talking to the dog all the way, she spun gravel in the vet's driveway and parked at the back door.

Dr. Knight came out and joined her at the rear of the van. She clicked the door open as she said, "He can't move."

One of Dr. Knight's volunteer assistants came out and stood beside him. Lynn could not remember the boy's name.

But they didn't even bother to carry Orson inside. After a quick check of vitals and reflexes, Dr. Knight looked at her, shaking his head. "I'm so sorry, Lynn, but I think this is it. We could shoot him up and you could take him home again, but very soon…" He stopped and wagged his head, stroking the old dog all the while. "I think it would be a lot easier on him if we put him down right now."

"I figured." Lynn ignored her tears and crawled up in the van. She laid her cheek against her furry friend. "Time to go see Paul. I'm sure he's waiting for you on the other side of the bridge." She sat and raised his head to her lap. He licked her hand, staring at her with trusting eyes. He sighed and was gone within seconds of the injection in his leg.

Dr. Knight smiled sadly. "I'm sorry, Lynn, so sorry. He was a magnificent pooch. And a good friend, I know. Do you want to take him home to bury him or shall I cremate him?"

"Cremate him. I'll scatter his ashes on the lake like we did Paul."

"Okay. You want some more time with him?"

"No, he's gone." She laid Orson's head back down and

scooted out of the van so that the young assistant could step forward and pick him up.

"I'm so sorry, my friend." Dr. Knight hugged her. "You want someone to drive you home?"

"No, thanks. I'll be okay." At the first turn out, she pulled over and dissolved into tears all over again.

# Chapter Two

The entire family but for Lillian gathered at the big house for supper and a sob fest. A friend was gone, and like Grampy, Orson was not coming back. He'd gone over the bridge. When people or animals or anything else died, there was no coming back. If G'ma said it once, she said it ten times. So did Phillip. Each of Phillip's children talked with their mother, who pretty much said the same thing as the others.

After they went home, Lynn left the dessert dishes in the sink and staggered up to her room on the north side of the loft. Surely the well of tears would be drained dry by now. Until she saw Miss Minerva curled in the middle of the bed as if waiting for her.

"The dog is gone and now you can come up here, is that it?"

The cat yawned wide, pink tongue curling, surrounded by very sharp and very white teeth. Minerva finished her stretch, all four legs, claws extended and retracted as she relaxed. And purred, eyes slitted, the pink interior of her ears nearly transparent against the lamplight.

Lynn fought to keep her eyes off the dog bed waiting at the foot of the bed. She should have asked Phillip or Tom to gather up Orson's beds, toys, and bones, but she'd not thought of it. Tomorrow she would wash and pack everything away in a box on the chance that there might be another dog living here sometime. Her eyes brimmed, but other than making her nose run, the storm may have subsided.

She changed into her jammies in the bathroom as always, threw her dirty clothes in the hamper, and wrapped herself in her robe. Resolutely she kept her gaze from straying to the other side of the bed. She'd even thought of moving into one of the other bedrooms, but after two years, surely she didn't need to do that now.

Propping the pillows against the oak headboard, lamp lit on the stand beside the bed, she climbed up on the high bed and scooted her backside into the pillows. She'd found her reading habits had changed, too. No more gore, psychotically evil villains, coarse language, downers in general. Cozy mysteries, heroic biographies, whatever book her reading group had chosen for the month and a good devotional and teaching of some kind or another were now her reading materials of choice. She had loved dog, horse—well, general animal stories starting when she could first read page one and kept on reading. A lot of other people must be saying the same thing, because there was a plethora of animal stories available both in print and e-books.

Before Paul left, she'd volunteered at the library in Detroit Lakes, but since, she'd not had the energy. Coping with life and the family business seemed to take far longer than it used to. Tired. She was bone-aching tired. But sleepy? No. Burning eyes from all the tears, yes, but...She opened her latest book, flipped to the bookmark, and settled in to read. That was another difference; she could read in bed without feeling guilty that she was disturbing Paul. It used to be that she would read in her leather recliner downstairs and come up when she was finally sleepy. He would roll over and mumble good night, having gone to bed after the news.

No snoring. Orson always snored and snorted when he dreamed he was chasing. Paul had snuffled but that was more comforting than disturbing. No bedroom noise allowed her to hear an owl hoot. A dog barked, probably at Phillip's; his hunting dogs liked to bay if the coyotes started to sing. Orson used to but hadn't been able to hear them the last couple of years.

She tipped back her head. Another hole in her heart. Some might say, "Only a dog," but somehow Orson had been a living connection with Paul. Tonight it felt like the two holes in her heart were bleeding into each other.

Phillip had offered to come back after Maggie got home, but she'd declined, sorry now that he'd not done what he wanted.

Alone in the house, this big, solid house. The refrigerator kicked on. The owl did another flyby. *Lord, I know you are here, but right now . . .* A furry paw tapped her hand and a whiskered nose nudged her fingers. She rubbed the cat under her chin and the purr chugged into a gentle rumble. Miss Minerva turned around and curled right into her side so Lynn not only heard her, but also felt the vibrations.

She laid her book aside, read her *Jesus Calling* for the day, and rolling on her side, one hand petting the cat, she slipped into a peaceful sleep. The strange ways by which God provided slipped through her mind.

The next morning she was fine until her feet hit the floor and a cold black nose did not come to rest on her knees. No thumping tail, no whimper to say, *Good morning, let's go for a walk.* Fighting back the tears—again, she stumbled through her morning routine—and after dressing (which took some serious self-talk; the bed had looked so inviting, or at least oblivion did), she made her way down the split-log stairs and into the kitchen, where the cat was sniffing the dog dish, water bowl, and then looking out the window to the deck.

"I know, my friend, he's gone and he's not coming back, until we scatter his ashes on the lake, just like we did not so long ago."

Miss Minerva left her window spot and came to twine her supple self around Lynn's legs. Each meow seemed to end on a question mark.

Lynn leaned over and, picking her up, she tucked the cat under her chin and went to the window to look out over the lake. A silver trace of fog hovered over the water, soon to be dispelled by the sun that would leap into the day track any moment. She waited. There was something infinitely refreshing and restorative to see that first moment when the golden rim backlit the trees beyond the lake. While the land wasn't flat, like the Red River Valley not too far to the west, the hills could be called gentle and rolling. People from places like Colorado and Vermont often snorted at even calling the terrain hilly.

She sniffed and, blinking, blotted her tears with the cat's head. That was just enough time for the sun to catapult, as if shot with a heavenly slingshot, into the new day. The fragrance of coffee floated from the kitchen and the burble of the coffeemaker ceased with a hiss. "When do you think the loons will be back?" she asked the limp form in her arms, to be answered by a purr rumble.

Miss Minerva never minded being carried around, which was a good thing, since Miss Priss dressed the cat along with her dolls and carried them around. The dolls she dragged by an arm until she was large enough to hold them. The cat, while compliant, had never permitted dragging.

The return of the loons always meant winter was truly gone and spring had dug in to stay. The two seasons habitually argued through the month of April and sometimes even into May. Snow was not an unknown on Mother's Day and even later. But this year spring had arrived early. Lynn poured her coffee, fetched cottage cheese and applesauce from the fridge, and plopped the toaster down with her usual two slices of bread. While she used to make full breakfasts for her family, after Paul died, bacon and eggs and all the trimmings were only for company times. She couldn't count how long since she'd made Paul's favorite coffee cake or waffles or even omelets. Maybe it was time she invited the grands for a real Saturday breakfast before she lost her touch with pancakes from scratch. While generally not considering herself a snob, she insisted that real pancakes, and also pickle relish and coffee, be made from scratch. Mixes were good for many things but not the three aforementioned.

She spread the cottage cheese on the toast, broiled it to hot, and layered homemade applesauce over the top, one of her favorite breakfasts and even good for her. She'd learned the idea years earlier at a Weight Watchers' class. Taking her breakfast out to the leather recliner facing the lake, she sat down, waited for Miss Minerva to make herself comfortable, and leaning her head back, she closed her eyes.

"Lord, I am having a hard time thanking you for this morning, but you said you appreciate praises, especially when they are a sacrifice. Lately, so much of what I used to love to do has become a sacrifice. Forgive me please, and I do thank you for the beauty of the lake this and every morning, for this furry critter on my lap, for food to eat and even the desire to fix it. I hope Paul and Orson are playing fetch together and enjoying their reunion. I know you know how much I miss them. Did you miss your Son like this when He visited hell in those three days?" She sniffed and heaved a sigh. "Thank you for not letting me go. At least I know that you don't change. Thanks again. Amen."

She dug a tissue out of her plaid flannel shirt pocket, and after blowing her nose, she picked up her rapidly cooling coffee. Elbows propped on the leather arms, she sipped, sniffed, and when she realized that her mind was ambling back along the memory road, she jerked it to the present, set the coffee cup down, and attacked her breakfast. Sitting here like this was too dangerous.

"Get moving!"

Miss Minerva jumped to the floor, throwing a disgusted look over her shoulder.

"Sorry. I didn't mean you. What is on my list for today?" If she didn't keep lists, she would mess up and not get something, or sometimes anything, important done for the day. That was another one of those frustrating things; she'd never been forgetful like this. Surely she couldn't be slipping into dementia, not at fifty-two.

The next afternoon after a brief wait and a close scrutiny from Dr. Eleanor Alstrop, accompanied by a plethora of questions, she got dressed again and joined Dr. Eleanor in her office. Taking the chair, Lynn mentally prepared herself for bad news; she was getting very, very good at that, what with all her experience. No way could she feel this cruddy without something major.

"Menopause?"

"Why are you so surprised? You have all the symptoms, and you're fifty-two; plenty of other women have it start in their late forties." The doctor templed her fingers and smiled at Lynn over the tips. "Didn't you suspect?"

"Obviously not."

"But you've been skipping periods?"

"Well, yes, but that was just a relief." She reminded herself to drop her shoulders; the tension was giving her a headache. "So now what?"

"So now you have to decide to hormone or not to hormone."

"Today?"

"No, we'll get the lab results back, see where your scores are, and then proceed." Dr. Eleanor pulled a booklet out of her bottom drawer and motioned toward a shelf of books. "Take this one, and if you want more information, I keep up on all the latest research. Letters from various schools are right there in those white three-rings. You can and should go online, too. Get all the information you can and then we'll talk again. In the meantime, I suggest trying the yam and/or soy products and see if they help. I'm in favor of natural methods if at all possible." She paused and gave Lynn an observing study. "You realize nothing will change overnight? There is no happy, one-size cure in this situation."

Lynn shook her head, making a face at the same time. "Well, I guess I should be grateful it's not cancer or some terrible disease, but..." Her voice trailed off, and she glanced around the bookshelves that held more pictures than books and a collection of Eskimo carved soapstone animals. She blew out her breath. "So, where do I get those yam and soy products you mentioned? I've never been much of a fan of soybeans. Tofu makes me gag."

"There are other ways of using soy than just tofu. Although if you season tofu with poultry seasoning and fry it, it'll taste just like chicken."

"I always think someone suspect when they say something tastes just like chicken."

"Me, too. I'll call you as soon as the results come back. But while I have you here, how are you doing emotionally, regarding the grieving, that is?"

Lynn closed her eyes and drew in a deep breath. "I figured that all this stuff I'm feeling might be due to the grief. That's one reason I came in. Shouldn't I be over the grieving by now?"

"It's how long since Paul died?"

"One year, nine months, and a day or two. Not that I'm counting or anything."

"Still get angry?"

"At times, nothing like earlier."

"Uncontrolled crying?"

"If you mean, can I stop it or keep it from starting, sometimes. But I've learned that the tears do stop and that I might as well just give up, cry it out, and it'll go away. You never know what will trigger it. Paul's dog had to be put down two days ago. That was horrible." The tears welled immediately. "That house is mighty big for one person and a cat. I heard every sound. Packed up all his things the next day and put them out in the garage in case I get another dog."

Dr. Elly was nodding slightly and frowning just a bit.

"What? You going to tell me to go out and start meeting men? Someone said that the other day, and I felt like swinging whatever I could get my hand on. Like I want another man in my life."

"Paul would want you to be happy, and if falling in love again happened, I think he would be the first to encourage you."

"No matter how much I miss Paul's hugs and humor and presence, uh-uh. And besides, where would I meet any new men?"

The doctor shrugged. "When the time is right, you can be sure God will bring the right man to you. After all, He did before, didn't He?"

"We always thought so. But it wasn't supposed to end this way. We'd grow old together and enjoy not only our grandkids, but the great-grands and maybe do some traveling and learn about retirement and..."

"And go through menopause and possibly serious illnesses and..." Dr. Eleanor smiled. "I know. But right now, we're dealing with this one thing. I do have an idea. Are you serious about that house being too big?"

"Well, yes, but no, I'm not selling it. Phillip already suggested that, in the hopes it would make the finances improve."

"The plumbing business is not good anymore?"

Lynn shrugged. "The boys are doing a fine job, but like everything else, times are tight."

Dr. Eleanor pulled another pamphlet out of another drawer and handed it across the desk. "A friend of mine back east decided to check into shared housing after her husband died."

"Shared housing?"

"Makes a lot of sense when you think about it. Two or three people sharing a house, each with a private bath and possibly a sitting room or some such. Not family members, which is a good example, but the people are related, so something different. There are even nonprofits springing up to assist people who are interested to find each other. Women in their late forties, early fifties, who have a career, are the largest group taking part in this. It can be not only financially beneficial but emotionally as well."

Lynn took the pamphlet and barely glanced at it before sticking it in her purse. "Well, it's not like I don't have family nearby." She pushed herself up with her arms, getting that instant flush that could make her sweat in a snowstorm. "Good thing I have AC in the van."

"We'll see if we can get on top of that. If you could keep a journal of what happens when, that might be helpful." She stood. "I'm here if you need to talk. There's no crime in either talking with a counselor and/or trying some antidepressants for a bit. If you have a headache, you take something and it helps. Same principle."

"Thanks, my friend. See you in church on Sunday?"

"Choir is singing, I'll be there for sure."

Out in the van, Lynn slumped in the seat, staring at nothing. *Lord, why do I feel that my whole world is coming crashing down on me. You promised you never leave. Then why do I feel so very terribly alone?*

# Chapter Three

R*ead the book, go online, then we'll make a decision.
Why can't she just tell me what is best and I'll do it? If it
doesn't work, we'll try something else.* The argument ham-
mered in Lynn's head all the way home.

Phillip met her at the car. "We have a mighty unhappy
customer; I'm on my way over there now to see what we
can do."

"Is it our fault?" Now why did she ask that before she
even knew what the situation was? "The name doesn't ring
a bell."

"That's because they are new here; the inspector said everything in that old dump passed inspection, and now their
hot-water tank blew up and there's a leak under the kitchen
sink, and she says her husband sat down on the toilet and it
nearly fell through the floor. They found a work order that
we had done some plumbing on that house."

"That was years ago, so theoretically they are not *our* customers." Even as she said it, she realized her son—so much
like his father in so many ways with this sense of taking care
of the world's plumbing—would automatically assume responsibility. Or at least do all within his power to make the
lady happy. Or at least content. They were going to have to
have a serious discussion about this sometime. Although she

seriously doubted that conversation would make any real difference.

"I know, I looked it up. Could you call and see if you can talk her into a more rational frame of mind? It'll take me half an hour to get there, and I have another call I'd like to do on the way; you know that first cabin north of the Bradbury turnoff right on the lake?"

"Bradbury turnoff. I remember. Sure, oh, what is her name? She's always so apologetic when she calls. She's back for the season already?"

"Yes, and she can't get the water valve to turn on. Shouldn't take but a minute."

"You drained all the pipes and winterized that place, didn't you?" How she hated not being able to pull a name up right away. She used to. "Well, tell her welcome home from me, and I'll get on this other one." She headed for her house rather than the office. Since the computers and phones were synced, she'd be able to pull up the phone number.

She stepped up on the deck and the realization of no happy hound to greet her made her want to sink down on the step and howl. Or go throw rocks in the water. Or herself in the water. That thought followed on the now familiar heat wave. The lake water would probably turn to steam. She shucked her sweater off and went to stand at the edge of the deck where the breeze off the lake could hopefully blow her cool or at least comfortable. Stripping down even further was a distinct possibility.

Right. And she who would much rather bite the woman's head off was supposed to make nice. Appease the woman, something she used to do quite well. How could she possibly be sweating? It was not hot out, barely even warm, though after the winter they'd had, anything above forty felt like summer. Not sure if she was mopping sweat or tears, she dried her face and turned back to the house.

She made *the* phone call, assured the woman that the water heater was indeed twenty years old by their records, and yes, they had done some work on that place but not in the last seven years. No, it was not the plumber's fault if there was rot around the toilet. The inspector should have caught that. Yes, they could install a new toilet as soon as the floor was repaired. She'd given the woman a phone number for one of the members of their church who took on small jobs like this and always did better-than-expected work. George had the same philosophy they did. Go the extra mile. Always give more service than the owner expected.

Christ's admonitions made good business sense, too. Paul had organized a small group of like-minded businessmen at church several years before he died. They met once a month to encourage one another and study more on letting God be the CEO of their businesses. She was praying Phillip would join the group and Tom, too, but so far they kept saying they were just too busy.

Phillip's white panel truck, with PAUL'S PLUMBING lettered in bright blue, pulled in beside the house two hours later.

"Thanks, Mom, Mrs. Henderson was sweet as could be when I got there. I don't know what you did or told her, but if you could pass on the skill, possibly by injection, I'd be happy." Phillip poured himself a cup of coffee. "Any cookies?"

"I think the jar has already been raided." She raised a finger. "But..." She went to the side-by-side refrigerator and pulled a bag of cookies out of the freezer side. "Put these in the microwave for thirty seconds or so."

Since she'd quit drinking anything with caffeine after four, she filled the hot pot and fixed herself a cup of tea.

"What are you doing for supper?"

She stared at her elder son. "It will soon be that time, won't it?"

Phillip gave her a strange look. "Mom, you always have meals planned in advance. What did you learn at the doctor's?"

She blew on her orange spice herb tea and sipped, both of them leaning against the counter. "After a comprehensive Q and A, blood work, et al, Dr. Alstrop determined that I am in full-blown menopause."

"So-o?"

She tried to stop the sigh but it wouldn't stop. "So, these abominable hot flashes, the frequent and disgusting tears, and even the forgetfulness are all symptoms of the big M."

"So what will you do?"

"My assignment is to read, research, and see her in a week. After I have learned both sides of the hormone or not hormone debate, we will decide what I am going to do."

"Oh." His arched eyebrows admitted to his confusion. "Well, at least it is not life threatening."

"Not to me, but possibly someone else when I lose my temper, which is another symptom. I guess different women react differently to this thing. I thought the tears were still left over from grief, and well, they might be, but it could be this as well."

His phone sounded like a duck call, making her shake her head while he answered. "I'll be right there." He snapped it closed and set his cup in the sink. "You want to come for mac and cheese with ham? Maggie has supper ready. She said for you to come, whether you feel like it or not. Besides, she wants to know what the doctor said, too."

The thought of going out again, even across the field, almost buckled her knees. *No* was a seldom-used word, especially with her family. She pushed her hair back off her sweaty forehead. "Tell her I'll call her tomorrow. But right now all I want is a bowl of soup, some leftover corn bread, and I am going to curl up with a good book. *The Truth About Menopause.* A real page-turner. I might even go online and do the suggested research, and you know how much I like doing that."

"You're sure, even if it is going to cost me a valuable arm or something?"

She waved him off. "I'll be fine. Miss Minerva has moved upstairs. She slept on the bed last night."

"Really? You want me to send Rowdy over?" Rowdy was a rambunctious year-old Lab who had a knack for chewing on all things wooden—table legs, chairs, sticks he brought in. He well lived up to his name. His saving grace was he could fetch a duck or goose from anywhere in the lake, having been taught by master Orson, in spite of his age.

"Thanks, but no thanks. When and if I get another dog, it will not be a hunting dog. Just warning you."

"All I ask is no yapping ankle biter."

"I promise." She locked the door behind him, something else she'd started doing only recently, when Orson was losing his hearing and couldn't be depended on to announce either two-legged or wildlife visitors.

After taking a bag of frozen soup out of the freezer, she heated it, warmed the corn bread, and took her supper into the family room to watch the news, something Paul used to do all the time and she now did sporadically. Tonight was not a good night to watch the news, neither national nor local. The old camp song came to mind, "dadeeda in Africa, rioting in Spain...hurricanes in Florida, and Texas needs rain."

Those were all the words she could remember, but the tune kept playing and replaying in her head. The phone rang, she answered with "hello" instead of the business name, but when no one responded, she did not wait for the sales pitch, instead slamming the phone back in the stand. She really missed the days when slamming a receiver could give some measure of satisfaction. Why did she never check for phone numbers? They had that service.

Miss Minerva leaped up into her lap and circling, along with claw digging, made herself comfortable. Since usually Orson was at her feet, this was another new behavior.

Lynn stroked the cat and relaxed to the purring engine that took over. She picked up her book and started to read: "Chapter One—Dispelling the Myths of Menopause." Sometime later she woke with a start, stabbed the off button on the remote, and turning out the lights, she headed upstairs, cat at her heels. She should have gone to Phillip's house. Quiet did not inhabit that house. Instead, all of it congregated over here.

The next morning, she'd turned on the TV in the kitchen to watch one of the morning shows when the hostess announced, "Next on our lineup is three women with a story to tell about a new trend that is really an old trend all dressed up to fit today. It used to be that aging sisters or cousins would share a home, or an older woman invited a younger member of the family to come live with her, or the program that kept America laughing for many seasons, the slob and the neatnik sharing an apartment. But today there is a new twist, so let me introduce Susan, Alicia, and Denise, who are sharing a house in Baltimore, Maryland. We'll let them tell their story. Now, Denise, how would you like to start?"

Lynn poured herself another cup of coffee to go with her

toast and sat down to watch. Amazing, first the article and now this. All three women had good-paying jobs, one had a dog and one a cat, and the picture of the house didn't look anything out of the ordinary. One of them traveled a lot for her job, one of them liked gardening, and one liked to cook, so they each did what they liked best, sharing the general living spaces and having their own room and bath. *Could this house work for something like that?*

When the hostess asked if they had any advice for others who might be considering such a move, they all said, "Don't be in a hurry."

And some of the individual comments resonated with Lynn.

"We agreed in the beginning that if someone had a gripe, they needed to get it out on the table for discussion and not let it fester," said one. "That has been a wise decision."

"So you've not always gotten along?" The hostess leaned forward, elbows on her knees, hands clasped.

"Be real. When you put three strong women together, who are all working out their own issues of being single and getting older, of course there have been touchy situations. But we figure we are all adults and grateful we have made this move. We needed to do the work to make it work for us," said another.

"I've heard of others who have attempted shared housing and disbanded before a year was up."

"Like in anything, there are horror stories. That's why deciding if you like each other is so important," the first one added.

"And not hurrying. Give it a trial run," said the third, who seemed more reticent than the others.

"Family approval, i.e., kids and friends, is helpful but not absolutely necessary."

"Thank you, ladies. Our time is up, no matter how much I'd like to continue this fascinating topic." The hostess looked toward the camera. "And now, after our break, we'll be..."

Lynn clicked the TV off and sat staring at the blank screen. Miss Minerva lay curled in a spot of sunshine. The geraniums blooming in the window needed to be moved out on the deck to harden off before being planted in their summer home outside. As usual, thoughts bombarded her from every direction. She should be working on the books, going online and searching for information on shared housing and on menopause, going for a walk, checking in with Annie. Strange, neither of her sons had called. Her thought patterns reminded her of some of the computer games the kids played with shapes appearing and disappearing all over the screen and one was supposed to knock them out, all of which yielded total frustration to her rather than any kind of fun.

The grands had realized that asking G'ma to play computer games was not going to happen. However, if they took out a board game or cards or dice for Farkle, she'd be right there. Most of them had learned their numbers playing games with G'ma.

*One hour. I'll spend one hour on menopause research.* She booted up the computer, hit Google, and scrolled down looking for the best sites. Skimming through them. A phone call interrupted her after far more than her allotted hour.

"Mom, we're out on the Murphy job; we just ran out of thread sealing compound and we're only half done. If I call in the order, can you go pick it up?"

"Where?"

"The Plumber's Friend in Detroit Lakes. I'm sorry, I know I ordered extra just in case, but we still ran out.

We can move to another part of the job, but then we are stymied until we have the compound." At her silence, he added, "I'll owe you big-time; you must have something you can collect on."

If she ever checked the list, the men in her family were so far in favor's debt it would take a year of full-time work to catch up. Not that she really had a list. "It'll take me half an hour to get ready. I didn't plan on going out today." She said the latter rather explicitly.

"Sorry, but Annie can't. Maggie has to sleep since she's on nights again."

"Need anything else while I am in town?"

"Not that I know of, but keep your phone handy."

She snorted as she clicked off. As if her phone hadn't become a permanent appendage. While she dressed for town instead of staying home, she thought of Mary Rousch at the library. When they both had time, they could do lunch. If anyone knew of someone in their area who was also interested in shared housing, she would be the one to ask. A walking, talking encyclopedia known thusly to all was their librarian Mary. One who gathered information like a giant magnet.

On her way out the door, again being struck with no four-footed companion to tag along, she stopped and called the supply house. Yes, the order was ready; they'd had everything in stock. Funny that Maggie hadn't called to ask if she could keep Miss Priss while she slept. Some of her best G'ma times were when she had one of the kids at a time. Cookie baking was often a favorite activity, and with Miss Priss, whose real name was Caitlyn, dress-up was a close second. Miss Minerva took about as much as she could stand and then would hide who knew where.

After a brief stop at the grocery store on her way back,

she delivered the threading compound and returned home. This time her research was shared housing. The phone again. Sometimes she was tempted to ignore it, but checking the screen, she grinned instead.

"G'ma, can I come bake cookies? Mommy is still sleeping and I just got home and..." She dropped her voice. "I don't want to wake her up. She's grumpy if I do."

Lynn rolled her lips together. "See you in a minute." And clicked off, smiling and shaking her head at the image. Miss Priss was on her way. As always when she knew one or more of the children were coming, she stepped out on the back porch to watch them run along the path that crossed the large open field between the two houses. The little towhead with a pink bow in her hair—she loved hair decorations— waved and picked up her speed.

Lynn blinked back the tears that burned the backs of her eyes and immediately caused her nose to run. Joy or sorrow, her tears had no rhyme or reason, other than the big M. She dug a tissue out of her pocket and blew her nose. Miss Priss would ask immediately why she was sad.

"G'ma," she yelled to be heard. "I got a new purse." She waved a shiny pink plastic bag, which would no doubt be of the latest princess ilk. Miss Priss devoutly believed in princesses, and according to her daddy, she was his.

"Beautiful." Lynn wasn't making any definitions of what she was referring to. She braced for the leap into her arms, surely not typical princess behavior, whatever that was. The smile beamed up at her made her hug the little one again. "So how was preschool?"

"Arnold brought a big worm in his pocket, and the girls shrieked and ran." She shook her head. "It was dumb. He wasted a good worm."

In this family if you couldn't put your own worm on

your own hook, you didn't get to go fishing. And if you didn't go fishing, you would miss out on a good amount of the family entertainment. Miss Priss slid her hand into her grandmother's. "I hope we are going to make peanut butter cookies, and I want to mash them with a fork."

"If that is the kind you want, no problem. We could make chocolate chip bars, too, if you like. They can be baking while we form the others."

"Okay. Daddy likes the bars best." She swung her purse with her other hand. "Did you know that next year I go to kindergarten?"

"I figured."

Blue eyes stared up at her. "What if I don't like it?"

"Do you like preschool?"

A nod and a serious look. "Most of the time, until some boy does something really, really stupid."

"Girls don't do stupid things?"

She shrugged. "But we listen better." Her smile widened. "Miss Minerva. You want to play dress-up?"

"How can we bake two kinds of cookies and still play dress-up?"

"I just wanted to see her run. I think she got tired of playing dress-up. Last time she scratched me. All she had to do was say she didn't want to play anymore. She didn't need to get mean about it." Miss Priss boosted herself up on a stool. "Can I wear a apron?"

"Of course you must." While they chatted, Lynn took all the ingredients and a mixer out of the pantry and set them on the table. Mentally she ran down the list of ingredients and double-checked to make sure she had everything. "The peanut butter is on the bottom shelf; you want to get that?" Fetching the princess apron she had made for this particular grand, in pink of course, she tied the apron strings and dropped a kiss on the curly blond hair that caused more than one argument over tangles. Getting the hair washed had taken coercing, bribing, and strict orders until they found a no-tangle product that even worked on curly hair.

"Can I start the mixer?"

"Wait until we get the ingredients in. You remember how to crack the eggs in?"

"Can we use a bowl like before? Daddy said he didn't like chewing on eggshells."

Having made certain there were no shells in the dough, Lynn rolled her eyes. Leave it to Phillip. "Sure, that's always the best way to learn." Cooking with helpers always slowed the job wa-a-y down but she'd not trade it. Both the brothers had helped in the kitchen, and Travis now did some of the cooking and baking. He said he was going to be a chef someday. Davey would rather catch the fish than fry them, although he, too, had become a good assistant in the kitchen.

She let Caitlyn measure the sugar and unwrap the butter cubes, then turn on the mixer. "Now, don't go sticking the wooden spoon or spatula in the bowl while it is running, right?"

"I got whapped good last time."

"And?"

"And the beaters got bent. That was a tough wooden spoon, huh?"

"Could have been your fingers."

"Nope, my fingers didn't go near that bowl. The spoon did."

"Okay, shut it off and dump in the eggs." Step by step, they mixed the dough, added the chocolate chips, minus a few that made it into two willing mouths, and shelled and broke nuts. Lynn spread the dough in the jelly roll pan and stood by while Caitlyn slid the pan into the oven. She stepped back and dusted off her hands. "Now we have tea."

By the time the boys got home from school, the peanut butter cookies rested on the cooling racks, the bars were in a flat plastic container, and the two cooks made hot chocolate with marshmallows to float in it.

"You didn't wake Mommy, did you?" Caitlyn greeted her two brothers as they burst through the door.

"You think we're stupid or crazy?" Travis stared at her as if she was the crazy one. "G'ma, are we having supper here?"

"What did your mom say this morning?"

"She said she forgot to ask and Dad was supposed to, and I don't know if he did or if we are going out for pizza."

Davey spoke around the cookie in his mouth. "Not going for pizza."

"Why?"

"Daddy has a meeting."

"How do you know?"

"He said."

Lynn kept her smile to herself. Travis tried to be the boss, but while more quiet, Davey observed, listened, and forgot nothing. She took the corn bread casserole out of the freezer, along with a frozen peach pie, and turned the oven back on. Nights like this they ate early so Maggie could sleep until supper, then spend the evening with her kids before getting ready for the late shift. Everyone was glad when she wasn't on the night shift.

Thinking about the day on her way up the stairs to bed that night, Lynn realized it had gone from sad to study to hurry, hurry to the sublime and closed with the wild. All in all, a perfect day if she could ignore the tears and the sweat.

Was thinking about bringing two other women into this messy, busy life even half a good idea? It would certainly take some special kind of people. However could something like that even begin to work out? Surely even the thought was a menopausal fantasy.

# Chapter Four

"Please, Lord, let this dinner help us mend the rips in our marriage."

Angela Bishop stared at the face in the mirror. Dangly earrings just the way that Jack liked them. His favorite little black dress that he'd bought for her on one extravagant shopping trip. Strappy, sparkly heels that brought her five foot three up to five six and made her legs look far longer than they were. Even her deep auburn hair, colored just the way he liked it, managed to behave and stay in the French twist at the back of her head.

Tall, slim, sexy. She brightened the red lipstick and rolled her lips together. Checking the diamond-decked watch that she never wore for fear it would get lost, she saw she was ready on time. Learning to be punctual had been a hard lesson, but she had perfected it. She grabbed a wrap from the drawer, and after winking at that woman in the mirror, she strolled down the stairs.

Jack said he'd meet her here, right now. Where was he? So much for her grand entrance. She picked up the wrap she'd been trailing behind her and draped it over her arm.

"Oh, wow." Accompanied by a wolf whistle, Jack skidded to a stop on the hard wood floor. "Angela, is this gorgeous creature really you?"

She ignored the reply she wanted to make and smiled seductively, tilting her head slightly to the side. Employing every sexy hint she'd ever read in the women's magazines or seen on the computer, she ran the tip of her tongue over her glistening lips and batted her false eyelashes. Ones she'd learned to apply just for this night. He'd wanted a sexy, beautiful, successful wife and she'd worked hard to become just that.

Pitching her voice down just a bit, she smiled again. "At your service." At the bottom of the stairs, she did a slow pirouette, trailing the shawl and throwing a glance over her shoulder, lashes at half-mast. She'd even learned to wear contacts since he'd complained about her glasses. "Are you ready?"

"Am I ever."

His throaty answer made her smile again. It must be working. Imagine Angela Bishop a vamp at age fifty-one. She laid one hand on his arm, bright red acrylic nails with a sparkly embedded on one forefinger tip, glinting in the light.

"Here, let me." He took her wrap and laid it around her shoulders, fingertips caressing the back of her neck. "Your chariot awaits, m'amselle."

Once he had her seated in the low-slung red Porsche, his latest purchase, he was whistling as he crossed in front of the car to the driver's side.

She had to admit Jack looked good, too. The black suit he'd paid far more for than half her wardrobe, with a white silk shirt, open at the neck to reveal curly chest hairs, set off his dark good looks as a heart-stopper. Who would ever dream looking at them, they were celebrating twenty-five years of marriage? While their two children were planning a family get-together to celebrate, she and Jack had opted to have this one night together, just the two of them.

He torched off the motor and paused. "Where are we going?"

"To the Mansfield." She had set up this date, making reservations at what she knew to be his favorite restaurant. It was too high priced and too upscale to go to regularly, but once in a great while . . .

"Sparing no expense, I hope."

"That's right." She smiled at him and purred, "You're worth it."

He patted her knee and shifted the Porsche to drive. Four on the floor. A man's dream, and a middle-aged man at that. Was middle age what was prompting his restlessness these last couple of years, his demand that she go out and get a job so they could have a better lifestyle? But perhaps she was feeling middle-aged as well, because she was going along with it, carefully remaking the old Angela into the kind of woman he raved about who worked in his office at the bank. Sexy and successful. Two of his favorite words when referring to women. And slim. Angela now weighed fourteen pounds less than when she graduated from high school.

"Did you get my shirts at the dry cleaners? I have to leave for a short trip in the morning."

"No, I had two showings this afternoon and then I forgot. I'll pick them up in the morning."

"My flight is at eight." His tone bit.

"Why didn't you tell me?"

"I asked you to get them."

"But you didn't say . . ." She cut off her reply. "Let's not argue tonight, okay? I'm sure you have plenty more shirts to make this trip. How long will you be gone?"

"Three days, four at the most. I guess I'll have to buy shirts if I need more."

Since when had he played the martyr role? "Where are you going?"

"Seattle. I have back-to-back meetings with marketing and mergers and acquisitions."

Was that a hint of pride she now heard in his voice? Since he'd given up sharing much business talk with her, complaining that she was never around to listen when she brought it up, she wasn't really sure what this meeting entailed.

"I'd like to go to Seattle again."

"Someday maybe, but not this trip. I'll have no time for sightseeing or anything."

"Will you see Charles and Gwynn?"

"No time. I've not even told them I'd be in the vicinity. This trip came up so unexpected. Rush, rush, rush. Why they didn't tell me before, but according to Ken's boss immediately above him, there's a problem and I'm the man to handle it."

"Good for you." She patted his knee, earning a quick grin. Why was it that lines on a man's face and silver sideburns looked sexy, but women were not to age? Another of those questions she'd seek answers for someday. She leaned back in the seat and stared out the windshield.

He switched the dial to light classical, something they both enjoyed, and for a change, peace seemed to settle into the car interior, the black leather both smelling and feeling luxurious.

"Maybe I should think of getting a new car, too. A Lexus maybe? Sedan would be good for taking clients to see the properties."

"If you can afford it, go for it. Although you might give it a lot of thought. They're expensive, you know."

Her eyebrows arched in spite of herself. And this little

number had not been expensive? She'd never known the
sticker price, but then perhaps he had leased it, something
she might consider as well. After all, it would be a business
write-off. Whatever had happened to those years where
they talked over finances, trying to figure out whom to pay
and who would have to wait? They'd laughed and loved
together, did family things with Charles and Gwynn, like
sports and canoeing up at the lake property. With both
of their children married and no grandchildren at this
point, they had all seemed to drift in different directions.
Although they had worked together to create the family
celebration...

"Four days?" She turned to stare at her husband. "The
celebration the kids set up for our anniversary is Saturday."
*With a special something going on at church on Sunday.* But
they were keeping that part a secret, so she couldn't mention it just yet.

"No problem, I'll be back Friday night at the latest."

"Are you sure?" She fought to keep her tone calm when
it wanted to go up an octave, bordering on shriek.

"Of course I'm sure. I told the board I had to be back."

She stared at him, shock registering. He'd forgotten.
"Wasn't it on your calendar?"

"Oh, I'm sure it was, er, is." He gave her his toothy smile,
sure she would acquiesce like she always had.

*No arguments tonight. Just nod and smile. Tread softly.
Drop a brick on his head later.* That thought surely didn't
help peace, but it did make her laugh inside. *Breathe deep,
tonight you are celebrating, just the two of you.*

He pulled the car in front of the Mansfield and stopped
where a valet opened her door and greeted her with a smile.
She let him help her out while Jack came around the front
of the car and tossed the young man the keys.

"Be careful with my baby here." He patted the roof, took his ticket, and held out an arm to escort her inside.

When he greeted the maître d', the familiar response reminded her he'd been here before. But they had only been here once before, years ago. Jack always said they could not afford this kind of place. But back then, that was the truth.

The gentleman smiled mirthlessly. "Going all out?"

"Nothing too good for my girl." His hand at her back guided her to follow the man with the leather-bound menus who seated them in a booth, shook out the fancy folded napkins, and placed the stiff, white cloths on their laps before opening and setting the menus in front of them.

"Thank you, Henri."

"You are welcome, and if there is anything else you need, feel free to call me. I'll take care of it."

Was that a tip Jack passed him? Jack, or at least the Jack she used to know, had been stingy with tips. "Henri?"

"Ah yes, I've brought clients here before."

"Oh, your expense account must have expanded somewhat."

He ignored her comment and studied the menu. "Would you like me to order for both of us? I have a special idea in mind."

"If you'd like." Another strange behavior. This was turning into a night of strange behaviors. Why did she feel like he was showing off?

He beckoned the waiter over, the two conferred, and the waiter left with a smile and nod to her. "Now," said her husband. "Why don't we go dance while they prepare our supper? Oh, and I ordered a bottle of extra-nice wine since we are celebrating."

"Thank you." She nodded. "I didn't reserve a wine, but I know you don't care for champagne."

They both put their napkins on the table, and he took her hand to lead her to the spotlighted dance floor. No recordings in the Mansfield or even a piano player. A six-piece ensemble played a waltz, and she let herself relax in the strength of Jack's arms. For a moment she could forget about the strange behaviors. They'd always danced well together and tonight was no exception. As they swung and blended with the music, she heaved a deep breath and let herself rest her cheek against his shoulder. Surely this would lead to a night of making love, something they'd not had a lot of lately.

The waiter brought the bottle of wine; poured some in a glass; and Jack swirled the goblet, inhaled the perfume, and nodded to the man to pour. They used to make a joke out of things like this because their only identification was with red house wine or white.

Somehow she got the idea if she brought that up to laugh over, he'd not think it funny. He'd reacted that way lately to a lot of their family stories, as if they were no longer humorous and he would rather forget their earlier life.

At least there would be lots of reminiscing when the whole family, including their church family, met to celebrate.

He lifted his glass to touch hers. "To our new lives." After the elegant clink, they each sipped and savored. Or at least he seemed to. Actually, the wine was red and dry, and to her it tasted like medicine. The yucky kind that you chugged fast and followed with several glugs of water. Immediately. She ordered herself to not be silly and took another very small sip, glancing at the bottle. There was no way he was going to pour any more of that into her glass.

She nibbled on the assortment of breadsticks, crackers, and crunchy breads in the basket on the table. As bad as the wine was, these were delicious. Their salads arrived; the waiter ground the obligatory pepper on the Caesar salad and she savored the crispy crunch with a tangy dressing. The chef certainly knew how to prepare a good salad.

"More?" Jack held up the wine bottle. His glass was empty.

"Ah, no thank you. Not yet." Another sip to go with a smile and an immediate bite of bread.

Here came Henri with an assistant and some kitchen equipment. They set up next to her table and with broad gestures prepared the entrée. A column of flame flared eighteen inches into the air as the other restaurant patrons were watching and pretended they weren't. This, she knew, was flambeau, but it had never been done for her before. With a flourish, the chefs folded up their equipment and left.

The food certainly lived up to its reputation. Small rosettes of the tenderest steak in a delicious wine sauce. "Oh, this is so good," she murmured after the first bite. "Thank you."

"Glad you like it. They are famous for their Steak Diane. One of my favorites here."

*Huh?* Another intriguing comment to file away for later pondering. She asked, "Have you heard from Charles lately?"

Jack shook his head and downed another swallow of wine. His glass was nearly empty again.

"What about Gwynn?"

Again he shook his head and finished off his glass.

"Ah, won't you be over the alcohol limit, dear?"

He did a brushing motion. "No problem, it'll be dissipated by then, and besides, you could drive. You can drive a stick shift, right?"

"Not for a long time." So far he'd not allowed her to drive his baby. In fact, she'd hardly ridden in it.

They danced again while their table was being cleared, but for some strange reason, the feeling of closeness was no longer present. He danced more like it was a chore than a delight. Despite all the surface glamour, this evening was beginning to seem weirdly wrong. She wanted to mend her marriage and bring Jack back to the intimacy they knew once upon a time. What was happening here?

Back at the table she caught him checking his watch. "Do you have somewhere you have to be?"

"Oh no, no, not at all." He smiled but it never reached his eyes. "Now, how about we share a dessert, unless you want a whole one. Their crème brûlée is really good."

She ignored the feeling of unease she kept getting. "Share, huh? Can we not afford to each have one?"

"Of course we can," he snapped, and signaled the waiter. "Two, please."

"Of the usual?"

"Yes."

"Jack, I meant that as a joke. You know, how we used to joke about not overspending?" She reached for his hand, but instead of taking hers, he withdrew his.

"Oh, well, I—I guess I overreacted. Sorry."

*Sorry, my foot. You're furious. What is going on here?* She took another sip of wine to make nice. It didn't taste any better than before.

He poured the remainder of the bottle in his glass, only a small amount.

"Look, why don't you take mine? I really would rather

have tea with my dessert." She pushed her glass over toward him.

"You sure?"

"Oh, my, yes. I've had plenty." *And besides, since I'll be driving, I will not take any chance on being forced into a sobriety test.*

Conversation lagged, with her trying to come up with a topic for conversation that couldn't be answered with one sentence or one word. Jack was normally a real talker, especially at his most charming and after a glass or two of wine. Maybe after so much wine, he became taciturn. He rarely drank so heavily. She heaved a sigh of relief when the dessert arrived and put in her order for the hibiscus rose tea.

"If this is as good as it looks..." She picked up her spoon and broke the burnt sugar crust to scoop out the rich velvety crème. Her eyes closed, the better to appreciate the texture and flavor. "Oh my."

"I knew you'd like it."

"Eating this is a decadent delight." She savored another spoonful. "This is the best I've ever tasted. I'd come here just for the dessert. I so want this evening to be a memorable one. Just think, as of tonight, we have been married twenty-five years. Hard to believe, isn't it?"

Jack took more than one sip from his wineglass, more like a big swallow. While he nodded, he did not answer.

She licked the spoon, looking at him at the same time. Sultry was the effect she was hoping for. She huskied her voice. "Let's do another twenty-five, what do you say?"

Jack stared at her. No smile, no nod, no affirmation.

The silence sent a chill through her. Something was absolutely wrong here.

"Angela, I've been wanting to tell you this, but I couldn't

find a good time." He drained the glass, set it down, and laid his palms flat on the table. "I need to find out who I am."

*Find out who I am?* That was so 1960s. The chill deepened.

He cleared his throat, firmed up his voice. "This afternoon I filed for divorce."

# Chapter Five

"Are you ready, Miss Rutherford?" the elderly Realtor asked quietly.

Judith Rutherford stared at her home and swallowed. *Ready? Never.*

They stood together on the sidewalk in front of the stately three-story old home. Rutherford House, listed on the historical sites in the town of Rutherford, Minnesota, was an icon of the area and family owned since 1893, when lumber baron August Rutherford built the house for his bride. Family owned until Judith's father died and she discovered that in reality, the Heritage League owned the Rutherford House, according to a trust she had never seen. Her father had promised that he would provide for her. She had always assumed that meant the house was hers, there being not much else left from the grand estate.

*I have to get some backbone here,* Judith told herself when she would far more easily melt into a puddle or, as the case may be this day, become a sheet of ice. She shivered in spite of her heavy wool black coat. Like the house, it too had seen better days. "I lived here all my life."

Mr. Odegaard flinched. "I know. I've known you since before you were born."

Judith was well aware of the friendship between her father and the Odegaard males, one of whom was this Realtor and brother to the head of the Rutherford Bank. Had she not known better, she might have suspected they were in cahoots regarding the Rutherford legacy, since the bank was also the financial arm of the Heritage League. As an only child, Judith understood far more of the intricacies of the family history, some mythical and others supremely valid. She should know; she'd been the caregiver for both of her parents since *the accident*. While history used BC and AD as time markers, *the accident* did the same in this once-thriving town.

Judith forced her mind to focus on the here and now. Her mother died five years ago, and her father had been wheelchair bound since he'd broken his back those long years before, although twenty-five years was not really long in the overall scheme of things. She'd been a young woman when the forest fire roared through the town, leaving this house as one of the few untouched structures. Her father fell during the firefight and a broken back was the result. He had run his business from his home thereafter.

"Ready as I'll ever be." She drew a deep breath. "Would you like another walk-through?"

"No, I know you have catalogued every artifact down to counting the spoons. As soon as we can come to an agreement between the Heritage League and the bank, this house can go into the national directory. Your father's wishes to turn this into a living museum are coming true." He shuffled one foot. "I know this is such a personal question, but have you been provided for?"

"In a manner of speaking. I have a trust that was separate from that of the house and business, from my grandmother on my mother's side." That in itself was a miracle. More than once, really many times, her father had tried to persuade her to join that trust with other family investments that he controlled. There was some clause in the trust that forbade that from happening.

She'd considered fighting the trust that she was, in name only, administrator for. The trust that gave the house, the only remaining property of the once-thriving family, to become a heritage center rather than hers to sell and thereby gain sufficient funds to live on. Her father had promised that if she remained at home and took care of her parents, she would be well provided for on his death. She had dreamed that perhaps then she could leave this place that held so few good memories for her and begin a new life, somewhere where she was not bound by the strictures of the family history and family name.

Not that she was bitter or anything.

"How long before I have to be moved out?" All right, so she had dreamed of moving out. But not on these terms.

"I really do wish you would stay on as caretaker at least. I know your father intended that you should; he said so. Once we have the living history museum in place, we will need a knowledgeable administrator. You're perfect for that. I guess I assumed from the way your father talked that you were in agreement with that."

"He did not mention anything like that to me, Mr. Odegaard."

"Perhaps he simply assumed it."

"Perhaps." He did tend to assume she would do whatever he wanted. "And how long do you think it will be before that is in place?"

"I wish I knew. The paperwork is horrendous between the state and the national historical societies. I know you did as much as you were able, but the inventory of furnishings was only one small aspect."

Judith nodded. The cold winter that should have moved on and left spring in charge was still fighting for supremacy. Snow was predicted for tonight. The thought of remaining as caretaker in a house that no longer belonged to her made her jaw clench. *Provided for. Right.* How cruel when one's own father did not live up to his word. Especially after she laid aside all her hopes and dreams to make her ill and aging parents' remaining years as comfortable as possible, even to being an assistant in the family business. A business that had it not been run into the ground, she had often considered taking over.

But according to her father, women were not capable of running a business. In those last months that had surely been a joke. Judith shivered in spite of her heavy coat. "So basically, I can leave immediately. "

"Immediately? Oh, please do not leave immediately." He turned to look at her. "Miss Rutherford, we have to find someone to be caretaker, someone dependable. That will take time. Are you sure I cannot convince you to remain for, say, six months at least?"

Judith heaved a sigh. "Let me think about it. I'll let you know in a week if that is all right." The thought of remaining in the house tore her in two ways.

"Oh, thank you. I will be hoping you agree to stay." He reached out to shake her hand. His hand was cold and bony. "We will be in touch. Is there anything I can get you in the meantime?"

Remaining polite was growing more difficult by the moment. She should have invited him in in the beginning, but she'd been afraid he'd stay around forever. And stop her packing. "No thank you." Hoping she wasn't appearing rude, she moved toward the wrought iron gate that opened to the walk up to the front door. Green shafts were just starting to break through the soil. The daffodils that had lined the walk for years were as anxious for spring to come as she was.

"I will call you," he called to her.

"Ah, ah, yes, thank you." She sent something that she hoped resembled a smile and pushed open the gate as if the hounds of heaven were after her. As she heard his car door slam and the engine start, she heaved a sigh, but did not allow herself to slow down until the sound of the motor disappeared down the street. Putting one foot in front of the other was like pulling her feet out of gluey mud, the kind they had in the Red River Valley less than a hundred miles to the west.

Since she'd been forced to let the help go several weeks after her father died, due to lack of money to pay them any longer, she dug a house key out of her leather purse and finally was able to open the door. Going around to the side entrance from the garage would have been far easier, since the front door was so rarely used any longer, but she hadn't been thinking clearly.

She shut the door behind her and leaned against it. Admitting to not thinking clearly was almost as bad as not brushing her teeth the required two minutes. "Judith, you must not let Mr. Odegaard or anyone else befuddle you like that." Her voice disappeared in the dead air of the entry hall. Ignoring the ornate mirror over the walnut table and the flowers that were wilting in the vase, she made her way back to her retreat, the sunroom, the one room in the entire house not tainted by all the vultures that had been circling for the carrion.

She felt the peace of this usually sunny room sink into her soul. Totally out of character, she draped her heavy coat over a chair, loath to traverse back down the hall to the coat closet, at least right at that moment. Instead she crossed to the fireplace and flipped the switch for the gas log to ignite and pour warmth into the room immediately. Several years earlier, she had insisted, and for a change her father had finally agreed, that all the fireplaces be refitted with gas logs. At least they still had the look of the original fireplaces so the historical value of the house was not seriously compromised. Those last years he had suffered from the cold and acquiesced to changes.

Suffice it to say, her father wrote the book on stubborn.

Oh, for the years when she would ring for Mrs. Winslow, who ran the house, or Mindy, their last maid, and before long a pot of hot tea would be brought into the room, along with whatever she had pleased to eat. Mrs. Winslow was the last one to go and she had been ready to retire anyway. The job had gotten to be far too much for one aging lady.

"Well, if you want tea, go fix it and be grateful for the microwave." This talking out loud to herself was getting to be a habit. One that she would have to discard when she left Rutherford House or people would think her going batty in her later years. Not that forty-seven was old. According to statistics, she was only getting into middle age.

In middle age and she had yet to live, apart from this house and those who used to live here, too. Sometimes she felt like if she turned fast enough she'd see her father wheeling through the widened doorway. He disdained using the motorized wheelchair. Perhaps that was something she could sell. Judith shook her head. Surely there was someone in need of that chair. She would call the senior center in the morning; they would know.

Back in the sunroom, after carrying in her tray of tea and toast, she settled near the fireplace, staring into the flickering flames. Did even the flames ask her the questions ricocheting in her mind now in the silence? *What am I going to do? Where am I going to live?*

Staying here and carrying on as always was far and away the easiest of all possibilities. And also the most impossible.

"I will not stay in Rutherford. I will not remain in this house." Her voice dropped in spite of her personal orders to be strong and firm. "I can't, dear God, I can't. Haven't I given this place enough of my life?" Even her backbone refused to obey and she slumped in the chair. Leaning her head against the pillowed back, her eyes drifted closed. *What can you do, other than take care of stubborn, cantankerous old men?* The miserable little voice that lived somewhere where she couldn't evict it taunted her when her defenses were down. But it was right, what could she do? She had to find some way to earn a living; the inheritance would not last long if she used it to solely support herself. At least through the years since her mother died, she had reinvested it, and not into the Rutherford company, in spite of her father's wishes.

The one thing she had stood up for, and even when reeling in terror, she had persisted. Her mother's mother had been very wise in the way she set up the trust so that her father had not been able to touch it even when his wife was alive. At least not the principal.

*Oh, Mother, I never blamed you for leaving. But...* She sipped her tea, now gone tepid. At least the cozy kept the teapot relatively warm. Her mother had knitted the cozy in a double layer that insulated the china well. Strange how today so many of her memories returned to her mother. It was as if now that her father was gone, there was room for the good memories of her mother to return. For so long her mother's memories had centered around those last excruciating months and the agony of watching her dear mother die an inch at a time.

All the while trying to keep up with her father's demands.

Her mother's death was an emotional devastation, her father's a financial one.

He had promised to provide for her in return for her years of service.

And she had believed him. Calling herself names did nothing to facilitate the situation. She'd been through this miasma countless times.

She rose to stand in front of the mirror that reflected the beauty outside into the room. She took the pins out of her sedate bun and let her hair fall down behind. Two feet long. Nearly three. She ought to cut it now that he who insisted she not cut it was dead. Staring at the gaunt face that looked to have aged ten years, she shook her head. "Is it too late to start a new life?"

That night she sat down in front of the fire, teapot in cozy beside her and a yellow pad on a clipboard. At the top of the page she wrote: "To Do with the Rest of My Life." She poured herself a cup of chamomile tea so she could go to sleep sometime before 2:00 a.m. and stared at the page.

The grandfather clock out in the hall bonged the hour.

She stared at the page.

And finally wrote: "I can choose to stay here and take care of the place." That would indeed be the easy way out. But it would no longer be her home. Not that it was now either. She stayed here on sufferance.

"I can go somewhere else, but what will I do?" She stared at the words she had written. Where and what? Two huge words growing more so all the time.

Leaning her head back, she closed her eyes and let her mind free float. She saw herself growing into a young woman, dreaming of going away to college. While her two friends were dreaming of boys and marriage, all she wanted was to be an anthropologist or an archaeologist on a dig in some faraway place, like Egypt or Africa.

After one year at the University of Minnesota, she'd not gotten too far away from Rutherford, and she'd been forced to remain at home and take care of her parents. One took care of one's family, the creed of the Rutherfords through the years. It was supposed to be short-term and then she would return to school. And now twenty-plus years later, she was nothing and she had nothing.

When the phone rang, she thought to ignore it but instead checked the face, a familiar number, at least not a crank call.

"I suppose you are sitting in that big hulk of a house all by yourself," Melody, her cousin and best friend, announced without even a "Hello and how are you."

"I finished all the cataloguing and turned the paperwork over to Mr. Odegaard, the executor, today."

"And now what will you do?"

"I have no idea."

"Well, you should have enough money to do pretty much whatever you want."

"Sometimes life does not work that way."

"He screwed you again."

"Not my way of putting it, but in the long run, you are right."

"Well, that…that…," she sputtered to a close. "If he weren't dead and buried, I'd be tempted to take care of him myself."

Uncle Sebastian had long ago ceased to be even an addendum to Melody's favorite people list. She made her opinions known with no compunction.

"So he left you with nothing?"

"Pretty much. I have my own personal possessions, my car, my clothes, and the fund that Mother left to me." She looked around this, her favorite, room. She had chosen and paid for the furnishings in this room. They were hers. The furniture in her bedroom the same, only that had been given to her by her mother. That was it.

"But I thought he promised you would be cared for. I thought the estate was yours."

"No, he signed the house and furnishings over to the Heritage League with the provision that they turn this into a living history museum of life in the early 1900s. I can remain here as caretaker if I so desire. He expected that was what I would do."

"Come live with me."

"I can't do that."

"Why not? The children are grown and gone; it is just Anselm and I rattling around in this big old house. You could have you own quarters. Be as free as you like. We want to do some traveling, so you could go with us or stay here. Surely if you want to find a job, that would be easier closer to the cities like we are."

"What would I do?"

"Well, you pretty much ran your father's business these last years."

"True, but I never received a paycheck or paid taxes or anything that an employer could look at and see what I have done. I have no references, business that is." She leaned forward and poured herself more tea. "Since my father signed off on everything, it is like I am a zero on the register of life."

"But you did all the work besides taking care of him."

"You know that and I know that, but how would I prove it to a prospective employer?"

"Have you thought of going back to school?"

"Funny you should say that. I wrote it on my thinking pad. I'm sure my meager credits are not applicable any longer."

"You could live here and go back to school."

"I could. I am writing that option on my think pad."

"Where would you like to live, if not here?"

"I have always wanted to live on a lake or an ocean or a river. To wake and see the water every day sounds like a bit of heaven."

"Well, there are enough lakes in Minnesota you could probably have one of your own, mosquitoes and all."

Melody never had cared much for water, especially not after that summer she almost drowned at Bible camp. Judith stared down at her list. "Someday I want to have a dog, too." Another desire her father had squelched.

"We have Bozo, we'll share. Look, Judith, at least come and visit for a while. Put your things in storage, get moved out of that house, and perhaps you'll have a different perspective. Your father's ghost is probably watching every move you make there. If anyone could die and come back to influence and make his daughter miserable, it would be Uncle Sebastian."

"I'll think about it. And thank you for calling. You were just what I needed."

"You want me to come and stay a few days, help you get out of there? I can, you know."

"I'll let you know. I guess I've made so many decisions in the last few days that I am about decisioned out. First thing, I need to decide if I will stay on here as caretaker or not."

"Not."

"Thanks. Tell Anselm hello from me." When they clicked off, she counted the bongs of the clock—10:00 p.m. Perhaps she'd sleep better tonight. The chamomile tea might help with that. And maybe she'd wake up in the morning with some decisions made.

Or maybe she'd choose to stay in bed. After all, anything could happen.

# Chapter Six

"I am more and more thinking this idea of house sharing is the way I should go." Lynn sat back in her chair and looked across the kitchen table at Phillip.

"Have you counted the cost?" Phillip was studying his mother, staring in the same way he would ponder a clogged sink.

Lynn stared right back. "I'm working on that. We need one more bathroom so that each of the other bedrooms have a bath. I figured you'd look at it inside and out and give me an estimate. Far as I can tell, that's the only addition to the house."

"What about garage space for two more cars in the winter?"

She flinched. She'd not thought of that. "Do you think the hot-water heater will be sufficient or do we need a newer, larger one?"

Phillip was in his deep-thinking mode, arms crossed, staring toward the floor but most likely not seeing anything. She waited with all the patience she had cultivated through the years of working with his father. The two were far more alike than different. Perhaps Phillip laughed a little more readily and he was right-handed, not left. He had inherited something from her.

"You might consider the newer instant hot ones. This one is what, ten, fifteen years old?"

"At least. I'd have to look it up."

"Will you furnish the rooms or would they bring their own beds and things?"

"Good question. If they were buying into the house—some places do the financial side that way—they would bring their own, but since we don't have a suite for each, I guess it could go either way. I have the furniture."

"Have you talked with anyone who does this? I mean, what if you don't get along?"

"I'll do interviews, ask for referrals, check financial statuses. The book I got has a list of questions to ask. And then I pray about it. You know, if we're not happy with the situation, I can give notice that they have to move. I mean, we all know that life changes and sometimes in an instant." How well she knew that. She'd dreamed of Paul again last night and realized she was also crying when she woke up. Just the thought brought the tears burning at the back of her eyes. Would this never go away? She sniffed and reached for a tissue from the box on the counter.

"You okay?" Phillip asked softly.

"Yeah, or I will be."

"You know, if you really want to do this, I think we should all sit down together and talk about it. Any chance Lillian could come home for a weekend?"

"We can ask."

"Have you mentioned it to her yet?"

She nodded. "She said to do whatever I thought best and she'd ask around to see if she could find someone who was doing shared housing. I mean, she'd shared an apartment while she was going to school and that worked all right."

"Somehow it seems different when it's a group of students or younger people just getting started."

"Your age bias is showing."

Phillip heaved himself upright. "I'll check and see when Mags has a day off. We can Skype with Lillian if we need to. We'll ask Annie to come stay with the kids so we don't have a bunch of interruptions. I'll ask Tom to do the same."

"Thanks." She watched her eldest go out the door. She could tell just by the set of his shoulders that he was not yet convinced this was a good idea.

The day of the meeting, she baked two apple pies and one chocolate meringue and lasagna as only she could make it (the kids all said so). The French bread with garlic and Parmesan cheese was waiting under the broiler. The table was set in the dining room, not here in the kitchen, as if it were a holiday of some sort.

Perhaps it was. She'd made a rough estimate of the bathroom expenses; priced the new water heater; and talked with Hank, their local contractor, about building a two-car garage, getting two estimates, one for making it two story so they could eventually finish the second level into a mini-apartment, a guest suite or game room, or something. She'd talked with Ron at the bank about a possible loan, feeling pleased when he told her that whatever she needed was available to her. There was something to be said for banking for many years at a local bank. And having grown up with the bank manager. She had all the papers in a file folder waiting on the antique buffet that once belonged to her grandmother, then her mother, and now it was hers.

*Any changes I make to this house will only increase the value of it*, she reminded herself while breaking the romaine lettuce for the salad. If she could ever get the garden in, they would soon have fresh lettuce. That morning she had listened to the inner idea to plant mixed lettuce seeds in an oblong pot and set it on the south-facing windowsill to sprout. Getting a head start on the growing season. Paul had built her a hotbed for starting seeds, but since he died, she'd just not had the energy to get out and do that. So many things she'd let go by the wayside. Would she ever get back to them all, or were they for a reason or only a season?

With everything in order for the supper, she headed upstairs to put on a clean shirt at least. As always tomato sauce had managed to splatter on her white T-shirt. That's what happened when the cook forgot to put on an apron.

Sometime later with the five of them finally seated at the table and all the food in place to be served, they bowed their heads for grace. For a change, perhaps to make this a more formal occasion, she started the Norwegian prayer that her mother had not only taught her but her children. *E Jesu navn, gdr vi til bords.* At the amen, she nodded. They needed to use the old ways more often so the traditions did not get lost. "If you pass your plates, I'll dish up the lasagna." She had cut it into hefty pieces in the kitchen before bringing the huge pan to the table. She did not know how to make a small amount of anything.

Another one of the lessons of widowhood that she had not succumbed to, cooking for one.

"So, did you get that Peterson place finished?" Phillip asked, looking toward his brother.

"I thought we weren't going to talk plumbing tonight." Maggie rolled her eyes at Josie, who sat across the table. The two younger women always tried to keep family meetings on track.

"Oh, right." Phillip passed the bread basket on around. "Maybe this weekend we can get the dock out."

"We have to repair that off wheel first. I have the canoe up on sawhorses so I can give it another coat or two of varnish."

The two wives shrugged.

They might as well give up, Lynn thought.

"Hey, Mom," Maggie asked, "did you get that flier in the mail about the quilting, needlework, and craft show in Minneapolis? I'm sure dreaming of going."

"How can you get time off?" Lynn's attention deserted her remodeling ideas and zeroed in on the new topic, one very dear to her heart.

"Far enough ahead, I can ask for it. We had such a great time the last time we went." She looked at her sister-in-law. "You want to go, too? It'll mean a night or two in a hotel; I think the show lasts three days, but we needn't stay for it all."

"Oh, how I wish. I studied that thing and the calendar, and there is no way. You'll just have to teach me what you learned when you get home." The three of them had attended a similar event in Fargo, just one time, but Fargo was less than an hour away, and Minneapolis, four on a good day.

"Can I get anyone anything else?" Lynn asked, looking around the table. Maggie stood and started to clear the plates.

"Just leave them in the sink and we'll have dessert later."

"Big brother said you made both apple and chocolate pies. Do we really have to wait?" Tom practiced a pout.

"Come on, take your coffee and we'll turn on the news while we wait." Phillip stood.

"Don't get too comfortable; we'll only be a minute." Lynn handed Phillip the file folder as he walked past her. "Just in case you want to start thinking before we get in there."

"Are you saying watching the news is a nonthinking activity?"

Her shrug precluded any need for words.

In the kitchen, the girls were already loading the dishwasher.

"I can do that later." Maggie waved a hand. "You go ahead and cut the pies. I know both of them want a slice of each."

"I'll start the coffee," Josie said.

Through the years the three of them had become a well-oiled team on kitchen routines. When possible they canned and froze food together; baked Christmas goodies, using all the Norwegian recipes they so dearly loved; and cooked other times when large quantities of food were needed. All the kids joined them with Christmas baking.

*If I do the shared housing, will I have to give up traditions like this?* Lynn paused in cutting the pie. She gave a small headshake. No, these family times were too important. The other women could take part or not as they pleased.

Lynn fetched the coffee mugs from the rack on the wall and went back to serving the pie. "Whipped cream or ice cream?"

"Phil will want whipped on the chocolate and ice cream on the apple."

"Tell him to get his own then." Josie nudged Maggie and the two swapped grins. They always said Lynn catered to her family far more than she needed to. Lynn figured she didn't cater half as much as her mother had. So perhaps it was a generational thing, one that maybe shouldn't disappear altogether.

Josie filled the coffee carafe while the others set up a tray, and Maggie carried it into the family room, where the television was now on the sports news. Both guys groaned at the same time when the hockey scores were announced.

"We can turn that off now, right?" Josie asked as she poured coffee into the mugs.

"Yes, we must." Maggie answered a question before it could be asked. With the pie distributed, the women sat down and the clink of forks against plates was accompanied by hums and smacks of appreciation.

Tom waved his fork. "I think she's trying to soften us up."

"Whatever gave you that idea?" Lynn grinned at her boys. She had finally realized that no matter if their ages said they were men, she knew they would forever be her boys. "You want more?"

"Later." Phillip set his dish aside. "Let's get this discussion under way." He pointed to the folder laid open on the carved pine coffee table that was heavy enough it needed two men to move it. Paul had cut jack pine off their land to make the table years earlier. Paul. Always Paul.

"Before we get into the expenses, et al, I want to know if any of you have serious concerns about my idea." She watched as both couples glanced at one another before answering. Obviously this had been an item of discussion. Waiting was never easy for her and this was no different. But she nibbled at the pie she was eating in small bites.

Tom looked up from studying his pie crumbs. "Define serious concerns."

"Flat out against it." Why did she feel she was laying her life on the line? Each of them looked at her and shook their heads.

"You're not flat out against the idea?"

Maggie looked at the others, then said, "You know that we all love you and want you to get to do the things you want."

Lynn combined a shrug and a nod.

"Within reason, of course." Tom, as usual, managed to inject a bit of humor.

Lynn deadpanned, "Of course." But she knew her eyes were twinkling.

"So, our concerns are the funding, and..." Maggie pointed to the folder. Heaving a sigh, she sucked in a deep breath. "...And we are being incredibly selfish; we don't want our lifestyle here to change. I mean, like all our traditions and being able to let the kids come here without advance planning and..." While the words came in a rush, she smiled when Phillip took her hand.

Lynn felt her shoulders slump in relief. "I don't see that any of that would change. I'm sure they will have careers or jobs, too. Probably, they'll be gone through the workweek. One story I read, one of the women wanted the safety of something like this because she travels for her job all the time and not worrying about her home was a plus for her."

"Good point." Josie nodded.

Lynn stared each of them right in the eyes, moving around the circle. "I know two new women will make a difference, but it could be a good one, you know. They will most likely be working since they are single, and we always have room for more at all our celebrations and traditions. If they want to join in, they will be welcome. And...when I talk with them, more like an interview, we will discuss this. This house has children in and out, dogs, cats, gardening, fishing, church, all the things that make up our lives."

Maggie sat back, more relaxed, smiling.

Lynn continued, "It would be different if I were wanting to move away, but for some reason, this whole idea appeals to me. Through the years I have learned that when God wants me to do something, He sends an idea, but then persists if I try to ignore it. Or blow it off. This is like that." She paused and watched all four of her family relax and nod or sort of smile or shrug. "You can be sure I have been praying about this, and I hope you have, too."

"What does Lillian think?" Phillip asked.

Tom replied, "She's all in favor, looking for other people who have done this that we can talk with."

"Figures, she doesn't live here," Phillip muttered.

Lynn shrugged. "Be that as it may, were she to come home, there will be a place for her to sleep." She pointed to the folder. "When Hank gave me the estimate for the garage, I had him give me two. The second one is for a two-story garage that we could finish in the upstairs as a guest room or whatever is needed."

"Connect the garage to the house? Like where?" Phillip spread out the schematics and studied them a moment.

"An enclosed breezeway. It doesn't have to be heated. Hank says it's a good security feature for someone living alone; you don't have to go outside when you leave the garage."

"We might want to plumb in a shower and stool in the main level, sort of like a mudroom." Tom looked up at her. "And you say a loan is already approved?"

The discussion continued with all of them taking part, figuring out answers to construction questions she'd not even thought about.

Phillip sat back. "Did you set a time with Hank? We'll have to pour that flooring first, you know."

"I gave him a possible."

He nodded. "I'll bring the Cat over in the morning, get that spot graded off. We could start on the footings as soon as we finish Peterson."

Tom asked, "How much more there, do you think?"

"I'd say most of a day. You want to take that and I'll do the Cat?"

Tom nodded, then looked up at his mother. "If that spot is okay with you, we'll have to dig out that flower bed but if you want to connect to the other garage..."

"Wait, don't we have to get a building permit first?" She waved her hands, fingers spread.

"You take the plans Hank drew up in tomorrow and tell them we need to start immediately." Phillip rolled up the schematics. "They'll approve, and we'll be well under way. We have to do this while we have some slack time and the weather is okay. You want a tub with a shower in that third bedroom? It will be a pretty tight fit."

"No room. A shower will be fine. I can order the fixtures tomorrow when I'm in town."

Lynn went to bed that night stroking Miss Minerva, who had decided she should have Paul's pillow. For some strange reason, she felt like she'd been run over by a truck. An eighteen-wheeler for sure.

When her men got their teeth into something, they took it and charged ahead. Good thing she had some money stashed so they didn't have to wait on the loan. *Lord God, if you are not behind this, will you please bring it to a halt? Now before we start the garage?* Not that any of the improvements were not good for the place. And she and Paul had talked about another bathroom, but...

She lay in the peaceful darkness, listening as if she fully expected God to answer right now. An owl hooted. Off in the distance the coyotes struck up a chorus. *Thank you, Lord, for this amazing, wonderful peace. I've not felt it for a long time. Thank you.* She was almost asleep when another thought burst into her mind. *How am I going to find these women to move here? Lord, I'm throwing you this one, too. I have no idea. What if this is all for naught?* The peace settled her back down with nary a ripple.

# Chapter Seven

N̲ot even one tear.

Angela went down her to-do list again. Pure rage had settled into determination so profound she had no doubts that what she was doing was right and proper. Even though thoughts of revenge had backhanded her more than once. After all, God said revenge was his province. Even when it was a husband gone crazy?

The phone had been ringing when the taxi dropped her off at the house. He'd said he would pick up his suitcase in half an hour.

"I don't want to see you."

"Fine, I'll pack and be gone in fifteen minutes."

She'd shut herself in the family room with the television on and the earphones in place so she wouldn't even hear him. After that she had stuffed all of the rest of his clothes, other than his suits that she left on hangers, into black garbage bags and lined them up in the hall. His remaining suitcase she had filled with all the paperwork in the desk and some other personal items. He'd been lucky she'd not thrown them all out on the front lawn. Other people had been known to do that. Had he said he was thinking of divorce, she would have suggested counseling. Christians just didn't make abrupt decisions and throw away their marriage vows. But when she finally asked if there was someone else, the empty silence made her shut off the connection.

It was still hard to believe that he had actually thought he could live at their house until he found an apartment. *The nerve!* That phone call the next day had almost made her find something to drink. Maybe it was a good thing he wasn't closer to home. Stupid things like that were what kept her from crying. That and her job.

And here their children were planning a splendid party to celebrate a twenty-fifth anniversary, one that wouldn't happen now.

*I shouldn't have to be the one to tell the kids. I didn't do this!*

He did not respond to her text that he needed to be the one to tell Charlie and Gwynn and in person. Even though their father... no, that was not worth pursuing. With news such as this, the social media would never do. Would Jack think he could text or e-mail such a devastating bomb? Quite probably.

On this Thursday morning, she dumped the remains of her cold coffee in the sink, slapped her notebook closed, and returned to her bedroom to make sure her makeup was perfect and she'd not forgotten her jewelry, like she did on Tuesday. The mirror confirmed she was ready, so she smiled at the face, the image she had grown into because Jack wanted a fashionable and successful wife, promising her that when she changed, their marriage would be the best anywhere.

*Right!*

A memo waited for her when she arrived at work. It asked her to stop by her superior's office at her convenience. She looked at her assistant, who shrugged also; put her things away; and strode down the hall. She paused before knocking on the door, pulled her jacket down, and after a deep breath, she knocked and entered at the command. "Good morning."

He pointed to the chair in front of his glass desk. "Have a seat."

*Now what?* She took another deep breath to calm her rampaging mind.

"We have a slight problem here, and I have a feeling you are not aware of it."

"Slight problem?" Her voice wanted to squeak but she choked that back.

"You know that Maple Street strip mall?"

"Of course, the one I've been pushing through in spite of so many difficulties. Why, just last Friday, I beat out another brush fire."

"The St. Cloud Investment Company wants out. Their excuse is this has taken too long and they are opting to use the escape clause. They will no longer be any part of the funding."

"They can't do that."

"Yes, they can. As always, money talks."

"But they were the ones who caused all the delays." Angela felt like banging her head to clear it. "Surely there must be..." Her voice trailed off as he shook his head.

"We all did our best here, but sometimes things like this happen."

"So what do we do?"

"Shut it down."

*And there goes my commission. The one I was counting on to carry me once the divorce is final.* "So what do we do, call the other investors?"

"A letter will do but a phone call is polite."

From the look on his face, she realized she would be the one making the phone calls. "Do they get their money back?"

"Check all the contracts. What has been spent cannot be refunded."

At least she had not paid the last bill for all the permits that were no longer needed. It was a safe guess that the county would not agree to refunds. Perhaps right now the official slowness was a plus in her favor.

Her boss leaned forward. "So, what else do you have in the works?"

*Not much* was not an appropriate answer. "I'll have to see where we are on the other projects." Over and over she had heard, "Do not put all your eggs in one basket." Yes, that was a cliché but that's why it was a cliché, because it was so true. She had given the Maple Street project all she had, all her time and energy plus a fair amount of her own money with all the driving and entertaining possible investors.

Despair not only sounded dismal, it tasted worse.

"Setbacks like this are common in our business. You did your best, so you tie up the loose ends, suck in a deep breath, and go on to the next. You've done well for one so recent into this business; don't lose sight of that."

"Thank you." She rose with all the grace she could dig up from clear down to the tips of her scarlet toenails, sort of smiled, and retreated. Back straight, smooth walk, head high.

"I'll see you Saturday." The arrow quivered between her shoulder blades. Tell him now or...She escaped out the door. Down the hall to her office, shut the door securely, and collapsed in her chair.

*Five minutes, Lord, can I have a five-minute pity party?* But when she closed her eyes, all she could see was a brick wall collapsing, one brick at a time. Was the wall her short but successful career, up to this point, or her whole life?

Forty-eight hours until the party was scheduled to start.

Option one: go forward, play the devoted couple, and not tell anyone about the pending divorce until months from now. Could she play the game? Good question. But again, it all depended on Jack. Would he do a no-show or play the game?

Oh, he can play the game. After all, she'd had no hint. At least not to this degree.

But will he show?

He loved his kids; surely he wouldn't destroy them like this.

She picked up her phone and hit speed dial for his number. When he clicked on, she heard, "Excuse me, I need to take this." She heard him walking, a door open and close, and then his voice.

"This better be quick, I'm in a meeting."

"Okay, this is the quick version. Since there is no time for our children to change the plans for the anniversary celebration, Saturday afternoon at three p.m., I believe we can act like all is normal, get through the weekend, and then deal with all this after. The alternative is for you to call them and let them know your decision. I have a hard time believing you would be so cruel as to do that."

"Of course that is what we will do. I'm surprised you'd think otherwise. I'll be back in town Friday night. They'll be staying at the house?"

"Yes. Perhaps you'll all be on the same plane. Charles said not to worry about meeting them, he's rented a car."

"In playing out this drama, do you want me to stay at the house Friday night? Explaining a hotel might be...?"

She groaned. He had one-upped her. "I guess." She'd have to hide all the bags and put a few personal things back out.

"My flight is supposed to arrive at nine. Don't bother to meet me, I'll take care of it."

"Good. Enjoy your meeting." She clicked off and dropped her cell on the desk. At a knock on the door, she raised her head from her hands. "Come in."

Her assistant stuck her head in. "You need anything else?"

"Is it that late already?" She checked her watch. "No, you go on home. We'll deal with all this tomorrow."

"Anything I should know?"

"Tomorrow."

By Sunday night, Angela was sure her face was near cracking. Charles and Gwynn and their spouses had left for the airport by six. They would be exhausted in the morning before work, but they were young and tough. Tonight she was feeling anything but tough. With a promise to see her tomorrow after work, Jack had hauled himself off to a hotel and peace again descended on the house.

No one had commented on the tension she felt so keenly, but she had caught Gwynn studying her several times. She'd probably grill her mother later; she was too busy being the hostess to do much else.

But the party was lovely. So many old friends came, the music was good for dancing, and the barbecue on Sunday afternoon raised the bar for backyard celebrations. Their smart children had catered both events.

Angela stared at their last family portrait taken at Gwynn's wedding. It included spouses and was now enlarged, touched up with oils, and hung over the fireplace in a perfect carved frame. That had nearly undone her. The tears that did trickle down her face could only be expected, and she'd not melted into a puddle like she feared. Hugging her children was easy; somehow she'd managed to evade any hugs from Jack.

Jack could have earned an Oscar for his performance. She would certainly cop best supporting actress.

Monday morning she was almost ready to leave when the doorbell rang. Checking the peephole she saw a man in uniform, like perhaps a sheriff's deputy. She opened the door. "Good morning. How can I help you?"

Stone-faced, he handed her an official-looking packet. "Divorce papers, ma'am." He touched the brim of his hat. "Have a nice day." Did an about-face and left.

Angela stared down at the package in her hands. Surely there was some mistake. But the name and address were hers. She alternated between burning fire and deep-freeze cold, the two flipping like a cartoon.

This only happened in movies, and bad ones at that. She turned back into the house. Could one go into shock over something like this? "Breathe, Angela, breathe!" She did as she ordered, but now all she felt was dizzy. Sinking down on the chair by the table in the entryway, she leaned forward to put her head between her knees. All she needed to do was faint.

*Slow down! Breathe!* She repeated the instructions until she dared lift her head. The world had stopped spinning. She stared at the packet, realizing she was shaking her head.

Never had she felt so alone in her entire life.

Whom to talk to? As she ran down the short list of her closest friends, she realized that she'd not paid much attention to friends once she started on the grand remodeling program, herself being the one remodeled. Physical trainers, style trainers, a business coach, and going through real estate classes in half the normal time—all had left no time for friends. Besides, she'd had a vague feeling that the women at church, who had congratulated her on the new look and life, had withdrawn after she kept turning down requests and invitations.

Who was left?

She hit speed dial for the office. "Hi, Sandy. I won't be coming in today. I got most of the cleanup done and I really feel shot."

"I'm not surprised with a weekend like this one. I wanted to suggest that you plan for today off before we left on Friday. By the way, your kids sure did a great job on the celebrations. I hope mine can manage something like that one day."

"Well, you needn't worry about it for some time." Sandy's kids were still in grade school. "So, I'll see you tomorrow." She almost asked if Sandy knew a good divorce lawyer but said good-bye before she could say anything. Shame was slithering in like the sidewinder she'd seen in Texas one time. How could she do all this without letting anyone know?

All her normal planning techniques flew out the windows of her mind. "I can't do this. I just can't!"

She tossed her cell phone into the basket on the table and headed for the stairs. A shower, surely a hot shower would wash away, wash away, wash away what? Or perhaps crawling back into bed to reclaim some much-needed sleep. How could she have failed so terribly when all she wanted to do was make Jack happy?

# Chapter Eight

I truly can't stay here any longer."
The face in the mirror looked ten years older than a year ago. Judith turned away and sank down in her chair, then stared around the room full of antiques and heirlooms. How quickly could she pack up and get her things in storage? A week? What would she take with her? Melody assured her that she was more than welcome to come with no restrictions as to length of time. Their phone conversation still made her smile and feel a warmth cuddle her heart.

"You can use us as a place to regroup and decide what you want to do with the rest of your life. You do understand that you are welcome forever?"

"Thank you, but we shall see. You know what they say about long-term guests and three-day-old fish."

"Well, since you are family, not a guest, I guess that just doesn't apply here at all. Oh, and something special, there is a big quilting and needlework expo in Minneapolis in a couple of weeks. I already got my tickets and I'll get yours, too. I'm using a coupon I have for us to stay in a hotel right near the center. Half-price."

"Leave it to you, the coupon queen."

"Oh, and don't put your sewing machine into storage. I

have a couple of projects for us. How long since you did any crocheting or...what else was it you used to do?"

"Mother and I did cross-stitch; well, she did more needlepoint, but we always did it together. I'm sure I have at least one unfinished project, and she was working on something just before she died, in spite of how weak she was. I put all that stuff in a box up in the closet. I'd almost forgotten I should pack some of the sewing room for me, too. Melody, you are good for me."

"Glad to hear that. See you in a week? Ten days? The sooner the better."

Judith picked up her notebook and stared around the room again. She'd go room by room and note what things to put in storage, what to pack, and what to leave. At the top of the list: pick up packing boxes. While she had been cataloguing the furnishings of the house, she'd sorted and given some things away, tossed others that were too worn and of no use any longer.

For the next two days she worked from whenever she woke, usually before dawn, until she dropped into bed at night. She made arrangements for a moving company to store the furniture she did own, packed her own boxes, and went up in the attic to find furniture to replace the things she was taking. The movers would put that in place also.

Again, Mr. Odegaard tried to talk her out of leaving, but after apologizing once, she just smiled and stood her ground.

"But what will we do for a caretaker? I thought for sure you would agree to stay."

"I gave you my decision within the week like I said I would. We had not discussed any further than that." *And it is no longer my problem.* Funny how she was divesting herself from the responsibilities of the Rutherford House.

She was ready the day the movers came, and by the time they left, while sparse in the sunroom and her bedroom, all the rooms were furnished. She put her overnight case and purse in her car; did another walk-through to make sure all was well; and after dropping the keys off to give to Mr. Odegaard, she drove by the house once more with a good-bye wave and headed out of town. "Good-bye Rutherford, good-bye old life." Three o'clock, not bad.

Ten miles out of town she gave up, pulled into an empty parking lot, and let the tears roll. She cried for her mother, for what could have been with her father, for her love of the old house, for her dreams of living comfortably either there or elsewhere. But hardest of all to bear was the betrayal. Her father had lied to her. When the tears finally dried up, she leaned her head against the steering wheel. What a simplistic, trusting fool she had been.

Not only was her old life gone, she had no idea what she wanted for her new life. For the rest of her life.

She tipped the seat back to rest her burning eyes for a minute. *Oh, Lord, how am I going to get through all this? At least I have my mother as a good example.* Her mother had been a saint—first of all to put up with her husband and then to live in trust that in spite of all her pain and weakness, God had a plan. She kept reminding Judith how much God loved her.

But if God really loved her, why did He permit her father to treat her like he did? What kind of parent lied to his daughter after using her as nurse, caregiver, secretary, and whatever else his life needed. Chauffeur, at least after Robert left to go help his brother. She shouldn't have been surprised when he was furious with Robert for leaving. Deserting him, he had said. She sucked in a deep breath, the one thing that kept her from boiling at times. Another breath and she could feel her shoulders and the rest of her body relax. *I will get going again in just a moment.*

A rap on her window jerked her out of a deep sleep. She turned to see a uniformed officer staring at her.

"Ma'am, are you all right?"

She nodded and pressed the button to roll down the window. Blinking, she nodded. "I'm fine, I guess I was more tired than I thought." She caught a yawn. "Excuse me."

"Perhaps you should get out of the car? You know, walk around."

"I assure you, Officer, I've not been drinking."

"Better safe than sorry. Fresh air will help you really wake up." He waited for her to open the door and step outside.

She trapped another yawn but missed the one immediately after. Long shadows showed her she'd been sleeping for perhaps a couple of hours.

"Someone called in when they saw you not moving, afraid you'd suffered a heart attack or something." All the while he talked, he observed her carefully. "You moving?"

"I am." She did as he'd suggested and walked around the car. He was right; the fresh air was helping.

"Could I please see your driver's license? Standard procedure, you know."

"Of course." *Don't get upset. He's just following procedures, they have to do that.* She reached in the car to dig her wallet out of her purse and handed the license to him.

"Thank you. You know it's about to expire?"

"Really?"

"Didn't you get a notification?"

"Officer, as crazy as life has been since my father died..."

"You are Mr. Sebastian Rutherford's daughter? Of Rutherford House?" At her nod, he smiled. "My folks used to take us to Rutherford for the logging and lumber industry. I remember touring that house and being in awe that people really lived that way any longer."

"Well, it is now a living history site, so you can take your children there and continue a tradition."

"Really? That's good news." He handed her back her license. "Good thing you stopped when you were tired, but a woman alone in a car...Well, even in Minnesota, that is no longer safe. A motel would be far wiser."

"Thank you, Officer Benson, you have been most kind." She got back in her car and put her license back in her billfold. He waited until she drove away, hand raised in a farewell wave.

*So do I continue on to Melody's or take his advice?* She stopped at the next fast-food place, got some coffee and back on the road. Her cell rang.

"Where are you?" Melody sounded concerned.

"I...well, I hit a crying jag and then fell asleep until an officer tapped on my window."

"Do you want us to come get you?"

"Don't be silly, I'll be fine. Got some coffee; I should be there in an hour, depending on traffic."

"Anselm and I can leave right now."

"Melody, I'm fine." At least she would be when she mopped the tears that bombarded her at the thought that right now someone cared enough to come get her. "Seriously, I think it was a reaction to the crying; after all, I did leave a whole life behind."

"You're not a crier."

"I guess I am now. I might stop and get something to eat, too, so don't worry."

"Call me."

"Yes, ma'am." Judith hung up as her cousin giggled. Between the coffee and the conversation, she drove the remainder of the way without any other incidents, other than slow-and-go traffic, which should have been over by this time. No wonder Melody was worried.

Before she even parked in their driveway, Melody and Anselm both came out the door.

"I was this far from calling you again." She held her fingers half an inch apart, then threw her arms around Judith.

"I'm sorry, I should have called you again, but I hate to talk on the phone and drive, especially when you see so many red lights in front of you." Oh, how good it felt to be greeted like this. While Melody and Anselm had come early for her father's funeral and stayed a couple of days after, since then she'd come to realize the friends she used to have in Rutherford had drifted away through the years as more and more of her time was absorbed by her parents, but mostly her father. He did not share well.

"I heard there had been an accident earlier." Anselm hugged her next. "Leave your car for now, Melody has supper all ready. We can unload later. We're just glad you're here and safe."

Judith leaned back in and grabbed her purse. Now she was glad she'd not stopped for even a snack, let alone supper. Melody was an excellent cook, something she'd never had to learn to be. Ever since the cook left, she'd been eating ready-made food from the grocery store or a restaurant. She could make sandwiches and salads, which were mostly her favorite foods anyway. Since a caretaker would be living in the house, she'd left the kitchen and all the supplies. She had emptied the refrigerator and given the perishables away.

"You want to wash up while I get the food on the table?" Melody said.

"I do, thank you."

The guest bathroom, like the entire house and Melody herself, welcomed guests with comfort and peace. The walls wore textured layers of various peaches over a creamy base. Peach-and-cream towels, even peach soap with a bud vase holding a Peace rosebud and a bit of baby's breath. Judith picked up the vase and inhaled her mother's rose garden. Thanks to her mother's love of gardening, Judith had followed in her footsteps. Cut flowers, the results of her choices even though she'd had a gardener to do the hard work, graced each room in Rutherford House. She'd planned on a greenhouse so she could cut flowers during snowstorms if she desired, but when her mother died, the joy went with her.

Why was it today so many of her thoughts returned to times with her mother?

"You sit there." Melody pointed to the chair where a box wrapped in bright floral paper of pinks and purples and tied with a sparkly ribbon took up much of the plate.

"Melody, I should be the one bringing you gifts." Judith smiled at Anselm, who waited to pull out her chair. "Thank you." How many years had it been that someone other than a servant seated her at a table? She was usually the one seating people.

"I saw this and I thought of you." Melody's grin reminded Judith of when they were girls and loved to surprise each other and their families with gifts.

Anselm seated his wife and patted her shoulder as he moved to his own chair. "You know Melody. Nothing pleases her more than someone liking the present she found for them."

"I know. Can I open it?"

"Of course. But it is really no big deal."

Judith slid the ribbon off and didn't bother to try to save

the paper. After all, her father was not here to chide her for wasting something. From inside the box she lifted a purple coffee mug with fireworks on one side and the words *Freedom at Last* on the other.

"Highly appropriate." She thought she was smiling at Melody, but when she had to sniff and Melody was blinking, Judith sucked in a deep breath. "Whew, that was close."

"Right. No tears at supper." She lifted the lid on a casserole and the fragrance of mac and cheese made Judith smile. Melody met her with a wide grin and lifting eyebrows. "I know. Tonight we have comfort food." She pointed to the individual salad molds of green Jell-O, carrots, and mayonnaise, one of the things Melody's mother used to make for their tea parties. Three little girls playing tea party, including Macy, Melody's younger sister, only with real food.

"And she has pulled out all the stops." Anselm started to push back his chair, then paused. "Let's have grace first and I'll bring in the rest of the feast." He held out both hands, and after a gentle squeeze, he started "Come, Lord Jesus..."

The two women chimed in with the childhood prayer they had all grown up with. At the amen, he smiled at Judith. "We are glad to welcome you here, too; only as far as we're concerned, you are not a guest, but a beloved sister."

That did it. Judith watched his retreating back through a liquid veil. Blinking failed to stop or even slow the flow.

"It's okay, Jude, we just want you to understand that for us, family means we stick together."

Jude, Judy, names never used in her father's presence. Her mind took off for a moment. He used to call her something, a nickname when she was little, before all of life changed in Rutherford. What was it? Or perhaps she made it up. *No!*

"What is it?" Melody's voice came soft and easy on the ear.

"Do you remember my father calling me a name not Judith?"

"When we were little?"

"Yes." Her mind kept digging for it, but the more it dug, the further off the memory floated, tantalizing but leaving. As her mother always said, think on something else and it will return eventually. "Homemade rolls!" One sniff and who cared about a stupid name?

"She said comfort food." Anselm set a basket with a cross-stitched linen towelette folded over the rolls.

"That's the one I made for you." Her eyes widened as she smiled at her cousin.

"Of course. I treasure it. And your mother's needlepoint is on the rocker in the living room."

Anselm returned with another steaming dish in one hand and a plate of pickles in the other. "Green bean casserole, made to order, the traditional way." He sounded like a waiter announcing the works of a great chef.

"I haven't had green bean casserole since—since I don't remember when."

"Did you ever learn to cook?"

Judith shook her head and shrugged. "No, not ever. Guess I better start learning." She lifted a roll and inhaled the scent before putting it on her plate.

The conversation while they reveled in the meal caught them up on all that had happened since her father's funeral and of other things during his last days, along with the happenings of the family. When they finally laid their napkins on the table, Judith wasn't sure if she could even stand, she was so full.

"Dessert later." Anselm picked up his plate and silver.

"Good. Much later, I hope." Judith fought to keep from groaning.

"I'll go unload the car while you two clear the table, okay?"

Judith looked up from gathering plates from the table. "Don't bother with the boxes in the trunk yet. Anything I'm going to be needing is in the car."

"Your sewing machine and the projects?" Melody asked.

"Yes. And clothes. I didn't bring a whole lot. Well, some are in the trunk, too."

Melody stared at her. "You didn't get rid of everything?"

"No, but I put most things in storage until I have a place to live."

"We can turn your bedroom and the one next to it into a suite, almost like a mini-apartment, only you'd have the whole house, too." Melody followed Judith into the kitchen, both of them carrying things from the table. "You go sit down, you can be company tonight at least."

"Sorry, if I sit down I will most likely be out before my back hits the cushion."

Judith took over loading the dishwasher, since right now she was having a hard time remembering her name, let alone where things went in Melody's recently remodeled kitchen. "How's your mom?"

"Loving her new digs. We moved her to a retirement complex where she has her own apartment, lovely place. Much against her better judgment, she is seeing, as she puts it, a gentleman friend."

"My word. Aunt Kit?" Kit was short for Catherine, her own mother's youngest sister. Her husband, Don, had passed away not long after Judith's mother died.

"I know. But he is delightful, and they share so many interests, opera being one of them." She wrinkled her lip at the idea of attending operas on a regular basis. "They are talking of a trip to Italy in June. As he said, they have no time to waste and plan to use up every moment they have left."

Judith looked around the kitchen, then poured soap in the dishwasher and shut the door.

"At least you know how to load a dishwasher. Just push the start button. Every machine is different."

"I can clean things, just not cook them fit for human consumption. Where's Bozo?"

"Mom asked if he could come stay with her for a bit, until she gets used to her new place, said she feels safer that way."

"Someday I want a dog or a cat. Or if I can find a place in the country, I would like chickens, not many, but a rooster and hens. I've been reading up on them in magazines, but when I mentioned it to Father, he about leaped out of his wheelchair in total disgust."

"Why didn't you just get some? What could he have done about it?"

"Made my life miserable."

"Miserabler, you mean?"

"Something like that." The two adjourned to the family room, where Anselm had started a fire in the fireplace and was placing more chunks of wood on it as they sank into the cordovan leather chairs. Judith heard her cell beep and checked for the message.

"Oh, good grief, someone broke into the Rutherford House. Mr. Odegaard wants me to come back and identify what might be missing."

"Will you go?"

"No. He has a complete inventory, right down to the canned goods." She heaved a sigh. "I suppose I should go. Obviously someone needs to be there." *And that someone should be you until they find a caretaker.* Guilt was a heavy burden.

Melody stared right at her and brought her back to the new reality. "Don't you even think about it!"

Well, she did think about it. Constantly. But Melody was right. She had not abandoned them; they had abandoned her.

# Chapter Nine

With a divorce pending, income dribbling in and perhaps drying up, Angela had no idea what to do next. The last week had passed in a haze. Yes, she had shown two properties, both private homes. The offer had been accepted on one. The parties were still negotiating on the second house. Her stab at commercial real estate development had failed with only the slightest possibility it might not be dead. Her possibility meter was fast slowing down.

There was no way she could afford keeping the family home. Jack did not want to buy her out, probably for the same reason. And so she was also getting their home of fifteen years ready for the market. She sent Jack the list of repairs, none of which were major. He had yet to agree to pay for them or do them.

If Jack wanted the divorce, he was going to have to pay for it.

One minute she wanted no part of him, to never, ever even see him again. The next she contemplated what she needed to do to bring him back. After those two options, she usually slid into a puddle of tears.

"Where is your pride, woman?" she demanded of the face in the bathroom mirror as she prepared to go to work. She had informed her assistant, Sandy, of the disaster, then ordered her to show no sympathy or even compassion. That's the way it had to be to keep their relationship normal with no leaks to anyone else in the office.

"I'll try," Sandy said with a sniff and a swallow, blinking all the while. "But..."

Angela held up a hand traffic cop–style. "It's the only way I can maintain." She dropped her voice. "I need this job and I need to make these sales. And more. I cannot do that giving in to the tears. So please..." She stopped and sniffed before pasting some semblance of a smile on her face. "We can do this. We can."

"All right. So be it." Sandy straightened her shoulders and gave an emphatic nod. One nod. "You have three calls to return, an appointment to show a house at eleven, and an appointment with a possible seller at two."

"Thank you." Angela glanced at her watch. An hour and a half to get prepared, which included finding some backup properties to show if the buyer did not like the one they were walking through. She returned phone calls, one from the seller of the one house saying their last counteroffer was their final one. She thanked them and called the possible buyers back. They said thanks but no thanks and gave their reasons. When she offered to search for more properties for them, they said they'd get back to her.

Right. One of the calls was for a short sale. Short sales were a lot of hard work for little money, but anything was better than nothing. She arranged the appointment and set Sandy to researching the short-sale lists for her. A couple wanted a second look at a property out in Rosedale, so she drove out and met them there. Should she tell them the traffic around Rosedale had become much more congested in the last few years? Not a chance. They came from Chicago. They knew traffic.

By the end of the day, Angela dragged herself home to the emptier house. She had assigned herself one room at a time to stage for the showing. She was now on the master bedroom. She'd started with Gwynn's room, then Charles's and their bathroom. Those were the easiest. So far the packed boxes were gathering in the guest room aka sewing/craft room that she had appropriated after the children left for school and marriage. Preparing that room would be a nightmare.

*Walk away.* Where had that thought come from? *I want out.* That was Jack's line. Why was she the one doing all the work when he was the jerk? Jack the Jerk, a perfect name.

Her phone buzzed; she had it set on vibrate, so she checked the face. Deep breath. "Hi, honey, good to hear from you."

"Mom, what's going on?" Leave it to Gwynn to cut right to the chase.

Angela collapsed into her leather recliner in the family room. "Why, what do you mean?"

"I talked with Dad."

"And?"

"And he seemed weird."

*—er than normal?* But she kept the sarcasm to herself. "How so?" She stretched her neck from side to side to try to alleviate the pending headache.

"Evasive. Like he is keeping some secret. I don't think he wanted to talk to me." Her voice cracked.

Daddy's little girl was getting a dose of Jack the Jerk. Angela slammed her head back against the cushion. So unfair. What to say?

"Mom, are you there?"

"Yes, I'm here. Gwynnie, just ask him. You know he has always said you can ask him anything."

"Somehow I get the feeling that old adage of his is no longer true." A pause. "So what is going on, Mom?" Another pause, this time from Angela's side. "Mother, tell me!"

Angela pounded her fist on the arm of the chair. *Why, why do I have to be the one to dish out such disgusting news?* "How many times have you tried talking with him?"

"Three. I gave him every chance to tell me and he sidestepped every time. This just isn't like him."

Not the Jack they used to know, but now...?

"Mother, do not give me the runaround or I will be on the next plane to Minnesota, job or no."

Angela knew that tone; Gwynn did not make threats lightly. "Give me a minute, okay? Tell me something good about your life."

"That bad? Is he sick?"

*Only in the head.* "No, your father is not sick. Look, I need to do a potty run and then I will call you right back."

"Promise?"

"I promise." She clicked off the phone, did what she needed, and swung by the kitchen for a glass of water. The dread of this talk parched her mouth. Back in her chair, she hit speed dial. Gwynn answered before the first ring was done.

"Are you sitting down?"

"Mother, you're stalling."

"Your father has decided he needs to find himself and has filed for a divorce." The words stumbled over each other in her rush to get it said.

"*What?* A divorce after twenty-five years of marriage? How can he? Surely you didn't agree to it."

"It doesn't matter whether I agree or not. He filed. I was served the papers."

"When did all this happen?"

"He told me at our anniversary dinner." Angela shut her eyes to try to stem the pain. *Stay angry!* "I'm sorry, Gwynn. I had no idea." The sounds of her daughter crying shattered her heart all over again.

"B-but, oh, Mom, I can't talk right now. I'll call you later."

Angela laid her phone down and stared at the portrait above the fireplace. The perfect family or so everyone said. Should she call Jack and tell him what had happened? Nope. He wanted to find himself, he could go looking without her help. She was not going to be the buffer any longer. Gwynn and Charles were going to be hurt. She'd help them pick up the pieces if she could, but not him. Right now she could be totally furious with him and disgusted beyond belief. Something she'd read about men in midlife who did this very thing said they often realized their mistakes down the road and wanted to come back. But some bridges could not be restored after being burned.

He said he'd taken everything he wanted to keep and to do with the rest as she willed. His high school trophies went in the trash. She thought a moment and moved them to the giveaway box. Someone could take the engraved plates off and reuse them.

She'd lined up boxes in each room, labeled them KEEP, DONATE, and DUMP. She'd made a box for each of the kids, too. Those would go in storage until they could pick them up or pay for the shipping, should they decide to. There were no boxes labeled JACK. She left enough books, photos, and figurines on the bookshelves to be attractive. The goal for every room.

Charles called the next night. "Dad won't talk to me."

"Oh, really? Any idea why?"

"Probably because I yelled at him."

"You talked with Gwynn?"

"Yes. What are you going to do?"

"I am getting the house ready to sell, trying to move some real estate, and in between, thinking what I want to do with the rest of my life."

"Would it help if I came back?"

Angela heaved a sigh. "Much as I would love to see you, the physical labor here is keeping me sane. Once the house sells, which I think will happen rather quickly, I'm going to look for an apartment and move. But everything will be boxed by then so the house is showroom ready. Stuff will go in storage, but I am being rather brutal in the sorting. After all, empty nesters downsize a lot of the time. I'm looking at it that way for right now."

"Do you know what Dad is going to do?"

"Nope. He took all he said he wanted." The fact that he'd taken no furniture made her wonder if he moved in with someone else. So far, Sandy and the kids had not asked if there was another woman. She was surprised at their lack of interest.

"I'll come if you want."

"Thank you. I know you would. How's Gwynnie doing?"

"Alternates between anger and tears. Mom, he never calls either one of us."

"I'm sorry." What more could she say? She didn't hear from him much either.

"Mom, do you have enough equity in the house to give you some cushion?"

"All depends on what we can get out of it. Not enough to buy another place since we have to split it. Don't worry, okay? I'll be fine." Charles had always been the worrier in the family. He liked things planned out, in order, no surprises.

"You'll let me know if you need some help? I mean, we can send you some money..."

"Thank you for the offer, but really I'm okay." *Or at least I will be if I can get some properties sold.*

"What happened with that shopping center?"

"Fell through, the major investor pulled out. It's a long and boring story."

"Sorry."

"Thanks for calling, Charles, I'll keep you posted." After they hung up she allowed herself to relax into the chair, but when her mind took off again, she heaved herself to her feet and continued with the sorting. Good thing she'd gotten rid of a lot when she was doing the big Angela makeover. From happy little homemaker to successful career woman. And she'd done it. She could do this.

The next day she got an e-mail from Jack. "Schedule the repairs and send me the bills."

She blinked and read it again. "Okay, I will do that." She called a man from their church who had helped them before, read him the list, and agreed that Saturday would be a good time. One more thing down. She thought a moment and called him back.

"Sam, you have a trailer for hauling things, don't you?" At his yes, she added, "Good, I have some boxes that need to go to storage, a lot of boxes." At his "no problem," she made a note to check into a storage unit in the morning. Downsizing was going to become her standard reply when asked why she was selling the house.

That night she slept better than in weeks. Perhaps it was because the kids now knew and she didn't have to worry about keeping secrets any longer.

Her good news in the morning: the couple loved the Rosedale house and had put the money down. It was going into escrow, and she had a couple who were supremely happy. Closing was scheduled within twenty-one days, a record. After jumping through all the hoops, she closed on a short sale, and two new clients walked in cold looking for a house. She listed one new property, the cute little bungalow of clients in a divorce situation wanting out now. All in all a promising and productive day.

She and Jack met at the attorney's office, agreed on a fifty-fifty split on everything, including the outstanding bills, and signed the papers. "I do not have any money to pay attorney fees," she said at the close of the meeting, staring at Jack.

"I'll pay them."

She watched him. The kids were right, he was hiding something. He must want out mighty bad if he agreed to all this without a fight over anything. Maybe she should have asked for more. She turned to the attorney. "So what is the next step?"

"I'll prepare the paperwork for you both."

"How long until the house is ready for the market?" Jack asked.

"I plan to list it next week, why?"

"For how much?"

"I'm going for top dollar. Ralph is listing it and we are looking at comps to see how the market is for a house like ours." *Ours for not much longer. The end of a life, or at least a marriage.*

"Will you have it appraised?"

"If you want to pay for it."

"I think we should."

*We? Since when was there a we? You've not done one iota to make this happen. We!* At the rate her jaw was clamping, she knew she better get out of there. "I'll schedule it and send you the bill. Still at your office?"

"Yes."

*No thank you, kiss my foot, or anything. Jack Bishop, you are certainly not the man I married. When did you change?* All the way down the elevator and to her car, she thought about Jack. He'd not made direct eye contact with her at any time in the meeting. The urge to do something, anything, to punch a hole in his boat, into his dream for finding himself, made her clench the steering wheel with both hands and shake it. Just get through this; sound advice but something sure was bothering her. He was being too agreeable.

*There, all done.* Angela walked through the house that was hers yet in deed only. A decorator could not have done a better job, but then showcasing came easily to her. She'd helped a couple of her clients do the same thing and they always got top dollar. Even the front door had been repainted. Inside and out, all was ready.

When her phone played Pachelbel's Canon, she checked the screen. Jack. "Hello." She almost added, *Now what?*

"I want to buy you out."

"What? You said…"

"I know what I said, but I've changed my mind. I want all the furniture, everything just the way it is now."

"Are you insane?"

"I'll add another five thousand to your half for all the work you've done and another five for the furnishings."

"You want me to pull it off the market?"

"Yes, is that so hard to understand?"

"If I were you, I would not get sarcastic." After he mumbled something, she continued, "Let me get this straight, you want all the furnishings, not just the furniture. Curtains, everything."

"Yes." He cleared his throat. "I walked through it yesterday while you were at work. I want it left just like that."

She clamped her jaw. "You kept a key."

"Yes. I want to move in soon, within two weeks. Can you be out by then?"

"Slow down. Five thousand is not enough for the furnishings. Make it ten since you want everything that is in the house right now. What about some of the things in storage?" She looked around the room, then through the living room. "I will take my personal things and that includes some of the furnishings you saw, like pictures, my mother's china . . . I need to furnish an apartment, you know." She knew she was thinking on her feet and her feet were tired, along with the rest of her.

"So?"

"So, I will take this off the market. Then you and I and my lawyer will talk tomorrow and iron out the small stuff. You have agreed to ten for the furnishings and five extra on my half of the house value. And you will pay me five thousand tomorrow as surety and the remainder when I turn over the keys." *Where are you going to get the money, buster? I have no idea, but that is your problem, not mine.*

He stuttered on a reply, cleared his throat, and said, "I agree."

"Fine. My lawyer will draw up some papers tomorrow to make sure all is legal. When I move out, we will clear my name off the title. Are you sure this is what you want to do?"

"I am."

She sat in her chair after the conversation, mulling it over. Talk about a strange conversation from a man who said he couldn't afford to buy her out. What had transpired in the few weeks since that conversation? This wasn't the time of year for a bonus. Her part of their mutual debt would be around twenty-five hundred. And they would not have to pay real estate fees; looked like she was coming out with more than she thought possible. Her father would have said, "God is providing." Much as she'd been distancing herself from her heavenly Father... She shook her head. Mercy was all she could think. What great mercy.

All accounts had to be changed, and she would no longer be banking where he worked, that was for sure. A thought lightning bolted her. He better not be taking money out of their remaining joint account to pay her. She'd not put any more money into that account since he moved out, not that she had much to put in. Angela rubbed her forehead. This was all too bizarre for words.

After the phone call canceling the sale of the house, in which she dodged questions, she put out the lights and headed up the stairs, her little notebook with lists in her hand. For some strange reason she felt like her whole world was flipping and spinning out of control. Her phone announced a text. Meet me at the bank and we'll go through the safety deposit box and clear up our accounts. Two p.m.

She texted back. Ten, I'm busy in the afternoon.

See what I can do.

*And if you can't, I'll take care of it all myself. Like I have been for years. Jack, you have trained me well. You jerk.*

# Chapter Ten

Y ou want me to do what?" Judith sat gaping at her
cousin.

Melody's smile turned into a chuckle, possibly even a giggle. They'd had a history of giggling when they were little
girls, but giggles had vanished for Judith years ago. About
the time the two families quit getting together. "Just do as I
tell you, it's not hard."

Judith shook her head as she picked up the pile of quilt
pieces. It looked haphazard; not like something that could
be salvaged, let alone made beautiful. "This is not beginner
work."

"I hate to be the one to break the news, but you are not a
beginner." The two had sewing machines set up on the dining
room table and patterns, books, and fabric scattered all over
the place. Even the room looked haphazard. Melody held up
the pieces for step one. "Just do as I do and you'll be fine."

"Famous last words." Judith stretched her neck to each
side, pulled her shoulders back, and huffed out a breath she
did not realize she'd been holding. Step by step, one by one,
they put together pieces of fabric that looked so—well, so random. The resulting quilt blocks were gorgeous. This was more
pleasant than she was about to admit. Time not only flew by
but the piles of in-progress and finished blocks grew, too.

"Amazing what we can accomplish when we work as a team like this." Melody had a trail of quilt pieces reaching clear to the floor and piling up, not taking time to cut threads until she finished. When she handed the train to Judith, Judith took it to the ironing board, along with scissors, and clipped and pressed seams.

"Do you have a quilt frame?"

"No, and my quilting machine is in for repair. I don't quilt by hand much any longer; it's more fun on the machine."

"Let alone faster."

That night after supper while they sat in front of the crackling fireplace, Judith cross-stitching and Melody working on the needlepoint Judith's mother had started, Anselm looked up from the book he was reading. "My belly is calling for coffee or tea and dessert."

"Let me finish this row."

"I'll get it. Coffee or tea?" When both women answered tea, he shrugged and headed for the kitchen.

"To continue our conversation..."

"Which one?"

"The one about what do you want to do with the rest of your life?"

"Interesting, isn't it? Here I am nearly forty-eight years of age and I really have no plans."

"What about dreams?" Melody shook her head as Judith shrugged. "Nope, not good enough. Way back you dreamed of college and becoming either an anthropologist or an archaeologist."

"I didn't get to go to school long enough to make up my mind, either."

"So what is stopping you from doing it now, if those things still interest you?"

Judith laid her hoop in her lap. "You really think I

could?" She had to clear her throat. Did she dare even
think of such a thing? Slowly she shook her head. "I really
can't afford to go to college now. I need to get a job of
some kind, but I don't have any kind of résumé. Who
would hire a forty-seven-year-old single woman with no
documentable skills?"

"Hogwash, to quote my father."

"Hogwash to which problem?"

"The work résumé for one. Sure, you'd have to put one
together, but..."

"And I have no college degree. No piece of paper to show
I went to school."

"No, you don't. But..." Melody paused. "We need to start
with lists. But before that, if money were no object, what
would you do?"

"You said dream and this is way beyond belief. I'd live on
a lake somewhere and go back to school." She tipped her
head against the cushioned chair back and let her eyes close.
"A lake where I could see the sunrise or the sunset, hear the
loons call, and I'd have a dog beside me. And chickens. I still
remember that short time when Momma kept chickens. I
would drive to the campus every day or..."

"Or some of your classes you could take online, if you
wanted to get a job. But with money no object, you wouldn't
need to worry about that."

"Yeah, well, in dreams you can do anything." *Nothing like
real life, the life I am living.* "Besides, I'd love the classroom,
the discussions, the people, even the homework; you know,
the academic atmosphere. I have always loved learning, and
that is one thing where my father and I agreed. He made
sure I learned a lot."

"Ain't that the truth," Melody muttered into her yarns.

"Ah, a bit of sarcasm there?"

"Not difficult to find some when you talk about Uncle Sebastian."

"Hard to believe but he did have a good side, too. Shame that the bad so overwhelmed the good during his last years." She sniffed, then reached for a tissue, and after blowing her nose, she heaved a sigh and nodded. "So, dear cousin, you did get me dreaming. I'm surprised at what came out. Shame the money thing is so real and anti-dreaming."

"You know that both our mothers believed the same thing, *where there is a will, there is a way*. They raised us on that adage."

"I think mine got buried in reality."

"But that reality is over and your new life is beginning, or rather, has already begun." Melody leaned forward. "You can always live here and go to college. We seem to have a plethora of schools within driving distance."

"But no lake with loons." A smile tickled Judith's mouth as she mentioned that part of her dream, the dreams she didn't know she had.

"You want to eat at the table or where you are?" Anselm held a tray with teapot and cups.

"What are we having?"

"Ice cream on those brownies you made and hot fudge sauce."

Judith groaned. "I sure hope you have chopped nuts and whipped cream to put on that sundae."

"Sorry, just plain." He paused with the tray. "Well?"

"Right here." Melody inhaled. "You made Constant Comment tea! What a sweetheart you are." She moved her project off the coffee table so he could set the tray down. "Anselm, my sweet, you spoil me rotten."

❀     ❀     ❀

The next day on their way to the quilting and needlecraft show, Melody asked her again. "Did you think about school and your dreams?"

"I did and I followed your orders to start with lists." Judith patted her leather purse. "All in here. You know, I've never been to a show like this."

"What a shame. Someday I want to attend the biggest of the big in Puyallup, Washington. I have friends who have gone, and they say that this one is good but that one is incredible." She followed the signs into the parking lot of the convention center. "I brought my fold-up cart along and my credit card. You will find notions and all kinds of things here that you don't find anywhere else. Wait until you see the vendors. Talk about creativity." After they parked, she retrieved her fold-up cart from the trunk and handed Judith a bottle of water. "You did bring another bag, didn't you?"

"Ah, no."

"Fine, I brought you one. It folds out bigger than it looks." She pointed off to the west. "That's our hotel. We'll check in after our day on the floor and we're too exhausted to go any farther. We can even do room service for supper if we want."

"You have it all planned."

"Major campaigns require major plans. We have our first Make It and Take It at ten o'clock."

"Make It and Take It?"

"You'll see. Since I already have our name tags"—she pulled them from her purse—"all we need is that big program with all the maps and things. I assume it's basically laid out as the last time, so..." She grabbed two of the newspaper-like eight-page programs and, handing one to Judith, led the way.

Never had Judith seen so many excited women. Why,

the walls could bulge out and back in with all the energy in this huge hall. While her eyes would rather stop and look at each booth, she knew better than to lose Melody, who was plowing through the crowd with iron determination. Thank goodness her cousin was tall and wearing a bright red jacket.

In one of the hallways off the main floor, the relative quiet felt like a balm. Judith blew out a breath; it seemed like not enough air to breathe as they hustled on their way.

"Did you see anything you want to go back to?" Melody checked the program to make sure that the room number and class matched. "Some of the demos are really worthwhile, not that most anything here isn't."

Most of the chairs were already taken. To get two together took some doing. An assistant came around with kits and greeted each of them, inviting them to come look at the finished samples.

By the time the hour had disappeared, Judith's speed-quilting project was nearly half finished, like most of the others. She now knew how to sew together strips accurately, then offset and sew them together, creating a tumbling blocks pattern. It was so easy when one knew the tricks.

"I have included complete instructions in each of your packets. I hope you have a great convention, and I am teaching another class tomorrow at eleven. No, it will not be the same." She held up the sample of lovely ribbon embroidery on, of all things, a pillowcase. "Hope to see you back."

As the women filed out of the door chattering and laughing, Judith felt like she might just bob above the others, she was so filled with delight. *I've not had this much fun in years, and to think I hesitated about coming.* They headed back to the main convention floor.

"The quilting section is over there, if you would rather

do that next." Melody pointed to the far end of the football-field-length hall.

"I—ah..." Judith had no idea what she wanted, and it was so crowded.

"What I thought we would do was make a quick tour of the whole thing, then come back to the places where we want to spend more time."

Judith stared at her. "You have to be kidding, right?"

"No, why?"

"Because my brain is already on overload. We saw that there was a demo on stabilizers back there." She pointed to where they had come from. "I would like to watch that, and besides, there were chairs there."

"Of course, but surely your feet don't hurt already?"

"When you said comfortable footwear, I didn't know you meant hiking shoes."

Melody shrugged and grinned at the same time. She'd perfected the action. But she led the way back to the demo site, this one on various kinds of stabilizers to use. Since cross-stitch did not use stabilizers, Judith was curious as to what they were used for.

"This is all new to me," she said as they sat down. The woman next to her had a cart like Melody's. Many women had them in various designs. "Did you buy that here?" Judith asked.

"By the door as you come in. They have a pickup room where you can leave your bags and get them at the end of the day, too."

"Really? People buy that much?"

The woman pointed at her cart. "More than half full. This afternoon I will probably pack all that in one huge bag and leave it at pickup."

"I see." Watching the demo, Judith realized that the

product could help her and decided to buy the sample pack, along with all the info on where to purchase or order the product should she want more.

By the time Melody allowed them to stop for lunch, Judith's bag was nearly half full, a lot of it free samples. "You didn't tell me about all this."

"Why should I? You wouldn't have believed me." That shrug-grin thing again.

"Right. When's the next Make It and Take It?"

But Melody was obviously thinking lunch, not about making anything. "Turkey sandwich okay? And a bottle of flavored tea?"

"Whatever." Judith glanced across the table. A woman over there had a really good-looking salad. "How about that?"

"Will do." She set Judith's bag on the chair, her cart beside it, and away she went, no lagging in her steps.

"I'm exhausted. Are these chairs taken?" asked a woman beside Judith's right shoulder.

"No, they're free. Please join us."

"Thank you." The two women sat down, one older, one younger, both looking a bit jaded.

"How about I go get our food?" the younger one said. "What would you like?"

"Anything and a superlarge coffee, I have the sweetener here."

The younger woman left.

Judith smiled. "Sounds like you feel the same way I do."

"If you mean in need of a chair and a drink, you are right on."

"You been before?" Was Judith the only one in the world overwhelmed by all this?

"I take it you haven't?"

"No, and I am amazed beyond anything I even thought of."

"My name is Lynn Lundberg." The woman extended a hand. "Welcome to your first quilt and needlework show, and I hope you love it so much you have to come again."

"Judith Rutherford. And I have a feeling that if I live any-where in Minnesota, my cousin is going to force me to come again. Not that it will take much force."

"Why, Lynn, you came after all. Those chairs taken?" a new woman said with a smile.

Lynn waved a hand. "Join us. Just leave these chairs free."

"I can only stay a minute. Need to rest my feet."

Judith smiled at the lady and her friends across the table and reached for her cell phone. But instead of checking for messages, she shut it off and slid it back into the assigned pocket in her purse. If someone did happen to call her, she'd not be able to hear them in here anyway.

Melody set the food on the table. "You didn't say what kind of dressing, so I got two, raspberry vinaigrette and ranch. And I couldn't resist the bars. They were crying out our names." She laid down two clear-wrapped bars with chocolate chips and topped with coconut.

"I haven't had one of those in ages. What a treat." Judith dumped the croutons and dressing on her salad and dug in, surprised by how hungry she was. Mrs. Lundberg and her friend chatted until her younger friend returned with a tray of food.

"Good seeing you, Lynn. I'm feeling recharged. There's a booth I need to find that I heard has some great punch nee-dle embroidery patterns and kits."

Mrs. Lundberg said good-bye to her friend, and she and her other friend talked as they ate their lunches.

Judith paused, halfway through her salad. For some rea-son she ignored her mother's training and listened—eaves-dropped, actually—because she had just heard a comment about a lake and looking for housemates. Again against her mother's dire warning that curiosity killed the cat, she asked, "Where do you live, if I may ask?"

"On Barnett Lake near Detroit Lakes." Mrs. Lundberg leaned back to include her. "This is my daughter-in-law Margaret Marie Lundberg. Maggie."

"Nice to meet you. I'm Judith. I know this is a crazy question, but are there loons there?"

"Oh yes. When we're out canoeing, we often see an adult swimming with her babies on her back."

Judith's heart took a little skip. "Really? I've lived in Minnesota all my life and I've never seen that. Their call is so haunting."

Maggie smiled. "Up where we live, it's a way of life. Mom has remodeled her house to try something new; she's even given it a name, like they name cottages in England. Loon Rest."

"That's beautiful. Trying something new?" *Judith, you are so out of line!*

"Well, my husband died," Mrs. Lundberg said with a smile that trembled just a little.

"I'm sorry to hear that," Melody said.

"Thanks. But I have a big house and I feel the need to do something different."

Maggie leaned over. "Understand, that's in spite of having her grandchildren right across the field and the family plumbing business right there and still going strong. My husband and his brother run that."

"Now, Maggie, you know it's not that I'm lonely, because really, I'm not. Still sad at times, but..." Mrs. Lundberg shrugged with her hands. After a sucked-in breath, she continued, "So I read about something called shared housing, and it intrigued me." She looked at Judith, then Melody. "Have you ever heard of that?"

"Families have been sharing houses forever; this is differ-ent?" asked Melody.

"Different in that the people who do it are usually not related. For instance, I met two women who were friends before they decided to buy a house together. But they were single and could see the sense of it. The convenience."

"I see." Judith nodded. "And my friend's daughter went to graduate school for a PhD, so she and three other grad students bought a house. They anticipated being in school five years, so in the long run it was quite a bit cheaper than renting. When one graduated, she would sell her share to someone new."

Mrs. Lundberg nodded. "Exactly. There are many ways to go about it, but the bottom line is the same. Usually there are private quarters for each person, and they share the rest of the house. That's what I have set up. I have a big log house, so it wasn't hard. I'm looking for two single women who want to do this."

Maggie wagged her head. "We have no idea how to go about finding these women, but Mom insists that God will bring the right ones together."

"I take it you are out in the country?"

"There is a convenience store, a veterinarian, and a pizza place in Barnett, about a mile or so from our house. And Detroit Lakes nearby has basic amenities."

"One of the don't-blink-or-you'll-miss-it so-called towns," Maggie said with another smile. "Oh, and the grade school is there, too, where my three kids go."

Judith was almost afraid to ask her next question. "How far are you from a city—not just shopping, but higher ed?"

"Higher ed? There's a community college and a satellite of the University of Minnesota about an hour away."

*Loons! And a college!* And... Judith was practically hyperventilating. "And what are your requirements of those you want to share with? Or do you already have people in mind?"

"Well, single women. I only have space for two and I have a guest room for visitors. Each suite has a fair-sized bedroom, a full bath, and a view of the lake. We're building a second garage that will be ready before winter."

Maggie picked up the thread. "Actually, it is almost ready now, and the view is gorgeous. We put out a dock in the spring and take it up at freezing. Flowers, gardens, and Mom has the most fabulous kitchen. We're hoping this can become a real family kind of thing."

Judith made sure her mouth did not hang open. Was there any possibility that this might be the answer to a dream she just discovered forty-eight hours earlier? "Now I really am asking for too much. Can you see the sunrise or sunset?"

"The house faces east. I love to sit on the deck and watch the sunrise, and the reflections in the evening are just as spectacular." Mrs. Lundberg studied Judith. "Do you think you might be interested?"

Nodding slowly, Judith barely more than whispered, "I think so."

# Chapter Eleven

"So you are serious about coming to Barnett Lake next week? And of course you are welcome to stay with me, try your room out, if you will." Lynn smiled at Judith Rutherford.

The show was over, and Lynn and Maggie sat with Judith and her cousin at breakfast before heading home.

Judith bobbed her head. "If I change my mind, I will call you. I'm going to check with several colleges in the area regarding their classes. I am sure by this time that I will be starting from the beginning. I think credits that don't end in a degree expire after ten years. Not that I remember a whole lot of that first year anyway; been a lot of years in the meantime." Judith glanced at her cousin. Melody did not look overjoyed. Apparently this was an abrupt change in plans of some sort. What plans Lynn could not guess.

Lynn asked, "Do you use a GPS?"

While Judith shook her head, Melody answered, "I'll bring ours."

"How about I e-mail you the directions, just in case? For some crazy reason, people in our area seem to have a bit of trouble with GPS. It leads them back along a dirt track that ends at a tree. Perhaps the reception isn't the best or something."

Judith asked, "I thought of another question last night. Do you have a dog?"

Lynn could feel her smile slip. "We did but had to put him down about a month ago. Old age. He was my husband's dog."

"Will you be getting another or would you mind if I got one?"

"You don't want a little yappy thing, do you?"

"I have no idea what I want; I've never had a dog in my life. Or a cat either."

Maggie whispered a sad "oh."

They said their good-byes a few minutes later and all headed for their cars. They were no sooner on the interstate than Maggie commented, "You've made your mind up about her, haven't you?"

"Have I?" Lynn studied her daughter-in-law's profile. "Do you have objections?"

"I thought we had agreed that you would ask for references and investigate those applying before making up your mind."

"I can still do that."

"You know Phillip is a stickler for wise business sense."

"There's something I've realized; this is not a business venture but a life. And from the sound of things, Judith has had a rather restricted one."

"You also agreed to not make a final decision until you saw the two women together. This is the first person you've even talked with."

"It came about in a rather strange way, you have to admit. Looks to have God's hands all over it to me."

Maggie rolled her eyes. "I don't really want to be there when you talk this over with Phillip."

"Since I am convinced this is all God's plan, we'll just

have to wait and see. So, now let's change the subject. What part of the show did you like the best?"

"You didn't spend a whole lot of money there. I'm proud of you." Melody checked her rearview mirrors and changed lanes.

Judith snickered. "You more than made up for it."

"Actually, this time I was more careful than the first time I went. That's where I bought my quilting machine. You saw the good show deals they offer."

"I could have watched the machine embroidery demonstrations for hours. I'm surprised that intrigued me so." Judith willed herself to relax. How long had it been since someone else had been the driver, except on the way to the show?

"You can try out mine. I have all the instructional DVDs and a lot of simple patterns. I can tell you, it is an expensive hobby."

"Any chance of a rest stop break? That coffee . . ."

"No problem. There's a rest area three or four miles ahead."

Melody pulled into the rest area and they both went in, but Judith finished first. She walked out to the curb to wait and looked around a little. According to her conversations with the Lundberg woman, this part of the country looked much like the area where that house was situated—rather thick woodland with open glades and some cleared pastures. And a lake. And loons. Judith could certainly live in this.

Back in the car and on the road again, Melody seemed awfully quiet.

"You tired?" Judith watched the woodlands spaced out with houses and farms fly by. Obviously this land was all trees not that terribly long ago. In the Rutherford area, there had been huge trees when her great-grandfather first hacked his way in.

"Aren't you? You know if you want to kick back and sleep awhile, you can do that."

Judith let her eyes drift closed, but images of a log house, a lake complete with loons, a dock, and reflections would not leave her alone. "You think I am making a mistake? If I go west, I mean?"

"I was hoping you would be closer, not farther away. Like preferably where you are, in my home. But if this really is your dream, then what can I say? I was the one who forced you to dream."

"Forced me? I don't think so. Allowed me, encouraged me is more like it. I really need to see if I can get into the university. You think they have grants and financial plans for someone my age? And with so little income?"

Melody hooted. "What do you think you are, over the hill and worthless or something? Good grief, woman, we are in the prime of our lives now. Not only changing horses in midstream, we are setting out on whole new adventures." She paused. "Regarding the finances, though, that might be to your advantage when applying for grants, etc."

"You said 'we.' What is your new adventure?"

Melody smiled. "Not sure if other than all I am doing through church and civic stuff, but if there is a change, you will be the second to know."

"Anselm will probably figure it out before you tell him."

"True, for a man he is very intuitive."

"You better treasure that man, dear cuz," Judith warned. "You got one in a million."

"I know. I have to be very careful to not let little things bug me. He is a man of God but can be bullheaded at times."

"Can't we all?"

"Are you saying I'm bullheaded?" Melody looked her way.

"Not at all. Keep your eyes on the road." Judith heaved a sigh, and she could tell her smile was both inside and out. "Thank you for dragging me to that amazing show. You opened my eyes to a whole new world. Made me wonder if, just possibly, I have some of my mother's artistic abilities. Remember how she used to arrange the flowers? I can remember her drawing pictures for us to color. Remember?"

"I do and I think my mother kept some of those. She used to groan that her sister got all the talent. I'll have to check that box."

"The box?" Judith frowned.

Melody nodded. "A box of mementos. She kept all kinds of memory things in a box for me; well, actually for each of her children, all personalized for each of us, too. She went through all the old pictures and made sure she kept the important things like graduation hats, 4-H ribbons, honors of any kind, our report cards."

"I want to see yours. Mother kept a lot of things and I kept those boxes, but there is no order like that. Oh my word!" She thought a few minutes half watching a long white barn and well-kept buildings, followed by many, many trees that whisked by. "What will I do with all the things I kept if I move to Lynn's house?"

"A storage unit until you decide; surely they have storage units around there."

"I kept my bedroom furniture because Mother and I bought that together. And I have her chair."

"The rocker she did the needlepoint seat and back for? I remember that seat; beautiful handwork."

Judith felt elated and sad simultaneously, an odd sensation. "Yes. I can hardly bear to sit in it; it makes me cry and realize how much I miss her. Probably more now, which is crazy."

"Just remember, your room always waits for you here. And I expect you for holidays, at least. Just think, soon your life is going to revolve around school holidays. I'll help you research first thing in the morning. After all, two computers are better than one. When we go visit Lynn, we'll go on over to the college campus and get your new life rolling."

"You really believe this is all going to happen, don't you?"

"I do. You don't?"

"Dreams coming true are a little hard for me to accept right now. We shall see."

# Chapter Twelve

M om, I have something to tell you."
Lynn knew well that guilty look of her younger son.
"What? Can't be that bad."

"I hope not but Josie said..."

*Do not roll your eyes, smile.* She even tried to keep a mother's exasperation look at bay. "Now you have my curiosity in full force. For Pete's sake, just tell me. I promise not to ban you from apple pie for the rest of your life." Hoping to make him smile didn't work. What could it be? "Tommy!"

"Well, I put your sharing your house idea up on my Facebook page."

"You didn't. You're teasing, right?" At the slight shake of his head, she ordered herself to breathe. Which she did. She'd heard making oneself breathe could bring on patience and right now she really needed a bucketful.

"It seemed a good idea at the time. You know, see if anyone else has done it, what their experiences were. I could go take it off maybe."

She could have sworn they just hit a time warp and he was ten years old again. And then suddenly the room became very warm. Unbearably warm. On impulse she walked over to the thermostat; there was nothing wrong with the room temperature.

"Mom? Are you all right?"

Hot flash. She sighed. "Just getting old."

"I probably should have asked first, huh?"

*Breathe.* "Might have been a good idea. What if we get a whole lot of cranks who... ?"

"I didn't put your address or anything stupid like that. Or even your name, come to think of it. And only my friends and their friends can see it." He held up a hand, back to adulthood. "But here's the interesting thing. You remember Charlie Bishop? He came home from college with me a couple of times, I taught him how to ice fish and he caught the season's record."

"And your father promised to never let him come again? We all laughed at that threat, from your dad, no less."

"Right. Well, after graduation we kind of lost touch with each other, until Facebook a year or so ago. Been keeping in touch somewhat. But he responded to my post. Said his Mom has just been forced into a divorce, his dad turned into a jerk, and she doesn't know what she is going to do. His dad is buying her out on their house and she has to move rather abruptly."

"Interesting." *Oh, really, come on.* Her inner chider went into full force.

"You could talk with her."

She could tell that this son of hers really wanted a positive answer.

"After all," he pressed, "what can it hurt... to just talk, I mean."

"Give him my number and have her call me." This can't be any more a strange way to meet than at the quilt show. *God, I get the feeling you're at work again.* Sometimes, like now, she was almost sure she heard a heavenly chuckle.

"Thanks, Mom."

"Where does she live?"

"Here in Minnesota, St. Cloud area, I think. He and his sister are both in Seattle."

"You want a piece of apple pie?"

"You have some?" His face brightened immediately.

"One piece left of the apple cherry." She opened the refrigerator door and brought out the pie. "Ice cream, too?"

"Why not?"

"Probably because it isn't even dinnertime yet."

"I better call Phillip and tell him I'm a bit delayed getting back."

"I'll bag up some cookies; that'll sooth the savage beast."

A few minutes later, on his way out the door, he threw over his shoulder, "Her name is Angela, Angela Bishop."

Nice to know. Four more days until Judith Rutherford arrived. And Lynn had not even had time to unpack her bags of treasures from the quilt and needlecraft show. And the garden really needed weeding. Time to call in the short troops. She texted Maggie and asked if the kids could come after school to help her weed, then headed outside to bring out the rototiller and get the weeds between the rows done, at least. After Paul died she had invested in a lightweight one that she could use and kept the heavy-duty one for digging up in the spring and on new places when she added more garden or flower beds. Would either of the women be interested in gardening? Maybe she should make up a questionnaire for them to fill out.

"You did *what*?" Angela glared at her phone, or rather glared at it in place of the son whom she wanted to do more than glare at.

"You heard me." Charlie spoke with all reasonableness, as

if suggesting she move to some outlandish place where not knowing anyone was an everyday occurrence.

"Right. I heard you, but don't be silly. I have a job here and I need to work, in case you thought I was independently wealthy."

"But, Mom, you told Gwynn on the phone that you needed to start a new life and maybe in a new place."

"I was just running off at the mouth."

"So what is happening now at that real estate office? Can you make a living there? A decent living?"

What could she say? The short sale fell through, one couple backed out of searching for a house, and the potential seller changed his mind and went with another agency. She had zero income until the one in escrow closed. She'd not found an apartment she could move to. The ones she could afford were not palatable and the ones she liked she couldn't afford. Sometimes she wanted to do Jack bodily damage. He refused to give her an extension, said he needed the house now.

Lately, overwhelmed was her only recognizable emotion. No, fury was the other.

"So will you call her?"

"Charles Edward Bishop, do not put any more pressure on me at the moment."

"Please call her and I'll stop bugging you—for now."

She could tell he hoped she'd be reasonable. After all, he was trying to help. Not like some other male she knew.

"Okay, I will call her. Only because she and her family were so good to you those years ago. But I can tell you right now, this just isn't going to work. You don't just pick up and move a real estate business."

"Thanks. I'll tell Gwynnie to keep on praying."

"Yeah, well, I'm glad to hear someone else is praying, too.

Right now I don't seem to be getting any answers." Or heavenly help either. She thought of the day before when all the
real estate transactions came tumbling down and she had
no further options other than cold-calling, which she hated.
Maybe crawling back into bed and pulling the covers over
her aching head was the best remedy.

Lynn stared at the pad of paper on her lap. At the top: "List
of Questions to Ask." "Maybe I should just do a checklist for
each of us to fill out." Thanks to Tommy, she had gone online and started looking for other people embarking on a life
change like this and discovered there was a whole world out
there of communities, of bloggers, and of nonprofits formed
to help people do this. Shared housing was nothing new, but
it was growing more popular all the time.

She wondered if there were other people in the Detroit
Lakes area who were already experiencing the situation. It
seemed most of the houses and communities she had re-
searched were in cities with access to public transportation
and all kinds of entertainment. She looked out over the lake
where a flock of mallards settled on the smooth lake surface;
their duck chatter could be heard on the slight breeze off
the lake. She'd be hearing loons anytime now.

Miss Minerva wound herself around Lynn's legs and
chirped permission to lap sit.

"Sorry, I'm busy."

The cat jumped up anyway and bumped her head on
Lynn's chin, a demand to *pet me, pay attention to me*. Lynn
held up her pad of paper and scribbled, "Must love animals,
no smoking, light drinking," and watched the flock of chick-
adees squabble at the bird feeders. Life in the country was a
far cry from city life, different in just about every way imag-
inable. Her phone sang and Minerva jumped down, glaring

over her shoulder as she stalked off. Settling on the deck railing, she took up bird-watching, too.

"Hello, Paul's Plumbing."

"Oh, sorry, I must have the wrong number."

"Whom are you calling?" This wasn't the first time this had happened. But the calls had been transferred to her once their help left the office.

"Lynn Lundberg."

"Speaking. How can I help you?"

"Ah, well, my son said I should call you regarding your idea of sharing your house."

"Are you by any chance, Mrs. Bishop, uh..." She couldn't remember the first name. "Sorry."

"Yes, Angela Bishop. My son, Charles, visited you several times."

"Yes, I remember Charles well. Fine boy. Well, he was boy then. Tommy told me about you yesterday morning. I was hoping you would call." She softened the business voice she'd answered with. "Do you do Facebook?"

"Not as much as Charles does. He and my daughter, Gwynn, text all the time, too."

"Do they expect you to do the same?"

"They do." Her voice took on a bit of a smile.

"I know, mine too, and my two sons live near here, one across the field, the other less than a mile away. My daughter teaches school. Tommy said your two are really far away in Seattle."

"Right. And some days it feels farther away than others." They chatted for a while before Angela asked her first real question. "I am a real estate agent and this makes me wonder why you want to share your house."

"I have a rather large log house, and since my husband died, the house has felt even larger. We talked about my selling it, but the term *downsizing* makes me gag. I love my house, but one person living here alone seems a waste. And besides, help with the mortgage would be another solid reason."

"So a housemate will pay rent."

"Yes, I know sometimes women buy a house together, but not here."

"Have you advertised?"

"No, I hope I don't have to. I'd rather God brought the right people here since this seems to be His idea anyway." There, put the faith questions right out there.

"The thought of moving away from this area seems overwhelming on one hand and a welcome reprieve on the other." Angela paused, obviously thinking. "Is there any chance you could send pictures and maps?"

"I could, but the best idea would be for you to come see. I'm warning you, though, if you want city living, this is not it. Detroit Lakes is the closest real town and it's about ten miles away. We're about forty-five minutes from Fargo."

"There are real estate offices there, of course."

"Yes, some very good ones." Then for some strange reason, Lynn asked, "Is that what you want to do with the rest of your life? Sell real estate, I mean."

Angela heaved a sigh, audible even over the phone. "I wish I knew."

"You are welcome to come visit, spend the night if you'd like."

"Could my kids come visit me there?" She sounded like a little girl lost.

"Of course. And your grandchildren, too."

"Perhaps someday, but right now, they are career focused. Charlie has always talked of going back to your house. He so loved it there but he is a confirmed city dweller."

Lynn flipped to her calendar. "When would you like to come?"

Another sigh. "Would tomorrow be too soon? I don't know about spending the night."

Lynn swallowed and kept her voice level when it wanted to squeak. "That will be fine. If you want directions..."

"No, I have my GPS. I'll see you after dinner tomorrow. Can I let you know then if I decide to spend the night?"

"The bed will be ready for you." They did their good-byes and Lynn sat staring at the lake. Miss Minerva jumped back up in her lap, knocking the pad of paper to the deck floor. Lynn sat stroking the cat and thinking about the phone call. Talk about a hurting woman. In fact, from the brief histories they shared, both Judith and Angela had been through some pretty traumatic situations in the very recent past. Was this good or bad in regards to building a shared house with the three of them? Or were there other people to interview, too? *Lord, I wish I knew what you are doing in all this.*

# Chapter Thirteen

Judith pulled into a graveled circular driveway and parked in a wide spot beside a nice little black sedan. Was this the place? Surely so, two-story log house on the shore of a lake. The two-bay garage beside it was so new you could still smell the lumber. Too bad they had not made the garage of logs as well, but the cedar shakes that formed the siding were good enough. Judith had managed enough renovations on Rutherford House to know a thing or two about construction. This new building was very well constructed.

And the lake. Transfixed, Judith walked out across the green lawn to the water's edge. *Oh my. The lake.* A slight breeze tickled the surface and made it shimmer. It glowed. Yes, this was exactly her dream. No loons that she could see, but Lynn had said they were there. And ducks. Five mallard ducks puttered around at the water's edge nearby. Blue water reflected blue sky. And beyond, the sharp contrast of dark evergreens and pale green deciduous trees just beginning to come into foliage.

The yard was clearly loved and well cared for. Judith could see no weeds, and that was the first thing she looked for. Properly tilled beds, full, well-established grass. *Good. Good.* After her father laid off the landscape gardeners, the Rutherford House grounds that had once been the pride and envy of the region had all fallen into neglect, for Judith could not handle the herculean task. So she had arranged for the local garden club to take over the grounds of the Rutherford estate. Her father objected strenuously to strangers rooting about in his yard, but Judith insisted. The women, and a few men, took to the project with alacrity. They pruned, planted, tilled, mowed, and used some of the flower gardens as experimental plots. Now once again nestled amid lush beauty, Rutherford House enjoyed its former dignity and glamour. Did her father—or Mr. Odegaard, for that matter—realize the half of what Judith had accomplished for that estate? Obviously not, or if they did they were ungrateful fools. She turned back toward the house.

Two women came down off the porch to greet her. No two women could be as contrasty as these two were. The one was superthin, almost too lean, well dressed, well coiffed, very upscale looking; she seemed aloof, almost cold on first approximation. Beside her, Mrs. Lundberg was graying, normal build, very casually dressed, and sort of downhome bouncy-cheery. She oozed "Grandma."

Lynn smiled and extended a hand. "Welcome, Judith. I'm Lynn Lundberg. This is Angela Bishop, another potential housemate. Please join us. We're in the middle of a hot discussion about how much flour goes into lefse dough."

Judith laughed. "The fate of the free world hangs on this decision, doesn't it?"

Mrs. Lundberg and Mrs. Bishop looked at each other, grinned, and nodded. Mrs. Lundberg said, "You'll fit right in. Come and sit, please."

Judith took the three wooden steps up to the porch, or veranda, or deck, or whatever you'd call it. She settled into a wicker papasan chair with a velveteen pad that was even more comfortable than it looked.

Mrs. Lundberg handed her a glass of clear pink something over ice. "Raspberry lemonade. The raspberries are homegrown. The lemons, not. How is your cousin?"

"Pouting, but she'll get over it. When I left Rutherford House, she intended for me to settle near her, ideally in her spare bedroom. Instead, if I come here, I'll be farther away than before."

"Would that create a problem?"

"No." Judith said it firmly, but was it really true? Melody was certainly disappointed, but it wasn't like Judith was moving to Mongolia or something. Would Melody come visit her here or expect her to make the long drive? Melody had hardly ever visited when she was at Rutherford House. That probably answered the question right there.

Mrs. Bishop's voice, a purring alto, sounded absolutely sexy. "My son and Lynn's son are friends. They reconnected through Facebook and"—she shrugged—"well, here I am. I drove out here the day after I first phoned Lynn and liked what I saw. This is my second visit."

Judith gazed off momentarily at the shimmering water. "*A dream come true* is such a trite phrase, but it pretty much describes this setting. Mrs. Lundberg, I understand I'll be paying rent, but are there separate charges for grounds keeping; you know, landscaping and maintenance?"

"No additional charges, especially no landscaping fees. And please never call me Mrs. Lundberg again. I'm Lynn and this is Angela." She chuckled. "My grandchildren and I love to garden. Well, not exactly. I'm the one who loves gardening. They pull weeds just to get to the cookies and pie following."

"In short, you bribe them."

Angela laughed. "Bribery works wonders. I used it all the time on my kids. Still do." She frowned and cocked her head, listening. "Speaking of which..."

Judith heard it, too. Children's voices. It sounded like a whole classroom full, all chattering like blue jays. The happy gang came pouring around the corner of the house and toward the women on the porch. Judith cringed and tried not to let it show. She was not all that into small children, especially not five at once. They all wore child-type daypacks on their backs, and curiously, the two tallest boys had sticks of firewood stuffed into their packs. At least a grown-up was accompanying them, a jovial fellow also with a backpack.

Lynn was grinning. "This is my mob. Angela, you've met Phillip. Judith, Phillip is my elder son."

The man stepped forward, smiling, and shook her hand. "How do you do, Judith?"

"Where's Tom?" Lynn asked.

*Oh, dear, there are more?* flitted through Judith's thoughts.

"Fronting down Mrs. Sturtevant."

"Fronting down?" Judith frowned.

He grinned. "Family slang. My dad invented it. The opposite of backing up. Mrs. Sturtevant's drains backed up, so my brother, Tom, is snaking the line."

"Ah." "Snaking the line" Judith understood all too well. She was intimately familiar with snaking lines. Some aging pipe or other in Rutherford House was always backing up. Usually tree roots were involved.

Lynn pointed. "Tom's children are those two, Douglas, Daniel. Doug and Dan." Each grinned and waved as he was introduced. "These three are Phillip's. The tall gangly one there is Travis; he plans to become a chef. That's Davey, and this is Caitlyn. Miss Priss, to her parents and me."

"I'm gonna be a ballerina," Miss Priss announced. "Soon as I grow up."

Angela smiled. "A worthy ambition! But then, so is becoming a chef."

Judith had absolutely no idea what to say to these children. She rather envied Angela in a way, for Angela could at least come up with something.

Phillip explained, "We're headed for the park. We're going to roast marshmallows and make s'mores. You ladies are invited, of course."

Judith pasted on a smile. "Perhaps another time. Thank you."

"I'd love to sometime," Angela said. It sounded so much warmer and friendlier than Judith's response.

One of the boys—was that Doug or was it Dan?—boasted of making an A on a math test. Lynn exclaimed something very positive. Lynn doted, that was for sure. Immediately the other four had to tell of their latest triumphs, eagerly talking and certainly not taking turns. And they had that habit all children have that annoyed Judith no end; if you didn't respond to a child instantly, that child kept repeating until you did. "G'ma, G'ma, G'ma, G'ma, G'ma..."

On the plus side, they all had nice little triumphs, at least for that age group.

In a few minutes the children all waved good-bye; the safari and their simple native guide trooped away around the house. The noisy chatter faded.

Thank goodness that was over with. Lynn had mentioned she would be introducing the mob who came and went through her kitchen. Judith faced a question that was minor at the moment but could easily become a monster: Did she really want to share her life with five noisy children? But then, the placid lake stretching out before her resumed its siren song.

Lynn said, "Angela, you explained that your husband filed for divorce."

The gaunt woman (yes, that was what she was, gaunt) studied the decking a moment. "Lynn, Jack is a man obsessed with youth and good looks." She shrugged. "And I admit, he's extraordinarily good-looking—movie star handsome. Slight graying at the temples and the physique of a thirty-year-old, right down to the six-pack abs. He spends hours a day at the gym and an hour a day in the bathroom just grooming. Taking a gorgeous woman out in public, to see and be seen, is extremely important to him."

Judith could not imagine that mind-set. Surely this Angela couldn't be telling the truth here. There was more, something deeper, that she wasn't admitting.

Lynn nodded sadly. "Sounds like he found someone younger."

"I'm sure of it, but I've never seen any direct evidence of it. Except... I was trying to mend our marriage and took him to the fanciest restaurant in the area; we could not afford it when we were raising kids, and I knew he loved that kind of thing. You know, glamour, a place that in theory he never went. And yet, he knew the maître d' by name, and when he ordered flambé, he didn't have to say it; the waiter knew. Even then I wasn't really suspicious; later, I started sorting things out. And since I left, I've discovered he was systematically draining our accounts. I froze the ones I could; something about stolen horses and barns."

Judith wagged her head. "I can't imagine a person like that."

Angela's voice dripped bitterness. "Imagine it."

As the three continued talking, no one said much more of substance. Judith listened with one part of her mind and with the other tried to weigh these two women. Lynn. She seemed soft and motherly, but detectable beneath it all was an iron core. And this questionnaire she had them fill out. It smacked of micromanaging. Her father had micromanaged, so Judith knew it when she saw it. And authoritarianism. *Do it my way or else.* Judith had spent a lifetime under the thumb of an authoritarian micromanager. She truly hoped she was dead wrong about Lynn Lundberg.

And there was Angela. Judith's first appraisal seemed correct—this woman was aloof. Or maybe not; she seemed more wary than aloof. Guarded. Judith had dealt with a lot of high rollers, schmoozing wealthy people who might contribute to the Rutherford House renovation or some other local charity, and this woman did not "feel" like a wealthy person. *Silly thought, Judith!* Yes, but there it was. Judith had developed a sort of sixth sense about this, and she trusted her feeling now. Angela was either a very wounded woman or a phony.

But she could give this situation a try. If it didn't work out, she could always move back to Melody's, figure out something else. As she watched the vivid colors of the sunset reflect off the ripples in the lake, she made her decision.

# Chapter Fourteen

So this is the day they move in?" Maggie asked as she poured herself a cup of coffee.

"They should get here midafternoon." Lynn stood with the refrigerator door open, staring at the inside. "I've planned an easy supper, the rooms are ready, and why am I so nervous? I can still back out."

"I wondered if you were. I would be. In fact, I am, too. On one hand, I want them to love it here like we do, and on the other hand…"

"Do I really want to share all this with two women I don't even really know?"

Lynn set the half-and-half on the table and poured her own coffee. "I've been trying to guess what all the problems could be and all I get is a headache, and that reminds me about health issues. Are there any? What do we do if there are?"

"The old what-if game?"

"Right."

"Someone I dearly love told me probably more than once to let God take care of the 'what ifs' and I am to deal with one minute at a time." Maggie poured half-and-half in her coffee and added a bit of sugar.

"I hate it when I have to eat my own words." Lynn sank

down into her chair like the state of Minnesota draped over her shoulders. "You suppose the other two are as scared of this as I am?"

"Scared? Lynn Lundberg scared? I doubt it. Apprehensive is sure understandable. Kind of like getting married, I'd guess. Well, no, not really. Permanent houseguests, but that's not right either. How will you divide up who does what?"

"The things I read said everyone needs to be upfront and honest about likes and dislikes and what really is impossible, i.e., smoking. I won't tolerate that, as everyone knows. Not even smoking on the deck, like some people go outside to smoke. I am so glad none of my kids smoke."

"Or chew. Bleh." Maggie made the appropriate face.

"Well, at least most women do not chew." Lynn glanced at the counter. "Minerva, get down. We talked about a lot of that when they were here to visit together that time."

"Do they both like animals and kids?"

"They said they do, but Judith has never had kids around, at least not like here. Minerva!"

Maggie nodded. "I'll see that the kids stay home until folks are settled in." She reached over and covered Lynn's hand. "I told them that eventually they will get to do sleepovers at G'ma's house again. Miss Priss was the most concerned about that." She glanced up at the clock and drained her coffee cup. "I told Phillip I'd run some errands before dinner. Better get on it." She reached down and stroked Minerva. "At least no one is bringing a yappy dog."

Judith arrived first. She got out of her car and stretched, smiling at the sight of the tulips blooming in a bed beside the graveled driveway. Her mother used to insist on red tulips lining the walk to the Rutherford House after the daffodils were finished. Back in the days when they had gardeners. The movers were supposed to be here by three to unload what she had marked for here and then take the rest to the storage unit. She would be so glad when this day was done. Leaving Melody and Anselm was hard. Even though it wasn't as if she'd not see them soon again.

She waved to Lynn up on the deck. "What a lovely day. Is Angela here yet?"

"Nope. She called to say there had been a bit of a problem." She pointed out toward the driveway. "There's your truck."

Lynn showed them where to back in, and within an hour, the furniture was in place, the bed put together, and they'd even moved the boxes from the trunk of the car into the hallway.

"You guys in need of coffee or iced tea?" Lynn asked, but when the two men turned down the offer, she sent them on their way with a bag of cookies. Obviously, Granny here loved to bake. She asked Judith, "You want me to go with you to the storage lot?"

"You don't mind?"

"Nope, supper is ready and I just got another call from Angela. They are still an hour and a half out."

Once in the car, Judith looked at Lynn. "I still can't believe I really am doing this."

"Join the club. We are all embarking on a new life adventure, that's for sure. I'll help you make up your bed when we get back."

The gate would not open at the storage lot. Judith tried, Lynn tried, the younger of the movers tried.

Judith dialed the number for help. No one answered. "So now what?" Getting the churning to stop in her middle would be one important thing.

Lynn pulled out her phone, searched her contacts database, and dialed a number. "Merv, you have any idea where Penny is? We can't get into the storage lot."

A voice so loud that Judith could hear it said, "No idea where she is, but he is over at the hardware store. You have the number?"

"Yep, thanks." Lynn looked at Judith and shrugged while she located the number and hit send. "Hey, Jason, Lynn here, could you pass the phone to George? We're stuck at the storage gate." They chatted and she closed the call. "He says he'll be right here. Take him about five minutes."

The fellow named George arrived in a white pickup and used his key on the gate. It slid open, and the men unloaded and were on their way in less than half an hour. Judith snapped the lock shut on her unit and they returned to the car.

"Sorry about that." George was huddled over at the gate, working on the box as they drove out. He grinned sheepishly. "Welcome to Detroit Lakes."

"Reminds me of Rutherford that way," Judith said. She asked Lynn, "You want an ice cream or something?"

"No thanks. We better get on home in case Angela's estimate was off." Lynn pointed out landmarks as they headed back to Barnett Lake. They pulled into the drive and parked in front of the new garage. "So, did you get signed up for school?"

"I did. The semester starts June first. I decided to not go full-time this semester. I couldn't get one of the classes I wanted, so I am only taking three."

"That gives you two weeks to settle in and get ready."

"I thought of going to Melody's over Memorial Day weekend. Visit my mother's grave and leave flowers there. I always took flowers from the grounds at Rutherford House before."

"You are welcome to take some from here, and the hot-house geraniums are usually blooming then. We can put them in buckets so they last."

"Thank you, but Melody said I could cut from her yard, too." She paused. "Will I be able to help in your yard and garden?"

"Judith, this is your house now, too. There's plenty of things that need to be done, so I thought we could see what each of us likes best or dislikes the least and sort of move into that." Yes, this woman seemed to be a natural micromanager, just like her father.

They drove in right behind a moving truck and Angela was stepping out of her car. Whatever reservations Judith harbored would have to be put aside for the moment; the die was cast, as they say. They repeated the same move-in drill, but it seemed to go faster with Judith helping.

Judith said, "You told me you have dinner waiting. Tell me what you need done for supper, and I'll have it on the table when you get back from the storage lot. Or I can go along and we'll get it done super quick."

"Warming up dinner won't take long. Hop in." Lynn slid into Angela's front passenger seat, so Judith climbed in back. She had to scrunch aside a lot of blankets and bedding on the backseat.

Angela looked about at the end of her rope. "Thanks for helping me."

"You are welcome," Judith replied. "It appears you don't have much to put in storage."

"I know. I left some in St. Cloud. I wasn't sure what to do with it, so I figured I could decide later."

"So this Jack is in your old house?"

Angela grimaced. "I just learned that he has a housemate already. I imagine they will be married once the divorce is final. Seems she's pregnant."

"And I take it this is a surprise to you?"

"Total shock. He's a master at hiding things, or so I have discovered. Or else I'm terribly gullible."

*Or some combination of the two*, Judith thought, but she didn't voice it.

They continued in silence to the storage lot.

George was still working on the automatic opener. He straightened and grinned. "You're back. I should have this fixed by the morning."

"Surely not that long. Can't you find the parts?" Lynn asked.

"That's the problem, all right." George smiled at Angela. "Welcome to Detroit Lakes, ma'am. This is a great place to live."

Back at the house, supper preparation went swiftly. Angela and Lynn heated the food and Judith set the table. She was gratified to observe sort of abstractly that they worked together naturally and efficiently.

"We need the wineglasses; they're out in the mudroom on the shelf over the dryer. I have a bottle of sparkling cider in the fridge so we can have a toast."

Angela came out of the bathroom. "Dinner smells wonderful. Where do you want us to sit?"

"Up to you." Lynn pointed at the end chair. "I usually sit there since Paul died. That was his place for all our married life. Thanks for setting up the dining room table so formally, Judith. It feels more like a celebration that way."

One thing the former mistress of Rutherford House knew was formal dining. And she loathed it. But sometimes there was a place for it. Judith sat down. "Your cat isn't real happy about having new people here. I got the evil cat eye."

"Miss Minerva likes to think she is head of the house, and sadly, we did not seek her permission."

"We used to have a cat," Angela said, "but when she died, we decided to not get another one since we were both working and not home during the day." She sat down on Lynn's left. "I'm left-handed."

When they were all seated, Lynn said, "We say grace here; we've not talked a lot about beliefs, but…"

"Oh, I'm glad." Judith held out her hands and Angela nodded, too.

Lynn lowered her head. "Thank you, Lord, for safe travel, for this glorious day and bringing us all together. Thank you for this food, and I ask for a good night's sleep for my two weary friends. Amen."

"Thank you. Weary doesn't begin to cover it." Angela trapped a yawn. "Sorry."

"You sure make wonderful potato salad," Judith said after the first mouthful. "Do you suppose you could teach me to cook?"

"Of course." Lynn passed the pickle dish around.

"Are the rolls homemade?" Angela stared in wonder at her roll.

"I had some refrigerator dough that needed to be used; makes it easy, you know."

Judith nibbled a pickle. "I guess you made these?"

"My daughters-in-law and I work together on the canning, freezing, and pickling. Makes it go much faster that way. I'm thinking that might be the last jar of those.

"Would anyone like dessert?" Lynn asked when they were about finished eating.

"Sorry, not tonight." Angela stood and picked up her plate and silver. "I promise to help clean up tomorrow night, but I am so tired, I can't think."

"Not to worry. We'll take care of it all. I'll come help you with your bed in a minute. Okay?"

"You needn't, but thank you." She took her dishes into the kitchen and headed down the hall to the bedrooms.

Lynn waved an arm toward the dirty dishes. "I'll do these and you go help her?"

"Thanks." Judith knocked on the half-open door and looked in to find Angela sitting on the naked bed, dissolving in tears. "What is it?"

"My bedding is in a box. Somewhere."

"No big deal. What size?"

"Double. I took it out of one of the kids' bedrooms. I left our king size in the master bedroom. What a stupid thing to do."

Judith returned in a minute with the bedding Lynn provided in hand, including a mattress pad and a quilt. "Queen size, but it will tuck in easily. I'll get you a pillow..." She stopped.

Angela was sitting in a recliner, sound asleep, tear tracks on her cheeks.

Judith went ahead and made the bed, knelt down and removed the sleeping woman's shoes, then pulled the lever for the recliner. She tucked the quilt around Angela's body and left the room. Perhaps she and Lynn would be able to get her to the bed after a nap.

"How did she ever make it driving here?" Lynn asked after Judith described what had happened.

Judith wagged her head. "To crash like that seems strange for the little I know of her. She's a pretty determined woman."

"I agree. Let's take coffee and pie out on the deck and watch the evening settle in. But you better get a jacket. It turns chilly really fast. We'll make your bed after."

They had just settled around the glass-topped patio table when Lynn paused.

"There, you hear it?"

Judith tilted her head. "So distant. What is it?"

"The loons calling. The mating call. You get to recognize their various calls after a while."

"Haunting." This is what she'd dreamed of; curiously, in real life it seemed oddly different from the dream.

"Wild and free. Good thing the mosquitoes aren't out yet. Still too cold for them."

Judith smirked. "What a pity. Do they spray around here?"

"Not out of town this far." Despite that the evening had cooled off, Lynn flapped the front of her T-shirt rapidly, fanning herself. Judith didn't get hot flashes. Yet. She had that to look forward to and she had never even married.

"Do you swim out there?"

Lynn nodded. "Of course, off the dock mostly. You want to stay out of the reeds; that's where the bloodsuckers lurk."

Judith shuddered. "I'm afraid I am a pool baby."

The breeze off the lake kicked up, and they went inside to run the dishwasher and make Judith's bed, then together got Angela from the chair to her bed and tucked her in, clothes and all. A strangely weird end to a strangely weird day.

# Chapter Fifteen

When Lynn finally made her way up the stairs, Miss Minerva leaping ahead of her, she got ready for bed in record time and crawled in. *Lord, help them sleep as if they've been here for a while.* She'd warned them of the coyotes' singing but hoped nothing would wake them again. She read for five minutes rather than her usual fifteen and turned out the light. Oh, the bed felt so good.

She woke to a cat in full fright mode screaming on her chest. "What is it, Minerva?" Surely that wasn't the coyotes howling. It sounded like a hound baying. Right by the house. No one in their area had a hound, not even a beagle. The sound came again, horribly sad. It sounded like it was on the deck or by the entryway. Call for help or go see? Lynn grabbed her robe from the foot of the bed and stuck her feet in her moccasins. Turning on the hall and stair lights, she made her way downstairs. Nothing on the deck.

A whimpering noise caused her to flick on the porch light and open the door. She sucked in air. "What are you? Whose are you? Oh, you poor thing."

The end of the dog's tail quivered, and he stared up at her, long filthy ears and eyes to break one's soul.

"Are you injured?"

His tail thumped. He whimpered again.

She held out her hand, palm down, and his big black nose gave her hand the sniff over. The tail thumped again. She patted his head and a long tongue swept across her wrist. "How come you're not afraid? Who do you belong to? Are you lost?" She knelt beside the dog. No collar, no tags. He lurched to his feet and wagged some more. "How did you get so filthy?" Where could she put him? She couldn't leave him outside to howl all night. "You want to come in?" She stepped back and held the door open. "Are you hungry?"

Lynn heard a growl and a hiss. Miss Minerva was not happy.

The dog was half in but scrambled back and out.

"I'll be right back." She shut the door and headed for the mudroom, where she had not gotten rid of the leashes. He sat on the steps, waiting for her, his tail in full swing. She slid the leash around his neck and led him into the mudroom. No dog food, so cat food would have to do. Filthy as he was, he wasn't bone skinny.

After she fed him, he curled up on the rug and was soon snoring. Hopefully they would find the owners right away.

Lynn went back to bed, but a pathetic howl woke her just as Minerva landed on her chest.

Lynn blinked herself awake, unseating the cat as she threw the covers back in order to leap from the bed and grab her robe at the same time as her feet found the slippers. It was morning, but she'd wanted the others to sleep in. She was down the stairs and heading for the kitchen when Judith charged into the room.

"What was that? Wolves?" Judith was wide-eyed. "It's not wolves, is it?"

"A dog howling, long story." Lynn pulled the door open to have a hound greet her verbally and dash to the door. "Okay, fella, okay, I'll let you out and perhaps you'll go back home, wherever home is." She opened the door and stood back to watch. Down the stairs he went and barely made it to the gravel before he peed a river. "Well, at least you are house-broken."

Judith stood right beside her, gaping. "Where did that dog come from?"

"I have no idea. I couldn't leave him howling on the front steps, so I brought him in, fed him cat food. I gave him a couple cups. He gobbled that so fast, I'm sure he's been without food a couple of days, at least." She watched him, nose to the ground, white-tipped tail waving over his back, while he inspected the yard, reading all or anything that had traversed recently.

"He's big. And terribly dirty."

"Right on both counts. Sure wonder who owns him; bet they are searching high and low. But I've not seen any signs or heard of a missing dog." The hound raised his head, then turned and trotted back to the steps, tail wagging.

"Do people often dump unwanted pets along your road? They did in Rutherford."

"Far too often. We have a good humane society in Detroit Lakes."

"Look, he's grinning. I don't know dogs well; it's a hound, right? The baying. Is it a bloodhound or a beagle? Those huge, droopy ears…"

"A basset hound." Lynn looked down at the dog. "You go on home, big dog. Your folks are missing you."

He climbed the three steps and stared into the house, then up at her. Obviously he knew where the food might be.

"He looks kind of pudgy. You know, round."

"Actually, he's a bit on the thin side as bassets go; Tom had one once." Lynn started to open the door but shut it quickly. "Will you please go through and close the other door to the mudroom? If he gets in the house and chases Minerva..." She shuddered.

"Of course."

As soon as the other door was closed, Lynn opened the outer door. The dog sat looking up at her, tail in motion; he looked inside, then up at her again. Lynn walked in and held the door open. "Come on." In he came. "You have good manners, fella. Someone spent time training you. How about you stay in here and I'll go round you up some breakfast." He followed her to the inner door but stopped when she said no. When she closed the door again, he whined, but at least he didn't bark or howl.

"I found the coffee last night; I hope you don't mind if I make some," Judith said.

"Not at all, go ahead. I like mine about medium. I'm going to call and see if my son Phillip can send over some dog food." She glanced at the clock. Six fifteen. He would be up by now.

He answered on the second ring. "You okay?"

"Yes, just have a slight situation here. Did you hear a dog howling last night, two-ish?"

"Nope. Why?"

"I have a guest here, a rather large basset, and he was howling fit to raise the hardest sleeper from the front door. Filthy, but agreeable and mannered. Well socialized. You noticed any posts or anything about a lost hound? Oh, and he's hungry. No tags or collar. How about running some food over for him? He does like cat food..."

"Probably likes anything edible. He didn't chew or destroy anything in the mudroom? Sure, I'll bring some right now. How are your two ladies doing?"

"Judith woke to the howling, I think Angela is still asleep, although how anyone could sleep through this guy's demands is beyond me."

"See you in a minute."

Lynn hung up. "Kibbles are coming."

Judith looked down at her nightclothes. "Oh my gosh, I'm not dressed!"

"Don't worry, you're decent. I'll just take the sack from him. He'll be in a hurry anyway." The murmur of dripping coffee and the aroma sent Lynn to the cupboard for the coffee mugs. "I have a coffee cake in the bread box to warm up."

"When do you have time for all the baking?"

"When I get uptight, I bake." She heard the truck tires on the gravel and headed to the back door. The dog's tail drummed against the dryer and he followed right behind her. Lynn opened the door and watched her son step down from the four-wheel-drive pickup and bring a bag of kibble to hand her.

He studied the pooch. "A basset hound, eh? A real handsome basset hound." He handed her the bag.

"A hungry, filthy basset hound." The dog stood right beside her, staring up at Phillip.

"What if you can't find the owners? Or someone dumped him?"

"I don't know, I've not thought that far."

"Wonder if he hunts?"

"Maggie will strangle you if you bring home another dog."

"I know. See you later." He headed back to the pickup.

A whimper and increased tail wagging said the dog knew what was in the bag. Lynn poured the kibble in the dog dish she had set out the night before and refilled the water bowl at the wash sink. "There you go, fella. Enjoy." She wrinkled her nose. *Pee-uw.* "You not only are dirty, but you smell bad." He looked up from his dish and wagged his tail again before returning to gobble the kibble as if she might take it away from him.

"So what are you going to do with him?" Judith asked when they sat down at the square pine table in the kitchen with coffee and warmed-up coffee cake.

"Make some phone calls first. Take him to the vet and see if he is microchipped. I'll have the vet check him over, maybe even bathe him, since I have no desire to try that myself right now. His toenails are pretty long, too. He's not had the best care."

"This is so good!" Judith worked the coffee cake in her mouth. "But you say he's been trained. Doesn't make sense, does it?"

"Nope, sure wonder what his story is."

"Surely he's not dumped. How could someone dump a dog like that?"

"How can people dump any animals? I guess people figure, *Oh, there are homes along here, someone will take them in.*"

"So sad." Judith turned full attention to her coffee cake.

"Not just sad, it makes me furious. I would love to catch someone in the act and dump a load of buckshot into their vehicle."

Judith's eyes went wide. "Really, you would do that?"

"Who knows? You want eggs and bacon or dry cereal, hot cereal, toast, what would you like?"

Judith cleaned up the last crumbs of her coffee cake. "I think I want to go get dressed first, if that's okay."

"Good idea."

Judith glanced at her. "But you said everyone on their own for breakfast and lunch."

"I know, but if I'm making mine, fixing for two or three is

not that big a deal. I am going to have bacon and eggs over easy."

"Sounds heavenly to me."

Lynn paused, stared at nothing a moment. "I think I'll check on Angela, just quickly. Listen at her door."

A meow in grumble mode announced Minerva. "But first," Lynn corrected, "I will feed Her Highness, whose nose is seriously out of joint."

"She doesn't like dogs?"

"She and Orson were good buds, but this one is an intruder in her domain."

"I see." Judith nodded. "So it's not just humans who are territorial."

"Have you had cats?"

"'Cats and dogs are dirty pests.' Direct quote from my father. 'Certainly not something for children.' End of discussion. But I always rather wanted a pet."

"How sad. I think all children should have pets." Lynn shrugged. "But that was long ago and perhaps Miss Minerva will win your heart." The cat appeared at the sound of her name and curled around Lynn's ankle, nearly tripping her. "Or repulse it." She gave Miss Minerva a brief stroking and walked back to Angela's door, listened a moment, then gently tried the latch. It slid open. She peeked in to see Angela sound asleep. She closed the door again.

When she returned to the kitchen, Judith had put on jeans and a cute sweatshirt. A true Minnesota girl, she was wearing flip-flops in this chilly spring weather. She had gotten the skillet and toaster out. "I did learn how to make a simple breakfast. Basic survival after the cook left, but you have so many wonderful choices." She stepped aside and sat down.

"The coffee smells very good." Lynn smiled. "Oh, and

Angela was still sleeping. Or at least she wasn't moving around."

Judith nodded. "I heard the toilet flush earlier."

"As soon as we have breakfast, I'll make some phone calls." Lynn grabbed the pad of paper by the phone and started a list, beginning with the veterinarian. She put the bacon on.

"Can I do anything?" Judith asked.

"No, I don't...wait. See that piece of notebook paper on the fridge, with all the names and numbers on it? Can you use it to look up the numbers of the calls on my list? I'm sure they're all there somewhere."

Judith pulled down the piece of paper with its jotted names and numbers all askew and laughed. "I'll bet every refrigerator in the world has a phone book like this." She sat down at the table. "Vet. Knight?"

"Yes. That's Herb. Most business interactions in this area are first-name basis." Lynn turned the bacon and started the eggs. She happened to notice out of the corner of her eye that Judith was mostly watching her cook. She had also noticed that Judith was uneasy when the kids came by during her visit. Lynn could teach Judith to cook; she could not teach her to like children. Was this going to be a problem?

When they sat down to eat, Judith said, "You make it look so easy."

"It has become easy. Our family has always worked hard and played hard. They're good eaters, even the less-than-successful recipe attempts."

Judith ate in silence. Then said, "You mentioned the dog's toenails. And the fleas and ticks and bathing. There is so much to pets besides—well, you know, calling 'din din' and they come running. Like the commercials. I feel disadvantaged. Like I spent my whole life in a sterile lab jar."

Lynn opened her mouth in amazement and closed it again. What an alien world. After breakfast she started her call list. Judith had written all the numbers in a small, neat hand. The woman was well organized and efficient.

Ten minutes later Lynn sighed and laid aside the phone. "Nope, no one has heard of a lost dog. The humane society and the vet in Detroit Lakes are all posting his info. I'll make up cards and post them on bulletin boards at the feedstore and a couple of other places. We have an appointment with Herb at eleven. You want to go with me, er, us?"

"Sure. Maybe my father wasn't totally wrong about pets. You know, he's going to stink up your car."

Lynn probably couldn't teach her to love dogs, either. "I'll spray it after."

The phone rang. "You have a dog, G'ma?"

"Sorry, Miss Priss, he's not to keep."

"Oh. Can I come see him?"

"After school if he's still here." She clicked off after the good-bye and smiled at Judith. "You remember Phillip and Maggie's daughter."

"Of course. She's a charmer."

"When she wants to be. She's a bit of a tyrant or at least tries to be. Her folks are working on that."

A whimper from the mudroom. When no answer came, the next was a tentative *woof*.

"I suppose he has to go out again. Sure wish we had a kennel to put him in." She pushed back her chair and stretched, arms behind her.

Judith stretched, too. "You do what you need to do. I'm no cook, but I can surely clean up. Lynn, I really enjoy your kitchen. It's so friendly."

Lynn smiled and thought about it a moment. "'Your kitchen.' It's ours now. Communal space. I'm really going to

have to make a major adjustment about that; ceding terri-
tory in a way. I take it the Rutherford House kitchen was not
especially friendly."

"No, and neither was Cook. She did not like other people
in her kitchen. I guess I'm going to have to make some major adjustments, too. But then, we expected that."

"Yes." Lynn crossed to the door to the mudroom, where the
plea was becoming more insistent. "Okay, fella, out we go."
Outside, he sniffed until he located the perfect spot, did his
business, and charged around the yard, then returned to sit at
her feet. The sun on his coat revealed a tick embedded at the
edge of his right eye, a swollen tick. "Oh, rats, I haven't had
to remove ticks in a long time." She started to leave him outside, but he glued himself to her jeans-clad leg and scooted in.
"Sorry, this is as far as you go. I'll be right back."

A drop of oil on the tick's head and it would back right
out. Then she'd dispose of the tick without leaving the head
under the skin to fester. After finding the bottle with the
eyedropper that they used to use—sometimes not throwing
things out right away was a good thing—she dug out a collar,
buckled it on his neck, and attached the leash for control; he
might not appreciate her ministrations. He didn't like it, but
he submitted. By the time she was done, she'd removed two
ballooned pests and a couple that were still brown. His ears
were a mess, and he had fleas. He licked her hand.

"Don't do that, guy. You might have a family waiting."
She turned to see Judith by her shoulder. "This is just oil. It
won't hurt him."

"I had a fleabite once," Judith mused. "My body did not
like it; it hurt. Do fleabites hurt on dogs as well as children?"

"I don't know. They itch, I'd guess. Herb will give him a
flea bath as well as a soapy one. You sure you want to come
along?"

"I should stay here and finish unpacking. But yes, I'd like to come."

"I'll leave a note for Angela." Lynn glanced at her watch. Past ten already. "I really hope she's not coming down with something."

The dog jumped up in her SUV without a problem and immediately climbed up on the backseat, looking at her like he was saying, *Well, I'm ready, what you waiting for?* A dog who liked to ride in a car, but then, don't they all?

At the vet's, there was only a small floor-mop-type dog waiting, who immediately started barking at the basset.

"Dodo, hush." The woman looked at Lynn apologetically. "Sorry, he doesn't mind terribly well. You're Phillip's mother, aren't you? I'm Agnes Rosen; he was out to fix some damage left from winter repairs, and he opens my house every year."

"Mrs. Rosen, of course. I am—Lynn's the name—and Phillip always enjoys working for you. He says you make strawberry-rhubarb pie much better than mine. I think we met last year. And this is a friend Judith."

"Howdjidoo. We met? My memory just isn't what it used to be, so frustrating." The yapper sat in her lap and watched the basset, who had stretched out on the floor. "That's a handsome dog."

"He showed up on my front steps in the middle of the night. You've not heard if someone is missing a dog, have you?"

"No, sorry." She started to reach down to pat the dog on the floor, and her yapper went into full frenzy. "Oh, hush." She tapped the little dog on the muzzle. "No, Dodo, behave yourself."

"Come on in, Mrs. Rosen." Amy, Herb's assistant, beckoned the woman from the open door to the treatment rooms. "And how is Dodo today?"

"Right now, he's not even limping. But he was before we came. I think he got something in his foot, but I couldn't find anything."

A few minutes later, Mrs. Rosen reappeared and the receptionist, Lydia, showed Lynn into a treatment room. Judith tailed after them, so Lynn introduced them.

Amy came in smiling cheerfully, so Lynn introduced Judith to her as well. Amy squatted and extended her knuckles for the introductory sniff. "So what is this dog's name?"

"I have no idea. He showed up at my house in the middle of the night. I talked to Herb this morning, and he said to bring him in. We need to chip him first and then see what's up. Surely someone is missing their dog."

The basset tried to head out the door, head down, no wag in the tail, but Lynn brought him back with the leash. "Looks like he's not excited about this."

"I wouldn't be either." Amy frowned as she stared down. "He's a mess."

"I agree. I took five or six ticks off him already. That's why I asked Herb to schedule for a full grooming. Look at his feet."

Amy nodded. "I'll weigh him and get his vitals. Wonder how long he's been on the run." She led the dog away. He left the room eagerly, returned reluctantly.

Dr. Knight entered the room, smiled at Lynn, and studied the dog.

"May I introduce my new housemate Judith Rutherford."

He extended his hand. "Good to meet you and welcome to Barnett. You a dog lover?"

Judith accepted the handshake. "I have no idea. I've never had a pet in my life."

His bushy eyebrows arched. "Really. Rutherford, Rutherford, no relation to the town of Rutherford?"

"Yes, that was my family. They're all gone now, and the
house is being turned into a living history museum."

"Well, I'll be. Interesting." He turned his attention to the
dog, who had plastered himself to the floor. "Sixty pounds
and you need at least five more." He stroked the dog's head.
"You're not looking too good right now, young man. Let's see
if we can help you out." When he stood, the dog did, too, so
Dr. Knight scooped him up and, with a grunt, set him on the
stainless steel examining table. "Lynn, you want to hold him
or shall I call Amy back in? She's setting up the bath."

"I'll try. But I can already tell you, he does not like his
ears or teeth or feet examined."

Of course, just to show them, the dog sat without moving
through the entire exam, then snuffled the vet's ear.

"He's fairly dry mouthed for a basset, and he looks to be
a purebred. Not chipped. No collar and tags, either?"

"Nope." Lynn got mad all over again at the thought of
someone abandoning a lovely dog like this.

"Noble of you, but if someone really cared about him, I'm
sure they'd have put out the word."

"Don't say that. I don't think I'm ready for a new dog yet.
A lot going on at the moment, and of course, Orson." Lynn
sniffed back the tears that still surfaced when she thought of
bringing Orson here not that terribly long ago.

Dr. Knight nodded. "He looks to be about five or so, ear
mites, fleas, and I think we should worm him, too. Since we
have no idea whether he has his shots, I'll do rabies, and he
should have at least a nine way. You want to spend this kind
of money on him?"

"Not really, but what are my choices? I called the shelter,
and they're so overcrowded now that they asked me to fos-

ter him. We can't let him be around our other animals if he has something or gets something, and you know Phillip's dog will welcome a new playmate."

He lifted the dog down and kept the leash. "We'll call you when he's ready to go home. Good to meet you, Ms. Rutherford. Any time you decide you need a pet, let us know. We usually know what's available around here."

"Someone must want their basset back," Lynn muttered as they left the office.

"How could they not? One look into those big, brown, sad eyes of his and..."

"Oh, great, not you, too. Let's go get the postcards you wanted, and we can stop at the feedstore for kibble. I'll give what's left to Phillip when his owners come for him."

Judith stood beside the car, staring at the door handle. Thinking, obviously. Then she slid inside.

Lynn twisted the ignition. "What are you thinking about?"

Judith grimaced. "I hate to say this, but I'm hoping the former owners never show up."

# Chapter Sixteen

A ngela thrashed her way out of the sheet and a quilt. A
quilt? Where was she? Heart pounding, she sat up. She
did not have a revolver in her hand, pointing it at Jack
and...and who? Someone, of course. She was not screaming, threatening to kill them both. A dream. What a terrible,
awful dream. And so real. Vivid. Did she really feel that way
about him, them?

Yes, the room was strange, but she had moved in here
the night before, or rather yesterday. No clock. No noise.
She'd been up to the bathroom during the night, thanks to
a night-light put there by Lynn Lundberg. What time was
it? Phone? Purse? She stared at herself, still in her clothes.
When she crashed in that chair...someone had made her
bed and put her to bed. Right after supper. Her mouth felt
like she'd been chewing on sawdust.

After another trip to the bathroom, she eyed the bed
again. What if she just crawled back in and pretended the
world did not exist? At least for a few more hours. Back on
the edge of the bed and staring around the room, she discovered her purse on the far side of the chair. Get out her
phone or not? Why was that such a major decision? Boxes
lined the wall, hopefully one including her own linens. Or it

was at the storage facility. Some of these boxes could probably go into storage.

Decisions. Decisions. She flopped back on the pillows, but as soon as her eyes closed, the dream attacked her again. Jack and Jacqueline. Wasn't that cute? The gun felt heavy in her hand. Her heart rate leaped to pumping mode. *No!*

Bed was too dangerous. She picked up her phone. Twelve thirty. No wonder her stomach just grumbled at her. Twenty text messages. Ten phone calls. Battery almost out. She dug out the cord from her purse, found an outlet, and plugged it in without reading or responding to anything. Now that was a first, not at least reading the texts and seeing who called.

After retrieving her travel kit out of the suitcase, she adjourned to the bathroom. The shower did its best to wash the dream away, the travel away, and the tears. *But I didn't want this new life. I was happy in my old life!* Happy? Well, she thought she'd been happy or at least content. But frustrated, if she was honest. Yes, mostly with Jack. Had her intuition been picking up on more than she realized or was willing to even contemplate?

But by the time she was dried and dressed and on her way to the kitchen, the state of despair had taken up residence on her shoulders again. She read the note on the table and did as it suggested. Made herself coffee and cut a piece of the coffee cake, then took cup and plate to the kitchen table, only to pick it up and head for the deck and the sunshine that glittered the lake. Stretched out on a lounger, she sighed. Did she really live here? Or was this another dream, only this one a bit of heaven?

*A revolver!* She'd never hoisted a revolver in her life. Her dream must have been the fruit of too many crime shows. A dog barked in the distance beyond the trees. Birds twittered and sang in the trees where a hammock stretched between two trunks, oak maybe, or maple. As if it mattered.

"How could he do such a thing?"

The slight breeze lifted her bangs. *Just do one thing at a time,* she ordered herself. *You cannot let your mind dwell on the past.* Someone had said that to her lately. She couldn't recall who.

"I know you are not supposed to hate anyone, but right now I hate that man and that—bimbo, whatever she is."

A soft, plaintive *meeow.*

She looked around and saw a fluffy gray cat watching her through slightly slitted green eyes. "So do you hate anyone?"

This time a chirp and she would swear a shrug. Did cats shrug?

"If your husband dumped you for a younger woman and then kicked you out of your house, wouldn't you hate him?"

The cat licked the pad of her right front paw, her fluffy tail curved around her.

"Not worth hating, is that what you mean?"

A yawn showing pink tongue and white needle teeth.

"I agree. Boring. And yes, it made me tired, too." *But I failed as a wife. I really did. I tried to be everything that he said he wanted; I changed my whole life around, every aspect of it, just to make him happy, and look what it got me. For all my careful attention to appearance, all my establishing a glamorous and lucrative career, I could not make myself younger. And he wants a young woman.*

She let her head rest on the cushion and crossed her legs at the ankles. With the sun kissing her closed eyes, all she could see was light through her lids. Ducks were quacking down on the water. A house finch sang, and two other birds sounded like they were scolding each other; maybe the lady bird didn't like what the gentleman bird brought for a nest. Or maybe he, too, was trading up for a younger lady. It happens.

Looking at this house and property from a Realtor's perspective, there was much to praise. The house was picturesque, well built, well landscaped, and certainly situated well. If she had to live somewhere other than her own home (equally well built and landscaped but stuck in the middle of a gated community), this was pretty darn nice.

Back in the good old days, when she'd been a housewife and mother and gardener and reader and cook, she'd maintained feeders and a birdbath in the backyard and enjoyed the birds. But the makeover took all her time and energy, and many things she enjoyed suffered. Including her friends. They had finally quit calling and inviting her to lunch or a party or even checking in on her. She worked on Sundays after she got her real estate license, but when she did go to church, they'd all said things like, "We need to get together sometime. I'll call you." And they didn't, neither she nor they.

"I really messed up."

The cat rose and padded over to the lounge. Effortlessly, she leaped up and stood, tail in a question mark, never taking her gaze off Angela.

"Well, look at you. I know you have a name, but I don't remember it. I'm Angela and I guess I am going to live here now. At least for a while." She had a hard time believing she'd be here, well, for the rest of her life. But then, who knew where they would be in, say, five years or even one year? After all, she thought she'd had her life all mapped out and look what happened.

"Life changes, did you know that?"

The tip of the tail twitched. The cat wore a bib of white and a few white hairs at the end of her tail. The white toes on one back foot looked like painted toenails. How could she go so long without blinking those emerald-green eyes?

"You have a name. I know you do. And you are a good listener. You want some crumbs?" She held out the plate.

The cat moved closer and sniffed the plate, then came around to sniff her fingers. She sat back down.

"Is that *no thank you*?"

A slight sound. "You carry on a conversation, don't you?"

*Chirp.* Those whiskers twitched.

Angela set the plate back on the side table and watched the cat watching her. "I'd pet you if you wanted." She opened her hand, palm up.

The cat sniffed her fingers again, then her wrist. The green eyes studied the woman, and without a sound, she jumped up on Angela's legs. The kneading began at once. Angela stroked the cat's head and back. So silky and—shedding. Oh, well. She continued to stroke her, letting batches of fur loose on the breeze.

The cat turned around a couple of times and curled up. The purring started out softly but escalated as Angela continued to pet her.

"Well, cat, it looks like I have made a friend. Thank you. I need one." She stared out over the tree-lined lake. Houses could be seen among the trees and docks, proclaiming where the land was used. The deep green of pines, lacy tamaracks, and deciduous trees of all shades, most still leafing out, guarded the shore. Bright green lawns ran down to the water or sand in some places, small boats were tied to the docks, and canoes were either turned over on docks or farther up on the beaches. Two canoes rested on cradles on the dock below her. A ladder at the end of the T-shaped dock looked as weathered silver as the floating dock.

A car drove in, tires crunching on the gravel drive. The

cat leaped off her lap and headed for the steps leading down to the earth.

Angela stayed where she was. Two female voices, car doors slammed, and a dog barked. A *dog?* Lynn said she didn't have a dog. What had the note said? They'd be back later was all and to make herself comfortable. She had done that. She should have been unpacking. She should have returned texts and phone calls, too, but since the phone was in her room, she found it delightful to not even hear it. Maybe she should go throw it in the lake and cut off all connections to her former life.

The dog barked again, a deep *woof*, obviously a big dog.

"No, you don't bark at the cat." Sound carried remarkably well here.

Curiosity got the better of her, and since her chair was now in the shade, Angela forced herself to her feet and took cup and plate with her through the sliding doors to the house. Windows banked the entire east wall of the house, all with wood frames, including the doors. Since she became a Realtor, Angela noticed things like that. And appreciated the value and beauty of a house so thoughtfully crafted. She started to slide the door closed, but Lynn called, "Leave them open, but the screens. It's too beautiful a day to have closed doors." Angela pulled the screen door into place and continued to the kitchen. Lynn and Judith were just setting their purses down on the kitchen table.

"Should I let him in?" Judith asked.

"Minerva's outside, so yes, we'll see how he does." Lynn slid the kitchen window open. The curtains moved slightly.

Angela smiled. "So that's the cat's name; I had forgotten. She introduced herself to me just now."

"You feel better now?" Lynn asked.

"Sorry. I've never slept that late in my life, or at least not since—well, who knows." Angela set her mug and plate on the counter before opening the dishwasher. "Is this clean?"

"Yes, I'm afraid we got involved this morning and didn't empty it. We want you to meet our newest guest." Lynn nodded toward the floor.

"A dog? I thought I heard one bark. Why, he's handsome, a basset, right?" Angela looked from the dog to Lynn.

"You didn't hear him howling last night, or rather, sometime early this morning?"

Angela shook her head. "I don't think I heard anything. I have a vague recollection of someone helping me to bed."

"You were really out of it." Judith smiled across the center island. "We were afraid you might be coming down with something."

"Yeah, exhaustion, I guess. So what's the story here?" She watched the dog casing the joint, giving everything the sniff inspection.

Angela kept only half an ear on the narrative as Lynn and Judith described finding the dog. She had become something of an expert on reading body language. A person can say whatever they want you to believe, but body language says what that person really thinks and often what that person is ready to do. Angela saved more than one sale that way. So why was it that Jack had so completely snookered her? There surely had been signs, probably plenty of them, but she didn't pick them up. Willfully blind, as the psych folk say. *Angela, you fool.* And she was depressed all over again.

"And so there he is." Judith waved a hand toward the dog. "Not only immunized to the gills, but clean and flea-free." *Yep.* Her body language and Lynn's as well said that the dog was as good as theirs.

"Anyone else as hungry as I am?" Lynn opened the steel

refrigerator door. "We have salad and sandwich makings and leftovers from last night."

Judith smiled at Angela. "And homemade bread."

"There's sliced ham or turkey, cheese, etc., and salad."

By the time they'd finished making their sandwiches, the dog had returned to the kitchen and cleaned out the cat's dish. He sat looking at them, as if assessing who they were.

Angela left her plate on the counter and went over to him, holding out her hand. He gave her hand, her sleeve, her jeans, and her shoes a sniff over, his tail wagging slowly, then sat in front of her. "So now what?" His tail swished faster. He nudged her hand.

"I think he is saying *pet me*." Lynn set down her plate, too. "His ears might be a bit tender because the vet cleaned them and put in the meds. He had ear mites along with fleas and possible worms."

Angela bent over and stroked the dog's head. "Hey, boy, you need a name. You are so soft and silky. But then so is Minerva."

"Let's go outside to eat. We need to talk about what to do about the dog." Lynn led the way outside and closed the gate to the stairs.

"Are you serious, *we* need to talk?" Angela couldn't believe she'd said that. Never had Jack asked her opinion on something; he always formed an opinion and then assumed it was hers as well. This was going to take some getting used to.

The three sat down at the glass-topped wrought iron table while the dog explored the deck.

Lynn began, "Look, if we are to live together, we have to learn to make decisions together. Discuss things, agree, disagree, work it out. Like if one of us is allergic to dogs, then we wouldn't keep him. Or can't stand the animal, or..."

Angela looked across the deck at the big, sad eyes, the comical jowls. "How could someone not want him around?"

"Well, we're taking a gamble; he might have some really bad habits. We don't know anything about him, you know. And from what I've heard, bassets are known for being stubborn and independent thinkers." Lynn held out her hands. "Let's have grace.

"...And, Lord, help us make a decision about this hound who might be a gift from you. Amen."

"I hadn't thought of that." Judith stared at her plate, then across at Lynn. "I mean, well, I guess we didn't pray much at our house. Until my mother died, we attended church regularly, but sort of..." She shrugged. "With my father and his wheelchair, it was easier to stay home, especially as we had to let the help go. For a while I went myself and then fell out of the habit."

"Me, too," Angela said quietly.

"We belong to the Lutheran church in Detroit Lakes, but there are a variety of churches, and if you want, you might choose a different one. But I hope we can have that bond, too. Let's eat."

"I think we should name him Homer," Judith said after a few bites and murmurs of how good the sandwich was.

"Homer. Kind of a strange name." Angela really liked this bread. *Homemade, huh?*

Judith shrugged. "Well, your other dog's name was Orson, right?"

"After Orson Welles, you know—*Citizen Kane, The War of the Worlds*. Paul enjoyed his movies and named his puppy Orson."

"Homer wrote *The Odyssey*," Judith added. "I remember reading that in school. This pooch has obviously gone on an odyssey."

"Any other suggestions? Some people with rescue dogs try a variety of names to see if their new dog responds to any of them." Lynn looked toward the railing where the hound, now stretched out on his side with his jowls sagging, seemed already to be sound asleep. "Homer works for me."

Angela shrugged. "No problem here. Homer it is. How do you teach a dog his name?"

"Use it a lot and give rewards when he responds. We can go online and look up basset hounds, learn what we can. The first thing is going to be getting him and Minerva together."

*Good luck with that. Bassets are stubborn and independent? That cat is even more so. She takes life on her own terms.* Angela almost smiled at the way the cat coolly, emphatically, made her desires known. She finished her sandwich and stood up. "Well, I need to go start putting things away. I have an intense dislike of boxes, unless they are empty. You want us to break them down?"

"Please. By the way, have either of you ever been out in a canoe?" When they both shook their heads, Lynn smiled. "Another adventure if you want to try. And Phillip has a boat and motor, it's just not back in the water yet. Boating?"

"When I was a kid, we used to have a rowboat. Jack talked about buying a boat, but it never happened." *So much never happened.*

On the other hand, Angela reflected as she put her dish in the sink, she was somewhat relieved that they never had a boat. Jack had even looked at some boats. One was a sleek little runabout, what the dealer called a cigarette boat, very expensive. Jack had even taken it out for a spin, the dealer beside him. He had really looked good, too, a handsome young man tooling about in a fancy motorboat; Angela had to hand him that. And isn't that what life is all about, looking good as you operate expensive toys? Jack certainly thought so. Now that she was alone, Angela was not so certain.

So what *was* life all about? For years, she had striven to look good for Jack. Fifteen pounds thinner than her high school weight, professional hairstyle, snazzy clothes and heels. She was wearing bedroom slippers at the moment, and she liked the feel much, much better. Frankly, she didn't care how she looked, and the realization was so powerful it stopped her in her tracks. She didn't have to be a fashion plate anymore, and it was intensely, gorgeously, brilliantly freeing. She was free! Oh, how she loved that.

She left the kitchen just as she heard Lynn out on the deck scream, "Grab him!"

Here came Minerva with Homer hot on her heels. Sharp claws rattling on the hardwood floor, the two raced past her up the hall. Angela paused, waited. She heard Homer's wild yelp, and here he came back down the hall, Minerva hot on his heels.

Smiling, she continued to her room and to the boxes waiting.

The first carton she slit open was shoes. Her three-inch spikes, the silver French stilettos, the sexy white Calvin Kleins that looked so good with her midnight-blue velour sheath. She dug out two pairs of flats and her canvas sneakers and closed the box back up. She set it over near the door. This was the first of the boxes that would go to the thrift shop tomorrow.

# Chapter Seventeen

Judith consulted her campus map. Here was the student center, so that building right over there must be Solon. The main campus of the University of Minnesota's Duluth campus was much bigger and more varied than she would have guessed. It was also tightly concentrated, with nearly all the campus buildings crowded into what amounted to a sprawling city block, not spread out across two cities the way the Twin Cities campus was. The campus was well laid out, too; for instance, the student health services sat in the midst of the student housing, the handiest place for ailing students to reach.

She had earned her only college credits on the Minneapolis campus; she'd loved the academics, put up with the big city. Duluth was awfully far from Detroit Lakes and only somewhat far from Melody's. Again doubt grabbed her. Was this the right way to go? The wrong dream?

And here was Cina Hall, just as the map promised. She entered and crossed to a desk just inside an open door. A blond woman in her thirties smiled from behind the desk. "May I help you?"

"I have an appointment with Meredith Pollan. I'm a few minutes early."

She glanced at her computer monitor. "Ms. Rutherford?"

"Yes."

"Dr. Pollan can see you now. Let me take you." She stood up and walked out into the hall, so Judith followed her. The hall's walls were covered in ruins—photos three feet wide showing ruins from all over the world. A few, Judith recognized. That was Machu Picchu; everyone recognizes that one. Another was the narrow defile leading to the stone city of Petra. Some were Indian ruins, but she couldn't identify which ones they were. Wouldn't it be marvelous if someday she could? Just look at a tumbled pile of adobe and say, *Why, yes. This is Walnut Canyon. And that's Tuzigoot.*

They entered a door at the far end. A woman about Judith's age looked up and smiled. She was seated behind what had to be the world's most cluttered desk. Stacks of papers, some dark gray rocks, a lovely Southwest Indian pot, a phone, and a big computer monitor. In fact, the whole room was similarly cluttered with papers, books, and artifacts. On a table against the side wall sat a computer with two monitors.

Judith dipped her head toward the setup. "Two monitors?"

"Most of the people in the department have a dualie for research. Steve over in geology has a three-bee. You can put two images up for comparison, run two sets of figures simultaneously, or a data sheet and an image. Many uses. Meredith Pollan, Ms. Rutherford." She extended her hand for a handshake, so Judith obliged. She was not a thin woman nor was she stocky, but rather square built and not an ounce of fat. She was remarkably tanned for someone in Duluth at this time of year. "Please have a seat."

Judith settled into a nice comfy chair. "When I arranged this appointment, I sent you my transcript. I have no idea exactly what information you'd need."

"Right here." From several inches down in a pile at her right, Dr. Pollan pulled out Judith's envelope and opened it. "So you are interested in a career in anthropology. I saw that the credits you are transferring are very good." She looked up at Judith. "Thirty-six credits in core courses, so you completed your freshman year with a 3.2 GPA. Excellent."

"But that was a long time ago."

"Math, history, and English haven't changed too much. I see you earned these at Twin Cities. You've moved?"

"I have. I live near Detroit Lakes now."

She shook her head. "Five hours? Six?"

"About." *But I don't want to go back to Minneapolis because there are too many memories there. I had a healthy mother and father then.* "It's more or less the same distance either to here or to the cities, and I like this campus. It's compact, easy to get around in. And you have a very good anthropology program."

"We do indeed. And your letter said you want to know what courses to take to complete your AA over at Detroit Lakes."

"That's right. I've signed up for this next semester's courses, but I can still change some of them." She handed Dr. Pollan the registration receipt with the courses listed.

She studied it a moment, nodding, her short salt-and-pepper hair bobbing just a bit. "Good. Good. By the end of this next semester, you'll have nearly all your core courses under your belt. I see you've not had 1602 and 1604 yet. You'll need both of those courses to go into upper division work." She clarified, thank goodness. "Biological anthropology and archaeology and cultural anthropology."

"They sound fascinating." Judith smiled. *No, this was not a mistake after all.* "I can hardly wait."

Dr. Pollan simply looked at her for a long moment. What

was going on in her head? A gentle smile slowly spread across her face. She pulled out her keyboard tray and clickety-clicked rapidly, then swung her desktop monitor around so that Judith could see it. "You are computer literate, I presume."

"No computer whiz, but not a Luddite, either."

"Good. In addition to your major, you may want to declare a minor or a second major. You will also need elective credits, and only six hours each can be applied to your major and your minor. Here are some of the recommended electives. What do you see there that you'd like?"

Judith ran down the list. She saw no reason to reject any of them. This was going to be great! "Linguistics would probably help as much as anything. And...." She pondered. "I think I would choose geology. I realize it's a science and I don't have a science background; I would really have to work, but it would be very interesting and probably quite useful."

Dr. Pollan sat back in her chair. "Ms. Rutherford, I teach a large number of beginning anthropology students, and I also advise most of the entering freshmen who are interested in the field. They all want the maximum number of credits for a minimum amount of work. It is so refreshing to find someone who chooses a subject because she actually wants to learn about it. Geology would be an excellent choice, and we have a course for nonscience majors that should suit you well."

"What is the difference between them, science and non-science?"

"Geology for science majors requires four semesters of calculus. This course does not. Could you sign up for geology and linguistics instead of these two?" She pointed to Judith's list.

Judith didn't have to think long about that. "Yes! Absolutely."

Dr. Pollan tick-a-ticked her keyboard a few moments. "Oh, good. This will give you an additional four credit hours this next semester. Hm. I wonder." More clickety-clicking. Again she pointed to her screen. "This course is a good basic one that you'll need, and it is available online. You can take it at home."

"Perfect."

The woman worked her computer another minute. "There. You'll get the link to this course before the semester begins." She sat back. "When you complete your AA, will you be moving near Duluth here to finish your bachelor's?"

"Frankly, I don't know. My life has been in turmoil lately." *Has it ever!*

"I ask about residence plans when I advise incoming students because finding a good living situation is a great help."

"They are up in the air. None of us knows if our present arrangement will work." *Enough of that subject.* "Thank you so much, Doctor. You provided exactly what I wanted: advice on what to take to make the most of my college time."

"I'm more than glad to help a willing student. Do you have any other questions?"

"Uh, what kind of questions?" Judith had several, but were they the right ones?

"Well, let's see. For instance, I talked to an advisee yesterday morning, an incoming freshman, who wanted to know how she could get the autographs of all the hockey players. I'm going to take a wild guess and say that you have no particular desire to collect college athletes' signatures."

Judith laughed. "You got that right. I do have one major misgiving."

"Yes?"

"It's been years since I did anything scholarly—you know, academic. And my classmates are all so much younger than I; learning comes easily for the young, not easily at all for the—well, the mature. Should I be taking a full course load this fall?"

"An excellent question! The short answer is yes. For starters, you may seem to be the oldest cookie in the oven and you're afraid you might get burned. In truth, the university has many transition students such as yourself, people who have been riffed or laid off and are trying to develop marketable skills."

*That's me!* But before Judith could say that out loud, the woman continued, "You have the advantage over your younger classmates, Ms. Rutherford, believe me. You're not just stacking up credits as so many do; you *want* to learn. I think you'll do very well and be very pleasantly surprised. Also, getting your feet wet in academia, so to speak, should be easier in a community college atmosphere—smaller facility, smaller classes. Not to mention that you certainly don't strike me as being a wild party animal eager to become the next prom queen."

Again Judith laughed. *Party animal?*

The woman scuffed around inside her desk's lap drawer—without actually seeing the inside, Judith suspected it was just as cluttered as the surface—and brought out a business card, handing it to Judith. "This is my direct number. Please call me if you encounter problems or difficulties; I'll help you iron them out. Ms. Rutherford, you are truly going to enjoy your new academic life; I'm confident of that. I look forward very much to welcoming you into our department."

Judith glanced at the card. "Thank you, Dr. Pollan." She stood up, and Dr. Pollan stood, extending her hand. They shook, and Judith walked out into the long sterile hall with all the ruins on its walls, wildly elated. She had had misgivings since the beginning of this crazy idea; would she fit in at all? They evaporated. Almost. *"I look forward to welcoming you into our department."* Her heart did a little tickle.

Signs helped her find the Kirby Student Center as young, young classmates laughed and churned all around her. There didn't seem to be many of them, but then, Judith realized, this was either the end of the semester or very close to it.

Other signs directed her to the resident dining center, but she didn't go there. She was not a resident. Instead, she walked out to the food court. Quite an array of choices greeted her, everything from fast burgers to Chinese.

Eventually she chose Thai, mostly because Cook had never ever done anything the least bit Asian. Her father did not approve of Asian culture or cuisine. Oh, he collected Asian art pieces if they were strikingly expensive, but as a lifestyle? Never. In a way she was suddenly entering a whole new world of exotic choices. In another way, the very thought terrified her.

*Mm.* Thai food was surprisingly tasty; at least this dish was. Something with pork, snow peas, onions, and broccoli florets in a delicious sauce. As she ate her stir-fry and rice, she looked around the food court. The next time she was on campus she'd try the Italian place over there. And maybe the Dog Shack. How silly! The high-society Judith Rutherford eating a hot dog! She almost laughed out loud.

Why not? She was Judith Rutherford, student, now. Maybe she'd sample the Dog Shack next.

In fact, if she wanted to fit into the campus scene, either here or at the Detroit Lakes Community College, she was going to have to learn to eat pizza and drink beer. No. Oh no. No, some things were just really too extreme.

She spent another hour simply walking around the campus. She found the bookstore, but they did not have the fall semester's textbooks shelved yet. Come back in August, she was told. No, she would get them online from the bookstore site. They did, however, have a couple of books for general reading, popular nonfiction works on geological subjects—one about the eruption of Krakatoa in Southeast Asia, one on the great Galveston hurricane in 1900. She bought them both.

She walked down to the sports complex, Chester Park, with its track and baseball fields. Also other types of fields devoted to sports she knew nothing about and the tennis courts. She did not particularly enjoy the game of tennis. She didn't even watch Wimbledon on television. Would she become the superfan that all college students seemed to be? Probably not.

She realized eventually why all the buildings were connected by corridors and breezeways; in the winter, people didn't want to go out into a blizzard with every class change. The more she wandered about, getting lost now and then, the better she liked this campus. It was neat and tidy. Sensible. Efficient. Complex.

She liked to think of herself as sensible, efficient, and complex also. Liked to think? She *was*. All those years of taking care of her parents and her father in his cranky dotage, she had to become neat and tidy and sensible and highly efficient, and she had learned a lot of arcane, complex things. And the bitterness of being betrayed by the old man slapped her anew unexpectedly. Would she ever get over it?

The old man had messed her up royally. He had snarled at her all the time, making certain she knew that she was failing to fully please him. And surprise! She missed the old reprobate terribly.

She eventually came to the parking lot where her car sat, so she got in it and drove away, not toward the hamlet of Barnett and Barnett Lake, but south, down to Melody's.

Just think, loons. Quiet. Rutherford House had been quiet, sometimes too quiet.

Should she have taken over as caretaker? Absolutely not. She was certain of this now. And the word *betrayal* brought to mind their housemate Angela. Talk about betrayed! Twenty-five years of marriage, and you discover your prince in shining armor is a pig. Was there any stability in the world, anything you could grasp and know it would not betray you?

In church, the preachers—there had been three so far since Judith had started going to that church—claimed that Jesus was the only person upon whom one could depend totally. He seemed very, very distant just now, certainly not close enough to lean upon.

Memorial Day would be here in two days. Just think. In forty-eight hours she could pay tribute to the bitter, thankless old man who destroyed her past and her future. *Wonderful.*

Up ahead, red brake lights flared on. All of them. Cars and trucks slowed to a crawl and before long stopped completely. With a sigh she turned off the engine. She wouldn't be going anywhere for a while. Northbound traffic came through at a trickle. Something big had happened ahead.

Her cell phone broke into song. She dug it out. "Hello?"

"This is Melody. Are you all right?"

"If stationary is all right, I'm absolutely peachy. Why?"

"News radio just reported a huge pileup on 35 South east of Cambridge. I just turned on the TV. They're showing a live feed from a helicopter. What a mess! I was afraid you were in it!"

"I'm sitting behind it."

"Oh, I'm so glad! Anselm and I were worried you were caught in it; apparently, there are a number of injuries."

"I can see the news chopper way up ahead there; it just climbed above the trees; now it's below the trees again. I'm going to be really late getting in, Melody. There are no exits for miles. I'm trapped."

"That's all right. Just get here safely."

"Thank you." And then Judith thought of the flowers. "Do we have flowers for the graves?"

"We do. I'll cut them tomorrow so they're fresher."

"Excellent. Thank you. And wait until I tell you where my dreams are going!"

"I can't wait!"

"Well, you'll just have to." They both laughed and good-byed each other.

With nothing to do but sit there, she dug her two new books out of the trunk and opened the first one, the one about Krakatoa. Simon Winchester. She recognized the author's name; she'd read one of his books long ago, *The Professor and the Madman*, and had really enjoyed it. Why had she not done more light reading as she tended her father? Years of good reading potential wasted, she regretted that.

The driver behind her blew his horn, startling her. The line was moving! She tossed her book aside and cranked the ignition. The traffic was dismally poky, and it took nearly ten minutes to go half a mile, no doubt because gawkers were slowing to look at the mangled trucks by the roadside that had not yet been hauled away. But then they passed over the wet road where fire trucks had washed away the gas and oil and broken glass and probably even blood. Traffic opened up again and she was back to speed.

When was the last time she had ever been so thoroughly

immersed in a book? Years. And what had captured her attention so completely that she hadn't noticed the line moving? Subduction zones! When the traffic had stopped she had no idea what a subduction zone was, and if you had asked her if she cared, she would have said, "No!" And here she was eagerly learning about subduction zones. She regretted all over again losing so many years when she vegetated in Rutherford House.

Melody, Anselm, and their dog, Bozo, all greeted her warmly as she drove up to their house. Anselm carried her overnight bag upstairs, and Melody brought out a big dish of beef stew, setting Judith up at the kitchen table. "Okay!" Melody plopped down across from her. "Tell me where your dreams are going!"

Judith divided her time between telling about her day and savoring the stew. She was really hungry; delicious as it had been, the Thai food had long since left. "I was about a hundred pages in when traffic started to move again, and the author was explaining about subduction zones. Melody, I'm an alien on an alien planet. This isn't me. I've totally changed, and I can't say when it happened. But...well, there it is."

"And I couldn't be happier for you! You're blooming late, but at least you're blooming! Now, how do you like that shared living arrangement?"

"I hope it works. One is rather aloof, and the other seems to think we're not just housemates but one big happy family and she's the matriarch. And she's rather messy; that goes against my grain. However, I'll be taking classes at Detroit Lakes and one online, so I think between commuting and studying, my days will be pretty much full. Too full to get bored or irritated." Judith wagged her head. "From Rutherford House to a couple rooms. What a change."

"Well, if it doesn't work, you know, a room here is waiting for you."

"Thank you."

Anselm came in from the mudroom and sat down. "Are you girls all settling in yet?"

"So far, so good. And it's a pretty time of year there."

Melody beamed. "Judith is going to be a world-renowned anthropologist and discover new ruins."

Anselm bobbed his head. "Congratulations! Does the world know about this yet?"

"The world! *I'm* not even sure of it." Judith sighed. "I'm about the same age as Dr. Pollan, my advisor. She has years of research and publications behind her, and I haven't even taken freshman anthropology yet. It's daunting."

"But it's doable!" Apparently Melody harbored no doubts whatever. "That's the important thing. And Anselm, they found a dog. Rather the dog found them. Judith, tell him about it."

She did so, and then, very weary, excused herself and went to bed. She expected to toss and turn a lot; she'd been doing that lately. Instead she fell asleep quickly and slept through to morning.

The next day Anselm went to work and Melody made reservations at their favorite restaurant for Memorial Day dinner. That afternoon, Judith and Melody cut the flowers for the graves. They laid them in a huge Eskimo cooler with a bag of ice. The flowers pretty much filled the cooler.

Flowers. For her father. Judith should be starting to mellow; instead she was getting angrier. Should she mention anything about it to Melody? No. But all those years she'd lost were starting to eat at her big-time. Now that she saw what her world could have been like, the loss began to really weigh on her.

Her father had the money to hire a nanny. Judith should have left home and completed her education, going against his wishes if necessary, not trying so hard and so long to please him, because she never could. She should now have a desk stacked high with important business, and some rocks that meant something to her and weren't just rocks, and maybe an Indian pot or basket or something...and a dualie in the corner! How she envied Dr. Meredith Pollan!

At the very least she should be president of the board of directors caring for the Rutherford House. She should own it! She'd earned it, God knows.

That night she tossed and turned and did not sleep well again.

The next morning Judith felt like she was in a fog. She nibbled a roll for breakfast and drank too much coffee. Melody and Anselm chatted merrily about a shed he wanted to build out back. Judith listened to them yak and didn't even hear what they were saying. She wished she could get back to her new book. Her new life. Instead she had to go honor her father.

Anselm put the cooler in the trunk of their car and Judith climbed into the backseat. She had her new book in her purse, but she couldn't read it on the road, thanks to the motion sickness she had apparently inherited from her mother. Mom could get sick on a porch swing.

Betrayal. Loss. That was all she could think about. It was consuming her and she didn't care. She wanted it to consume her. She was such a pitiful excuse for a failure. An old woman with nothing. Nothing.

The fog swirled around her brain and made time pass and made time stand still. Now, finally, they were at the cemetery. The cemetery was flooded with so many visitors today that Anselm had to park out on the street. He and Melody

swung the cooler between them and headed for the Rutherford plot, Judith dragging along behind.

The Rutherford plot was something of a tourist attraction
in itself. A huge plot with twelve grave spaces, nine of them
occupied, it was surrounded by a black iron fence with
an arch over the gate. The fence was made of hundreds
of spears pointing upward. What was Judith's grandfather
thinking of when he had the fence installed; try to keep the
ghosts in and the living out? A marble statue of a serene-
looking angel with huge folded wings stood on a pedestal
in the middle, eight feet tall. The angel extended its right
arm out over the graves, and in its left hand it held a scroll
of some sort. Judith had been told once what it all meant.
She'd forgotten.

Judith half expected to find Mr. Odegaard at the gravesite
and dreaded the thought that she might. She didn't even
want to look at him ever again. Melody pressed a green plastic vase on a pick into the ground at the head of Judith's
mother's grave. Anselm poured water into it, and Judith
carefully chose flowers in complementary colors. She
clipped a couple of the stems shorter to create a more vis-
ually pleasing bouquet. *There!*

She stood up. *I love you, Mom.*

Melody pushed a similar pot into the ground at the head
of Judith's father's fresh grave. It still smelled damp, earthy.
Anselm poured some water in. There were no flowers that
Judith disliked—they were all beautiful—but some she liked
less than others. She chose flowers she liked the very least and
stuffed them into the vase without thought or effort.

She stood up. Stared at the nameplate. Sebastian Rutherford.

And she spat on it.

# Chapter Eighteen

**M**emorial Day weekend. A lot of the old-timers called it
Decoration Day. Lynn liked that. You decorated
graves. You flew the flag. You went to the parade, and so
many marchers were wearing red, white, and blue.

Lynn stood on her porch with her coffee cup, turned her
face to the sun, and breathed in spring. *Aaaah.* While she
would much rather work in the flowers and garden, the billing
needed to go out—on time. Paul had always been a stickler
for billing and paying on time. It was a good habit to have.

Lynn had a mountain of catching up to do for the plumbing business. But should she go check on Angela first or
not? Her natural inclination was to try to help whatever was
injured or hurting.

*Just go check. You don't need a reason to feel guilty be-
cause you didn't.* She went to Angela's door and tapped
softly. When there was no answer, she silently turned the
knob and peeked in. Pausing, she listened. Nope, that
sounded like deep sleep. She managed to close the door
without a click. *Lord God, what do you want me to do?* Her
reading that morning had talked about God's kindness and
the value of kindness as one of the fruits of the spirit. But
sometimes true kindness pushed on someone to help them
over a hard place.

Was Angela just recovering from stress, or was she sinking into depression? *How would I know? I'm not a doctor.* She headed to her office and settled into the chair, automatically turned on the computer, and pulling out her file of due bills, she attacked them with a vengeance. While she could do her banking online and pay some things that way, she'd not gone in and added new accounts in some time.

Homer barking caught her attention. She got up and went to see. He stood at the back door, tail wagging. The mudroom echoed with another deep bark. "It's okay, boy. That's a good boy. Guess you must feel this is your home if you are ready to announce visitors." She opened the door to find a package too big for the box, so the mail lady had brought it in. She had probably honked and Lynn didn't hear it. She picked it up and brought it in, with Homer leaping up to sniff it. When she set the box down, he gave it a good going over.

"Good boy, checking everything out." His tail whacked against her leg, something she'd already learned could be a bit painful. First dog she'd ever had whose tail was a lethal weapon. Orson's and all their Labs' tails could clear the coffee table in one sweep. She got out the box cutter and started to open it before she read that it was addressed to Angela. "Oops." Talking to the dog was a habit she'd learned a long time ago. She took the box off the dryer and set it on the counter in the kitchen. She snagged a chocolate-chip-oatmeal cookie from the jar, poured herself a glass of water, and returned to her bookkeeping.

The phone. Phillip on the caller ID. She picked it up. "What do you need this time?"

"How did you know I needed something?"

"You only call during the day when you need something." She smiled to herself.

"I can't get ahold of Maggie, and Jason over at the Plumber's Friend called to say the part we need today was in. Could you please go pick it up?"

"Now?" Of course it would be now. She saved her work on the computer, left a note for Angela, grabbed the outgoing mail, and, dog on her heels, headed for the car. "You think you should go?" Homer stopped right at the door to the seat beside the driver. "You want to ride up here with me?" *Lynn Lundberg, don't help him create bad habits. You know dogs should have a fence across the back and not sit on the seats. Safer for all.* She let him up in the front seat anyway. *Shame on you, Lynn!*

Phillip was loading his panel truck for a house call when she got there.

"Heard from Judith?" Phillip asked as she handed him the box of gaskets.

"She was going to check something at the university in Duluth. Not sure what. Then she was going to drive down to her cousin's for the holiday weekend. And apparently they would go to Rutherford to put flowers on the graves."

Phillip nodded. "You want to go canoeing tonight? Maggie is taking the kids to a movie and I passed on that."

"Oh, good, I've not been out yet. Let's go see if the eagles are back at their nest. If we take the big canoe, Angela could come, too. She needs to get out."

"Good. Stick something in the oven for supper, okay?"

"Now I know why the invite to go canoeing."

Phillip nodded toward Homer. "I see you got someone riding shotgun."

"He likes riding in the car."

"You need a fence. We have one back at the house."

"Bring it along tonight if you would. Thanks."

"I will. I'm assuming you've received no response to the feelers you put out. No owner has come forward?"

"And you're still snickering at my efforts, aren't you?"

"You got a dog, Mom; just accept that and enjoy him. Sure wish you'd let me try him on a hunt."

She snorted. Hunting indeed. "You have Rowdy. That's enough. Although Homer would probably do well. He seems to understand so much. He settled in mightily easily."

"How's your roommates thing going?" Phillip studied her a moment. "Something is worrying you, I can tell."

"I'm a little worried about Angela. Been praying for her. She talks to Minerva; I heard her out on the deck, but not much to us—yet, I hope. And she sure sleeps a lot."

"Depression isn't surprising in her situation." Phillip scratched his chin.

"Especially if they were close. I personally could go and dump a pile of chicken manure all over that guy."

"Uh-uh. Not long lasting enough."

He laughed and stepped back. She waved and put the car in gear. As she drove off, she looked at the big, goofy face beside her. "Like you'd be happy with a fence."

What time was it? Oh, good grief! Angela tossed her travel alarm aside. How could she sleep so much? True sleep, too, not the dozing, waking, dozing she used to do.

And she was still tired.

She dragged herself out of bed and made it, did her bathroom thing, and propelled her weary body to the kitchen.

Breakfast? Hardly worth it. Lunch. Compared to her fridge at home, this one was a cornucopia. Lynn did love to cook. She chose some good-looking stuff at random and arranged a plate for the microwave.

Lynn and Homer came bouncing into the kitchen with

their usual exuberance. Angela turned with a partial smile. "Good morning. Barely."

"Good morning. What are you having?"

"Leftovers from last night. And toast, I can't get enough of your bread."

Homer strolled over and plopped down beside her.

"Warm up enough for both of us, then, please." She nodded to the dog sitting by Angela's feet. "You have a friend."

Angela leaned over to pet Homer and got a slurp on her chin. "Eeuw, I really don't like dog slobber." She wiped her chin. "Judith seems to have taken it upon herself to walk him, but with her gone, I can do it. I'll take him out later."

"Good. Thank you." Lynn fetched another plate from the cupboard. "I love leftover pot roast. Well, I love pot roast no matter what." She set the table out on the deck and helped carry the meal out. Homer followed closely, riveting his gaze on the pot roast.

Angela and she sat down; it was cool and cloudy, the sky cover growing ever thicker, but still gorgeous out here. Lynn looked down at a monster-sized paw on her knee. "No, Homer, none for you. You already ate this morning." He answered with his well-practiced soulful whimper and sniff. Those lugubrious eyes rolled up toward her. His thick tail beat out an affirmation. "Sorry, fella, won't work." Resigned, he flopped down beside her. "Thank you, Angela. Great lunch idea."

"You're welcome."

End of conversation.

But then, Angela could not feel less like chatting.

As they were finishing their meal out on the deck and dark thunderclouds were gathering, she glanced at Lynn; she was being studied.

"Angela, are you all right?"

She shrugged. "All I want to do is sleep. I could go back to bed right now, I think. At least when I'm sleeping I can't think of the mess my life has become."

"Interesting. Why do you say a 'mess'?"

"I have no job, therefore no income."

"You had said you'd check with Realtors here."

"I know. But right now the thought of starting all over in a new place where I know nothing and no one and have zero contacts makes me realize, I don't really want to do that anymore. I was trying to become the successful woman Jack wanted, but I don't like the woman I became. I guess more precisely, I don't like real estate as a career. And obviously, after I changed everything, Jack didn't like the new me, either."

Lynn's mouth dropped open. "Wait. You became a Realtor just so you could be successful?"

"It sounded like a good idea at the time. And he seemed to like it at first."

"You mean Jack?" Lynn snorted. "Of course, but I don't even like to say his name, unless I put *jerk* behind it."

That made Angela smile. *Jack the Jerk.* She wasn't the only one to think it. "Thanks." She picked up the last half of toast and spread jam on it. "He likes his women thin—svelte, he calls it—so here I am, watching my weight carefully. On the other hand, I don't want to gain and be frumpy again."

"Hard to think of you as looking frumpy. You look good in whatever you put on."

Angela stared at her. "You mean that?"

"Of course. I never say something I don't mean. *Forthright* is a term I've heard used to describe me." She dabbed up crumbs with a dampened finger. "It would be easy to be domineering, but God seems to be working on that."

"You're a very strong woman."

Lynn smiled. "Right, on the outside. Marshmallow interior."

Angela giggled, then sobered. "I understand your Paul was still in his prime, and those photos of him, he looked so young for his age. The shock must have been especially bad since he'd not been sick."

"It still is." She changed the subject quickly. "Did you see that box addressed to you? It's on the counter."

"Why, no, I didn't look."

"There's a knife in the block by the stove." Lynn picked up their plates and carried them inside to load the dishwasher while Angela opened the box.

"From Gwynn and Charlie." She peeled back the box flaps and stared at the box within. It looked to be about basketball size. But when she tried to lift it out, it was stuck.

"Here, I'll hold the outer box."

Angela opened the card that was taped to the top of the dusty blue box. "To our mom, because we love you. Welcome to your new life." She looked to Lynn, shaking her head.

"Well, open it."

Angela slit the tape with the cutter and lifted up the lid. "Tissue paper."

"They didn't want it to break."

She peeled back the first layer of paper to find another envelope and pulled out a…"Fishing license!" Another layer yielded another envelope. "And a gift certificate to Cabela's for a fishing pole." Nestled on the bottom of the box was still another box. She opened it. "A fishing reel." She read its cardboard packaging. "For fly-fishing. Do they fly-fish here?"

"Sure do. And Phillip asked if we wanted to go out in the canoe tonight. How does that sound to you?"

"Are you sure? I mean, I don't want to intrude."

"Angela." Lynn took her hand. "There is no pressure here to perform for anyone." She blinked. "My friend, you can heal here and truly begin a new life. Your kids are wonderful, and they are welcome to visit. Charlie loved it here; those years ago that were only yesterday."

Angela stared at her. She sniffed and blinked, and in spite of her efforts, a tear rolled down her cheek. "I-I feel so worthless." She shook her head slowly. "So very worthless."

Lynn took her by the hand and led her over to the leather couch that faced looking out the window. She sat down and pulled Angela against her. "Now, cry it out." She picked up a box of tissues off the huge square coffee table and handed it to her.

"If I— If I start crying, I might never stop." The tears ran faster. She hiccuped.

Lynn wrapped her arms around her. "They run out eventually."

Angela let loose great gulping sobs, mopped, blew, and kept on crying, punctuating everything she tried to say with more huge sobs. "I-I didn't expect...I mean, I thought our life was all right and he...he was lying to me. I hate him and I hate her and I hate hating. I don't hate people!" She melted into Lynn as she had melted into her mother when she was a small child. She needed Mom now, she needed comfort, and there was no comfort, no peace in the whole world, and...Sobbing. She could not stem the sobbing. And Mother held her close, stroking her back, purring platitudes about God. She needed the cosseting if not the platitudes.

Homer sat by her knee, kissing her elbow, whining, his tail thumping. He lurched up onto the leather sofa cushions and snuggled his head under her arms to lay it in her lap. The more she cried, the more he whimpered, then sat back and, nose in the air, broke into a full-throated basset song.

Angela sat straight up and stared at Lynn, who was fighting to keep from laughing, then at the dog, who stared back at her and then gave another abbreviated howl, like a coda to his performance.

Still getting surprised by random sobs, Angela sat up away from Lynn's arms, feeling a bit awkward. She reached over and patted Homer, earning herself a hand lick. "This is one loving and lovable dog." She blew her nose. "I'm using up all yo— The tissues."

The room had darkened during her childish crying jag, and a distant rumbling made her look up. Lightning zagged in the east.

Lynn's eyes suddenly went wide. "Did you open your window?"

"I did." Both women leaped to their feet, one to charge down the hall, the other up the stairs.

"Check Judith's room, too, please," Lynn called.

Angela did so, even though she felt ridiculously invasive to be entering someone else's private quarters. What if someone simply walked into hers? If she trained the children in one thing, it was to respect others' property. But Judith's window stood wide open, ready to welcome the rain. Angela closed it and was impressed with how smoothly this wood-framed window operated. Excellent construction.

A howl from downstairs called her back. She found Homer cowering behind the sofa, whimpering and shaking. When the thunder crashed again, he howled so mournfully she called him out, sat back down on the sofa, and brought him up into her lap, petting him and crooning comfort. "Poor guy."

Lynn was out on the porch, simply standing there, head

up and eyes closed, inhaling deeply. She came back in. "Dog's afraid of thunder and lightning."

Lightning lit the room again and the thunder crashed right overhead. Homer yelped and tried to dig into the couch. Lynn laughed. "No, boy, you can't do that. Come on, it's all right." She sat on the other side of him and rubbed his back. More mothering. Now that Angela was attuned to it, she could see Mother in much of what Lynn did.

Lynn said, "I think there is something we can give him to make this easier. I'll ask Herb tomorrow." The rain continued, the wind churning the lake into a sea of whitecaps. The dock bobbed on the power of the incoming waves.

"I don't think we'll be canoeing tonight." Lynn leaned over and clicked the switch on the lamp. Nothing. "Well, good thing we have a gas stove, because right now, we have no electricity. The lightning must have struck somewhere close enough to take it out. If you have your computer on, go turn it off and your cell phone."

"I've never seen a storm like this over water. How utterly beautiful."

"Especially when we are in a solid house, wired to not burn down if lightning strikes. I'll get the fire going; the chill sure comes in fast, too." She looked down at the dog in her lap, who was now snoring softly. "Wore him out."

A chirp from the kitchen and Miss Minerva strolled into the room, tail straight up, and, ignoring the dog, she leaped up on the sofa and settled in Angela's lap. Homer raised his head and slid over the side onto the floor.

The rain still drummed on the roof, heard from even that high above them. Once the fire was snapping and crackling, Homer went to lie on the braided rug in front of it. The women moved over to the two recliners in front of the soaring stone fireplace and Minerva climbed back in Angela's lap.

"Looks like you've made a good friend."

Angela smiled. "You don't mind sharing?"

"Not at all." Lynn dug into the quilted bag beside her and pulled out her knitting. The click of the needles, the soft crackle of the fire, and the rain drumming on the roof and the windows—so homey, even if Angela's home was never quite like this. She realized now that when she showed a house she referred to as homey, it was not often like this.

Was this crying jag a turning point of some sort? Or a step in the right direction, at least? Angela would have explored that thought further but she fell asleep.

# Chapter Nineteen

Visiting the cemetery was not Lynn's favorite part of Memorial Day, mostly since Paul had been buried there. But honoring the family ancestors was not a problem. She'd been out at dawn to cut the lilacs, both purple and white, and now the house was filled with the fragrance. She picked enough to leave one bouquet at home on the kitchen counter. When Phillip arrived, he helped her load the buckets in her SUV and drove them to the cemetery. They weren't the first ones there. Since the gates weren't locked, people came when they wanted.

They greeted the other early birds and stopped at the earliest family plot, where they placed jars of lilacs on each of six graves. At the next, where the immediate generation before Lynn lay, they set out five jars. She and Paul had purchased the lot adjacent to his parents, but his sister had already volunteered to decorate those graves, so she moved to where Paul's marker lay.

"You know why I don't really have trouble coming out here, unlike a lot of people I know?" Phillip asked.

"No, why?" She arranged the vase with lilacs and turned from the rear of the car.

"Because they're not here. Their bodies were buried here but they are not here. And when I think of the celebration that went on in heaven when Dad went home, I'm glad for him." He laid a hand on her shoulder. "But sometimes I miss him something fierce, and that's what's hard to handle."

"Me, too." Like right now. She and Paul used to do this together. She sniffed and set the vase in the stand. Her last lilacs went on the small grave next to Paul's. She knelt there and rubbed the grass clippings off the marker. Amanda Lynn Lundberg, who at six months had died of crib death. Lynn stared down at it. "I am so certain God has a special place for little ones like this. Just think, she was a year younger than you, so she would be..."

"Thirty. You've been through a lot." He helped her to her feet and kept an arm around her shoulders.

"We never expect things like this to happen to us. I mean, there we were with our little son who was the cutest little towhead you ever saw and this beautiful baby girl. Healthy, laughing, she stole everyone's heart. Well, both of you did. We have that one portrait of the two of you." Lynn inhaled the potpourri of spring, the fragrance of lilacs, newly mown grass. "Life changes in an instant and we have no control over it. The amazing thing is that God holds us even closer when the pain is so devastating." She tissued away the errant tears.

"And then Dad died, also unexpectedly."

"But at least I knew then about grieving. The process wasn't such a shock. And I knew that when God got me through the first one, He wouldn't fail me this time either or any time." They strolled back to the SUV. "Now let's put these leftovers on some graves that no one ever decorates."

Back in the car on the way home, Phillip asked, "You have your stuff ready for the parade and picnic?"

"Pretty much. Just have to load the cooler and pack the basket."

"Is Angela going to come?"

"I hope so. She said possibly."

"What about the shindig later tonight?"

"Well, it will be at our house, so how can she miss that? We agreed before beginning this project that the house is to be used for family stuff."

When he parked the SUV and opened the door, they could hear Homer barking along with a howl thrown in for good measure. "Glad that dog is working out. See you in a while."

A bit later, Lynn tapped on Angela's door. "I'm leaving for the parade in fifteen minutes. You said you wanted to go along." No answer. She pushed open the door to see the mound of human still in bed. She stepped inside, walked silently over to the bed, and leaned in close, watching Angela's breathing. She didn't seem ill, just sleeping heavily. Lynn left.

Her phone rang as she returned to the kitchen.

"You ready, G'ma?" Miss Priss bounced, even on the phone.

"Got the cooler and the picnic basket all loaded, so anytime."

"Yay, Mommy says ten minutes."

"Okay, sweetie, see you then."

"Can Homer go along?"

"Not today. We'll take him out with other people in smaller doses first. Big crowds like the parade might scare him."

"Oh, bye."

And big crowds it was. They never tried to park downtown because it was easier to find on-the-curb seating farther along the parade route. They found their usual tree in front of a friend's house, unloaded the car, and Phillip drove off to park.

"I can hear the band!" The little girl jumped up from the curb where her two brothers and two cousins sat. Travis had his long-distance squirt gun at the ready. All had bags to pick up the candy to be tossed from all the floats.

"You go sit down before someone grabs your place," Maggie said after a flash hug from her daughter.

"G'ma, you could sit with us."

"That's okay, I'm right behind you. Curb sitting and your grandma aren't the best of friends anymore."

Her pixie face wrinkled. "You don't like parades?"

"Sure I do, just like lawn chairs better than curbs."

"There they come!" The boys all jumped up as the mounted sheriff's posse led the way with the flags flying above them. The huge U.S. flag half covered the rider in the blowing wind. The horses jigged, and spectators along the way stood with their hands over their hearts, including all the children. The Detroit Lakes High School band marched behind the horses, separated by a clown with a pooper-scooper.

Lynn felt her eyes go liquid as they always did when the flags went by. She mopped after she sat back down.

"Me, too," Maggie whispered.

After the high school drill team led by girls with spinning batons, the veterans still able marched while the trailer with the oldest of the veterans, some in wheelchairs but all in uniforms, returned the salutes offered by many of those along the way. Every time she saw them, as the numbers grew fewer, Lynn and so many others called out "thank yous" over and over. Part of her gratitude was the safety of all her men. Her father had never shared his experiences of the war in Korea but returned home a wounded hero and now was one of those no longer in the parade. Tom was still troubled by his experiences on active duty a few years ago.

He chose not to march, and when she glanced at him, he watched respectfully but was not cheering and waving like his boys.

"Here he comes," Travis hollered, and hoisted his water gun. A clown on an adult tricycle pumped up a water gun to spray kids and anyone else who got in his way. He zigzagged back and forth, bringing shouts of laughter and screams of "eek." Travis raised his gun. The clown laughed and the two dueled it out. Travis ran out of water to end it.

"You need a bucket and a pump," the clown hollered as he passed.

Lynn wiped her face. "How come I got so wet?" But she knew why. The clown in the crazy outfit was none other than Herb, the veterinarian. He loved dousing everyone.

Those on the floats for the organizations in town threw out candy, and the kids scrambled to fill their bags. The historical society wore prairie clothes of the early 1900s; the various class floats tossed candy; and everyone bantered, shouting insults back and forth, making everyone laugh. The swim team float looked like a big fish; the 4-H clubs had chickens and sheep along with kids; and two kids walked behind dragging their reluctant, head-wagging steers by lead ropes. A beautiful team of Clydesdales pulled a handsome buggy with a silver-haired couple, her with a parasol to match her lavender dress of the late 1800s, while the man sported a splendid frock coat and black top hat.

Two other bands marched and more horses and riders; various tractors, some huge and current, some old but restored; vintage cars with the drivers often wearing clothes of the period; and convertibles with the royalty followed by classic cars with the dignitaries. The parade closed with more horses, a pooper-scooper, and the skirl of bagpipes played by three men in full kilt regalia.

Lynn sighed. "I love parades like these." She took another swig from her bottled water. She hugged the little girl leaning against her knee and laughed at the boys playing and shouting with their friends from across the street. "I think you need your face washed," she said to Miss Priss, who had obviously been eating red candy, clutching her bag of goodies.

"We better get to the park if we want a table." Phillip started folding up the chairs. "I'm parked two streets over. Come on, guys, grab a chair." They joined others, lugging their stuff and heading for the cars.

"You should have had your panel truck in the parade, good advertising," someone yelled.

"If they don't know us by now...," Tommy hollered back.

Lynn climbed into the SUV. Memorial Day parades were all so alike and yet every one different. Two years ago she sat on the parade route with Paul. That was two years ago. What would next year's be?

The town's picnic, too, was unique and yet the same, just like all other picnics. Lynn enjoyed the food, the camaraderie. Two years ago Paul scooped egg salad and ham salad out of the tubs onto the rolls and doled them out. And he refereed the pickup volleyball. This year it was Phillip. Cherished memories, vanished times.

But in late afternoon as they arrived at the house, her house, with her children and grandchildren, she knew she had no reason to mope. Look at all she possessed!

"Sorry I didn't get up to come along." Angela looked up from the kitchen table as Lynn carried the cooler and picnic basket back in.

"You missed a great parade and picnic. Detroit Lakes goes all out for Memorial Day. One of the best parades ever, too." Lynn set her stuff on the counter and leaned over to pet the dog, who was dancing at her feet. "Did he wake you needing to go out?"

"No, I finally just woke up for the first time feeling like I was awake, like I finally had enough sleep. Makes no sense at all."

"I'd say that might be a step in the right direction."

"How can I help you get ready for tonight?"

"Well, the beans are in the oven."

"I know, I could smell them and stirred them."

"The hamburgers are all ready, hot dogs, too. Josie is bringing a relish tray and the hamburger fixings. I need to take the buns out of the freezer."

"I can do that."

"No, the freezer in the garage. We have both a chest freezer and an extra refrigerator in the garage."

"Okay, I'll get those."

"We set up everything on the counter and the tables on the deck. Unless the weather turns and we add another table in the big room."

"How many people are coming?"

"Oh, twenty or so."

"That's a crowd." Angela left to get the buns from the freezer. When she returned, she set three fairly large bags on the counter. "All these? You made all these?"

"Well, took me a while, but once you get known for something, you kind of have to stick with it or people get disappointed. Tommy has his secret recipe for the hamburgers and…"

"If you tell me someone makes the hot dogs, I'll…"

Lynn laughed at the expression on her friend's face. "I could say we bought them from a special place in town, but we didn't. The kids don't like his sausages as well as the regular kind, and most adults would rather have the burgers anyway. Sometimes we do a sausage cook-off, often on the Fourth or Labor Day. People bring the ones they made. I tell you, that is something."

"I've heard of chili cook-offs but not sausage. You want these left in the bags?"

As people arrived, the table was covered with dishes; the desserts were set up in the dining room; and chips, dip, veggies, and such began to cover the counter, too. The kids grabbed from the center island and all ran outside; the women gathered around the counter munching while they chatted; and the men took over the deck, helping themselves to the soft drinks and beer in the coolers lined up along the railing.

"Stay out of the water!" Phillip hollered to the kids heading for the lake. "It's too cold yet."

"He says that every year," someone murmured with a chuckle. Lynn introduced Angela to all the guests, and several of them hauled platters of burgers and hot dogs out to the table pulled up near the barbecue. When Phillip yelled, "Come and get it," and handed the hot-off-the-grill meat to be taken into the house, everyone gathered around the counter. Phillip said grace with everyone joining the amen.

Two years ago, it was Paul.

Phillip waved an arm and pointed. "Okay, kids first and then you all take the kid tables down on the grass. Do not feed the dogs. Okay? Mom, where's Homer?"

"In the mudroom. I'm not sure how he'll handle this many people. We'll bring him out on a leash after supper."

Lynn's mind could not help reflecting that last year Paul grilled the wieners and held Miss Priss on his lap while she devoured her hot dog bun, licked up the ketchup, and then ate the meat.

She joined Josie, who had taken Angela under her wing,

and some of the others at one table. "Whew. We didn't run out of food."

"Not yet," someone said.

Someone else cackled. "You never run out of food at the Lundbergs'. They would be horrified. Lynn might collapse from the shock."

"Oh, honestly!" Lynn wagged her head. "I know it is not my mission to feed the whole world, but when folks come to my house, I just don't want them to go away hungry."

"And take home plenty of leftovers."

"G'ma?" Travis showed up at her shoulder. "When can Homer come out?"

Phillip happened to see the exchange. "Let your grandma eat, for Pete's sake."

"Later, but you have to keep him on the leash."

"Okay." And off he charged.

When most people were done with the main food, someone made the rounds with a black trash bag, collecting the used plates.

Lynn listened in on several conversations. Angela seemed to be having a good time. Was she finally starting to heal?

Maggie sat down beside her. "All this food makes me feel almost guilty." She reached over and grabbed a chip from one of the bags lining the center of the table. "You did it again."

"Not me, it took everyone." Lynn patted her knee. "Aren't you getting chilly in those shorts?"

Tommy stood at the door. "The desserts are ready in the dining room. There is coffee for those who want it, and if you see anything missing, just ask."

"Where's the ice cream?" one of the bigger kids asked.

"That's for the Fourth of July, you know that."

Lynn caught Angela's questioning look and explained,

"We have homemade ice cream for the Fourth, made the old-fashioned way with hand-cranked ice-cream churns, salt and ice, and by then the local strawberries are usually starting. Some good, that's for sure."

"I'm going to have to diet tomorrow." One of the women groaned.

"Or not eat for a week," said another.

By the time the party broke up, not late because there was school the next day and jobs to return to, the kitchen was cleaned up, everyone took home some things, and Homer was stretched out on the rug in front of the fireplace, snoring.

"Welcome to holidays at the Lundbergs' in Minnesota," Phillip said to Angela as he carried a limp Miss Priss out the door. She had fallen asleep on the sofa.

Angela looked around the big, empty room. "I've been to family parties before, but not like this. How come no one even got into an argument? And I heard the men talking politics even."

"I don't know. We work together, we play together. All the kids are growing up together, and us old folks, er, older folks, you noticed there were several sets of grandparents...I guess part of the fun is that we have all ages. Not many teens here tonight. We have more younger kids. I know it can be a bit overwhelming at first."

"But people made me feel welcome. As if I'd lived here for years or was a long-lost relative."

"Good, I figured they would. I saw you talking with Betty; she'll get you involved in something in no time."

"I wish I knew what I wanted to do now that I'm here. Someone suggested I volunteer at the library. I think I'll go there and look into it."

"You step through the door and mention you're interested in helping, and Mary and her troops will have you busy in no time. You ever worked in a library before?"

"Volunteered at the school library when my kids went there. Actually, for all the years they attended."

"That was a few years ago."

"For sure, but I loved it, especially the little ones; well, that's not true, any ages." She nodded. "I think that's where I'll start, anyway."

Lynn leaned her head back, enjoying the quiet. "Hear the loons?"

"I do." Angela smiled. "Judith should be here."

"I always love when we're out in the canoe and see the mamas giving their chicks a ride on their backs. Something special about the loons."

"I don't know. Canoes tip over too easy. Since I don't swim terribly well, maybe I'll stick to the rowboat."

# Chapter Twenty

"I hate to see you leave," Melody whispered again as she hugged Judith good-bye.

"I know, but maybe I'll be back for the Fourth."

"No maybe about it. I'm counting on it."

Judith slid into her car and snapped her seat belt. "The road goes both ways, you know, and I will be in school, as close to full-time as I think I can handle in this summer of great change."

"Great change for sure. Drive safe and call me when you get there."

"Yes, Mama." Judith waved one more time and headed out the drive. At least she had waited until traffic had let up—she hoped. She slid the first CD of the novel Melody had given her into her player and sat back to be entertained on her way west. This was a first for her, listening to a book on the trip. She wondered if the book on Krakatoa was on CD. Another first for her. Even thinking about buying an audio book.

"Judith, you are indeed embarked on a brand-new life."

She stopped to potty and refill her travel mug, stopped again for lunch, and let the miles get eaten up by the novel, a historical about one of the queens of England. When thoughts of her actions at the cemetery tried to intrude, she slammed the door on them and kept her focus on the road and the story. The reader was doing an excellent job, which made the story even more enjoyable. This was almost as good as her mother reading to her. Almost but not quite.

When she drove into the new yard—*her* new yard—she saw Lynn and Angela out in the garden accompanied by a big-voiced dog who welcomed her home. She realized she really had missed walking with the goofy hound by her side. She waved and parked her car in front of the new garage next to Angela's, and once standing on the gravel, she inhaled a deep breath of clean spring air, stretching out the kinks of car sitting. Homer came barking from the garden, but when he saw her, his bark changed to a welcome whimper, yip, and dance routine. He leaped up, but when she ordered him down, he dropped to his feet and quivered all over, his tail whipping. She bent over and rubbed his ears, his head, and down his back.

"Boy, are you shedding." She dusted her hands to release black, white, and russet hair into the breeze, then went back to petting and talking to him.

"Welcome home." Angela and Lynn, still wearing gardening gloves, joined them, hugging her and petting the dog. "You have to tell us how everything went."

"Did you bring pictures? We have oodles of pictures of yesterday." Lynn's smile rivaled the sun. "Oh, I'm so glad you are home safe. You didn't get caught in that horrid accident, did you?"

"Sat on the interstate for better'n two hours, but I was reading and totally lost track of time. Never had that happen before. In fact, I've had all kinds of things happen to me for the first time." She lifted the lid on her trunk. "Melody sent you some specialty cheeses." As she lifted out her suitcase, Lynn grabbed the handle.

"You get your stuff out of the car; this calls for a celebration."

Angela and Judith swapped questioning looks. "What for?"

"You got home all right. We had a great day yesterday. The sun is shining and anything else we can think of."

Angela shrugged and reached for the box on the backseat. "They know how to throw a party here, let me tell you. I've never seen so much food in my life, homemade hamburger buns even."

"After driving in the crazy Minneapolis traffic, the quiet out here is pure heaven."

The two followed Lynn's roller wheel lines in the driveway and went in through the mudroom, too. Judith left Melody's gift on the center island and headed for her room with her purse and bag that included some books from Melody—several of them on audio—and her travel mug. She looked around her room. She'd not been fair in her description to Melody; this was not by any means a small room. She had room for her desk, a bookshelf, her mother's rocking chair and a side table with a lamp, a chest of drawers, and her queen-sized bed. Tomorrow she would hang one of her cross-stitch projects or maybe two. And a painting her mother had given her years earlier of a little girl with chickens around her.

Chickens. She had always loved chickens. Her mother tried to raise some as a hobby, but they didn't last long. Her father decreed they must go, for he was annoyed by the rooster crowing. To save the chicken project, they gave away the noisy rooster, for they could not bear to eat him. Her father banished the hens anyway.

On her way back to the kitchen, she eyed the empty hall wall. Maybe she could hang some of her things here? But to her own surprise, when she joined the others already out on the deck, she said, "Lynn, have you ever had chickens here?"

"No. Too many wild animals who enjoy chicken— raccoons, weasels."

"We had chickens when I was a little girl and I always loved them. I dreamed that someday I would have chickens again. Had I stayed at Rutherford, I would have done just that." She took the glass of iced tea and a lemon bar and sat down facing the lake. With a sigh and a smile, she leaned back and nodded. "I have a feeling that this place can become home very quickly."

"Why, thank you. I'm glad you feel that way. I always love coming home, the best part of any trip."

The three brought one another up to date; Judith told them about her excitement on the campus at Duluth. Angela announced she got up this morning at a decent hour.

"Not the crack of dawn but I heard the school bus. Homer came in and informed me that it was time to get up."

"Did he really?" Lynn asked. "Oh, how did he get your door open?"

"I must not have shut it tightly enough. But I was glad to see him. You gotta admit getting a slurp on the nose is a rather rude awakening." She reached down and patted the dog, who lay between them. His thumping tail echoed on the cedar decking. "You're a good boy, aren't you?"

"I have a confession to make," Judith said a bit later.

"Really?"

"I'm really embarrassed to admit this, but at the cemetery yesterday?"

They nodded.

"I spat on my father's grave marker." She looked up at both of them staring at her, mouths open, eyes wide. "Sorry, I mean, I…"

Lynn was the first to break into laughter, followed by Angela.

"Really, you think it's funny?" Judith stared at them, appalled both that she had done it and that she had admitted it. Then a chuckle started down in her midsection somewhere and finally bubbled out her mouth. "It isn't really this funny, is it?"

Both heads nodded in unison.

"Oh, it is!" Lynn sputtered. "Might be the healthiest thing you've done in a long, long time." She pointed to the lake. "Look, a flock of Canada geese landing on the water. We used to be a flyway for sky-darkening numbers of ducks and geese. We still get quite a few."

"Do you have a bird book?" Angela asked. "I used to know my backyard birds, but not like here with lake birds besides. I thought I saw an eagle the other day."

"You probably did. We have a pair that nest in a huge old snag up the lake." She pointed off to their left. "Phillip and I hoped to go see if they were back, but that storm came up. One of the reasons we like canoeing, you don't disturb the birds."

"I'm looking forward to learning how to paddle a canoe." Judith swirled her ice and remaining tea. "Anyone else want a refill? I'll get it." She pushed back her chair, making Homer jump. "Sorry, Homer." When he looked up at her, she asked, "Is he learning his name?"

"Seems that way."

Judith slid open the door and Miss Minerva paraded outside. She glanced over at Homer, and in all her regalness, she jumped up on Lynn's lap. Homer sat up, tail twitching, as the cat did her three times turn around and settle. The dog made a sound, not a whimper and not a whine, and lay back down, nose between paws, eyes on the cat.

Angela giggled and scratched behind his ears. "You sure learned a lesson here. You just tell us what you think, okay?"

"He probably will. We have two extremely verbal animals here." Lynn half shrugged and her hand automatically did as Miss Minerva fully expected. The purr motor did not start until the petting did.

Judith just shook her head and went on into the house.

So here Judith was, a bit less than forty-eight hours after she arrived back in Barnett Lake, prowling a hardware store again. This was apparently going to be a major feature of her new life. Not that she was a stranger to hardware stores, but mostly in the past she had scoured vintage hardware stores seeking replacements for small broken pieces in Rutherford House. This farm hardware store was *hardware* writ large.

Riding lawn mowers and three-gang garden tillers had taken over the front of the store. And so many grills. Simple ones, elaborate ones, gas grills, charcoal grills.

And a chicken coop.

Judith stopped cold, transfixed. Lynn continued to the plumbing aisles without her. A chicken coop. Skids beneath it to keep it above the dirt. She raised the door latch and opened it halfway. It did not swing out or swing shut. Well-hung. She stepped inside. Head high if you scrunched down, with nest boxes, roosts, and a smooth composite floor. Two vents. An actual ceiling fixture, not just a naked light-bulb hanging there. This was not a coop; it was a chicken mansion.

She went back out and latched the door.

A saleswoman in the store's cargo vest smiled at her. "You seem interested. We have a special on these. This week only, the coop comes with a waterer, that feeder trough, and enough poultry netting to enclose a six-by-eight-foot yard."

"You deliver?"

"Anywhere within the county, twenty-five dollars."

Judith didn't even ask the price. She handed the woman her credit card and followed her to a register. Her cell rang. She answered.

Lynn in the back of the store. "Can you please bring me a flatbed?"

"Right away." She signed the slip, grabbed a flatbed, and pushed it to plumbing. Reality had returned. That night in bed she realized she had not mentioned her purchase to Lynn. She had figured to.

A deep-voiced horn beeped the next morning as Judith, Angela, and Lynn sat around the breakfast table discussing the Fourth of July. Homer barked helpfully.

"Already?" Judith hopped up. "I believe that's for me."

It was! As she jogged out onto the porch, the driver was just climbing out of the hardware store's stake-side truck. Her coop and poultry supplies had arrived! But where to put them? Where would they be least conspicuous? Probably beyond the garage.

She glanced behind her. Lynn was standing on the porch step gawking. "Harry? Harry! Wrong address! We didn't order this."

The young man frowned at his invoice. "Says here you did, Lynn."

"It's mine," Judith said quickly. "I was thinking maybe behind the garage."

"But...but...it's a chicken coop. Chickens. We don't... chicken coop."

Never had Judith seen Lynn so flustered, not even when two dozen guests dropped in at once. Was her chicken idea—her chicken dream—so wrong?

Angela hopped down off the porch. "Chickens! What a

great idea! Fresh eggs, little chicks running around. I love it. What kind are we getting?"

Lynn shook her head. "We're not. This is a mistake, a...a..."

The driver named Harry turned to Judith. "Credit card payment here says your name is Rutherford. Any relation to the Rutherfords in the town of that name?"

"Direct descendant, yes. Rutherford House is now a public museum. Take your family and visit sometime."

The young man grinned. "Hey, I will. Gotta get a family first. I'll tell my girlfriend. Where do you want the coop?"

Beside Judith, Angela giggled. "Don't forget to tell her why."

Judith pointed. "Beyond the garage."

"Can do." Harry headed back to his truck.

Lynn had changed from agape to angry. In fact, she seemed very angry. "Judith, no! The three of us discuss things like this first. We're one household, not three separate kingdoms!"

Angela butted in. "Lynn, you must have said it a hundred times: 'This really is your home. You are not just renting a room.' All right. It's our home. But we are not your children. We're adults and sometimes we follow our drummers, not yours. Did you see how happy Judith looked when she heard the truck horn?"

Judith broke in. "My mother and I both loved chickens; this is a dream for me, Lynn. Please let me follow my dream."

"Besides," Angela added, "with three of us, feeding chickens, gathering eggs, and all will not be a burden on anyone. We can share the work."

Lynn's scowl had not softened. She turned and marched inside.

Judith drew a deep breath. "I may have made a huge mistake, Angela."

Angela shook her head. "This has been coming ever since we got here; I could feel it. I don't think she expected to have to share her matriarchal position."

"Matriarch." Judith smiled sadly. "She sure is that."

"Here?" Harry called, so Judith hurried around behind the garage, with Angela right behind her.

Angela stepped forward. *Good!* Angela was a Realtor. She knew where to put things. "If we set up the building there and paint it a cool brown, it will blend in well, hardly noticeable. Run the yard out this way with a gate there."

"Looks good." Harry frowned. "Is Miz Lundberg all right?"

"If she isn't, she will be. Do you need help with the coop?"

"Nope. Got the forklift right here."

Judith watched, fascinated, as the young man—surely not out of his teens yet; he still had a few pimples—casually threw some planks down between the truck bed and the ground. He walked up them to a big yellow blob of a machine like one of those riding lawn mowers. *Ah.* This was the forklift. He hopped on; started its engine; and expertly slid the forks under the coop, raised the load, and drove down the planks.

Angela was standing beyond some bushes, indicating exactly where to place Judith's dream. And she was right. Paint it brown and one would never notice it. The coop settled into place.

Harry used the forklift to unload the rolls of wire and big cartons with the poultry equipment. He drove it back up on the truck bed, blocked its wheels, and tied it down. All that heavy lifting, and one callow young man did it by barely raising a finger. With a cheerful wave from the driver, the truck rumbled away.

Judith grabbed the top flaps of one box and tugged. It took her and Angela together to rip the box open. She lifted out the shiny aluminum dome of a brand-new waterer. She laughed. "Some assembly required!"

"Wait." Angela raised a hand. "I have an idea. Let's pause on this until Lynn cools down and then get her to help. Get her involved from the very beginning. I'm hoping she'll feel a little better about it if she's in on it from the start. Almost the start."

Judith didn't have to think about that for long. "Good idea, Angela!"

Her cell rang. She answered.

"This is Phillip. Mom tells me we're in the chicken business."

"Phillip! I'm glad you called. I'm sure she told you I bought a chicken coop without a household conference. That's true; it was an impulse purchase. I wanted to call you just now and didn't know how to do it. You see, I am not looking for allies in a war, and I was afraid you'd get that impression. No, I'd just like to know the best way to approach Lynn. You've known her your whole life. Any suggestions?"

She thought she heard him chuckling. "Well, Judith, you have an ally anyway. I think when Mom got this house-sharing idea, she pictured two complacent people with no personal needs, desires, or opinions and they'd think exactly like she does. I won't tell her, 'I told you so,' that's for sure. But I can think it. Is your coop on skids?"

"Yes."

"Don't mark off a fence or anything yet. Tom and I will come over late this afternoon and pour some cement footings to get the skids up off the dirt. Did—"

"Oh, dear. It's big; the young man unloaded it with a fork-lift."

Phillip chuckled. "They're not the only ones with a fork-lift. Did you get chickens?"

"I have absolutely no idea how to go about getting chickens."

"Hold off on that. Did Harry deliver steel fence posts?"

"No. Big rolls of wire. Poultry netting for a six-by-eight yard, the invoice says."

"Yard gate?"

Judith studied the jumble of materials. "I don't think so."

"Tom and I will come by with what you need. See you later."

"I... Thank you, Phillip." She swiped the line closed. He had not offered any advice on how to approach Lynn. Oh, well. If the chicken coop killed this whole deal, maybe it was God's will. Lynn seemed to read God's will pretty well. But Judith no longer had the slightest idea how to recognize it, let alone respond to it. It certainly had not been manifest to her lately.

Angela motioned. "I'm going to dig up the geranium bed out front; it's what I was going to do anyway, before all this." She left.

Well, then, into the lion's den. Judith went indoors and paused outside the kitchen. Lynn had her back turned to her. She was mixing up a huge amount of dough of some sort; almost violently, it seemed. Quite likely she was getting started on hot dog buns for the Fourth. This was probably not the best time for a cooking lesson.

Who would know everything she needed? The hardware store. She got in her car and drove there.

The young woman who had first approached her was still working the front of the store. Judith flagged her down as soon as she pointed out the gardening section to an old lady.

"Where do I obtain chickens and supplies, like feed?" Judith asked.

"Miller's Feed. You go out of town on—"

"We bought cat and dog food there, I believe."

"Good. That's where. They sell farm supplies."

Judith got back in the car and drove out to the feedstore. And she noticed that this area was not quite the strange place it had felt like when she arrived. She was starting to know her way around. Was her increasing comfort perhaps a sign of God's will?

She spent a few minutes in the feedstore simply walking up and down aisles. What an amazing place. There was nothing quite like it in Rutherford. This store also sold chicken coops, both full-size and table high, but their coops cost more and they had no specials on. Judith felt a little better about her purchase. The toy section was almost all green tractors and yellow trucks and a huge case of miniature farm animals. And here were aisles of food. Dog, cat, rabbit, hamster, goldfish, koi, horse, calf, you name it—and yes, chickens. But not just chickens. This bag was for chicks; that one was labeled "laying mash." Judith had expected—you know, just plain old chicken feed.

She returned to the front and got a cart. She pushed it over to an older man stocking shelves. "Excuse me. I'm going to be getting some chickens and I'm not certain just what to buy in the way of supplies."

"Have you raised chickens before?"

"Not since early childhood."

He smiled and walked off toward the feed aisles. "Do you have the chickens yet?"

"No. We're pouring footings for the coop this afternoon."

Oh, my, that sounded as if she knew what she was doing! *Ha.* She tagged along behind.

He nodded. Maybe she did know what she was doing. "Do you have a brooder?"

She thought a moment. "For babies? No."

"I'd suggest checking want ads for grown chickens for starting out. Get a brooder and raise chicks after you've gotten your feet wet." He slapped a bag. "This is very good for hens, and it's a little cheaper than the name brands."

"I always thought chicken feed was cheap, as in 'that ain't chicken feed.'"

"It goes a long way, especially if you have an outside run." He laughed and slapped his hand on bags. "This stuff is good for chicks, and I recommend this laying mash if they're producing eggs. It provides minerals and amino acids they need. Just a side dish of it, so to speak."

"Thank you!"

"We have sawdust out back. If you spread sawdust on the coop floor you'll find it's easier to keep clean. My wife also lays down newsprint."

As he continued, Judith tried to keep it all straight. This was a far more complex process than she remembered. But then she thought about their pretty little speckled hen and the barred Plymouth Rocks, and…and…and she got excited all over again.

She wouldn't get feed yet, but she would get the sawdust and paper now. Assemble the waterer and feed trough. Have the coop all ready for its denizens.

On the way out she passed a huge corkboard with notices tacked all over it. *Oh!* There was a picture of very pretty, plump, tan chickens. Buff Orpingtons, it said, three years old. Free to a good home! The picture and caption took up the top half of the notice; the bottom half was cut vertically

into strips and each strip had a phone number. Judith tore
off one of the strips and pocketed it. She would call when
she got home.

*When she got home.* That surprised her; she was thinking
of this as home already. But what if Lynn was angry enough
to kick her out?

The paper came in a heavy roll that nearly tipped her cart
over. She managed to lift it into the backseat and toss her
big bag of sawdust into the trunk. A few more forays like this
and she would be ready to compete with weight lifters.

When she drove into the yard and parked in front of her
garage bay, another dilemma: Where to keep all the supplies and such? She could put the paper and sawdust in the
garage for now and ask Phillip later.

In the front yard, empty pots and flats were scattered
all over. Angela, on her knees, was just putting in the last
of several dozen geraniums. They lined the front porch, a
modest row of red that, in a month or so, would not be
modest at all.

And out back, a Paul's Plumbing pickup was parked and
the coop sat on the forks of a forklift even bigger than
the hardware store's. Tom and Phillip were pouring slurpy
cement into narrow rectangular footing holes lined with
boards.

Phillip did some final magic with a shovel and stepped
back. "These will be ready tomorrow. We brought another
sixteen feet of netting to lay on the ground; we'll wire it to
the vertical netting so that nothing can dig under the fence
to get your chickens."

She almost had tears in her eyes. "I am so grateful,
Phillip. Tom."

Tom joined them, grinning. "Actually, this looks kind of
fun. Know what kind of chickens you want?"

"I have a phone number here offering Buff Orpingtons. Apparently, getting grown-up chickens is easier."

Tom nodded. "We can set the posts this afternoon and stretch the netting after the coop is in place. That's quite a nice little chicken shack. I saw the price. We probably couldn't build it for that. Good buy."

"Thank you. I wish Lynn thought so."

Phillip stepped in front of her and looked her in the eye. "My mother has always run the show. This housemate thing was her idea, but she didn't think everything through. In this situation she can't be the only queen on the throne, but she'll adjust. She always does, even when Dad died. Still, it will be hard for her."

Tom chimed in. "You have serious adjustments to make. Angela's are even more difficult; she's been dumped. Rejected. That's always tough. Give Mom and Angela the room to make their adjustments, and make your own. We will support all three of you."

"Thank you."

The men went back to setting steel posts, squaring off corners.

Judith noticed that the coop had looked much larger in the store than it appeared here, nestled behind a bush. No matter. It was a good start to a dream come true.

*When people say "a dream come true," they surely don't realize how difficult and painful realizing dreams can be.*

# Chapter Twenty-One

Good morning, Lynn." Judith entered the kitchen to find Lynn already baking something. And it wasn't even breakfast yet.

"Good morning, Judith." No smile, no cheer.

Judith thought about this. Actually, she had been thinking about it almost constantly, and she could not see a clear direction to go.

She walked over to the stove and stood right next to Lynn. "When I was growing up—in fact, when I was an adult—my father would announce his decisions. There were never discussions, or meetings, or even him asking what we felt or wanted. Meetings and discussions are foreign ground to me. I didn't think of them and that offended you. I am very sorry. Will you forgive me?"

Lynn met her eye to eye for a long, long moment. "Yes. You are forgiven. Of course." And she turned, picked up an oven mitt, and peeked inside the oven.

Funny, Judith didn't feel forgiven. But she had done what she could and she had done it sincerely. She really was sorry she hadn't stopped to think. She opened the refrigerator and got out two eggs. Hen fruit. Cackleberries. Chickens. She smiled in spite of herself. Lynn's displeasure was the only cloud in her sky.

Lynn was indeed making hot dog and hamburger buns. She pulled two big sheets of buns out and put them on cooling racks.

Judith poured some coffee, leaned on her elbows, and watched Lynn.

Lynn paused to look at her.

Judith waved a hand toward all the buns. "I'm thinking about cooling racks of all things. Your cooling racks get the most traffic of any cooling racks I've ever heard of. Cook only had one and she only used it for pot roast. Hot dog and hamburger buns came from supermarket shelves, not Grandma's oven. And I'm rejoicing in how different my life suddenly is."

Lynn smiled, but it was not her usual cheery smile. "So much is different, that's for sure. For all of us."

"Lynn, I truly am sorry I acted impulsively. I'll try not to do it again."

"I know. And I truly forgave you."

What next? Judith could think of nothing else to say, so she made her breakfast as Lynn busied herself washing out bowls and bagging buns.

Then she returned to her room and started to call the number of the farm with chickens. *Wait.* She'd best make sure her pen was ready first. She went outside and around the corner of the house to see how her chicken coop looked.

And stopped cold. Phillip and Lynn stood nose to nose, and the conversation was not happy-smiley. Quietly, Judith moved closer until she could eavesdrop. This was wrong, so very wrong, but she did it anyway.

Lynn was saying, "You ask why I'm upset? I'll tell you why I'm upset. Judith admitted she made a big mistake, and she apologized. But you two! You betrayed me! You both know I don't want chickens, but you took her side! And helped her set up! When you know what my wishes are!"

*Oh, dear.* So that was why Lynn was so upset. Judith had made such a mess!

Suddenly Phillip reached out and engulfed his mother in a big bear hug. She struggled for a moment, then melted against him sobbing. "Mom, you know without a doubt we love you. We were not betraying you. You have two grown women—I might even say women old enough to be kind of set in their ways—and they are not always going to want exactly what you want, and not want what you don't want. Sometimes they'll want what they want. This is one of those times."

The sobbing continued.

Phillip purred, "What would Dad say about this? If we're at cross-purposes, let's do what he would want."

At first Judith didn't think Lynn was going to reply. Then she drew a breath so deep Judith could hear it. "He probably wouldn't give a hang whether there were chickens in his backyard or not."

Phillip chuckled. "Remember when Lillian decided to raise geese? We had goose droppings everywhere you walk. At least Judith's chickens will be limited in where they make deposits."

"And we never did get to eat any of her geese." Lynn hiccuped. Or was it a sob? She stood up straight and wiped her eyes. Phillip handed her a tissue and she blew.

Here came a Paul's Plumbing pickup into the yard. Tom got out. "Whoa. What am I missing?"

Lynn shuddered. "Nothing much. I'll explain, then."

Judith carefully backed away before someone noticed her. She hurried around to the front and into the house.

Angela was just coming into the kitchen.

How much should Judith reveal of what she allegedly had never heard? *Nothing.*

Angela stretched. "I can't believe I'm up and out before nine. I didn't even hit the snooze button this morning."

"Congratulations. Lynn was worried you might be ill. She would even go in and check on you now and then."

Angela froze in midstep between the counter and the refrigerator. She looked at Judith a long moment and then continued to the fridge. "You don't say." She set out the half-and-half and poured herself a coffee.

"I think the boys are here. I'm going to go see how my chicken project is coming." Judith went out the back door and walked across to behind the garage.

Lynn was standing aside watching as Tom sat at the wheel of the pickup and Phillip wired some of the poultry netting to the end post closest to the coop.

Tom put the truck in gear and very slowly, carefully backed up. Judith now saw that the truck was attached to a fence stretcher—or the stretcher was attached to the truck—and they were stretching the netting.

Phillip wired the netting firmly to the middle steel post, then to the front corner post. Tom moved the truck forward, then off to the side. They stretched the poultry wire between the corner and the center post.

Lynn went back inside. Judith stood gaping as these two boys—well, they were men, but half Judith's age made them boys—hung the gate between the two posts set in the middle of the second side. They set some braces to keep the posts straight. They had never built a chicken yard before, and yet look at it! Perfect.

They stretched the netting between the gate and other corner, then the netting on the other side. A tidy rectangular chicken yard, three sides of netting and the fourth side the coop itself, now awaited Judith's dream. But wait. Apparently there was more.

They stretched netting out on the ground inside the yard and wired it securely to the sides. Now raccoons and other animals that might dig under the fence could not come up into the pen to steal chickens.

Angela came out and stood beside Judith. "Wow!"

"It sure is wow! The Ritz of chicken coops!"

Finally the men came out of the pen and closed the gate behind them. They both looked mighty happy with themselves.

"That's beautiful! Wonderful! Thank you so much! Is there some way I can pay you or repay you? I would love to."

Phillip shook his head. "You mentioned yesterday how this is a dream of yours. We're happy to help you realize it. Now you just have to get some chickens."

Judith pulled that slip of paper out of her pocket. "I have a phone number here that I got at the feedstore. Someone is giving away some Buff Orpingtons."

Angela had her cell out. "What's the number?"

Judith handed her the slip of paper.

Phillip asked, "You need anything else?"

"As if this isn't enough!" Judith laughed. "No, I don't think so. I'll get some chickens if I can and appropriate feed for them. Thank you again!"

Phillip bobbed his head. "Mom, I'll be going into town. Need anything?"

From behind Judith, Lynn said, "Another twenty-five-pound bag of flour if you're near the supermarket." So she had come back outside; Judith had not noticed.

"Got it." Phillip nodded and jotted it down in a notebook.

Angela swiped her cell. "Those Buff Orpingtons are all taken, but the lady says someone named Franklin is moving and might be getting rid of some."

Phillip frowned. "Franklin. We put a tub and shower in for a Franklin. Hibdon Road?"

"Why, yes. I believe so."

"Young family, really nice people. Tell them their plumbers said hi."

Judith giggled. "I shall."

Lynn sounded sad, resigned. "I know where they live. I'll take you."

Should she accept the offer? Judith didn't have to think very long. *Yes.* "Thank you, Lynn."

Why did Lynn offer if she didn't like chickens?

Because Lynn had a big, big heart, bigger than her disappointments. That was obvious. Judith wished so much that she could be as magnanimous as Lynn and so able to bend with the punches.

Lynn had the number in her cell. She probably had every customer's number in her cell. She punched it in, talked a few moments, and closed the phone. "They're moving and have to get rid of their chickens. They'd like us to come over soon."

"Is right now too soon?" Judith asked.

Angela said, "I'd like to go along, but I agreed to help out at the library from three to eight tonight."

"We'll be back long before three. Let's go." Lynn headed for the garage. "No, Homer, you can't go along."

Judith had not even noticed that the woebegone-looking dog was hovering close, tail wagging.

Lynn drove and Angela sat in back, Judith in front.

Angela was grinning. "I am excited. This is so—so earthy! Real! Oh, I can't explain it."

Judith nodded in agreement. "I never expected to have it happen so fast."

They turned into a long driveway and stopped in front

of an open garage. A young woman came out of the house with two small children and a baby on her hip. "Thank you for coming; we caught them up last night and penned them. A couple of them are real escape artists. We're moving into town or we would keep them."

"We promise to give them a good home." Judith eyed the two boxes with airholes cut in the sides. "What kind are they?"

"Four New Hampshires and two, oh, shoot, they are black, can't remember the breed. We got them down at the feedstore this spring." She pointed to the feeder and waterer beside the boxes. "Those go, too."

"Are you sure you don't want some money for all this?" Judith made a sweeping gesture with her arm.

"No, we bought the chicks, but the others were given to us. You enjoy these; we sure did."

"Don't give our chickens away, Mom, please!" The little girl beside her looked up, tears starting to brim in her blue eyes.

"Maybe we'll get some in our new house. Depends on town ordinances."

"But they won't be *these* chickens."

The woman smiled guiltily. "She made pets of a couple of them."

Judith had no idea what to do, but Angela knelt down in front of the little girl so that they were eye to eye. "We promise to take good care of your friends. Can you tell me which ones are your favorites?"

"The big black one is Fluffy, and the biggest red one is Henny Penny."

"Oh, good! You know one of my favorite stories? The sky is falling! The sky is falling! Thank you for telling me."

As they loaded up the boxes in the back of Lynn's SUV

and waved good-bye, the little girl buried her face in her mother's skirt.

Angela watched behind them as the farm disappeared beyond the trees. "Fluffy and Henny Penny, eh? I sure hope those aren't the roosters."

"They're noisy. It's why my father got rid of them." Judith stared straight ahead. "I loved those chickens. I know exactly how she feels, but I wasn't allowed to cry. They were just chickens. You don't cry over chickens, right?"

When they brought the boxes out of the SUV, Homer was leaping and sniffing and whimpering until Lynn grabbed his collar. "Now down, Homer. Let's get you in the house." She hauled him up the steps and into the mudroom.

Judith and Angela toted the boxes around to the chicken pen, and Judith opened the new gate, entering her dream for the very first time. "Now what?"

Angela snickered. "You know what a pig in a poke is, right?"

Judith laughed, too. "When you buy a pig that's inside a sack. You don't know if it's fat or skinny or even a pig. Chickens in a poke—but then, I didn't pay for these."

They set the boxes down in the middle and closed the gate behind them. "Now what?" Angela stared at her box.

"I suppose we open the boxes and let the chickens find their own way out."

Lynn stepped up to the outside of the pen to silently watch.

Judith unfolded the flaps, opened them wide, and got her first look at what were now her chickens. Four reddish-brown chickens stared up at her. She left that box open and did the same with the other. The larger black one fluffed his feathers, his grand comb proclaiming his roosterhood. All but two of the chickens were nearly grown.

"Look, he's giving me the stink eye." Judith pointed to the

big black fellow in the second box and flashed a grin to Angela. "Think you're pretty hot stuff, don't you, boy? Do you suppose this is Fluffy?"

"If he starts crowing, you have a problem. You'd better name that big black one Fluffy. Just in case the little girl comes out to visit her chickens. But you have to have a rooster if you want eggs, right?"

And another distant memory surfaced. "No," Judith replied, "the pullets just start laying when they're old enough. But the eggs aren't fertile."

Angela wrinkled her nose. "Parthenogenesis?"

Judith grinned at the depth of Angela's vocabulary. "Think about it. We women lay an egg every month, and then we get our period." Judith held the gate for Angela, who was still laughing. "We are going to have to find six names, aren't we?"

They joined Lynn outside the fence, watching the newest residents of this lakeside home.

Angela shrugged. "We have two of them already, thanks to that little girl."

The chickens peeked over, hopped up, teetered, hopped down. One by one they fluffed their feathers and pecked at the grass, wandering farther with each step.

Judith was smiling. "This brings back good memories of my childhood."

Lynn looked at her. "I'm glad to hear that. Let the good memories blot out the awful ones of the later years. Is there feed and water in the coop?"

"Water. Not feed. Now that I know what they look like, I can buy the right stuff."

"And I have to get to the library." Angela pushed away from the fence. "Lynn, thank you for introducing me to Mary. So far I really love this job, even if it's unpaid."

Lynn smiled. Was the storm in her heart passing? "Most welcome. And I know your help is welcome there." She started back into the house, so Judith followed.

Lynn asked, "How long ago did your father insist on no more chickens?"

"Oh, I was eight years old or so, I'd guess. I was still way too young to mount a decent objection. Even in adulthood, I rarely took a stand. It was just easier to let him have his way. I got so tired of the constant anger." She cast one last look over her shoulder before going inside.

The rooster was strutting along the perimeter, sizing up his domain. The hens were already starting to eat the green grass.

"They are pretty tame." Lynn watched them a moment, too.

"I feel sorry for that little girl. I'd like their address. I'll take some pics and send them to her."

"What a nice idea. Let's have some iced tea."

Apparently the storm had passed. That pleased Judith immensely. So did chickens. So did the lake. So did everything. And to think she had once considered moving in with Melody.

Lynn let Homer out. Thank goodness chickens did not require as much attention as dogs did. Then they carried their iced tea outside and sat on the porch gazing across the riffling water. Lynn leaned over to look more closely at Judith's face. "You better put a hat on; your nose is getting a little red. You got any sunscreen?"

Judith shook her head. "Nor a hat, either." Why did Lynn's concern suddenly irritate her? *That's silly!* But there it was. She could feel anger rising.

"Surely we have some Paul's Plumbing caps over in the shop. You know, to protect your nose and cheeks. I'll have Tom get you one."

*But I don't like wearing hats. I never wear hats.* Judith kept it to herself, though. This posed a dilemma. They just smoothed everything over. She didn't want to create tension again. So should she just wear a cap to please Lynn, or... *Wait a minute!* Lynn was not her mommy. No wonder she was irritated. This woman was treating her like a child. Sure, her father had done that his whole life, but that was just how he was. She didn't have to let a landlady do it, too.

Then her very soul chilled, for here came two SUVs into the yard. The whole gang was here! All those children! Oh, dear!

Doors flew open; the children unbuckled, hopped out of their car seats, and came tumbling out. Maggie and Josie, the drivers, climbed out and headed for the porch.

Miss Priss came running up and plopped into her grandmother's lap. "Mommy says you have chickens! Can we see them?"

"You can," Lynn said. "But don't open the gate. Understand?"

"'Kay!" All five of them charged off.

Judith was irked all over again; they were her chickens, not Lynn's, thank you very much. On the other hand, she was relieved. The children were being directed appropriately, and Judith didn't have to interact with them at all.

"Oh, to bottle that energy." Maggie sat down beside Judith.

They heard barking and at the same moment, Doug, Tom's boy, came back screaming, "G'ma, one of the chickens is out and Homer is chasing it!"

"I'll get the dog," Maggie hollered over her shoulder, already off the porch and at a full run.

Judith ran hot on her heels. *Please don't let him hurt the chicken.*

Homer gave one more bay and allowed himself to be dragged away, Maggie now in charge.

"We didn't let it out, it was already out," Doug cried. "Honest! We didn't! And Homer took after it, but the chicken flew up on the back porch roof! See? There."

"Smart chicken." Judith watched Maggie drag Homer into the house.

Lynn wagged her head. "Mrs. Franklin said something about escape artists. But how?"

The boy named Travis (was he the future chef? Judith couldn't remember) pointed. "There, I betcha." He walked to where the fence met the coop. There was a gap of about three inches.

Lynn nodded. "We'll wire one-by-fours vertically to block the spaces on each side. He certainly is an escape artist."

"But how do we get him down?" Judith looked forlornly at her rooster.

"I'll climb up there and get him!" Travis suggested eagerly.

"Oh no, you won't!" Lynn barked. Her voice softened. "Those are his hens. When they go up into the coop near dark, he'll want to join them. He'll come down."

Maggie called to the kids, "Load up!"

Judith watched them pile back into the vehicles and buckle up. "Thank you for coming to visit the chickens." And she was almost sincere about that.

"Couldn't stay away." Maggie paused and added, "Priss would never let me."

Judith watched them drive away and suddenly thought, *That Josie, Tom's wife, never said a word. She is even more reticent than I!*

"I'm going to go start supper. Not to sound too cannibalistic, but I was thinking chicken potpie tonight."

"Sounds lovely."

Lynn headed off to the back door. She was barely inside when Phillip pulled around the corner of the house in his pickup and stopped by the chickens. *Oh, good!* Maybe he could fix the escape hatches.

He got out and joined Judith. "Just the lady I want to see." He walked over to the pen. "Nice birds. Five, huh? Nice number."

"Six." Judith pointed to the porch roof. His Excellency was pacing, giving them the stink eye. "Lynn mentioned plugging the hole with one-by-fours." She pointed to the gap.

Phillip laughed. "Ah. Yeah, we can fix that right away. Judith, normally I wouldn't talk about Mom's personal matters, but since you're all living together...well, I thought you should be aware. Maggie talked to Mom's primary care doctor this morning, Eleanor Alstrop, and told her how moody she is. They both agree, it must be a symptom of menopause."

"Of course. It would affect her moods. It never crossed my mind. I just don't think about those things."

"Exactly. And Tom and I are kind of hoping that you and Angela can cut her a little slack when she gets on a toot."

Judith nodded. "Certainly. I'll talk to Angela privately."

"Three strong women who are still virtual strangers, all under one roof, and in menopause or probably approaching it." Phillip sniggered, more like a snort. "This could get interesting."

# Chapter Twenty-Two

Angela awoke, stretched, seriously considered turning over and going back to sleep, but got up anyway, did her morning bathroom thing, and dressed for hot weather. Ever hopeful. She wanted summer to come in and get it over with.

When her phone sang, she took it out on the deck and glanced at the caller ID as she sank onto the cushioned lounger. "Hi, Charles, good to hear from you."

"I was beginning to think you fell off the continent or something. You do know the phone reception goes both ways."

"I'm sorry. I did e-mail you, though."

"What about the texts I sent?"

She flinched. "I've not been looking at texts because I had one from your dad and didn't want to see his name again."

"He was just checking to make sure you were all right."

"He called you?" Usually she was the one to maintain contact with their children.

"I know, shocked me, too. Even more so when he sounded concerned about you."

"Really." She heaved a sigh. "Can we talk about something else, like when are you coming to visit? Lynn and her boys both asked when, too."

"Her boys? Mother."

"They are half my age, and I wiped your butt. Boys. And you and Gwynnie are still my kids, so what can I say?" She stared out across the lake, immediately feeling a sense of peace start at her toes and blanket her all the way up. She could hear laughter from the other side of the house. What were they doing crossed her mind but not urgently enough to make her move.

"Mom?"

"Sorry. It's easy to just sit here and stare out at this lake; it changes all the time, like the clouds overhead."

"I always told you it was a beautiful spot. One reason I was so pleased you were moving there. So, did you find a job?"

"No, but I am volunteering at the library. Charles, I really enjoy it. Reminds me of all those years in the library at your school. By the time the two of you got through school, they were beginning to think I would be a fixture."

"Glad to hear that. Mom, you sound so much better, I can't believe it. You like living there?"

"*Like* is far too small a word for it. Took me a while; all I wanted to do was sleep and forget."

"Serious depression, I was afraid of that."

"Not surprising I guess. But between Lynn and Judith and this place, I'm coping better." She paused to watch an eagle glide on the thermals over the sky-blue lake.

"Talking with you makes me want to come there, but right now I can't take the time off, and our budget doesn't include airfare to Fargo, North Dakota."

"Wish I had the air miles to give you, but those were on the credit card your dad took. You might ask him." She paused. "Whoops, they're calling me; I better go." She tapped her phone closed and slipped it in her pocket as she walked around to the back.

"We need a picture!" Judith handed Angela a small silver digital camera.

"Of course!" She counted the chickens. Six. "How did you get the rooster back in?"

"Lynn's idea. Chased four hens into the coop and left the fifth out, squawking to get back together with her soul mates. The rooster came down to try to fix the situation, and we shooed him in with the rest at dusk last evening." Judith waved toward the top of the pen. "Phillip and Tom are going to lace netting into the top of the pen this evening. To discourage gate-crashers and hawks from getting in over the top."

Judith probably did not realize that Angela was a pretty darn good photographer. She not only set houses she listed, but photographed them to best advantage. She positioned the ladies carefully—"Move left a foot, Lynn. Judith, stand tall. I need you to block that dead branch." She fired off several from different angles, then worked four of the six chickens into a picture of Judith stooping low.

Already that morning Judith had been to the feedstore. She had two kinds of chicken feed and a mineral block of some sort. Did chickens really need all this, or had the salesmen at Miller's Feed seen her coming, you might say? And the boys (Angela loved that—grown men, fathers and lovers, but still boys, like her Charles) had already plugged Houdini's escape routes.

Angela sincerely hoped Judith would decide to paint the coop *after* three, when she had to go to the library. She really did not want to paint, although she would if she must. The three of them set up the chicken feed in two plastic bins at the back of Judith's garage bay. They stowed the sawdust bag in the corner. Mrs. Franklin's feed trough and waterer went into the other corner, backups in case they were needed. This hobby, if one could call it that, was accumulating quite a bit of stuff already.

Angela felt a wee little twinge of envy. Judith had a good thing going; all Angela had was a record of sleeping late.

She went to her room and pulled down her e-mail. Three from the kids. Two from Jack. She marked those two as spam. Five in reference to real estate. She realized her name was still out there on business cards and ads and no way to get it off.

Back in the kitchen, the three poured iced tea and all wandered out to the porch deck, Angela's favorite place to be.

Lynn sat back with a contented sigh. "I never get tired of this."

"Thank you for sharing it." Judith raised her tea glass, like a toast.

"Yes. It is so peaceful. I guess I really needed peace." Angela sipped.

"I love it no matter what season," Lynn continued. "Snow is beautiful. And a fierce storm viewed from right inside those windows... Wait until you see it."

"More than that thunderstorm that sent Homer into a panic?" Judith patted the dog, who was stretched out beside her.

"That was only a baby one." Miss Minerva jumped up on Lynn's belly. "Ugh, you're heavy." But she rubbed and patted the cat until the purr motor rumbled into song.

She looked toward Judith. "Are you ready for tomorrow?"

"Ready as I'll ever be. What I was thinking when I scheduled the first class for eight a.m. is beyond me, other than it was the only way I could get it. Their summer session schedule is limited and I was registering late."

"What is that class? I forget," Angela asked.

"Precalculus. Sometimes I wonder if getting a tutor would be a good idea. Basic math is fine for me, but this is higher stuff."

Angela shuddered. A precursor for calculus before 8:00 a.m. "And you're taking what online?"

"Social studies. It's needed for anthropology and archaeology."

Lynn nodded. "Good to get as many general credits as you can here. Lot cheaper than the university in Duluth. You know, Tommy is a math whiz. I'm sure he'd be glad to help you."

They chatted on, and Angela only half listened. She was thinking about this gang of three who were trying to live in harmony when they were all so very different. And with different goals. Judith was going back to school. Lynn was helping her late husband's business continue onward and upward. And what was Angela doing? Distancing herself from a handsome, totally egocentric man who had no conscience or ethics.

Just thinking about it made her sad all over again.

Her first day of school. Good grief, you'd think she was seven years old.

Judith drove to the Detroit Lakes Community College campus early. She had nothing really in the way of supplies, so she walked to the campus bookstore. It was not only open but busy already. Mostly the customers were students grabbing packaged snacks and juice boxes—breakfasts, no doubt.

They sold backpacks. She chose an inexpensive one large enough to haul her laptop around in. She hadn't thought to bring her laptop along today. Hers was a few years old; perhaps she'd be wise to buy a new one. Was there a place in Detroit Lakes or would she have to go to Fargo?

A pack of pencils, a pack of pens, a notebook, she paused. And picked up an inexpensive little eight-color box of crayons. Always on the first day of grade school she had started out with a new box of crayons. Smiling, she added that to her trove. Plus an appointment book. She would no doubt think of other things she'd need, so she could stop back here after class.

Still a little early, she found her classroom and stepped inside. And froze. This was not the lecture room of her old college days. She had just walked into an alien planet.

The room was wedge shaped and so big it probably made its own weather. A stage and lectern down front were no doubt where the instructor would be. The floor rose up toward the back at a steep rake, with four curved tiers of counters instead of desktops. Behind the counters were arranged at least fifty chairs at each tier; the room sat two hundred!

Other students were coming in now, young men and women in clothing much more casual than what Judith had ever worn to class. With a skirt and modest top, she was way overdressed.

Where should she sit? Off to the side, certainly. She chose a chair and settled into it cautiously. Here at her desk, and at each of the others, a number pad shaped like a television remote was anchored down. She was just going to have to swallow her pride and start asking questions.

A pretty girl with brown hair done up in a French roll sat two seats away.

"Excuse me?" Judith said to her.

She turned and smiled with amazingly white teeth.

"I have never been in a lecture hall like this one. What is this thing?" And she pointed to the TV remote.

"Oh. Sure. Most rooms have these now. Let's say the prof announces a pop quiz. First you punch in your number, like this." She demonstrated with her own. "And then when she puts the question up on the screen, you punch the answer. The little screen there will show you your score."

Judith stared. This was surreal. "My number?"

"Where is your schedule sheet?"

Judith dug it out of her purse.

The young woman pointed. "This number here. That's how you will be identified in everything you do."

Judith wagged her head, reminding her mouth to stay closed. "Thank you very much. My name is Judith."

"Tracy. Hi."

The instructor appeared, an older woman in black slacks, a blue shirt, and dark blazer. She looked quite professorial. Someone asked her a question. She answered, then talked to someone else. Finally she stepped behind the lectern, pushed a button, and a huge screen descended until it covered the wall at the back of the stage.

The woman fingered a keyboard and looked up at the ceiling.

Judith looked up where she was looking; a slide projector was bracketed to the ceiling, pointed at the stage. A little green light came on and the screen lit up with a blue light. A moment later, the professor's first slide appeared, filling the screen—the course name and number, PRECALCULUS 1114, and her name.

"Let's see how much you people remember, and I'll know where we need to review. Here's the first question; factor this quadratic equation and identify which of the three possible answers is correct."

*Factor...X squared plus three X...factor!* Judith whispered harshly, "My number pad won't work!"

Tracy smiled. "You have to put your number in first, so it identifies you."

"Oh. Right." She did that. Now it worked, but she had no idea which was the correct set of factors. She hit an answer at random, because already the next question was on the screen. Something about three exclamation points. That was three factorial, but Judith had forgotten how to use it.

She bumbled, she stumbled. Wait, she knew that one! But not the next. Ten questions in all. Her score popped up. Two correct out of ten. She had walked into the room with such high hopes, so much confidence.

The hope and the confidence were gone. Crushed. She was never going to pass this course, never.

Why, oh why, did she ever think she could be an archaeologist?

# Chapter Twenty-Three

S orry to bother you, but do you mind if I use your sewing machine? Mine is in the storage unit." Angela was poking her head in the door.

Lynn looked away from the screen with a spreadsheet on it. "Not at all. If you need a lesson on it, give a holler."

"Thanks, I'll bug you again if I have a question."

"What are you going to do?"

"Patch the pants I ripped working in the flower bed. That clematis trellis just reached out and grabbed me."

A little motherhood warning bell went off in Lynn's head. "Just the pants or you, too?"

"Uninjured, but thanks for caring. Sorry to interrupt; I'll let you get back to your work."

"You realize I'd rather do anything than enter data on a spreadsheet?" She glared at the stack of invoices beside her keyboard.

Angela stepped inside and leaned against the jamb. "If you'd like help, I'll be glad to. The real estate business would sink into the ocean without spreadsheets and meaningless data. I'm pretty good with mortgaging and finance, but bookkeeping, too. In college I actually considered bookkeeping as a career."

"I'll keep that in mind. You have a degree, right?"

"Liberal arts, and you know what that'll get you?"

Lynn shrugged.

"You learn to say, 'Do you want fries with that?' I got married instead. I'm off to the kitchen seeking sustenance. Can I get you anything?"

"Thank you, no." Lynn went back to her screen. With all the garden work and now when fishing was getting better, she hated to spend daylight hours in her office. So she worked nights.

So did Judith, apparently. She was holed up in her room studying. No, she wasn't. She was standing at the door in the spot Angela had just left.

Lynn smiled at her. "How is it going?"

"College in midlife is absolutely wonderful for masochists. I may be caught up for the moment. Going to go check on the chickens. You writing the great American novel?"

Lynn waved carelessly toward the monitor. "I hate spreadsheets."

"I did all the bookkeeping for Rutherford House. I can do that if you like."

Lynn spun her chair around. "You two are too much. Angela just said she has experience, too. I just hate to take up your time."

"I'm caught up for now. I'll be back in a minute." She paused. "I'm taking Homer with me."

*I'd rather be out there shutting the chicken door, sitting with Homer and studying the stars, the lake. Anything but here.* She turned her chair back around. Good thing her chair faced a blank wall instead of a window. Four more entries. It looked like the pile was multiplying each time she flipped one sheet over. She heard toenails on the hardwood floors and Homer bounded back into the room.

Sedate was not part of his makeup; when he moved, he moved, when he was tired, he crashed. *Oh, to be like that dog.*

Front feet up on her thigh, he looked at the computer screen, sniffed the keyboard, and drooled on her hand. "Thanks, buddy, at least you missed the keyboard." She rubbed his ears and neck, then commanded, "Down." His reproachful look was masterful, as only bassets have conquered. Slowly his feet slid off her leg and he dropped to the floor. "Good boy." She petted him again. He whipped his head around as Judith walked into the room carrying two cups of coffee.

Lynn raised her eyebrows. "I hope this is decaf."

"It is. I used to drink the leaded stuff right up to bedtime, but not any longer if I want to fall asleep right away, not hours later."

Lynn scooted some papers off the oak coasters one of her sons had made from a branch off one of their trees when he was in high school woodshop. She set the mug there. "Are you serious about helping?"

"Why not? I hear the sewing machine humming, and I was just going to read for a while or see what's on TV. You sort them and I'll enter them."

Lynn gave her the chair and pulled up a stool to sit on. To her surprise and delight, they whipped through the pile in a matter of minutes.

"Any more?" Judith asked.

"You are fast on that thing." Lynn glanced around the desk. "I don't think so. I have names to enter in the database for our newsletter."

"You send out a newsletter?" Judith looked surprised. "I used to do that for the Rutherford House, but when caring for my father grew so much more detailed, I quit."

"We make it newsy, family-style. I'll put a picture of Homer in it and maybe the chickens. Phillip and Tommy put in quotes, we include thank-yous from our clients. That kind of thing. We send some little promo item with the Christmas letter."

"You are amazing."

"No, just practical. We need all the business we can find. We put a bid on the plumbing for a small housing development going in at the other end of the lake. Ten houses or so. We get that, and we'll have to put on more help."

Again they exchanged chairs. Judith sank to the floor and crossed her legs. Homer immediately came over and, front feet on her legs, gave her his pleading *no one pets me* look, then rolled over for a belly rub.

Lynn snickered. "He sure has your number."

Judith gave her an arched-eyebrows look. "Just me?"

A few minutes later, Lynn rocked her chair back and stretched her arms over her head. "I can't believe I am done with those things. I always dread it."

"Is that pile to be filed?" Judith indicated a stack of papers with a brick on them. "Alphabetized?"

"Not yet."

"Well, let's get at it. Hand me half and you take half, and then we'll meld them."

"I feel guilty..." Lynn sat up straight.

"Oh, hush." Judith held out one hand and pushed Homer off her lap with the other.

Lynn hesitated only a moment. She never had been one to look a gift animal of any kind in the mouth. One could get bitten that way.

Less than half an hour later, Lynn slammed the file drawer closed and switched off the light as the two left the room. They headed for the kitchen, of course.

Lynn refilled her coffee and raided the cookie jar. "Thank you again for your help. I'm so glad all that is done."

"You're welcome." Judith perched on a stool and studied her coffee mug. "You mentioned that Tom is good at math. Do you think he'd coach me? I'd pay him, of course."

"I seriously doubt that; I mean, that he'd let you pay him. But yes, I'm sure he'd like to do that. I'll call him right now; he and Josie are still up."

Judith babbled something about not bothering them this late, but Lynn had already punched the speed dial.

"Lundbergs."

Lynn smiled. "Tom, Judith here needs some help with her math. Can you coach her?"

"Put her on."

Lynn handed Judith the phone. She had thought it was an easy question with a one-word answer. Apparently not.

Judith listened a moment. "Precalculus." She listened some more. "No. An old Sharp's. I can buy whatever calculator I ought to have." Pause. "Are you sure?" Pause. "Well, yes. All right. Thank you!" She handed the phone back to Lynn.

"Mom? Be there in ten minutes. I have to find my T81."

"Thank you. Whatever a T81 is." Lynn hung up.

Judith shook her head. "You Lundbergs do everything instantly, for sure! Phillip says 'footings' and presto. They're poured. You say 'hot dog bun' and instantly you have dozens of them on the cooling rack. Tom wanted to know what level of math I needed help with, and instantly, he's coming over with a graphing calculator. The instructor said we were going to need one; Tom already knew."

"I was thinking he'd be a good resource." Should she leave the two of them alone to chat in math languages Lynn didn't know? Or sit by and listen? "How about potato pancakes tomorrow morning? I have an urge to cook potatoes."

Judith laughed. "Sounds good! I'm going to run and get my textbook."

Potato pancakes and hash browns. That would be mighty tasty. And as she peeled the potatoes, Lynn thought about eggs. Having eggs right in your backyard would be nice; heaven knows they'd be fresh. No, she didn't like keeping chickens. She didn't want chickens. But as Angela said, they would not be her responsibility; with everyone helping (Miss Priss and her brothers as well, especially when they got a little older), it would not be a chore. If they wanted eggs for the whole family, they'd have to have more than five hens. That would mean a bigger coop, or build additional nest boxes in this one. Or...

Tom came in the back door grinning. "Hi, Mom." He gave her a peck on the cheek and crossed to Judith. "Good evening." He laid a very fancy calculator on the counter. It was at least six or seven inches long and about half that wide. In addition to the usual number pad, it had a row of key options Lynn had never seen before and a greenish-gray monitor screen in the top half. Amazing, and Tom knew how to use this?

Judith picked it up. "Yes. This is what the instructor has; well, something similar."

Tom smiled. "No doubt she has a newer model that costs twice what this did. But this has all the functions you'll need for precalc, and I put fresh batteries in it. Where should we start?"

Judith looked miserable. "Page one."

He laughed as he dragged Judith's text over in front of himself and opened it. "You'll be surprised how well you can do this."

"That would be a surprise, for sure."

Lynn busied herself with her potatoes. Judith frequently said, "Oh. I see," and Tom would say things like, "I knew you'd remember," and "Here's how factorials work," and "Wait; we can do it easier with logarithms. Let's review logarithms." And Lynn sang praises to God, silently, of course. She remembered the sullen, angry boy who returned from active duty three years ago, how much he had changed—a good change, a happy change.

She drained her potatoes, leaving a little liquid in the bottom in case they wanted mashed potatoes for dinner tomorrow, and put them aside to cool.

"So that catches you up?" Tom closed the textbook.

"It does! Thank you so much, Tom." She studied him a moment. "You should be teaching college-level math. You're brilliant at explaining something so that I can understand it. And believe me, if I can, anyone can." And then she asked a question Lynn dreaded. "Why aren't you?"

But Tom didn't duck it, and Lynn rejoiced all over again; he had healed so much in the last few years!

"I'm a wounded warrior, Judith."

"What's that?"

"I was in the Marines for four years—almost four years. Saw two tours of active duty, watched my buddies die, killed a few people myself. It messed me up royally. Dad hired me as soon as I walked out of the hospital, and Josie and the boys stuck with me in spite of it all. And Mom here. Things are looking up again."

"You're a fine plumber. But you're a fine teacher, too." Judith giggled suddenly. "And you put in great footings."

He laughed, too. "Great footings. My other marketable skill. Let's get together, you and me and the textbook, after your next class session."

"Thank you! Yes!"

Lynn was jumping up and down with joy on the inside and merely grinning on the outside. Being a teacher to a woman who wanted to learn was better than any tonic for her son. *Thank you, God! Thank you, God!*

She went to bed that night a very happy mother.

She woke abruptly. Homer was barking, a wild frenzy of barking and tearing around the house. Lynn rolled out of bed and ran to the kitchen barefooted. Angela and Judith came rushing in. Homer stood at the back door in full basset cry.

Lynn grabbed the five-cell flashlight from the shelf.

"Where are you going?" Angela cried.

"See what's out there." She snapped a lead on the dog's collar and opened the door. Good thing she braced; the dog nearly jerked her off her feet. She shone the spotlight toward the chicken pen. The gate had swung open and her light picked up two shiny eyes. The raccoon hissed and snarled as she came closer with the barking dog. She quickly slammed the gate shut and slid the hasp closed.

"What are you going to do?" Judith asked from behind her.

She headed back toward the house. "Call Phillip and have him come dispatch it. If we don't, it will be back. That's why we built the chicken coop so secure. I was afraid it might be something bigger. Homer, that's enough. You've done your job."

She handed Angela the lead and Judith the light. "For some strange reason I don't have my phone in my robe pocket. Silly me. Homer, you can stop barking now."

"But what if it's a female with babies?" Angela asked.

"Raccoons are cute, but they are destructive predators that eat chickens and chicken eggs, garden vegetables, all kinds of great delicacies. Homer, quiet!"

"You said you thought it might be something bigger."

"Coyote, fox, lynx, we've even had some big cats around here. That's why I put Homer on the leash. Or if it was a skunk, we sure don't want to clean him up after that."

They could see the truck lights coming in the driveway and not at a leisurely pace, either. Phillip jumped out of the truck and brought out his rifle. "I was dead, but Rowdy woke me even before you called. Must have heard Homer. The two of them probably woke all the dead. What's up?"

As he came across the yard, Judith trained the spotlight on the critter huddled up against the chicken house, snarling. The rooster and some of the hens were now squawking inside.

"He's a big one. How did he get in? He opened the gate?"

"I knew they were smart and dexterous, but this is amazing. We'll have to use something better than that simple latch." Judith stared at the chicken yard gate swinging open.

Phillip shook his head.

Judith watched the would-be chicken thief. "What will you do with it?"

Phillip grinned. "I thought we'd have raccoon stew for supper tonight."

"Oh, gag." Judith made a retching sound.

"You wouldn't!" Angela sounded sick already.

"He's kidding."

"Well, lots of people think raccoon is a delicacy. Lots of meat on that one."

"Thanks, son, we'll adjourn to the house while you finish up out here. Be careful, it could be rabid." At his look, she raised her hands. "Just doing my mother job."

He bent down and patted the dog. "Good boy, now we know the ladies are safe here with you on guard."

Lynn left the light for Phillip and turned the others toward the house. "Sorry, but you live in the country now. In the city you would call animal control, but we have to take care of things out here ourselves."

They were entering the house when they heard the gunshot, and a short time later, the truck left.

Lynn checked the clock—2:00 a.m.

"Well, I guess good night again."

"Hope nothing sets Homer off again. He about scared me out of my wits when he leaped up and charged out the bedroom door." Judith petted the dog. "I think you deserve a treat." He followed her to the treat cupboard and plunked his rear immediately, tail sweeping the floor, drool hanging from his jowls.

When the others headed for bed, Lynn turned off the light and climbed the stairs. Miss Minerva looked up from her spot on the bed, yawned, chirped, and closed her eyes again. "You missed all the excitement, cat. Have you no sense of adventure?" Lynn crawled under the covers. *Lord, thank you for our protection hound and the safe chicken house. And thank you I did not have to dispatch that raccoon.*

# Chapter Twenty-Four

"I had the worst nightmares last night." Angela poured her coffee and sank down on one of the stools at the center island.

"The raccoon?" Lynn held up a piece of bread. "Toast?"

"I guess. I dreamed I saw it explode and I threw up in the bushes. My mouth even tastes like I threw up."

Lynn set the butter, jam, and peanut butter on the table. "You want cereal?"

"No, thanks. This is plenty. I need to get showered. I'm working for one of the others who needed time off. Need to be there before we open."

The toast popped up, and Lynn laid it on a plate, pushing a knife over with it. "I have the quilters at church today; I was hoping you might go along. I think you would enjoy the group. Get to know more people."

Angela smiled. "Next time I will." She paused. "Lynn, I've been meaning to talk to you about something." Lynn looked at her questioningly. "Judith mentioned that when I was sleeping so much, you came into my room to check on me."

"Well, yes. I was concerned. We both were."

"And I appreciate that. But I am an adult, not one of your kids. If this is going to work, you need to respect my privacy."

"I— Yes, of course. I understand. I just wanted to help."

"I know." Angela smiled to ease the tension. "In fact, I do need your help with something. Have you heard of any jobs opening around here?"

"What kind?"

"I just need some money coming in is all." Angela shrugged. This not knowing the future was getting a little heavy.

"Are you strapped?"

"Not yet, at least not when the house money comes through. Of course, it would be nice if I could figure out what I am going to do with the rest of my life."

Lynn put two more slices in the toaster. "Check the job board at the college. And I'm thinking the library might have one, too. Not too many jobs get listed in the paper, but you can try. Come to think of it, there are classes at the college regarding re-entry women especially."

This was good marmalade. Angela slopped a bit more of it onto her toast. "I wish they had more paying jobs at the library. I love working there."

"Have you talked with Mary? She has more of an idea of what all is going on in this community than anyone else."

"Good idea. Thanks for the toast. Need anything from the grocery store?"

"Milk, two percent, and half-and-half for the coffee. I have that fake stuff here but..." She made a face.

Angela bobbed her head and jogged to her room. She felt better for having addressed at least one thing that had been bothering her. And Lynn had been so nice about it, too.

She stared a long moment at the face in the mirror. "You look haggard." She turned on the shower, and as soon as it warmed, she stepped in. If only she could wash away the lines around her eyes and the purple splotches under them.

How come she went from sleeping all the time to not getting enough sleep? Wasn't there some kind of happy medium somewhere?

Once she was dressed and had her makeup on, she fixed her bed, put her laundry in the hamper, and headed for the deck. She needed a lake fix to get some kind of calm back. The breeze played with the water, spoiling the reflections, but it didn't bother the ducks puddling about near the shore. Tail feathers in the air, they nibbled on the bottom grass and plants, then *bloop* and they'd be right side up again.

Homer whimpered at the screen door, and when she didn't answer immediately, he yipped.

"I'm not staying out here, but I guess you can if you want." She checked the gate to the steps to make sure it was locked and let him out, then returned to her elbows on the railing, gaze wandering around the lake. A couple was out in a canoe, three kids laughing in a rowboat, and the dock gently bobbed with the moving water. *Peaceful, oh, so peaceful.* She heard the screech of a hawk but instead saw the eagle floating in the thermals over the lake. Lynn said they were quite the fisher birds, but she had yet to see one dive to catch a fish.

Her cell rang, so she dug it out of her purse and thumbed it on.

"Hi, Mom?"

"Hello, sweetie. How's my favorite daughter?"

"You know Dad has been trying to reach you."

"Yes, I know."

"Mom. I don't know how to say this. Charles and I are really upset about all this."

"Gwynn, you're both grown-ups. You know these things happen."

"But to other people's families, not ours! Dad says he wants to try again, rekindle the romance, and he can't even reach you. Do you have to be so stubborn? Can't you at least talk to him?"

"Gwynn, I remind both of you, I did not initiate this. I did not ask for it, did not want it. Did not file for divorce. The burden is not on me, so don't call me the stubborn one."

"But you're the one who won't talk to him! He's changed, Mom. He's a new man."

Angela sighed heavily. "Look. Right now I can't even talk to him. I'm working on it, but I'm not there yet, all right? As for getting back together, forget it." *I've outgrown him, Gwynn. I see that clearly enough. And I am me again, at last, and not his artificial construct of a wife. I won't go back.*

"Well, at least talk to him. Promise me you'll talk to him. He wants it so much."

"Maybe. I won't promise, but maybe."

"Mom..." Her voice trembled. "You two are tearing us up. Please reconsider."

"First things first."

"At least think about it. And talk to him, all right?"

"Thank you for calling, sweetie."

"Yeah. I love you, Mom." She hung up.

Well, that certainly was not a happy call. She scratched Homer's head and bent over to rub his ears. "You be a good boy now. Thanks for saving the chickens last night. See you this afternoon."

She turned to leave and he padded along with her and back into the house. "Suit yourself." She grabbed her purse she had left on the counter, yelled, "See you later, call me if you need anything," and out through the mudroom door she went.

The workday went well. That afternoon when she was

ready to leave, she asked Mary if she could have a minute with her.

"Of course, come on." They settled into a corner, up in the open area of the old part of the building, the original Carnegie library. There were people at the tables on the far side of the room, but quiet reigned. "Now, how can I help you?"

"Mary, I love volunteering here and I plan to keep on, but I need a job. I would rather work here than anywhere but ... Any suggestions? Lynn said you have a better sense of what is going on than anyone."

"Well, I'm not so sure about that, but let me think. I take it you don't want to go back to being a Realtor?"

"Not in the least."

"As for here, there are no openings right now, but I'd hire you immediately if there were."

"Thank you." Angela kept from fidgeting through sheer force of will.

"You have a degree in ... ?"

"Liberal arts. My father said it wasn't worth the paper it was printed on, and he was right, but some companies just want a degree. I took classes in bookkeeping and office management at one time after my kids were on their own, but then went to real estate school because it would be faster and I figured I'd be good at it."

"Were you?"

"Fine, growing, getting good feedback from my boss..." She heaved a sigh. *Better be honest.* "... until a big commercial project fell through and things went downhill after that."

"I don't want to get personal, but are you married?"

"Not any longer."

"Ah. So you plan to stay here in our area."

"I do."

"Tell you what. Are you in a big hurry?"

Angela shook her head.

"Okay, then. Let me ask around. I'll keep my eyes and ears open and we'll see what comes up." She stood. "I would love to have you on staff here. Your years of experience in the school library show in all you do."

"Perhaps volunteering can pay off?"

"You never know." Mary smiled.

Angela left the cool of the library and stepped into the heat of summer. They were experiencing a warm spell, at least that's what people called it; she thought it more hot. Possibly the concrete in the town retained more heat than out at the lake. Probably that's why so many people headed for the lakes any chance they could. She knew there would be a breeze on the deck, so she did her grocery stop almost at a run.

*I need to get home.* She caught herself. Home. She had referred to Lynn's house as home. How had that happened so quickly? When she thought of the house she had lived in, it was surrounded by dark clouds and ugliness. Much as she had loved that house, it was no longer home. She stopped at a stop sign and waited for a car to pass. Had she divorced herself from it when she was getting it ready to sell? Or when did it happen?

Her phone beeped the text sound. Taking the ads for no texting to heart, she pulled over and hit the button.

Lynn: ETA?

She texted back, Ten minutes, and pulled back on the road. The driver in the oncoming car waved at her. *Do I know that person? No, people just do that around here. Angela Bishop, I think you have indeed found home. Now to be able to support yourself. The money from the house will not last you forever.*

Lynn said to pray for and about everything. *I used to practice that more but... There was always that but. Lord, you know I need a job. I don't need a lot of money, but I really need to leave the house money in the bank for emergencies. I need a job with benefits, like health insurance. I need to make a list.* She turned into the driveway and her heart leaped. She would have sworn it did. She was home.

When she came into the house, she found Lynn and Judith out on the deck. Lynn waved a hand. "Iced tea is fresh in the refrigerator. Come out and kick back for a while."

"Thanks. I need to get out of these clothes into something cooler."

"The breeze will help that."

She didn't bother to hang up her clothes, tossing them on her bed, but slipped into shorts and a tank top, her feet in flip-flops, and headed for the refrigerator. "Anybody want more?"

"No thanks. Did you have lunch?"

Angela thought a moment. "No, I guess I didn't. I couldn't wait to get home." She took her icy glass outside and sank down on a lounger in the shade. "Ahhh."

"Phillip called to ask if the two of you want to go out tonight, if the lake stays calm."

Judith whooped. "That would be marvelous. Yes!"

*Peace! Quiet water!* Angela hesitated. "As long as I don't have to get wet, I suppose so."

Lynn smiled. "Good. That's the best way to see the loons and the eagle's nest and shorebirds, although there aren't many of those around right now. And we have kingfishers nesting."

"And the peace." Judith stared at her iced tea glass. "Don't forget the peace. Escape from burdens."

Angela looked at her. "Your school is a burden?"

"Burdens are things you can carry. I am swamped. Buried, never to see daylight again. Angela, we've had two pop quizzes in precalc already; I scored twenty the first time and forty the second. And that is *with* tutoring! It'd be zero without."

"So already you're twice as good as you used to be."

"Those are failing grades!" she roared.

Angela shrugged. "You're only two weeks into it. I predict that all of a sudden it will click, you'll get into the rhythm of it, and you'll sail by with an A."

Judith sniffed. "And I predict that those rosy, rosy, rose-colored glasses are blinding you so bad you'll walk into a brick wall."

Angela sat erect and tossed her legs over the side. "Speaking of bricks, I thought I might make biscuits tonight, but I'm not going to turn the oven on. Too hot. Any requests for supper?"

Lynn said, "The salad is all made except for cutting up the tomatoes, and the chicken is breaded. It's on the middle shelf in the fridge."

"At least it's not raccoon." Angela shoved herself to her feet, leaving her flip-flops beside the lounger. She left the others laughing and went into the kitchen.

The wood floor felt cool to her bare feet. She got out the chicken, basking momentarily in the cold air, and brought out the bag of freshly shelled peas. She pulled the big cast-iron frying pan off its peg on the wall and dashed olive oil liberally into it from a cruet beside the stove.

The more she worked in this kitchen, the better she liked it. It was so well organized that very few changes were needed to make it uniquely hers. Rarely when she would show a house could she crow, "And look at this marvelous kitchen! Well designed and well organized. It will make cooking a breeze and getting creative a pleasure." She could certainly say that of this one. Except for the stacks of a latest project, of course. Lynn seemed to love to make a mess.

She got three potatoes out of the drop-open root bin. When was the last time one saw a root bin in a kitchen? Only kitchens that had never been remodeled since the thirties that she knew of. And yet this kitchen had one designed right into it, and she knew the Lundbergs had built this place. Mashed potatoes? Fried? If fried, thin sliced or chunked, home-style? They already had fried potatoes in various forms several times this week. She'd mash them. With sour cream, garlic, and chives, of course. She quartered them and dropped them into the two-quart saucepan.

She oiled a small iron skillet to sauté the mushrooms and onions she chopped for the peas. As they sizzled, she started a fire under the big skillet. When the oil began to move around on the bottom of the skillet, she laid the chicken pieces in. They sizzled happily. She set a splash screen over the pan.

No doubt they'd be eating out on the deck tonight, so she chopped and added the salad tomatoes, put the place settings and condiment basket on a tray, and carried it out. Judith stood up. "Here, I can set up."

"Thank you." Angela went back inside. She put the peas on, added the onion and mushrooms to them, and studied the stove. The meal was still plain. Mundane. They needed some little thing to jazz it up. She surveyed the canned goods in the pantry. *Aha! Cranberry sauce!* She opened a can and turned it out into a serving dish. She never made dishes with this many calories in her old home, and she reveled in her ability to at last cook large, so to speak. With élan and ritz.

The potato skins came off readily once they cooked. She

skinned about half of the potatoes, leaving the skins on the rest as she mashed, then whipped them with the salt, garlic powder, a dollop of sour cream, butter, and milk.

Heaping them into a dish, she sprinkled a bit of dried parsley over the top just because. The peas went into a smaller serving dish, and the chicken, golden brown, looked elegant layered on a plate. She called the ladies to the table, garnering tons of praise as they tasted the food. And that satisfied her immensely. It was not like Jack's praise. He would offer praise, but there was always the negative add-on: "Nice, but you know we're both paying attention to our weight" or "Nice, but I bet you can do even better if you try harder."

*Hmm*, the potatoes really were very good.

They were cleaning up after the meal when Phillip showed up.

"I'll get my stuff." Angela abandoned the kitchen and dug out her fishing equipment, her gift from kids who cared. The dishes would just have to do themselves tonight; the others abandoned the kitchen as well and headed down to the dock. Phillip had already piled the life vests, paddles, and oars on the dock.

Lynn explained, "Phillip is hyper-concerned about water safety. He got his kids drown-proofed before they were a year old. Now all three of them swim like otters. Wait till you see them."

"Swim...but the lake is still terribly cold. Shouldn't it be warming up by now?" Judith looked over the dock edge at the water.

"I suspect the locals swim in it before people from, say, Florida would. And by September it's quite nice." Lynn buckled into her life jacket. "Angela, let's you and I head out that way, and Phillip and Judith can go out that way."

"Dibs on the rowboat." Judith walked over and untied it. Phillip dropped the oars into the oarlocks and they crawled aboard.

If she had to go out in a boat, Angela would much prefer one that was not as tippy as a canoe, but well, here she was. She put her fishing gear in near the front, stepped into it, and settled onto the front seat. The canoe wobbled a little as Lynn put her own fishing gear in the back and climbed in behind it, giving Angela a bit of a fright. Just a bit. Angela pushed off as if she'd been doing this for years. In other words, smugly.

"Let's try that cove." Lynn nodded to the right.

They paddled over and Angela got out her box of lures. "Which one do you recommend?"

"You never know this time of year. Try them until one works. I used this one last time." With a practiced flick of the wrist, Lynn cast her line near a fallen tree. "You seem to be recovering beautifully from your old life. I am so glad."

"Thank you. I would not have guessed this change of scene would be so healing. Charlie still waxes eloquent about the time he spent here with Phillip and Tommy. At last I can see why."

"I hope now that they have an excuse, your children will come visit. It would be marvelous to see him again and meet your daughter."

"I'm getting vague promises from them. I hope so, too." Angela reeled the line in to change lures.

"Is your life here becoming more satisfying?" Lynn reeled her line in as well. Apparently she, too, had guessed wrong on the first one.

"Satisfying." Angela thought about that. "I like the word. And now that my life is so different, I'm beginning to see that my former life was not really very satisfying at all."

"For example...?" Lynn prompted.

"I'm finally no longer obsessed with making one more real estate sale; you cannot imagine how wearying that is. You land a sale and immediately you have to make another sale. And another. And I love not having to look gorgeous every moment. I see now that it was never my strong desire; it was Jack's expectation, even when we went to bed at night." She paused, thinking. "On the other hand, I've noticed that I'm gaining a little weight."

"It's not apparent."

"Jack would have noticed, believe me. When the children were growing up, I was pleasingly plump, you might say. He let me know he didn't like that. So once the children went into high school, I really started working on my weight, on my hair, everything. I dropped the twenty pounds I'd picked up after we married and then lost ten more besides that. Unfortunately, I see I've gained back three."

"So you can gain seven more is what you're saying and still weigh the same that you did as a bride."

Angela laughed. "I hadn't thought of it that way."

"And do you realize how many women would love to get back to what they weighed when they married?"

"True. It's not just the weight. All of it. Here I can wear flip-flops without getting some snarky comment."

"Less pressure, in other words."

"Exactly. And less judging. Shucks, no judging." She cast out her line. "And volunteering in a library again, and it's not just kiddy lit in the school library, real grown-up books. Besides which I'm recovering my joy of cooking. That is very satisfying to me."

"Well, we certainly appreciate it. You're a splendid cook. And you have the garden looking perfect."

"It's fun. I don't—" Her bobber dipped and she drew the line aside. "I have one!"

Lynn grabbed the net and leaned forward, extending it close to Angela. The fish flopped into the net, and Angela could at last get a good look at it. "That's not a walleye. Is it a trout?"

"No, a whitefish. A nice one, too."

Angela retrieved her lure and dropped the fish into the creel. She twisted around to look at Lynn. "Lynn, 'satisfying' does not begin to describe it."

# Chapter Twenty-Five

That was the most fantastic Fourth I've ever seen." Judith took her coffee mug to stand in front of the window beside Angela. "Fireworks all around the lake like that last night, and today it is back to placid." The sun had just leaped into the sky, making the blue even deeper as it traveled. While the men had picked up most of the debris from their own dock, the beach and lawn needed some more policing, decorated with pieces of red, white, and blue leftovers.

Angela would agree in spades. "I never tire of looking out over the lake, the sunrises like this, but all through the day. Always changing, no wind, puffs of wind, clouds, no clouds, birds, no birds." They both caught their breath as a flock of honkers settled on the water, their big gray bodies and black arched necks visible from a distance.

"Did you see the mother the other day with her line of goslings behind her?"

"As I said about my own kids: they grow up so fast."

They turned to grin at each other when the rooster crowed. His voice didn't crack for a change. "I think he's got it." Judith sobered. "You know where Lynn is? She's usually right here enjoying the view by now."

"Probably out in the garden. You going shopping to all the sales?" Angela asked.

"You have to be kidding. I do not go to any madness sales. Not after holidays and really not after Thanksgiving or Christmas. Melody talked me into it one time. I learned my lesson, and that was a fabric store. Women can get really pushy."

Angela half smiled at the thought. "I used to. A friend of mine and I would get up before dawn and be in line to open the stores. Not anymore, especially on some of those sales, they open in the middle of the night. Even if the merchandise was free. Besides, there aren't any morning-after sales in real estate."

"Maybe there should be. Like mattress sales to celebrate Washington's birthday."

The rooster crowed again and this time he had an echo.

Judith giggled. "That red one thinks he should crow, too."

"Phillip said it was about time to turn him into fried chicken. He's big enough."

Judith turned toward the door. "I'm going to let the chickens out of the coop and feed them. Are you at the library today?"

"Not today." Angela's cell did the two-toned signal for texts. She checked it and stuffed the phone back in her pocket. Jack. Her stomach clenched. When would she be able to get beyond reacting to these messages, let alone hearing his voice? The fury flared again, like a bonfire when someone threw on gas. She walked inside, dumped the dregs of her coffee in the sink, and went to stand in front of the fridge. "I feel like cooking. You want breakfast?"

"Sure," Judith tossed over her shoulder on her way out the door, scooping up the pail of kitchen scraps they kept for the chickens.

Angela decided to bake muffins, so she got out the ingredients and turned on the oven. She was just sliding the muffin pan into the oven when Judith came back.

"Lynn isn't out there. Did you know that Homer likes to lie at the fence and watch the chickens?"

"Really? Is her SUV out there?"

"Yes. Besides, if she goes somewhere she always leaves a note."

Miss Minerva announced her entrance with a demand for breakfast.

"Where's your mother?" Angela reached into the cupboard for the kitty food and poured the kibbles into Minerva's bowl. The cat strolled over, sniffed, and looked over her shoulder.

"No, you get the canned food at night. Kibbles in the morning. You know that."

Another sniff and she crouched down to eat one kibble at a time.

"I'm going up to see if she's in her room." Judith returned in a couple of minutes. "She's still in bed."

"Is she sick?"

"I have no idea. But how anyone can sleep with the rooster crowing and the birds having a community meeting in that tree off her window..."

"Perhaps she just had a bad night."

"Let's eat while the food is hot, and then I'll go check on her." The two took a tray with hot apple muffins and scrambled eggs out on the deck, where Homer joined them.

"After breakfast, I'll go pick up the stuff down there." Judith pointed toward the lake.

Angela shrugged. "That would be a good kid job."

"True. I forget about child labor. You think I should call Maggie and ask?"

"Why not?"

Judith wagged her head. "I don't know, guess I'm not comfortable doing that."

"All she can say is no. I know the guys are going somewhere this afternoon. Miss Priss is coming here so Maggie can sleep."

When they finished, Judith cleaned up and Angela headed for the stairs. She paused in the doorway, to rap or not, decided not to, then tiptoed over to the bed.

"I'm awake."

Angela leaned in closer. "Are you sick, Lynn?"

"Just had a bad night. Minerva came for me." She threw back the covers and swung her feet over the side. Once she was sitting, the cat eased into her lap and patted her cheek with the paw tipped in white toes. "I know." Lynn patted the cat and rolled her head from side to side. "Thanks for checking on me."

"Judith came up a while ago before she left for school. The muffins are still warm, and I'll scramble you some eggs, too."

"I better take a shower and see if I can get going. I'll warm it up when I get down there."

"You sure you're not running a temp or something? And by the way, you don't have to get up if you don't want to."

"Thanks, I know, but Priss is coming over later and I promised to have cookie dough ready."

"What kind? I'll start it. I'm in a baking mood today."

"Jack texted again, right?"

"How'd you know?"

Lynn snorted. "You always bake when he tries to contact you."

"Well, I guess that's better than hiding in bed. Tried that and it didn't help." She shrugged. "You want roll out, drop cookies, or bars?"

"Roll out, I guess. Or..." She scrubbed her scalp. "I can't think clearly yet."

"I should have brought the coffee up. I'll put a fresh pot on." Angela found herself humming as she went back down the stairs. Stopping at the floor, she stared at the east wall. Humming. She hadn't been humming since she couldn't remember when. Years ago? Possibly.

She assembled cookie ingredients and was just starting to cream the butter and sugar when the mob descended. All right, so it was only one little kid, but the energy and noise generated equaled that of a pretty hefty mob.

Miss Priss hopped up on a counter stool on her knees and draped her top half across the counter. "Isn't G'ma gonna bake cookies?"

"Yes, she is. She'll be out shortly and she'll take over."

When Lynn entered the kitchen, Angela abandoned the thought of baking cookies and just watched Lynn as she worked with her granddaughter. No, she wasn't working with her at all; she was playing with her, teasing, being teased, helping, being helped, loving, being loved.

The whirlwind departed a few hours later.

"I now know what being a grandma is like." Angela set the dishwasher to running and turned to Lynn.

"That was a pretty good intro, but wait until you have them all together. Now that can get wild." Lynn snapped the lid on the storage container full of cookies, some decorated with raisin faces, others with chocolate chips, red sugar sprinkles and variegated sprinkles. "She loves decorating cookies."

"What a cutie she is."

"True, but you didn't get a full dose of herself when in true princess mode. I read her the story of the princess and the pea one time, and all I could think was how appropriate. However, she can fish with the best of them and bait her own hooks, but she needs help sometimes getting the hook out. An outdoorsy princess."

What would Angela's grandchildren be like? Would she ever get any? While Gwynn and Charles had married, neither couple had mentioned starting their families and now she found herself wishing they'd get started. Now there was a major, major change. *Major* change! Angela really was becoming new.

Oh, how Judith dreaded this! To be honest, thanks to Tom's coaching, she did not feel completely overwhelmed anymore by math. But today incompletely overwhelmed was no help at all. She slid into her plastic chair that was designed to keep students from falling asleep in it, laid her pack at her feet, and stretched her shoulders.

Here came Dr. Stern, the bubbly math prof. Derailed by half a dozen students waiting for her at the door, she answered questions, nodded, answered more questions... *Come on, Dr. Stern, we're losing time here.*

Today was their first formal examination, and Judith would need every moment she could squeeze out of the hour. She opened her blue book and looked at it. A blue book. How long had it been since she'd seen one of these?

She got out four neatly sharpened pencils. Overkill? Not if you are so nervous that you break three leads. And she still had one pencil in her pack on reserve. She wrote the date, her name, and her ID number on the line on the cover.

Dr. Stern fiddled with her laptop. The overhead projector kicked into gear, and after a brief search (lower left corner of the screen), the title slide came on.

First exam
10 questions, 10 points each
Copy each question to your bluebook

Judith would have made *bluebook* two words there, not one. And she giggled when she realized she was editing her professor's slide. She hunched her shoulders and dropped them down, tensing the muscles, letting up. *Here goes nothing.*

The questions flashed up, three to a slide. Judith copied carefully and had time to double-check that she'd gotten it all exactly right.

A girl's voice called, "Dr. Stern! We haven't studied logarithms yet."

The professor snapped back, "This is advanced math. You're supposed to come in here knowing what they are and how to deal with them."

And thanks to Tom, who had drilled her on them, Judith did!

The screen went dark and Judith set to work, doing the problems she knew that she knew (including the one employing logs), then going to the tougher ones. She rejoiced that calculators were legal and she could punch the equations into her—Tom's—graphing calculator.

Moments later, Dr. Stern called, "Time. Close your books and pass them to the left." The hour was gone, the whole hour! Judith had hardly touched one of the questions at all. And then Dr. Stern sent ice water through Judith's veins by calling her number. "Stay behind, please; I want to talk to you."

*Oh no, now what?*

The professor's proctors carried the books forward and stacked them on the table beside the lectern. Judith waited until most of the others had filed out, then walked down to the lectern with feet made out of lead and encased in concrete.

"You asked me to remain behind."

Dr. Stern smiled. "Thank you. Find your book, please. They're stacked in general order, front, middle, back." She turned to address another student's question. By the time Judith dug out her blue book, the long line of students had dissipated.

Dr. Stern took her book from her hand and went through it, page by page, silently scanning each question. Nothing in her face betrayed what she was thinking. She could be a good poker player. Maybe she already was.

She flopped the book onto the stack and leaned forward on the lectern, both elbows. And she smiled. "Miss Rutherford, I was all prepared to ask why you thought you could handle this course. You failed the first two weeks and barely squeaked through the third. But I see you've scored at least seventy-five on this exam and probably higher. My aides grade the tests and we give partial credit, so you should come through this in the upper third of the class at the very least. I take it you're being tutored."

"I am, by a man who really should be teaching math. He works miracles." *And pours good footings.*

"Please understand I'm not denigrating you in any way by saying this, but your performance today is indeed a small miracle. You've come a long, long way." She stood erect. "Keep at it, please, Miss Rutherford. And incidentally, would you pass the word to your tutor that I will be looking for aides next semester? A good teacher would be a godsend."

"I shall!" Judith's heart sang. "Thank you, Dr. Stern! Thank you very much."

The professor turned away to address another student's question, so Judith left, her heart still singing. When was the last time it sang? She stopped in the middle of the sidewalk. *When?* The last time she was in college, all those years ago, and she aced world history.

Other pedestrians were pointedly walking around her, so she kept going to one of the memorial park benches and sat. With the sitting, she realized that thought made her howlingly angry. Her parents had been wealthy enough to hire the necessary help; Judith could at least have completed her bachelor's degree before devoting years to Rutherford House. She could be stepping right into master's level work now instead of starting out at the beginning again. Her parents had wasted her life and her brain and her dreams. They had minimized her, made her a servant, not because they could not afford servants but because—why? Why do this to their daughter? The fury burned.

But wait. Perhaps she had to reach middle age before she could appreciate success. She could at last pursue a dream, and she was in fact pursuing it. And succeeding against all odds. Even in math. Now there was a major, major change. *Major* change! Judith really was becoming new.

She stopped by Miller's Feed on the way home for some glass eggs. *Why?* To mess with her little chickens' minds! Yes, Judith Rutherford, high society dame, was psyching out poultry. She had read that you can put glass eggs in nests where you want your youngsters to lay when they start laying. Judith also picked up some laying mash, for her kids were getting to that age.

She stashed the mash and eggs in the corner of her garage bay and walked into the house. It was quiet. Very, very quiet. Angela had said something about stopping at the grocery store on the way home. But where was Lynn?

She walked into the kitchen and stopped. Lynn was sitting on a stool, staring at her coffee cup. Miss Minerva sat on the counter beside her. This was not good; Lynn always chased the cat off the counters. So Judith did it and headed for the coffeepot.

So far, Lynn had not said a word. This was not good, either. Her cheeks were wet.

Judith paused beside her. "What's wrong?" No answer. "Lynn, are you all right?"

Lynn looked up from studying her cold coffee. "Today is the anniversary of Paul's death." She sniffed, then grabbed for a tissue from the box always kept on the center island. "I handled this last year all right; I mean, I cried a lot, but that's to be expected."

"And today?"

"Today—today..." She shook her head. "Not today. I am so furious I could...I could..." A steely jaw and flashing eyes supported her words.

Judith gaped. "Furious about what?"

Lynn glared through her tears. "Paul! He left me. I know this makes absolutely no sense. I know it was an aneurysm. But surely if he'd gone to the doctor, they could have found something. If he weren't dead, I swear I'd kill him." She glared at her hands. "I can't stand this. I don't want to live the rest of my life without him. I want to go back to before. Before I get all the way awake, I reach across the bed and...and..." She kept shaking her head, as if it were weighted. "And he's not there, and he will never be there again. And..." Tears rained down her face.

Judith came around the island, wrapped an arm around her shoulders, and laid her cheek on her friend's head. "Go ahead and cry. Someone told me that tears are healing. Sometimes I get so mad at my father for all those years he robbed from me. I hate him."

"My mother always said not to hate anyone—how can you hate and love at the same time?" Lynn pulled a couple of tissues out and mopped. And blew and mopped and reached for more.

"I know I can hate and love; actually, I'm not sure of the love." Judith moved the box closer, pulling out one for herself.

"He left me! He was only fifty-four. Far too young to die yet." She crossed her arms on the granite and leaned into them. "Sometimes I wonder how I can go on without him, and then I ask, what are my choices? How could God do this to us? One of the church women told me, 'God must have needed a plumber in heaven,' and I wanted to deck her." She blew again. "Paul was such a man of God, like the Old Testament talks about a 'strong man of God.' Doesn't the world around here need that kind of man instead of hauling him off to heaven?" She was practically screaming. Judith pulled her in closer.

"What!" Angela stood in the doorway, two bulging totes in each hand. "What happened?"

Lynn sobbed and gulped. "Sorry."

"Lynn is being a normal human being. A grieving human being."

"Ah. Been there, done that, got the T-shirt." Angela abandoned all four totes, lowering them to the floor, and stepped in beside Lynn. "Lynn, I'm so sorry. I wish I could help."

Judith did not release her hug when Angela wrapped an arm across Lynn's shoulders. With her free hand she reached across to the tissue box and pulled another, handing it to Lynn. Lynn muttered something and blew, sobbed, her shoulders heaving.

And then Angela stepped behind Lynn and began massaging her back, working her shoulders.

Lynn covered her face with her hands for a few minutes before taking a deep breath and sitting erect. "I'm sorry."

"Well, don't be." Angela stepped back. "It's not only normal, it's healthy."

"Your massage felt good. Thank you."

"I used to calm the kids down with that. I had forgotten I know how to do it."

Judith stepped back as well. "Shall I help you put groceries away?"

Angela shook her head. "Nothing frozen, and the fridge stuff is okay for a while. They can wait. Let's just sit and unwind."

Lynn drew a deep breath, blew her nose, shuddered a sob, and stood up. "That would be nice. Let me get my knitting." Lynn headed for the sewing room.

Judith hurried to her room and returned with her laptop. "I'm doing homework, Angela, surprise, surprise. What will you do?"

"Read. Relax. I'm having to learn to relax all over again." Angela waved her book. "I started this today; it's quite good. Lynn's bookshelf has some great ones."

The three settled into the two leather easy chairs, with Judith on the sofa, where she opened her laptop and went into her file. Lynn's knitting needles sang a song of their own, and Angela draped one leg over the arm of the chair.

Presently, Lynn said, "I really am angry at him. With Paul. I didn't realize that."

Angela laid her book in her lap and looked steadily at Lynn. "You angry at him or at God?"

The knitting needles paused; Lynn studied her a moment. "Good question."

# Chapter Twenty-Six

Y ou're going to church with me?" Lynn's smile nearly cracked her face as Judith strolled into the kitchen, wearing a skirt and blouse.

"I said I would eventually, and I guess eventually arrived."

"Me, too. Can't be left out." Angela made a direct line to the coffeepot. After the first sip, she smiled. "What do people do without coffee?"

Lynn snickered. "Some drink tea, you know."

Judith added, "Energy drinks. The students buy junk food up the kazoo. My lab partner does diet cola. Lost without it."

"Like me without coffee?" She picked up a piece of coffee cake from the plate on the island and leaned back against the counter, cupping her hand to catch any falling crumbs.

"We leave in ten minutes." Lynn stared at the dog. "Do we dare leave you in the house?" Homer looked up at her, his tail wagging his whole hind end. "I don't really want to clean up any messes, you know." More wagging, then he plunked his rump down and lifted a front paw.

Angela shook her head. "I say the mudroom. Safer that way."

Lynn nodded.

"Don't you lock the doors?" Judith asked when they were loaded in the SUV and heading toward town.

"No, we've never had any problems, and with Homer, I doubt we would."

"We didn't used to either, but after some houses were robbed, the authorities strongly suggested everyone start locking their doors. I even started locking my car." Angela put her sunglasses on and buckled her seat belt. "So easy to forget when I am riding, I always remember when I am in the driver's seat."

"About the other day...," Lynn said.

"So you had a grieving time. What of it?"

"Well, sometimes I still cry in church. Just thought I'd warn you."

"At least you go. I quit going, which is far worse. If we can't cry in church..." Angela heaved a sigh. "But that's the way it is. People with their happy faces on and afraid to show how they hurt. My church, it was especially that way. Do you realize that saying *There, there, don't cry* is basically invalidating the crier's very real sorrow?"

"Someone said we shoot our wounded," Judith commented.

They parked next to Maggie's SUV and made their way to the front door, where greeters were smiling broadly and handing out bulletins. Lynn introduced Angela and Judith to everyone around as her housemates, and they filed into one of the back rows.

"Pastor Evanson is our senior pastor. Norm Nelson, our assistant, is on vacation right now." She handed each of them a hymnal, realized they both had picked up their own hymnals, and put these two back. They had both commented on her constant (and irritating—although they didn't actually say that, they sure implied it) mothering of mature women.

Would this simple gesture, handing them a hymnal, count as overmothering?

But Lynn didn't have a chance to ponder the question because the service began with the opening hymn. The service flowed as always, including the children's sermon with the kids gathered around Pastor Evanson, making everyone smile.

Pastor stepped into the pulpit, prayed, and then smiled out over the congregation. "Today we continue our study of forgiveness. We've talked about how God forgives. He not only forgets, but He moves our sin away as far as the east is from the west. Jesus died so that we are forgiven. Past, present, and future. He forgives us. So what, then? Who are we to forgive? Those who harmfully use you. Sin never happens to just one person; yes, our sin affects us, but it also injures those around us, the Bible says unto the third and fourth generation. Selfish creatures that we are, we think what we do won't hurt others.

"Families are destroyed when family members refuse to forgive each other. Marriages are destroyed when husbands and wives bear grudges and do not forgive. You will be destroyed if you do not forgive, for it will eat away at you like a cancer. Christ offers us the *free* gift. Turn to Him, tell Him everything, and accept His love and forgiveness, then go out and forgive others—before it is too late. Amen."

As they all filed out, Lynn introduced the two to Pastor Evanson as he greeted folks at the door.

He shook hands warmly. "So you have moved here to stay?"

Angela nodded. "Tentative at first, but yes, I think so."

"Welcome to Detroit Lakes, and we would be pleased to become your church home. You couldn't find a more lovely place to live than the Lundbergs'."

"Thank you. I agree as to the beauty. And the family." Angela smiled back at him.

He shook hands with Judith. "You look familiar. Have you been here before? Rutherford, did you say?"

"Yes, and if you've been to Rutherford to the Rutherford House, I was probably your hostess."

"Seems I heard your father died."

"He did. The house is becoming a living history museum, my father's dream."

"Well, welcome. Thanks for coming."

Lynn led the way out toward the car. "Paul and I used to go out for brunch after the service. You interested?"

"I would rather go home, sit on the deck, and study, if that's all right with the two of you." Judith climbed into the backseat, leaving the front passenger side for Angela. "From now on, I'll bring my schoolwork and I can study while you two brunch."

"And no one needs to cook dinner because we have plenty of leftovers. Every woman for herself." Angela settled in and pulled down her seat belt.

Lynn watched behind a moment and eased out into traffic. "I know one thing I want to do—go sit on the dock and dangle my feet in the water. The kids are gone for today, so it should be relatively peaceful, at least compared to most weekends."

Angela tipped her head back. "I wonder if Homer left us enough ripe strawberries for shortcake. I caught him eating them the other day. If so, I will make shortcake and..."

Lynn chimed in, "And I will go pick the berries."

Judith giggled. "And I will eat it as soon as it is ready. I know there's whipped cream in the fridge. There's something really special about the first strawberry shortcake of the season. We had berries in the back garden for years, but as we cut staff, that was one of those things that fell off the list."

"Well, we have gardens now. I'll fix that lettuce salad for supper."

Angela cackled. "And here we are planning our supper."

"But not dinner," Judith reminded her. "On our own."

They let Homer out and laughed at his vociferous and tail-beating welcome before opening the doors to the deck and heading for their rooms to change clothes.

Alone in her room, Lynn stared in the mirror. *I am enjoying life again. I did most of the time, but in spite of that crash the other day, I love having sisters around; at least they are beginning to feel like that. With everyone splitting up the chores, life is just easier. This house is alive again, too. Thank you, Lord God.*

After they ate, Lynn headed out to pick the strawberries. Homer tagged along, nose to the ground. He found the first strawberry. She watched him pick it carefully. If he would have closed his eyes in bliss, she would not have been surprised. A thread of pink drool gave it away. When he nosed for the next one, she ordered him out of the berry patch. "We need enough for shortcake, you big goof. Go find your bone."

He wandered off and she bent to the task, the sun hot on her back but her face protected by a wide-brimmed straw hat. They'd have enough for jam in a couple of days, but today she barely filled the bowl. On the way back to the house, she found Homer lying in the shade by the hammock where Angela lay reading a book. His gnawing the bone made her smile. "Good book?"

"Very. You should know, it is off your shelf."

"Doesn't mean I've read it."

Angela held it up so she could see the cover.

"I like her. I usually pick up all of hers. Maybe I'll read it after you finish. Once the garden starts I don't find much time for reading."

Angela wagged a finger. "The shortcake is on the rack on the counter. Have you noticed that sometimes the bread is on the floor?"

"I have, but..."

Angela stared at the oblivious dog. "I think he's doing it. I walked in the kitchen and he looked up from snarfing bread like he knew he was guilty."

"You think he could reach the countertop?"

"We should set up a motion-activated camera."

"Right." Lynn washed and hulled the strawberries, got out three dessert plates and forks, whipped some cream, and put it all on a tray to serve. She was just opening the screen door when a book slammed against her feet. "What's wrong?"

"I hate math! The prof explained it, the grad assistant explained it, Tommy explained it, and I still can't get it! Why did I ever dream of doing something that requires math classes?" Judith slammed her head against the back of the lounger.

Lynn dug her phone out of her pocket and handed it to her. "Tommy is number three on the speed dial. Let him help you."

"That's not fair to him, spending so much time on a hopeless cause."

"Hit the button; let him make that decision."

Judith glared up at her and snarled sarcastically, "Yes, Mo-ther!" When Lynn started to laugh, she glared harder. "Really, Lynn, your extreme mothering is wearing very thin." She pushed the button, left a message, and handed the phone back. "Satisfied?"

Was she really that bad? Even the boys called her out on her mothering mode at times. "Yes. I apologize for slipping into mother mode."

Judith took a deep breath and shook her head. "I apologize, too. I guess sometimes I need someone in mother mode."

"If Tommy can't help you or doesn't have time, we'll find you a tutor."

Judith looked up at her, a half smile curving her lips. "You realize you just said 'we'?"

Lynn shrugged. "I don't know, I guess. Why?"

"Because I've not had anyone in my life for years who not only said that, but believed it."

"Well, you got an older sister here who can be bossy but who sure means well."

Judith reached up a hand and Lynn took it. They smiled at each other, then Lynn leaned over and hugged her. "We'll beat this thing. If I can stand entering stuff in the computer, you can tough it out until you get it and then there'll be no stopping you."

That night after supper and shortcake, the three gathered on the deck in what was becoming their nightly ritual— stargazing. Tonight a breeze and several citron candles would likely keep the mosquitoes at bay enough to not drive them inside.

"Your pastor sure lays things out plain. No nonsense, here it is." Angela swirled her glass, setting the ice to tinkling.

"True, that's typical of the way he preaches," Lynn answered. "Sure made me squirm."

"You'd have thought he'd been reading my mind. I hate Jack and there is no way I can forgive him."

"When we said the Lord's Prayer was when it hit me. 'Forgive us our trespasses as we forgive those who trespass against us.' How can *as* be such a big word here? I mean, I've heard all this who knows how many times but…"

"But sometimes it just whacks you upside the head?"

"Something like that. I've always thought I was a very forgiving person. I don't bear grudges. Another verse that says 'quick to forgive and slow to anger.' I thought I was doing pretty good with that."

"And then what?" Judith asked.

"And then I had that meltdown and I had no idea I was so angry at Paul, and at God for taking him away." She released a deep sigh into the breeze. "I mean, I know he's in a better place, he got to go home to heaven, but the bottom line is— I want him here."

"Sometimes I would wish that I could turn back the clock to the before," Angela said.

"Before what?"

"Before Jack got so steamed up about changing our lives, becoming *successful*, lots of money, all that garbage."

"Were you happy then?"

"I thought I was, but looking back, he wasn't."

"Looking back," Judith chimed in, "all those years with my father so angry. He was a kind and loving man until the accident that crippled him. At least I remember good times when I was little. Melody and I played memory lane. We had lots of good times to talk about."

"I'm wondering if we are all caught in that trap."

"Of not forgiving?" Angela slapped at a mosquito. "Gotcha. Die, sucker. That 'sucker' is literal, of course." She trailed a hand on Homer's head and he quit snoring.

Minerva chirped at the screen door and Lynn got up to let her out. "Come along, Your Highness." Back on her lounger, she picked up her almost empty glass and swallowed the rest. "I really do want out of anger."

"That's part of grieving, they told me after my father died. One of the stages."

"But you are supposed to go through the stages, not get locked on one. Here it is two years later and look what it did to me." She stared up at the sky. *Lord God, show me how to let go of this and forgive Paul.*

Angela was staring not at the stars but at infinity. "At least Paul didn't do it deliberately. Jack did."

Lynn asked, "But what if you actively decided to forgive him?"

"I don't know. I don't know if I can or if I even want to. At this point I'd much rather get even. Or just walk away."

"True. Sometimes I feel like a little kid, screaming 'but it's not fair.'" Lynn stroked the cat, who had settled on her lap.

"My mother used to say that there are no promises that life will be fair," Judith murmured. "I understand that now, sort of, I guess. Still…"

"I wonder…" Angela's voice sounded distant. "I wonder if I really can forgive Jack. I have a feeling that he doesn't care how I feel, but…"

Judith snorted. "He's a selfish jerk who reneges on his promises."

"I know, but look how my life has changed. Had he not initiated a divorce, I'd still be locked into being a person that I don't even like. Trying to be someone I am not. I tried to be what he said he wanted, I really did. And I was good at it." Her voice dropped. "But it wasn't me."

Frogs chorused from the lake. A fish splashed. A dog barked somewhere in the distance across the water.

"Such peace. Lord, I do want to forgive Jack. I don't want to carry all this hurt and anger anymore." Her eyes brimmed over and her nose ran. She dug a tissue out of her pocket and wiped her nose. "Help me, please."

Judith wagged her head. "You guys make me almost wish I could forgive my father, but there's just too much. Twenty-five years! More. He ruined my life. I'm an old woman without a past and without a future." She shuddered. "No. I can't do it."

# Chapter Twenty-Seven

I*love* canoes!" Angela came slamming in the back door. Her wild arrival startled Judith, who was sitting at the kitchen table with Lynn, so much she almost spilled her coffee. "Well, maybe not love. But like."

Phillip entered behind her. "She didn't do too badly, either. She's finally getting the hang of it."

Triumphantly, Angela held out a stringer with three fish, each about a foot long, and laid them on the table.

Judith frowned at them. "Those are trout?"

"Walleyes." Angela pointed. "See how the two dorsal fins are arranged? Trout only have one fin there and an adipose fin near the tail—a little fleshy tab, not a fin with spines." She sat down, too.

Phillip flopped into a chair. "Fly-fishing can be pretty frustrating even for people who fish a lot, so we went after walleye."

"Phillip," Angela said, "thank you so much for taking me out! If it isn't something to do with real estate or makeup, I don't know anything about it. This is all new to me." She looked at Lynn. "It was amazing."

Phillip was smiling. "Our whole family enjoys fishing; glad you do, too."

Lynn added, "Phillip has been canoeing and fishing since he was five. He'd better know what he's doing."

"Five?" Angela sighed. "I never realized until just now how much Charles and Gwynn missed out on. Jack and I were always so busy..." Her sentence died unfinished.

*Her children missed out?* Judith thought, *I missed out, too! On so much!*

Lynn stood and crossed to the sink. "Now comes the interesting part. Bring your fish to the sink, Angela."

Phillip hopped up. "Oh, gee! Look at the time! Gotta go. G'night, Mom! Judith." He rushed out.

Judith watched him go. "What precipitated that?"

Lynn laughed. "He absolutely hates to clean fish. I'm afraid I spoiled him."

*Yeah, right. That generous young man is spoiled.* Judith walked over to the sink, too.

"This is a filleting knife; very sharp and no serration. If the restaurant is fancy enough, they'll serve your fish with the head still on it. Our house is not fancy." Lynn slipped her knife in behind the gill covers and cut off the head with crunchy, squishy sounds.

*Our house was fancy. The cook served some fish with the head still on.* Judith was in an alien world all right.

"Then we remove the internal organs. We stick the point of the knife in here and carefully cut open the belly. It isn't going to ruin anything if you accidentally cut the intestines, but it's nicer if you don't. Like this. See? And we clip out the anus here." Lynn had obviously cleaned a fish or two. She flicked the knife and it did just what she wanted.

She handed the knife to Angela. "Your turn."

As Angela performed surgery on her other walleyes, Judith thought, *Could I do that?* Yes, she could. The sorrow was that Cook never let her in the kitchen. She was always too little, even when she was approaching age thirty.

Come to think of it, she felt sad for Cook, too. The grumpy old woman spent her whole life and career—her *whole* career!—serving in the Rutherford House kitchen. She was good, very good. She could have been a major hotel chef or owned a restaurant. Why did she spend her whole life cooking for the Rutherfords? Not making that much money, either—Judith knew; she kept the books.

"If it's a fish this size, I usually just butterfly it. Catch a larger fish, and I'll show you how to fillet it." Lynn demonstrated with one fish and Angela butterflied the others. They applied a rub, wrapped the fish, and put them in the refrigerator. Dinner tomorrow.

Judith spent part of the next day simply reading, a luxury that until now she had not permitted herself. In fact, she had not yet finished the Galveston hurricane book, and this was the best part, too. The author remarked that a disproportionate number of women and children died. Well, yes. Men could swim in street clothes. Even women who could swim wouldn't have much luck in a raging storm, trying to swim in ankle-length wool skirts. And her thoughts pleased her. She was reading analytically, a good habit for doing well academically.

Around noon, Lynn went out to deadhead the roses and dahlias. Judith studied. After lunch Lynn went into town to the grocery and hardware store (and took Homer along—"we don't want Homer to think that every time he gets in the car, it means a trip to the vet's"), and Judith thought about her furniture. She'd made a formal study space, but her desk was too far from the window. She wanted more natural light. And over by the window here…someone knocked.

"Come in!"

Angela stood there grinning. "Let's go fishing." She was still glowing, like a child on Christmas morning. "That was a wonderful time last evening, fishing for walleye."

"I've never done that. Or paddled a canoe."

"It's not that hard, really! I can show you. Half an hour or so, not long; I know you have to study." She sobered. "Besides, I just got a call from my lawyer."

"Uh-oh."

"Not about me. Jack has not sent the money to buy his half of the house, so the lawyer hired a private detective to go nosing around a little. A woman named Marillee—I had to get my lawyer to spell that—wrote the check for his latest mortgage payment and now he's put her name on the deed as a co-owner."

Judith wagged her head. "That creep!"

Angela brightened. "Anyway, I'm going to put all that behind me and just go fishing. That's very scriptural you know. When Peter was so upset, he said, 'I go a-fishing.'"

Judith laughed. Several times she had wondered how they could possibly help Angela. Well, here was an opportunity. She'd move furniture later. "Sure. Let's go."

Angela gathered up her fishing equipment and they walked down to the dock.

The T dock was fairly large, maybe twenty feet by twenty feet. The canoe lay upside down on one side of it. Tied up on the other side, an inflatable rubber raft with a small motor on back bobbed in the water.

"Phillip showed me how." Angela gripped the edge of the canoe and flipped it over the side. It plopped into the water. Judith saw that it was tied to a ring in the dock and the paddles were lying under it. Well, at least that part seemed simple enough.

Cautiously, Angela crawled in and settled herself on the rear seat. The canoe only wobbled a little. "Pass me the tackle box, please, and the paddles."

Judith handed her the tackle box, the rod, and a net. "Why three paddles? There are two of us." She handed all three in.

"In case you accidentally lose one and it floats out of reach. You have an extra."

"Speaking of safety. Aren't we supposed to wear life jackets?"

Angela thought a moment. "I don't know where they keep them. Not in the mudroom." She shrugged. "Oh, well. We're not going out very far. Untie us, please."

Judith did so, tossing the rope into the front of the canoe. Then she climbed into the boat but carefully, reluctantly, as Angela had done, stepping in the middle only. The canoe moved beneath her feet too much; she didn't like this feeling. No matter. She was in. She sat down on the forward seat and picked up a paddle. "Which end goes in the water?"

Angela laughed. "That's about how much I knew about it, too."

Judith wondered how you were supposed to turn corners with this thing. But then the beauty of the moment seized her and she forgot about turning corners. The lake lay flat and glistening before them, with only a few wind ripples to give it texture. The sun skipped in and out among clouds, and the patterns of clouds and sunlight on the water were new and wonderful and constantly changing. *And look!* There was a loon way out there. *A loon!* Judith was not looking at it from her world onshore; she was in the loon's world now, a dream she'd had forever.

Behind her, Angela baited her line and cast it out. Judith laid her paddle across her lap and simply drank in the quiet beauty. Serenity. But this was a more peaceful serenity than what she had known at Rutherford House. It took her a few minutes to figure out why. At the house, she was always listening for the bell her father rang when he wanted something. Always. They had spacious, well-tended gardens and lovely rooms, but she could never just sit in them and enjoy the quiet. There was always that bell, an unpleasant expectancy; peace could always be shattered at any moment.

"I got one!" The canoe wobbled. "Oh, nuts, I lost it. Oh, well." The canoe wobbled slightly again as Angela cast her line out.

Judith smiled. No, that was not the same thing at all as an interruption at Rutherford House. That was simply joy being expressed out loud. She watched the loon.

But then her attention turned to a flat line of ripples approaching across the lake, a curious thing. The line was quite straight. And behind it the water was really bumpy.

"Angela? Turn us around and let's head back. You can fish from closer to shore."

"But I don't...well, I suppose, if you want." The canoe wobbled. "Okay, Judith, you hold your paddle in the water straight up and down; don't paddle, just hold it there; and I'll paddle and turn us around."

The line in the water was approaching quickly. And then it was here; it hit the canoe at an angle and they almost went over. From practically no wind to lots of wind instantly.

"Paddle! Paddle!" Angela cried.

Judith paddled! They were now positioned nose toward the shore, but the wind was driving them backward. They weren't approaching shore; they were getting farther out.

The wind picked up more.

"Maybe we should just turn around and paddle for the far shore," Judith called. "Then when this dies down, we can come back across."

"I think you're right! I'll turn us around."

Judith set her paddle vertically; she heard splashing and sloshing in back. The canoe began to turn. The wind caught then sideways, and they started to tip away from the wind.

"Lean into it!" Angela yelled. "Lean into it; it's going to blow us over!"

Judith leaned into the wind. Too late, she realized that was a serious mistake; the wind now had more canoe surface to blow against. It shoved the canoe sideways, and then they were tipping over in a terrifying sort of slow motion. Before she could lean on the other side or something, it was too late.

Angela screamed; Judith screamed; they were in the water!

The water was cold! Ice! It pierced Judith's clothes instantly. She was soaked to the skin with ice water. She gasped the biggest gasp she had ever gasped.

Angela was gasping, too, but she must have inhaled water; she was choking and coughing.

"Hang on to the canoe!" Judith cried. "Don't let go of the canoe!"

"It's going to sink, and..."

"It's upside down, but it's still floating; hang onto it!"

Cold! She was so horribly, miserably cold! They had only been in the water a few seconds and already she was shivering uncontrollably.

"Hellllp!" Why was Judith screaming for help? There was no one to hear her; no one ashore and certainly no one out here. And the cold... "Hellllllp!"

Angela managed words in between the coughing. "Help me! I can't hold on."

Judith was having trouble hanging on, too. Her hands were too cold to grip, her arms so cold they were stiff. Her legs were numb. Did she have feet? She didn't feel them. She was never, ever going to be warm again, never. The cold was even in her chest.

The upside-down canoe offered nothing to hang on to; its sides were smooth. Judith had been gripping the edge—the gunwale—but it was underwater, under frigid water. Her fingers were too numb to do that now. She groped underneath and grasped one of the crosspieces. She hooked her left arm over it and sort of locked herself onto it.

With a yelp and a moan, Angela drifted out from the canoe; she'd lost her grip.

Judith grabbed her and pulled her in, curled her free right arm around her, and held her.

"Helllllllp!"

It was raining; not just raining, but a drumming, slamming rain. And the pounding raindrops were curiously warm.

Something nudged into Judith and shoved her head against the canoe. What was happening? Her head went under; she forced it back up.

And suddenly she realized her right arm was empty! Angela was not there!

She wanted to cry out, *Angela! Angela!* but it came out as "Aaahnsssh...Aaahnshh!" Her mouth and voice no longer obeyed her.

She couldn't see anything because a huge gray blob right in front of her face blocked out everything. "Aaahnnssh!"

Hands were gripping her, pulling on her. "Let go!" Lynn's voice. "Let go!"

The words were supposed to be, *I can't! I can't feel... Angela is drowning! Find Angela!* "kkkaahhhnn... Aaaaahnnnsssh..."

*"Let go!"*

Without doing anything, Judith felt her arm slip free of that crosspiece. She was getting dragged up the side of the gray blob. She fell forward. She realized she was in an extremely awkward position, her cheek pressed against a flat surface, her hind end in the air, and her feet hanging down out there. And she couldn't move to change it. Besides, she didn't care anymore. *Angela! Find Angela!* "Aaahhnnsh..." So cold.

Was that she who was coughing or was it someone else?

Hands gripped her legs and tugged. She was going to slide back into the icy water feetfirst, and she could not move her arms or legs to do anything about it.

"Okay, Lynn, we've got her." A man's voice.

An engine kicked in; it sounded like it was moving away.

Judith could not feel her body parts at all, but she could at last raise her head to see what was going on. That inflatable boat they had seen at the dock was headed for shore. Lynn was operating it. And Angela was curled up beside her! Angela was safe!

And so was Judith. She, too, was in another inflatable being operated by two young men in navy-blue jumpsuits; they were soaking wet and didn't seem to care. They were all headed for shore, where two aid vans were parked. The vans' red lights flashed wildly, promising safety.

*Who? What?* This was all too much for her. And the heavy rain was warm.

They bumped into the dock. Strong arms lifted her up and out and onto a gurney, wheeling her into an aid van. She could hear the other aid van out there leaving, its siren growling up the scale.

"Lynn? Wanna come along?" a young man's voice asked.

"Sure!" The doors slapped closed, and this van also began to move.

Grinning, Lynn plopped down on a jump seat across from Judith. "That was sure close!"

"Whhhuhhh...?"

"I pulled into the yard and opened the car door. Homer jumped out, barking like mad, and ran out onto the dock. If he hadn't been barking at you, I would never have seen you two out there. I looked that way just as the canoe turned sideways and broached. Once it was upside down it became just about invisible. So I hopped into the Zodiac and hurried out to get you."

One of the young men slipped a cone-shaped plastic mask onto Judith's face. "And she called 911 on her way out."

"In this lake country," Lynn explained, "the fire department has a pickup truck with a Zodiac just for on-the-water responses. So we had two boats available, theirs and mine."

"Whhhuhhh..."

The young man was smiling casually, as if he did this sort of thing every day. Maybe he did. "Your core temperature—the temperature of your innards—is dangerously low. We're taking you to the emergency room, where they'll warm you back up safely. You'll be just fine. So will your fishing buddy in the other van."

Her fishing buddy. For some reason that struck Judith as particularly funny, but she was too cold to laugh.

Angela was safe. But her new fishing equipment, her gift from her children, was now at the bottom of the lake.

Amend that. Angela was safe physically. But would she ever venture out in a canoe again? For that matter, would Judith?

*Absolutely not!*

# Chapter Twenty-Eight

Angela walked in the library door to be greeted with Mary's "Oh, am I glad you're here! It's a madhouse today, and the shelving is way behind!"

"Good! I like it best when there's plenty to do." She tossed her lunch sack into the fridge and hustled out to the desk. Behind with reshelving, indeed! Three carts piled high and the drop bin half full.

She had developed a system. She grabbed a cart at random and wheeled it out by the stacks. She set all the books on the cart on end, arranged them more or less numerically or, in the case of fiction, alphabetically. Then she started at one end of the stacks, shelved her way to the other end, and did the fiction around the walls on the way back. She brought the cart back to the desk empty only to find two-foot-high stacks waiting for a cart.

A middle-aged lady with blue hair stepped up to the desk. "I am looking for an inexpensive rental. Can you help? I already bought a paper."

Their teenaged volunteer on the desk, Chrissa, pointed to Angela. "There's our real estate pro. She'll know."

Angela smiled at the woman. "There is a hair parlor on the edge of town, the Clip Shop."

"I saw that. Like the name."

"That's where I get my hair done. She's good. Also, she knows everything in the whole world about every person, cat, and dog in this town. Go tell her what you need. I'm confident she can give you some excellent leads."

"Hairdresser! Of course. I never thought of that, and we have a hairdresser like that where I come from, too. Thank you!" She left beaming.

Chrissa laughed. "So real estate pros send clients to the hairdresser's."

"More than that; sometimes we'd take Bess Walberg's hairdresser along with us on the bus on Sunday afternoon. She knew everything. She helped us sell a couple places that hadn't even been listed yet." Angela wheeled out the next cart.

"The bus?" Chrissa asked.

Angela started stacking and sorting. "On Sunday afternoons, Realtors go around to scope out all the open houses, see what's there. Our agency had seventeen agents. Rather than seventeen of us trying to find parking, we'd just rent a Crown bus for the day. Stock it for the party afterward, of course. Since I rarely drink, I was the designated driver. We'd go—"

"Wait! What?" Over by the monitor, Mary stared at her. "You drive a bus?" She sounded so intense.

Cautiously, Angela replied, "I have a commercial bus endorsement on my driver's license, yes. Is that bad?"

"It's wonderful!" Mary snatched up the phone and punched a speed dial number, put it to her ear, waited…"Rose? Remember that volunteer I told you about, Angela? She has a commercial endorsement on her license! We have a driver!" Pause. "Yes!" Pause, pause. "Right away!" She good-byed and thumbed the off button.

Chrissa was helping a patron, so Angela went over to Mary and lowered her voice. "What's going on?"

"We have a chance to obtain a used bookmobile out of Duluth, but we have to have a qualified driver before we can apply to get it. On the payroll. That driver would have to go over to Duluth, get checked out on the vehicle, and then bring it here."

"No problem. A bookmobile is just a glorified bus. Or a shamefully huge motor home. When would this happen?"

"A month or two. The system can't afford to hire a driver separately just for that, so it would have to be someone with library skills."

"I see. Like when I drove the bus, but I was also one of the Realtors."

"Exactly! Angela, we want that bookmobile so badly; this Detroit Lakes area has a lot of remote library patrons and some are not computer savvy enough to link into the system. And the children; the bookmobile is so useful in helping children find pleasure in books."

Angela's whole world brightened. *"On the payroll,"* she said. "Well, I'll gladly help if I can."

"And since you don't have small children, you could be on the road a lot with no problems. Out to schools during the week and rural areas on weekends. Perfect! I'll put together the paperwork to hire you."

*"Hire you"! Woo!*

It took Angela another hour to get the reshelving completely caught up, sprinkled in between with answers to patrons' questions. She stopped by Chrissa. "If you'll handle the desk another half hour, I'll take early lunch, and then I can do the desk over lunchtime."

The girl nodded. "Works for me."

She walked to the back room, started a pot of fresh coffee, poured the last of the old pot into her supersize mug, and retrieved her lunch from the fridge.

She sat down at the Formica table and got the Letter out of her purse.

Yesterday at dinner, Lynn had said, "I talked to Pastor Evanson for an hour. I told him about our difficulty with forgiveness. He suggested that we start working on it by writing letters to the people we cannot forgive: your father, Judith; Jack; and I am writing two—one to Paul and one to God."

"Good luck getting them delivered," Judith had said.

"Oh, not to send. We use them to organize our thoughts. Write them and eventually destroy them."

So here sat Angela with the Letter. Because her mind worked best in list mode, it was actually the List. She listed all the negatives Jack had generated one way or another and a separate list of all the positives that had come out of this.

Short list of positives. But look at how weighty each item was! Finding her true self. Finding true friendship in Lynn and Judith, something she'd never had before. Much, much less stress. And there were a few frivolous items, too: getting reacquainted with creative cooking; at last having some time to herself; and most of all to rediscover the real Angela, from weight to personal interests, not the phony, dissatisfying, let's-please-Jack version. None of that would have happened were she still the old Angela.

And as she pondered this, she thought that perhaps she should forgive Jack after all. His motives were selfish, and he obviously didn't feel like honoring his promise made at the wedding altar, but in the end, he had done her great good. Tonight she would write the Letter itself to him, forgiving him; it was a start.

What would be the next step, then? Lynn would have more ideas about that.

She thought for a few moments about that call from

Gwynn days ago and how distraught her daughter had been. She reached for a pencil to add to her list. She had been so wounded by Jack's perfidy that she had not paused to think about the effect on Charles and Gwynn. The kids were so torn up. On the other hand, what could she do about it? Jack was the one. Always it came back to that. Jack was the one.

And she was furious with him all over again. He was using the children to get to her. After destroying their world, he was using them, sucking them into the mess.

And then she reminded herself that they were her off-spring, but they weren't children, not anymore. They were adults, and they had the power to choose—choose to get sucked in and choose to back off. And yet, she had spent decades raising them; she still had an obligation to them; to herself as their mother, if not them.

So confusing and convoluted and all because Jack... there it was again. Jack.

She studied the Lists, looking for answers that were not there.

Forgiveness. That was the first step. Forgive. She would do that for the children. She even drafted the first paragraph before she put her empty lunch sack in the trash and went back out on the desk.

Chrissa hopped up and headed for the lunchroom. No, the bathroom. Angela took her seat as another patron stepped up to the desk.

Mary appeared an hour later with a fistful of papers. Between checking out books and answering questions, it was five minutes before Angela could see what the papers were.

"All this just to get hired?" Forms. Statements. Tax things. Regulations. *Good grief.* "Should I do this now or take them home and bring them back to you tomorrow?"

"Tomorrow is fine. Angela, I'm so glad you can do this!"

"Not as glad as I am to be able to do this for you." She folded them in half, ran back to the lunchroom, and slipped them into her purse. Then back out to the desk.

A towheaded boy stepped up, so short he could probably rest his chin on the desk. "Mrs. Bishop, I have to find out about fur trapping for Cub Scouts."

"Fur trapping. There's a computer open over there. Let's go see if we can find you some resources. We'll also check the shelves. I think we can learn a lot about fur trapping."

She spent less than five minutes showing him search engines. Being young, he grabbed the concept intuitively and cackled with glee. Then they looked up some book titles in the online catalogue and went to the shelves. Crowing "Wow! This is perfect, Mrs. Bishop!" he checked out four books and left.

*Mrs. Bishop.* Here was something else to think about. Once the divorce was final, should she keep Bishop or take back her maiden name? How would it affect the kids? She would run it past them both first, that was for sure.

Twenty minutes before closing, she reshelved everything in the carts. She would not leave undone work for the people who opened tomorrow. Then the flurry of checkouts as closing time approached. Finally she could gently shoo out the last of the lingerers.

The cleaning lady, Claire, came in. "Good evening, Angela!"

"Good evening, Claire. How is Doodie?"

"Much better. The incision is healing nicely. And the kids went through the yard very, very carefully, picking up anything he might gulp down. One paper wad blocking his gut was enough."

"I'm happy to hear it. Have a good evening."

"You, too." Claire headed for the janitorial closet and Angela walked out into the night.

And froze. Her mouth dropped open.

Jack.

He stood there smiling. "Angela."

"What do you want?"

"To talk to you."

"Talk to my lawyer. That's what she's there for."

"No! I need to talk to *you*." He stepped forward quickly and clasped both her hands in his. "I love you, Angela."

"*I love you*." She tried to think of the last time he'd said that. She couldn't. As far back as she could remember, never had he said that. Could it be that Gwynn was right and he was in fact changed? That he had somehow awakened to what he had lost?

He pressed on. "I saw a little café down the street half a block, a diner, and it's open all night. Let's sit down there and talk. That's all. Just talk."

She let herself be led down the street, past her car parked at the curb, to the gaudy neon facade of the Stop Inn Diner. Expressing forgiveness face-to-face would be better than writing a letter. Gwynn was right; she should at least talk to him.

And what would she do if he was as changed as Gwynn thought? Could she put the past behind? She was suddenly very uncertain and confused.

And hungry. She had been planning to eat leftovers when she got home, but since they were here...

"What would you like?" Jack pulled the menu off the clip and studied both sides. "How's their meat loaf?"

"Quite good."

The waitress appeared, pencil in hand.

"The meat loaf, but I don't want the gravy on it. And I want French fries instead of the mashed potatoes."

Good old Jack; he never simply ordered off the menu, he had to change it, presumably to improve on it. Same as he had done with his wife, Angela realized with a start.

"The Reuben, please." Angela smiled at her. The child didn't look sixteen and here she was working the late shift.

"Lettuce?"

"Please."

He watched the waitress leave. "I thought lettuce always came with it."

Silence.

Long silence.

She said, "My lawyer still hasn't heard anything about the house sale yet. Is there a hang-up?"

He cleared his throat. "My lawyer's working on it. Little snag, nothing serious."

Long, long silence.

"So, uh, Angela, how have you been doing? The kids say you're getting by okay."

No, she could not forgive him face-to-face. She would have to work out the Letter, find the appropriate phrasing. His unexpected appearance had sort of unhorsed her. "Doing fine."

More long silence.

He broke it with, "Your address is a box number now. That's the only one I could find."

"My lawyer didn't tell you where to find me, did she?"

"No, the kids did."

Anger boiled up all over again. She must not let it cloud her judgment.

Long, long, awkward silence. Minutes passed.

He leaned forward. "Look. I made a mistake. A big mistake. I'm sorry. But now I want to unmake it. I want you back."

She tried to arrange her thoughts, marshal an intelligent response. It didn't rise to the surface of her brain where she could articulate it. Good thing she was putting off the forgiveness letter; her brain was tongue-tied. "Well, uh, a decision that big would require a lot of thought."

He spread his hands. "What's to think about? I admit I made a big mistake. Now let's just start over."

"It's not that easy, Jack."

"Of course it is. I've changed. I want to start over. That's pretty simple, right?" He watched her expectantly, waiting for the answer he wanted to hear.

*Waiting for the answer he wanted.* Of course. She recognized that for the first time, this expecting the "correct" answer, the one he wanted. And she realized that in the past, she had always provided it, never once thinking about what she might want instead. He let her know what he wanted, and it was up to her to provide it. And she always had.

She watched his face. "Have you ever considered what I might want?"

He shrugged. "We want the same things; we've always wanted the same things. The kids are all upset and getting back together will take care of that. We want that."

"Why did you not want that when you filed?"

"I wasn't thinking. But that's all behind me. Now I just want us to be happy again."

"I'm happy now."

"Oh, don't give me that, Angela! A woman can't be happy without her man." He sat back as the meat loaf arrived. The waitress plunked ketchup down on the table and returned in a moment with the Reuben. She left.

He leaned forward again. "You need me. And I need you. The kids need us. See? Nothing more to think about."

She picked up her Reuben and savored that first bite. The

corned beef was juicy and not too salty, the sauerkraut mellow. They made great sandwiches here. In fact, she might make Reubens some night for dinner. All the ingredients were at hand in their pantry—even homemade bread.

He cut into his meat loaf. "It's not hot in the middle. I'll bet this was frozen five minutes ago."

*Of course it was. Do you think they keep their meat loaf ready for when you happen to walk in?* She checked herself. *Back off. Look for the good stuff. Forgiveness, don't forget.*

The Letter. She asked, "Your mailing address is the same, right?"

"Uh, no. I'm not at the house right now."

"Who is?"

He looked guilty, then defiant. "Doesn't matter. Soon as my lawyer works out the details, I'll move back in."

She thought about this. Flagged the waitress and asked for tea. Thought. And thought.

Cold in the middle or not, he polished off the last of his meat loaf and sat back. "You look very librarian-ish."

"Probably because I am a librarian."

"Picked up some weight. Eating well, huh?"

Anger. *Quell it, Angela.* Her tea came. She took her time dipping the bag.

He leaned forward eagerly. "So what about it? When can we get back together? I was thinking maybe even tonight. I'm in that motel on the edge of town. We'll have a good time getting back together. For old times' sake. And the kids."

She dipped the bag. The tea got darker than she liked, but she kept dipping.

"Angela?"

She kept dipping. Finally she pulled the tea bag out and leaned forward on both elbows. "You know what I think,

Jack? I think you haven't changed a minute. When I said
I was happy, you instantly called me a liar." She snapped
her fingers. "Just like that. But I was telling you the truth. I
am happy now for perhaps the first time since the kids left
home."

"I don't believe you. You're all alone."

"No, I am not. I have close friends now for the first time
in many years. Friends who support me and do their best
for me." She paused. "And I'm assuming that 'librarian-ish'
is a euphemism for frumpy. Right?"

"Well, uh, er, I wouldn't call it that. Not exactly. But—"

"But I'm not ultra-ritzy anymore. No longer arm candy in
your eyes."

"That's not it at all! Look, Angela, I want us back together.
What the kids want. So let's just do it instead of talking it to
death."

"And I finally rediscovered that I can think and function
as a human being, a fully human human being, and not just
an adjunct of you."

"Then start thinking straight. If you—"

"Thinking straight? You'd be surprised. Now I'm going to
think some more. This Marillee." His face went blank. She
pressed on. "Yes, I know her name. I would assume that
she's the floozy that you traded me off for. You showed her
around the house, and she liked it so much she wanted to
live there. So you rescinded your offer to sell your half and
asked to buy my half instead."

"You're just guessing."

"Now I'm going to guess you gave her half ownership of
the house in return for paying the mortgage because you
couldn't afford it just then. And now she's in the house and
she's kicked you out. Am I right?" She watched his face
a moment with smug satisfaction. "And I can see that I'm

right on. No, you're not going to buy my half of the house. I think you're broke. And probably in debt. And you need me to get back into real estate and make some money to bail you out and get your house back for you."

"Do you really...?"

"Am I wrong?"

"That's not...I mean...We...we have to think about the kids!"

"Oh, I'm sure you'll go whining to the kids about how stubborn and unyielding I am and how I'm ruining your life, but frankly, Jack, I don't give a rip. You forced me off onto a path I never would have chosen for myself, but I'm going to stay on it because I. Am. Happy!"

His lower lip trembled. She saw fury in his face that she'd never seen before. And she understood now, finally, that she had never seen it because she had always bowed immediately to his will before. This was the first time she ever opposed him, the very first time.

And it gave her strength!

He bolted to his feet and stormed out.

She stared at her tea. She was boiling inside and could not figure out why at first. Eventually she decided that it was a play of intense emotions at war with each other.

So what would she do next?

She got the Lists and the first paragraph of the Letter out of her purse, looked at them a moment...

...and tore them up into a bazillion little pieces.

# Chapter Twenty-Nine

J udith came out into the kitchen. Tom was there and Phillip. Both of them were wearing jeans that were wet and muddy to above the knee. Mud streaked their clothes and arms. And both were perched on stools at the counter wrapping themselves around pieces of Lynn's latest pie. This one was peach using the peaches from that farm stand down the road. And ice cream, of course. Peach pie must be à la mode.

She slapped a paper down at Tom's elbow. He jumped. Stared at it. Grinned wide. "I *knew* you could do it!"

Phillip asked with his mouth full, "What's that?"

"Her last regular exam and she scored eighty-nine. Out of a hundred, right?" He looked at her.

"Yes, and I stand a good chance of acing the final. I was terribly afraid I'd have to take precalc over again when I started the class. Tom, you are an amazing teacher! But then, I think I already said that." She sat down on a stool nearby.

He was smiling. "I think I heard that once or twice. And you told me when you came back from that first exam that your prof was looking for good math instructors."

"Dr. Stern."

"Yeah. So I made an appointment to sit down with her

and we talked awhile. Actually, what it was, she asked me to explain factorials, so I did. And then she asked me to explain logs, so I did. Then she whips this old slide rule out of her desk and said, 'Can you show me how to use this?' Sure, it's based on logs. So I showed her how it is set up and how to multiply, divide, take square roots and cube roots—you know, just the basic stuff."

"Tom, that was a job interview!"

"And she hired me."

Judith squealed. It wasn't a congratulatory squeal, just a disorganized, thrilled, and delighted one.

Phillip was grinning as broadly as everyone else. "He's teaching math lab sessions both winter semesters, Judith. And since he's at the school anyway, he's enrolling in the master's program. Someday this will be Professor Thomas Lundberg." Phillip stuffed more pie into his mouth.

Tom cut himself another piece. "It fits perfectly. Winter is always slow in the plumber's shop. Repairs, yes, and broken pipes, but for some crazy reason, we can't dig for new plumbing."

Judith laughed. "Of course. The world is frozen solid."

Tom scooped ice cream onto his pie. "I can teach the lab sessions and do some plumbing and still have plenty of time for ice fishing. My kind of winter." He paused and turned to look Judith directly in the eye. "You got me started. You showed me the way and even provided the door. Thank you, Judith."

That evening Judith settled at her desk by the window and just spent some time looking out. So Tom was also setting out along a new road in life. And he credited Judith with that. Was it true? Was she a helper as well as one being helped? True or not, the thought absolutely delighted her.

The next day, her biology course loomed, her other

nemesis. She had conquered one dragon, math, with Tom's help, but this biology...The biology she had learned those many years ago was not the biology she faced now. Then it had been all plants and animals, and of course, digestion and things. She had loved it. Now it was pretty much organic chemistry with a few life-forms thrown in. The structure of messenger RNA, the chemistry of foods going down and digestion going on and wastes coming out, in all the myriad animal and plant kingdoms and...What? The mushrooms and other fungi are not plants? They now have their own kingdom?

The previous session had been the last *how-am-I-doing* test before the final exam. Today she would get that test back. In theory, the test showed you your strong fields and weak areas, and of course, you would then spend your study time boning up on the weak fields before the final. But that was theory. She felt rather swamped by all of it.

She slid into her seat and flopped open her laptop. It was easiest to take notes on her laptop, then later print them out to study. Rereading notes in both electronic form and hard copy seemed to help her remember better.

Professor Thompson's graduate assistant returned the exams simply by shouting a name. That person called "yo" and raised an arm; helpful hands would then pass the test to its owner. Fairly efficient, just like Dr. Thompson.

Judith's came to her, folded in half with the grade concealed, as were they all. She opened the fold. A green-circled eighty-three greeted her. Eighty-three, B, better than she thought she would do but certainly not an A.

The doctor then began his lecture; Judith had to work to keep up as he expounded on the significance of the structural integrity of the double DNA helix and the value of apoptosis. She had no idea what he was talking about until she realized that the second *p* in *apoptosis* is not pronounced. She had read her text; now it made sense. She felt a certain heady flush of pride in working out that little factoid. The hour came to an end and she gathered her laptop and notepad (for drawing diagrams that she could not draw in Word) into her backpack. Like all the other students, she swung her pack around onto her back and stood erect. Like all the other students, she headed for the door.

Eighty-three. She would have to be content with that and hope intelligence lightning would somehow strike her before the final. And she believed in intelligence lightning like she believed in the tooth fairy.

"Ms. Rutherford?" Dr. Thompson flagged her on her way out.

"Yes?"

"I always want to learn what helps my students learn. Your scores have been rising all semester; this was your best score yet. What is making the difference?"

She thought about it. "Honestly, I don't know. A knowledgeable friend is tutoring me in precalculus. My grades in that course have come way up. Does that sort of success rub off on other courses?"

"Interesting. I wonder."

"Also, I'm getting into the swing of college better. Into the rhythm of it. I attended UM for one year nearly thirty years ago; I've had to get used to academic life again."

He nodded, smiling. "Are you being tutored in biology?"

"No, sir. Not that I couldn't use some."

"You know, one of the advantages of a small college is that your professors are here to help you. All you have to do is ask."

Judith sucked in a deep breath and nodded. "I'm not used to asking for help. I was raised to work it out myself."

"Well, if you need help, please know that my TA and I are both happy to. Our office hours are posted in the syllabus."

"Thank you, sir."

Her phone binged on her way out to the car. She checked the screen: *T Lundberg*. "Hi, Tom. What's up?"

"How did you do?"

"The best so far this semester, but it's only an eighty-three." She unlocked her car door and slung her backpack in, left the door open to let some of the heat out. "Clearly he thinks I should have asked for help a long time ago. Hey, but thank you for asking. Where are you guys working today?"

"Other side of the lake. Eighty-three ain't bad. Later."

*Not bad, huh?* She slid into her very hot car. Thank God for air-conditioning. She was waiting at a stoplight when her phone binged again. Lynn.

"I'm almost out of sugar; can you stop and get me a twenty-five-pound bag and three boxes of regular lids?"

"Sure, anything else?"

"Not that I can think of. Thanks. How did your exam go?"

"Got a B. Can you believe Tommy called, too?" *Do you know how wonderful it feels to have people who care enough to ask?*

"Of course. See you soon. Oh, and we caught the counter cruiser in the act. We set him up and he went for it. Later."

Judith chuckled her way to the grocery store. And sang her way home. She needed to call Melody tonight and catch her up on life in the west.

Homer charged up to greet her when she parked her car, his tail whirling in a circle. She had learned that language of the tail wagging; in a circle was the happiest, used for greeting those he loved. Side to side, swinging his entire hind end was a close second. He greeted most people with a gentle wag, and no wag was from severe scolding or total distrust, and then the ridge of hair on his back stood at attention. As he wagged all over, she cupped his face in both of her hands, his long ears wrinkling, his eyes dancing.

"Yes, I see you, and I say hello to you and thank you for the wonderful welcome. What have you been up to? Counter cruising, I hear." She reached over and rubbed chest and belly. She slipped into her backpack so that she could juggle the sack of sugar and the lids with both hands.

As she reached the back door, Miss Priss shoved open the screen door. "I didn't think you would ever get here."

"Hello to you, too. What have you been up to?"

"Helping G'ma. We picked raspberries this morning and we just made jam and we almost ran out of sugar." The little girl danced beside her as she entered the kitchen and set the sugar by the counter.

"To the rescue. Oh my goodness, but it smells heavenly in here." Judith gazed with admiration; brilliant red pints of raspberry jam decorated the counter, including the bowl with the skimmings in it.

"I baked that dough I had in the fridge, so we have fresh jam to spread on fresh bread." Lynn grinned at her. "Are you a heel or a middle type person?"

"Fresh bread? Definitely heel." She watched Lynn slice her bread loaf. "You are amazing. You stand in the kitchen, turn around three times, and suddenly there are delectable goodies. You don't even have to wave a wand. So how did you catch the counter thief?"

Lynn chuckled and opened a jam container. "It was Travis's idea. You know what paintball is?"

"Where people with more money than brains run around in the woods shooting colored dyes at each other."

"That's it. We got some neon-green paintballs, folded one inside a slice of bologna, and laid it out on the counter.

Someone snatched the bologna and exploded the paintball. Green dye all over his face."

Judith spent a merry little while laughing. She gripped Homer's face and examined it closely. "How did you get the green off?"

"Oh, the dye is washable and biodegradable. Harmless. Wait till you see the pictures from my phone."

"G'ma said we had to wait for you to have bread and *jam*! Pretty, huh?"

Lynn was slathering three pieces luxuriously in raspberry jam. She handed them out, the heel to Judith.

Judith started to take a bite, but Miss Priss raised a finger. "No! All at once. One, two, three." She signaled with one hand, her bread in the other, and they all took their bites just as she said. Or rather ordered.

Lynn and Judith rolled their eyes at the instructor and kept on chewing.

"This is almost as good as the first strawberry shortcake was." Judith vigorously brushed her fingers off on each other.

"That's going some. Is this enough for lunch, or do you two want more?"

"How are salads with raspberries on it and that leftover chicken we have?" Judith backed off her stool.

"I'll have cookies, please." Miss Priss licked her fingers.

"Right after you have salad," Lynn corrected. She looked at Judith. "Are you going to study?"

"My online social studies course. An original essay and three chapter reviews. The short answer being yes."

"You go do your schoolwork. We'll bring your lunch up to you." Lynn was smiling. "We want to encourage interest in school." She glanced at Miss Priss.

"Thank you, Lynn. This scholar appreciates it." She rubbed Miss Priss's head. "You make really good jam!"

"I make good cookies, too."

Lynn snorted. "Go do your schoolwork, Judith. Miss Priss and I are going to have a brief discussion about receiving compliments gracefully." Grandma's eyes were laughing.

Judith settled at her desk by the window. She saw quite a number of various boats out on the lake and it wasn't even the weekend. The chill of that canoe spill hit her unexpectedly. Would she ever get over it? She had seen Angela out in the canoe several times since their capsize. Phillip had taken her out a few days later and showed her survival tricks, and now Angela seemed perfectly comfortable fishing from the canoe. He had invited Judith, too, but she had demurred. She shouldn't have, but...

In a way, she envied Angela's resilience, her ability to work past horrific events. Her divorce. That accident. Shucks, being married to that guy; that must have required a lot of resilience.

And was Judith resilient? Not a bit. Just like her father. He never got over his wife's untimely death, and neither had Judith, not really. And he never moved an inch past his accident. Instead, he ruined Judith's life, insisting she take care of him forever while he sat there. Looking back, she should have just left. But that would have meant cutting herself off from the only life she knew, losing the security of her home and her family. Not to mention abandoning her father when he needed her. And Judith had never been a risk taker.

Could Judith change, become more flexible and embrace life better, like Lynn and Angela did?

She was mooning instead of working. She signed into the class site. First order of business: a thousand-word essay. She went down the list of suggested topics; she did not have to choose from the list—the instructor insisted this was just to get creative juices flowing. Basically she wanted students to describe how a person's culture shaped that person's attitudes, going into detail. But her list was boring topics, all of them. And then Judith's creative juices rose to the occasion. She pulled up a blank page in Word and typed in her topic:

Resilience as Shaped by One's Microculture

She was getting hungry. Judith looked at the clock. Gone, the afternoon was gone. The salad dish Lynn and Miss Priss had brought up sat empty beside her, her iced tea glass drained. She stared at the computer. How could she spend three hours and not even think of getting up? No phone ringing, no house noise—where was everyone? Her work completed for the moment, she ambled out to the kitchen; no one, and no one out on the deck. Hearing shrieks of laughter, she looked to the dock where all five grands, Lynn, and Angela were playing in the lake. Feeling both left out and grateful for the productive time, she went down the stairs and across the lawn to join them.

Now that she was used to having kids around, she was surprised to find that she enjoyed it. Well, in moderation.

"Go put your suit on," Lynn called with a wave.

"No thanks, I'm not much into swimming in lakes." The thought of bloodsuckers made her cringe. That and a gunky bottom.

"You can swim off the dock."

"That's okay. I'll just come and dangle my feet." She kept her gaze from the canoe. She knew she ought to get back on the horse, er, canoe to get over her fear. On the other hand, why? So far she had lived her whole life without going out in canoes.

There were more people than ever playing on docks or out in boats and canoes all over the lake. Sails of red and blue and white and stripes dotted the water. She sat down on the dock, Homer came to sit beside her, and she swung her feet into the lake. Travis jumped off the T of the dock, setting it to bobbing.

Lynn came out of the water to sit beside her. "It really feels good."

"Another time."

Miss Priss scrambled up. Something black on her leg. She looked down. "Oh, ick. G'ma, will you take this thing off, please?"

Judith closed her eyes. A bloodsucker on the little girl's leg—biology gone amok.

"Dad says you have to take off your own suckers," Travis yelled from off the end of the dock.

"I can't."

"All right, Travis, when she's bigger she will." Lynn reached over and pulled the horrid thing off and threw it over toward the reeds. "Let's go put some ammonia and salve on that."

"I'll take her up." Judith got to her feet and took Miss Priss's hand. "Do you need a Band-Aid, too?"

"No, I'm big now."

And resilient, just like the rest of her family, her microcosm. Maybe Judith should revise her essay slightly before sending it in.

Up at the house, she splashed on ammonia and applied the salve, watching as the child ran out the door and back down to the lake. No doubt to go right back in the water.

She debated. Go back down, go study some more, or bake that cake Lynn had gotten the recipe out for. She said it could all be stirred up in one pan. She looked at the card on the counter. Chocolate Wacky Cake. Lynn had made it before and it was really good.

*Mise en place*, Lynn always insisted. *Meeze ahn plahss.*
Judith and Angela both called it "mess in place" with a
smile. First, get out everything you are going to need, so you
know you have everything. Judith turned on the oven and
got out the cake pan, the measuring cups and spoons, and
all the ingredients, including vinegar, which had surprised
her, noncook that she was. She put the ingredients in the
pan, poured the water over it, stirred it, and slid it into the
heated oven. Carefully she set the timer for forty minutes.
By the time she put things away and wiped off the counter,
the time was half gone.

What to do while she waited? She fetched one of the
books that were required reading for her biology class.
*Guns, Germs, and Steel* by Jared Diamond. She had never
heard of the author, but apparently he was famous and
highly prominent. This was one of Dr. Thompson's favorite
books because to read it, he said, you should have a working
knowledge of biology, geology, geography, and sociology. It
was on Dr. Pollan's list of recommended books as well.

She was on page ninety-seven when all the lake lovers
came trooping in, laughing and teasing. "Oh, something
sure smells good." Dan, the youngest boy and a miniature
version of Tom, sniffed his way over to the oven. "What're
you making?"

"Wacky cake. I thought we could have it with ice cream."

Lynn nodded to her. "Good for you."

"I watched you before and followed the instructions on
the card." The fragrance of baking chocolate made her
mouth water. Chocolate cake just out of the oven—what a
way to celebrate her latest math score, if not her biology
score.

The timer buzzed. Judith reached for the oven door.

"Get a toothpick to check for doneness."

"Oh, that's right." Judith got a toothpick from the cupboard, gently pulled out the cake pan, and stuck the toothpick in. It pulled out clean. She set the pan on the rack on the counter and stared at it. Something was wrong.

"It's a little bit flat," Travis said.

"Well, sometimes those things happen. It will taste more like brownies this way, no problem. You go get the ice cream."

Angela sniffed above the cake pan. "Risen properly or not, it smells wonderful."

"By the time everyone washes up, it should be cool enough to cut. Ice cream on hot cake, what a treat for today." The kids scrambled for the downstairs bathroom and the women headed for theirs. When everyone gathered in the kitchen again, Judith had set out plates and forks.

The four boys picked up their forks and started pounding them on the counter along with their chant, "Let's eat cake. Let's eat cake."

Judith shook her head, laughing at them. "It's coming, it's coming."

She cut and put the pieces on the plates, Angela dished scoops of ice cream on top of cake, and they passed them out. Dan cut off a big bite and grinned as he put it in his mouth. His eyes got round, then his face scrunched and he spit it out.

"Dan, what?"

"G'ma, it's icky."

Lynn took a bite without the ice cream. "Oh. That's why it didn't rise right."

"Why?"

"You forgot the sugar. Now, don't panic, it's okay, we'll dig out the fudge syrup and crumble the cake in it, then the ice cream."

Judith stared at the cake. She picked up a crumb and tasted. "Sorry, guys. Euw, that's bad." *My first cake and I blew it.*

Davey frowned at his piece of cake. "Do chickens have taste buds?"

Judith wagged her head. "I doubt even the chickens would want it."

Lynn smiled. "We've all had things like that happen. No big deal."

"I passed biology and flunked cake baking. What a day."

"And I got a sucker on me. A big fat bloodsucker." But Miss Priss didn't seem to care at all.

Yes, this sprightly little girl would indeed go into Judith's essay.

# Chapter Thirty

"I love my new job!" Angela literally danced into the room. Judith looked up from her keyboard. "You were already working there."

"How can you sit there studying when the world is right outside that window?"

"If I go outside, I will get involved in that world, and right now I have to focus on this. Job?"

"I'm taking over the children's section, which is my first love, we're setting up a new help desk, and we won the bid for our bookmobile; I go over to Duluth next month and pick it up. Pure fun, and for that I get a paycheck, which relieves a whole different set of concerns."

"You were worried about finances?"

"It was creeping in." Angela stood in front of the window, watching the clouds pile up to the north. "Look at those thunderheads. Have you ever seen clouds more spectacular?"

"Please, no, don't tell me things like that. I won't look right now."

"You have far more self-control than I have ever had. I envy your discipline."

"My father forced me into it."

"Actually that is something you should be thankful for."

She could feel Judith's stare in her back and so turned around. "Just a thought."

Judith was still staring. "No, you are right. I think I should consider what other positive traits I got from him. And my mother." She went back to her laptop.

Angela wandered out onto the deck facing the lake. Lynn sat there doing a crossword puzzle and sipping a bright red raspberry-laced-something-ade. Angela turned around, went to the kitchen, and found the pitcher in the fridge. She poured herself a tall tumbler of raspberry something, tossed in a few ice cubes, and went back out.

She fully intended to go sit at the other end, so as not to disturb Lynn, but Lynn dropped her crossword puzzle magazine on the floor. "Come sit, unless you'd like to be alone and rest."

"I won't disturb you?"

"Heavens no. I only do crosswords when I'm bored."

Angela sat down beside her. "Late afternoon is just as gorgeous as morning or evening or stormy weather."

"It is." Lynn sipped a moment. "I have another appointment with Pastor Evanson tomorrow morning. Looking for suggestions as we take the next step, you might say."

"Oh, good. I look forward to learning what he has to say. I'm pretty much stuck in my rut, especially since Jack showed up and I could really see...uh-oh." Angela pointed. "That escape artist chicken is out."

"Oh, dear." Lynn stood up. "Miss Priss was here very early wanting to look for eggs. I'll bet she failed to close the chicken yard ga—"

Homer's loud howling from behind the house stopped her in midsentence. He was baying in an odd way. Angela leaped off the porch and ran. What was happening?! A chicken squawked. Not just one of their testy complaining squawks or even a *Help! A raccoon!* squawk. It was far more frantic than that.

Lynn arrived behind the garage a few strides ahead of Angela.

"*Homer, no!*" they both shrieked.

The dog had Henny Penny in his mouth and was shaking his head vigorously! His whole body rippled; those impossible ears flapped wildly.

"Let loose!" Lynn grabbed his head and jaws. "Let her go, Homer!"

Angela straddled him from behind and closed her hands over his windpipe.

Homer let Lynn pull the hen from his mouth. Angela stayed on him, holding him.

Lynn was near tears as she cradled the wet, bloody hen. "She's lost. Look. Her wing, her leg, that puncture wound in her back." She gripped the head, stood up, and swung the chicken suddenly in a circle. Angela had never seen a bird's neck wrung before. It was unnerving. Henny Penny made a few feeble kicks and went limp.

"Homer..." Lynn seemed to have run out of words.

Angela stood up, stooping to keep a firm hand on Homer's collar. "Well, it's obvious that Homer and Judith's chicken project cannot coexist. Which one are you going to send to a new home?"

"Neither."

"Lynn, Homer's a chicken killer!" Angela felt vaguely frantic herself, her nerves dancing beneath her skin.

"Homer is a basset hound! Bassets have been bred for hundreds of years to go after small game. He was being what he is, a hunter. I will not get rid of him for being what he is."

Angela gave up the argument. She was too overwrought anyway to mount a reasonable response. She looked over at the chicken run. The yard gate was ajar. Miss Priss had not quite closed it all the way and their escape artist had used the opportunity to get out, followed by the hens. Would it happen again? Quite probably. If not Miss Priss, then someone else; since it had been raccoon-proofed, the gate was not easy to secure.

Lynn took over Homer's collar. "I'll put him in the mudroom until we get the chickens back in."

Angela stepped back and watched Lynn lead/drag the dog to the house, then started walking back around to the front. And stopped cold. *Homer, being what he is.* Lynn did not penalize Homer for being what he is. He had shown his true colors: he was a destroyer who could not be trusted, and Lynn did not trust him. But in essence, she forgave him. Showed mercy.

*Jack is being what he is.* It rang in her head. Jack damaged his wife and children and wrecked his stable home, even his future; he stood to lose everything. He was a destroyer who could not be trusted. But Angela could forgive him, show mercy, as Lynn had done, and let him continue being what he is.

What a wonderfully freeing thought! Not forget, but forgive; not wish vengeance or payback, just forgive. She would tell the children about her forgiveness, but they must forgive him and Angela on their own terms, in their own time. After all these months the world was falling into place. Angela started scouting for chickens to chase them home.

Storm clouds gathered that made the job much easier; the chickens headed for the safety of their run. Lynn joined Angela on the deck. She said Judith had been quiet when she told her what happened. Sad, no doubt, but she seemed accepting. The storm came ferociously, and

Angela marveled at how powerful—and how brief—these storms could be.

That night the storm blew out, and the world smelled rain fresh, a fragrance compounded of trees and flowers and who knew what else, as the three gathered for their nightly stargazing. Judith had Homer beside her. She didn't hold what happened to Henny Penny against him. In fact, she seemed to have accepted it far better than Angela had initially.

"You better mosquito up; the breeze died," Lynn warned, slapping repellent on her legs and arms.

"Ta-da!" Judith held up a pink plastic bottle with a dispenser on top.

Angela frowned. "Baby lotion?"

Judith spread it over her arms. "A classmate says it is supposed to be the best mosquito repellent there is. We'll see." She started slathering it on her ankles.

"How come they don't bother me?"

"Because you're too skinny," Judith said with a grin. "They like blood with some fat in it. Like mine, for instance. Prime quality."

"You're not fat."

"No, but I'm middle-aged plump, and next to most of my classmates, I'm fat." Judith licked her lips. "Confession: for the longest time, Angela, I envied you, so lithe and rail thin, looking so good in a sheath dress. It's how I always wanted to be, but I never was. And then I started thinking about what it cost you to get that look and how it didn't make any difference in the long run, and I don't envy you anymore."

An owl hooted as it passed, its huge wings pumping soundlessly.

"Did you see that?" Angela asked, startled.

Lynn nodded. "Great horned owl. He lives in the trees on the other side of the road, not a stranger here. He or she, it might be a she."

"I heard hooting a few months ago, baritone. That was him? Her?"

Lynn nodded.

Judith looked at Angela. "You let little hints out here and there about what your marriage was like, and the more I heard the more I was afraid you'd go back to him."

Angela smiled. "Funny thing. Mary said she was hiring me just moments before Jack showed up that night."

"Our great God in action. He promises to prepare us for whatever is coming. I wonder…" Lynn's voice trailed off. The evening choruses were in full glory. The moon threw a trail of glimmer across the lake.

A bit later, Angela asked, "You wonder what?"

"I wonder if God tried to prepare me for Paul's death and I was not aware of it. The shock of that phone call, Phillip sobbing, I couldn't even understand him. I knew it was him because of his number, but…" She sniffed and reached for the tissues they kept at hand. "I kept saying, 'What? What are you saying?' Someone else took his phone and told me that Paul had collapsed and was gone by the time the ambulance got there. I guess Tommy kept on doing CPR until they dragged him off Paul and replaced him with a CPR machine."

Homer put both front feet on Lynn's hip, whimpering and trying to get close enough to lick her tears away.

She blew and continued, "The autopsy showed the aortic aneurysm. It just suddenly blew out, ripped open. The doctor said it happened so fast he never knew what hit him. And no pain."

*What to say?* Angela nodded.

Lynn smiled sadly. "I keep trying to find bright spots. You know, there aren't many."

"Yet," Angela amended.

"Yet. Yes. We had a second daughter; six months old, she died of crib death one night. We didn't talk about her. A bright spot is Paul finally gets to meet her."

"What was her name?"

"Amanda Lynn, after her grandmothers. I know I shall see her again one day, too."

"Well, don't be in a big hurry, okay? We got a lot of living to do first." Angela tried to envision losing a child. It didn't compute.

"So very true. But you know what a comfort it is to know that you'll see those you love again?"

Judith nodded solemnly. "I thought of that often when my mother died, but with her, I was so grateful she was finally free of the horrid pain she endured for so long. I could see her walking again and digging in her roses, smiling and laughing. Do you think there are rose beds in heaven?"

"Someone told me that all the things we delight in here on earth, like fresh strawberries, are just a foretaste of heaven. Rose beds specifically? Who knows?"

Angela sighed. So much heartache, all three of them. And yet, such a deep feeling of peace. "I cannot begin to thank God enough for what I am feeling right now. Peace."

They sat in silence awhile.

Did Angela dare to get extremely personal? She risked it. "Lynn, are you still angry at Paul?"

"I don't know. I hope not; one of the things Pastor Evanson and I will chat about tomorrow. I suspect anger is nothing more than a grief attack—again—with a big dollop of menopause. And that, I understand, is part of the process.

A friend told me her husband died ten years ago, and still, something can trigger tears all over again. But she also said, the tears don't stay around as long as they used to and that someone else told her that grief was like that."

"Interesting," Angela mused, "how often we help each other because of something we've been through."

"Or something we've learned about from others." Judith picked up her empty glass. "The day I can let go of all the things my father did in his anger and lashing out, that day will be a miracle. I need to get to bed; I have an eight o'clock again. One more week and finals." She stood up and stretched. "Good night, my friends."

They chorused good night to her as she left.

The moon (gibbous waxing was the descriptive term, Angela had learned) now sailed high enough above the land to be hidden by the trees. The sky glowed all around it.

"When do you start full-time?" Lynn asked a bit later.

"Monday. I am lucky enough to have the early shift. And we take turns on those nights that the library is open late. You ever go to the farmer's market in town?"

"Not really; got enough stuff here to eat."

Angela nodded. They sure did. "I was looking at the paper today and I am constantly amazed at all the things that go on around here. I'm thinking we might go to the concert out at the lakeshore park. Someone said they are really good."

"Good idea."

"I want to get more involved in this community. This is my home now and I finally have time for that." The baby lotion was working pretty well so far. "How are you coming with the quilts you were working on?"

"I'm thinking to set up the quilt rack so we can tie one off. We usually do that at the church, but perhaps we can do one here. If it were my quilt, I would just put it on the machine and go at it."

Angela stood and held out a hand. "Let's go set that up."

"Now?"

"Why not?" She pulled Lynn to her feet. "Then when anyone has some time, they can go tie knots."

Lynn was smiling as they went inside. "While we continue to untie our own."

# Chapter Thirty-One

Lynn glanced at her watch as she got out of the car. She was a couple minutes early, but that was all right. She would be happy to wait for Pastor Evanson. He came out of his office door; obviously he'd been watching for her. "I thought to go walking on the riverbank. It's a gorgeous morning."

"Good idea!" Lynn fell in beside him to walk the two blocks from the church down to the river.

Riverside Park. Just a small plot of land mowed when the city found some money to send the gang mower out; it wasn't often. Apparently, their pockets were a little short this month, but the grass was growing slower now.

Lynn took a deep breath of clean air. "I love this little place. I don't come here very frequently, but it's always quiet and inviting."

Pastor Evanson laughed. "You don't have to; you have peace and quiet in your home on the lake. So tell me where your mind has been going lately. You said you were angry at Paul for leaving and at God for taking him."

Lynn looked out across the river. Technically it wasn't a river, it was a creek. A puny but picturesque one. "I haven't made much progress."

"Let's start with Paul. His gravestone should say, 'This wasn't my idea.'"

Lynn laughed out loud at the thought. "I see what you're saying. He didn't want to go or intend to go. But, Pastor, if he had taken better care of his health, they might have caught the aneurysm in time to mend it. He was negligent and it took his life."

Pastor sat down on a park bench facing the water; Lynn perched beside him. "So, Lynn, how did your own MRI and ultrasound turn out? Any sign of aneurysm in your aorta? Phillip's okay?"

"Mine? I didn't...We..." And Lynn stopped. Of course. Why should she check something nobody thinks about? Except for this menopause thing, she was in perfect health. Until the moment of his death, Paul showed every sign of being in perfect health. And he didn't want to go. It was not his choice to leave her. She said quietly, "I see."

They sat a few minutes blotting up the peace.

"Now, Lynn, let's look at this anger toward God."

"I'm very sorry about that, but I can't help it. Why did he snatch away such a fine man, a man who loved Him and was doing good in the world, and leave all the creeps and crooks here?" Her voice was rising but she didn't mean it to. "It's not just! He's supposed to be a just God." She fought tears; the tears won. "I'm sorry. It's silly, but..." She sobbed.

He was smiling as he handed her a tissue. *Smiling!* "Not silly at all, Lynn. You are exploring one of the deepest mysteries of the faith: Why do the wicked prosper? It's so easy to say, 'Oh, well, this must be God's will,' and let it end there. But that's the lazy way out. I'm proud of you for tackling such a difficult question."

She blew her nose. "And I suppose you have it figured out."

"No one has it figured out. But I've pecked around the

edges of it a little. Let's explore this idea that God should leave the good people here to do good and take away the people who do bad, since you brought it up. Let's say that if you love God you live a long and happy life doing good. And if you ignore God, you die young. Where does that concept take us?"

Lynn was more of a doer than a philosophizer. She wasn't into mind games very much, but she could tell that this was an important one. So she thought about it, and the pastor gave her the time, sitting beside her silently. "The good, I guess, is that everyone would love God. That's what Jesus said everyone should do."

"I believe that's right. Everyone would love God; well, everyone sensible who can see the writing on the wall. And why would they love God?"

"Because it's, uh..." Her thoughts were jumbled. She wasn't sure how to say it or even what she wanted to say.

He said it for her. "If God rewarded His followers—His lovers—here on earth in ways you can see, then everyone would want to jump on that bandwagon. *For their own benefit*. Selfish. Love God for what it gets you. Not love God because He is the creator of the universe and the only being in all creation worthy of love and devotion. Love Him for the payback."

"But that's not love. That's manipulation."

"Exactly." Pastor Evanson handed her another tissue. "Jesus addressed this early on in His ministry, on the Sermon on the Mount. He said God makes His sun rise on the evil and the good and brings His rain to the just and the unjust. As far as you can see, He doesn't treat His believers any differently on earth. The payback comes later. Paul loves God. Not past tense, Lynn. Right now. That is the payback, and nonbelievers cannot see it. But it's very real."

Lynn was nodding. He handed her a third tissue, and between nose and tears, she got it soaking wet immediately. But this was good weeping in contrast to the weeping her loss had been dumping on her.

He sat up straighter. "I have an assignment for you. Do you have a concordance?"

"Paul did. Yes. *Young's*, I think."

"Look up *wicked* and see what the Psalms have to say about it. The fate of the wicked shows up in many other places, but concentrate on the Psalms, for now."

"I will." Lynn stood up, and her wet tissue joined the wad in her left pocket. Being a loving servant of God himself, the pastor handed her a fourth tissue. The thought made her giggle.

Her mind was racing with new thoughts now, fascinating ideas to explore. Just wait until she shared this with Angela and Judith!

And that thought stopped her in her tracks. They were not just renters. They were not strangers to come and go in her life. Today, they were sisters, to share their insights and hear Lynn's.

Part of Lynn's family.

"Lynn?" the pastor studied her, looking concerned.

She smiled. "Just counting more blessings."

"G'ma, G'ma! Come see!" Miss Priss charged through the mudroom into the kitchen. Lynn dropped everything and ran after her. Miss Priss grabbed her hand and tugged her along to the chicken yard and inside the chicken house. "Look!" She pointed into a nest box where one little brown egg nestled in the straw.

Lynn grinned. "Ah. One of the hens laid an egg already." The two bent close, gazing. "Go ahead, pick it up."

The child did so and grinned up at her grandma. "It's warm. It's not a glass one; it's a real one."

"Did you hear one of the pullets cackling? A different call than usual. That's what they do when they lay an egg. They announce it to the world."

Miss Priss held the egg carefully in the cup of her hands. "I wonder whose it is."

"Well, you watch tomorrow morning. Or if you hear any of them cackling at the top of their voice, go see who just left a nest."

Miss Priss carried the egg carefully into the house. "Where is Miss Judith?"

Lynn checked the clock. "Still in school. She has her precalc final today. She should be home soon." And tomorrow was the biology final, her bugbear, so most likely Judith would be holed up reviewing. Were it Lynn, she'd probably not sleep tonight but cram all night. But Judith was more disciplined than Lynn had ever been.

Lynn smiled. *Ah, exuberance.* "I need to can green beans. You want to help?"

Judith pulled into the driveway and parked. She put on her backpack—much more convenient than carrying it in hand—and walked around back to the chicken yard. Lynn must be canning green beans; the chickens were eagerly feasting on pointy bean tips. Judith refilled the laying mash tray. They should start laying soon.

She swung her pack off her back as she entered the kitchen singing, *"Freudig, wie ein Held zum Siegen, wie ein Held zum Siegen!"* She plopped on a stool.

Lynn and Miss Priss stared at her. Miss Priss blurted, "What's that!"

Lynn and Judith both laughed. Judith explained, "It's

from Beethoven's Ninth Symphony, and it's called 'Ode to Joy.' The words are from a poem in German. It urges you to go through life with joy like that of a victorious knight. I am happy and victorious!"

"Tell me!" Lynn paused from snapping green beans.

"Remember I got an eighty-three on the last biology test? I just learned that he grades on the curve. He makes the test too hard to get a perfect score on. Then he takes the highest score and uses that as A." She paused for effect. "The highest score was eighty-five!"

"Is that good?" Miss Priss quit snapping beans.

"I got an A! I still have the final exam, but I'm confident. And I feel I aced the online course. I'm on a roll!"

Lynn seemed just as happy. "Congratulations! We must do something special."

"Coming home to hear someone say 'congratulations,' being supportive, is sufficient for today. Thank you."

Miss Priss slid off her stool and tore across the room to throw her arms around Judith. "Good! You want to hear something else?"

"Of course." Judith grinned back at her. "What?"

"One of the hens laid a brown egg and it was still warm and G'ma said hens cackle when they lay an egg. Did you know that?"

"Really, an egg?"

"It's that one here on the counter in a bowl. See it?" Miss Priss scrambled back up on a stool and reached for the dish.

"I can see it. Yep, that is some egg."

"Will we get white eggs too?"

"I don't think so. You have to have leghorn chickens for white eggs. They are a white bird."

Lynn crossed to the fridge and pulled out sandwich fixings, setting them on the counter. "I made up tuna salad."

"'Cause that's my favorite," Miss Priss explained, "besides peanut butter and jam."

"Mine, too. Let me go change and I'll be right back." Judith grabbed her backpack and headed for her room.

Lynn called after her, "If you have any whites that need washing, I'm putting a load in and need more."

"Thanks, I do." They had learned that worked for all of them and made laundry easier too.

She dumped her pack on the bed, donned shorts and a T-shirt, pulled her white towel off the rack, and scooping up her white laundry, she headed back to the kitchen. *Doing so well in school sure makes a body energetic!*

She plopped her whites on top of the washing machine. Miss Priss was setting the lunch table out on deck, so she headed there.

Lynn came out with a pitcher of iced tea. "Studying this afternoon?"

"I figured more biology review after dinner for an hour or two and then I'll take the rest of the evening off to relax. I think I'm pretty much ready for tomorrow. And then it's over. Until fall semester in a few days."

"You never cease to amaze me. People like me used to hate people like you. Whatever happened to the all-night cramming?"

"Some do, I don't. This works best for me."

"Then tonight we celebrate. Angela will be home early and I'll go get the steaks out. Okay if I call Maggie and invite them all?"

"Tommy and his family, too?"

"I think he has a commitment, but I'll check."

In two glass sheet cake pans, Lynn prepared a marinade for the steaks.

"Roasting ears tonight?" Judith asked.

"Of course. Perfect with steaks." Lynn laid the meat in the pans and covered it. "And I was thinking home fries. I have the potatoes cubed and soaking in ice water."

"Love the way you think."

Judith settled herself to snapping beans. They had the last of them ready when Angela got back from work. She plopped onto a stool at the kitchen counter. "How did pre-calc go?"

"Smooth as a slug in mayonnaise!"

"Oh, gag!" Angela stared at her. "Where'd you get that?"

Judith grinned. "Hey, that's one of the least offensive; I'm learning a lot from these little college kids."

"I can imagine." Angela licked her lips, hesitated. "Want to go out on the lake? Fish half an hour? Something?"

*Nooo!* Judith's rigid, unchanging self screamed.

*Resilience. Remember?* But that meant changing, doing something she could not do. *Resilience!*

"I guess." She licked her lips. "Sure, all right."

Angela dug the life jackets out of the shed and they strolled down to the dock, Angela bouncing, Judith slogging as if on her way to the gallows. No. This was so wrong.

Angela flipped the canoe into the water, dropped in the paddles, and stepped into it near the front.

Judith handed her a tackle box and rod and laid another rod near the backseat.

. . . And lowered herself into the canoe as her whole body shrieked, *Don't!*

She sat down in back, tentatively. *Resilience. Remember that. You're putting your father's negative lessons behind you. You're improving your character.* She picked up her paddle as Angela pushed them away from the dock. *Passive suicide is a character improvement?* Her hands shook and she felt like throwing up. *No, please, God!*

Judith watched Angela tie on a dry fly. "Fly-fishing? Trout? Not walleyes?" At least her voice didn't tremble the way her hands did. She broke out in a sweat.

Angela was grinning; obviously she enjoyed this immensely. "Since we won't go to bed hungry if I fail to catch anything, I'm going for the bad boys. Go for the gold, I always say. Well, maybe not always. Go for the gold when it's convenient."

Judith paddled and J-stroked as Angela set a slow, casual rhythm; they cruised across to a cove. Then Angela shipped her paddle and flicked her rod, the lure whipping away over the water. The canoe glided silently. Ah, there was mama loon out there—well, Judith thought it was the mama. Even Mama was silent this late in the season.

*Hey, thank you, God, for seeing me through the semester! I am grateful. And next semester should be even better; I'm in the swing of it again. Thank you! Thank you.* Judith's heart sang and her body sulked, forced into an act of resilience.

Angela's rod whistled again; her fly sailed casually through the air and plopped near the fallen tree. Judith shipped her paddle and just soaked up the peace of this quiet evening.

*Peace.* Angela spoke often of at last finding peace. Lynn had always known it, probably, even in the depths of grief. And Judith was learning it. She smiled to herself. Someday little Miss Priss, now a constant maelstrom of activity, would be an adult, and she too would discover peace.

Off to the side, a fish leaped out of the water and splashed back in.

"Over here, turkey! My fly is over here!" Angela jabbed a finger, pointing, and they both laughed.

Judith dipped her paddle and started slowly gliding back.

If they hugged the shore and Angela fished her way back to the dock, she might catch something.

But she didn't.

They tossed their gear up on the dock.

"I'll help set up dinner." Angela got out and headed for the house. Judith stood up, stepped onto the dock, as the canoe did not bob much at all, and pulled the bow painter in to bring the canoe's nose around ninety degrees. Ninety degrees reminded her—analytic geometry next semester *and* first-semester calculus. Silly as it sounded, she felt almost ready. In fact, she was rather looking forward to it. She dragged the canoe up onto the dock nose first and flipped it upside down, so that rain would not collect in it.

Miss Priss was in the kitchen with Lynn when they went inside. "We're going to have a big dinner!"

Judith grinned. "We sure are. Hmm. Maybe I should make a wacky cake."

Miss Priss made such a face, they all burst out laughing.

That night under the stars, after all the others had gone home and things were back to normal, Judith broke the long but comfortable silence. "I did it."

"Which it are you speaking of?"

"Right now I was thinking of us paddling out on that lake again in the canoe and I could finally force myself to do it; not only do it, but relax and enjoy myself. It's a first."

Angela gaped. "I didn't know you were still struggling with that. You got past that on your own? Why didn't you say something when I asked you to go?"

"Asking for help was not permitted when I was growing up. I was expected to automatically know how to do anything. And emotional things, you never asked for help. You just didn't talk about them. I guess we were supposed to be strong enough to handle them alone." She thought about her father, locked alone in his grief when she was right there, locked in hers. But that was past. It was time to let go.

Angela wagged her head. "I was so scared the first time I ventured out after that spill. I really needed Phillip then. He is an excellent instructor, even when you're terrified. Now I feel confident out there."

"And that gives him great joy, Angela, although he'd probably never say that. Incidentally, both of you"—Lynn nodded to each of them—"he and Tom asked me if they could give you both the honorary title of Auntie."

Angela and Judith looked at each other, shrugged, grinned, and nodded.

"I think we are officially members of the family," Angela said. "I am honored."

"Me, too. I think that will be easier for the kids. All this *miss* stuff, sounds too southern for this northerner. Auntie or Aunt Judith. Nice ring."

Chuckles floated into the breeze.

"And acing finals! I never dreamed I could do such a thing."

"Wait a minute. What kinds of grades did you get that year you went when you were young?" Angela asked.

"All A's. But so much was different then. Now it's more complex, more—"

"That's it! Stop now! Studies show that returning students who have lived a bunch of years most often score higher than the younger classmates except in computer sciences. So, our experience and our desire count. Count a lot. Let alone the brain power."

They froze as the owl hooted and did a flyover.

Judith sucked in air. "Oh, I've not seen her up close like that. She looks so big. Another gift for today."

Angela laughed. "Bask in the feel-good, Judith. You earned it."

"Thank you. You know what I am going to do tomorrow? I made the appointment this afternoon."

"The way things are going, who knows?"

"I am going to go get my hair cut. Off with this long, wrapped, and pinned-up pile of hair. I'm thinking shoulder length. And the hair will go to Locks of Love."

"Look out, world, a new Judith Rutherford is on her way!"

"For the first time in twenty years, I'm dreaming. While I love the Auntie title and will keep it always—thank you, Lynn, you and the boys—I want to be Dr. Rutherford."

"Not medical, I hope," Lynn said with a groan.

Angela giggled. "I think she means archaeology."

"Something else I came to a realization about." Judith nodded as she spoke, as if to emphasize. "These last couple weeks I've been looking back, and I can see that I was so alone and I didn't even know I was alone. Distant father, deceased mother. Melody always so far away. Only now with my first true friends do I not feel alone; only now can I see the difference. Does that make any sense?"

"Absolutely. Even more sense than cutting your hair or taking calculus."

Angela snickered.

"I have a suggestion." Judith picked it up again.

"Okay." But Lynn looked at her suspiciously; it was more like a question.

"Those letters we wrote to the people we're supposed to forgive. I suggest we go get them and burn them in the fire pit. All of this over and done with. Closure, I guess I'm saying."

"God used burnt offerings all through the Old Testament. Incense rising to Him. I think this is a very good idea." Lynn lifted Miss Minerva to the side and got up. "I'll be right back, and I'll bring the fire starter."

A few minutes later they gathered around the metal fire pit and dropped their letters in. Lynn clicked the fire starter and laid the flame to the corner of each, then pulled the wire screen dome into place. The three locked arms and watched the flames. The letters curled, blackened, and the flames went out.

Judith left the trio and grabbed a box of tissues to pass around. "Lord God, thank you."

"Let this smell sweet to you," Angela added. She blew her nose and locked arms again.

Lynn simply let the tears run down her cheeks un-mopped. "Lord, you brought us together in such strange ways, we have to know it all came from you. And now this. You have made us not only friends, but more like sisters, sister friends. Thank you and may this be the beginning of our new life of adventures, the greatest one being, getting to know you better. Help us to walk always seeking your face."

The owl alit in the maple by the shed and settled herself onto the branch. Homer came to stand beside them, nosing Judith's hand. Miss Minerva chirped from the lounger. Frogs sang from the lake.

"I say we go have some of Judith's wacky cake and raise a toast to us, to the future, and to our God who always hears. Who knows what adventures are ahead."

"But Him."

Minerva padded over and rubbed against Homer. The three women looked down expecting the dog to explode but he didn't. Dog and cat followed them into the kitchen and both demanded treats.

Judith pointed at the two. "See, miracles do happen, to us and even to them. I don't think this is a someday home any longer. I think we all have a very real home. Since we now have six eggs, perhaps we should have omelets for breakfast. Thanks to my dream chickens."

"In our dream house, on a dream lake, with me as a librarian, Judith a brilliant student with big dreams, and Lynn seeing her home have family again. If we didn't know and experience all this really happening, we wouldn't believe it, either."

And away out on the lake, a loon called.

# Epilogue

Angela—Auntie Angela if you wish—smiled even though her seat was really not all that comfortable. She and four hundred other uncomfortable people sat in this huge auditorium, waiting for the graduates to appear. She glanced again at the brief program with dread; the shorter the printed program, the longer winded the speakers listed thereon. It was surely a law somewhere.

After a brief intro, the university's orchestra down in the pit launched into "Pomp and Circumstance." Actually, Angela was impressed. They produced a strong, broad sound. The graduates entered, some stately and some giggling, and filled the rows reserved for them. Being Rutherford, Judith was in the midst of the back end, alphabetically speaking.

Beside Angela, Lynn pointed. "There she is, third from the aisle on this side."

To Lynn's left, Miss Priss whispered loudly, "How come I didn't get to do this when second grade was over with?"

"Second graders graduate by going to third grade." Angela smiled at her.

"But when can I wear a hat like that?"

Angela frowned. "Lynn? Do middle schoolers have a formal graduation?"

"Not in this system."

"When you finish twelfth grade."

Miss Priss groaned. "I'll be *old* then!"

"That's okay, dear," Angela purred. "Graduation ceremonies allow for wheelchairs and walkers."

Beyond Miss Priss, Phillip burst out laughing.

"It's not funny!" Miss Priss pouted.

Tom, beyond Phillip, and Maggie and Josie at the end of the row, were snickering too. In the row ahead, Dan, Doug, Travis, and Davey twisted in their seats to look. Paul's Plumbing had closed for four days so that the whole clan could come to Duluth. Angela really liked that they all cared so much they put family ahead of profit.

Lynn shushed Miss Priss as a speaker in graduation garb stepped up to the lectern. The speaker said all the usual words of welcome and introduced the next speaker, Meredith Pollan, chair of the anthropology department here at the University of Minnesota–Duluth, who would announce the name of this graduating class's outstanding graduate.

Angela frowned at her program. Meredith Pollan. She had heard that name before, where?

Dr. Pollan stepped to the lectern and adjusted the mike. She appeared quite likable, with short salt-and-pepper hair, an enviable tan, and a build neither fat nor skinny. And for a brief moment, Angela regretted all over again trying to be so thin for all those years.

Dr. Pollan nodded to left and right. "Graduates. Parents, grandparents, siblings, friends, and whomever I missed there. Each year the university faculty convene to choose an outstanding student, one who reflects the school's mission, a person who exemplifies what student life should be. Sometimes it takes three or four votes to arrive at a winner. This year's outstanding graduate took it on the first vote."

Angela smiled. Not something that would carry any

weight on a résumé, but a nice feather in the cap all the same.

Dr. Pollan continued, "If faculty could build the perfect student, they'd make one who loves to learn; in fact, who takes courses not for the grade average boost but because the student wants that information. The best students follow advice offered by informed people and ask for help when they need it. The very best students prepare for an engaging career in a field they enjoy, a labor of love, and monetary reward is a distant second."

*That would be Judith.* Angela nodded to herself.

"Our outstanding student in this class brought to her school experience a strong background in historic site management and a strong desire to learn. In fact, she—"

Angela looked at Lynn and Lynn looked at Angela. Judith's Rutherford House was now a historic site.

"—brought all the attributes of an outstanding student that I just enumerated. By taking summer classes and heavy winter course loads, she completed her AA in Detroit Lakes and her bachelor's degree here in three years instead of the standard four, a massive accomplishment. She—"

*It was Judith!* Angela's heart swelled. She clapped her hands over her mouth to keep the happiness from bursting out.

"—plans to enroll in master's work here this fall. I present to you the outstanding student of this class, Judith Rutherford." She extended a hand toward the graduates. "Judith?"

Angela and all the Lundbergs leaped to their feet and began applauding with wild enthusiasm. Travis whistled piercingly. As Judith made her way to the stage, others here and there in the audience stood. And others. By the time she reached the lectern, she was receiving a full-blown standing ovation. Wisely, Dr. Pollan handed Judith a tissue as she stepped back.

The auditorium quieted and people sat down.

Judith blotted her eyes and nose. "I am grateful. And immensely honored. And even more immensely humbled. Because, you see, I have learned that a student who succeeds does not succeed alone." She was looking straight at the Lundberg clan. "So many others. For support, for guidance, for help, for understanding. For doing the dishes while I go back to studying. For feeding my chickens when I have a big exam that day. For being strong and true friends. Having such loyal friends is as new to me as is this degree. I treasure it all. I am so blessed by God. Thank you." She turned to the trustees seated behind her on the stage. "Thank you."

*Thank you.* It applied to Angela and Lynn as well, in spades.

The rest of the ceremony zipped past Angela; she couldn't even remember who the distinguished guest speaker was. How could so many life-changing things happen in three years? Angela glanced at Lynn, who hardly ever got hot flashes anymore, not that she missed that. And Angela weighed exactly what she'd weighed in high school.

Charles and Gwynn would be coming for a visit this summer. She could not wait to take them fishing. The guest speaker droned on. They'd need two boats; maybe she and Gwynn could take the rowboat and give Judith and Charles the canoe.

And now Judith walked up to receive her degree and shake hands with the personages onstage. She was grinning brightly, such a wonderful change from the shy, reserved, suspicious woman who had moved into their someday home. She was still quiet and reserved—of course, that was Judith—but she had opened up so much, broadening her world. She seemed much more ready now to handle the new things—not all of them pleasant—that life threw at her. Her cousin Melody ran down the aisle to the stage and handed Judith a gorgeous bouquet.

And had Angela changed as much as those two? She had to think about that. Yes, she probably had. The children said Jack had managed to get his house back and was considering remarriage. Had he matured? Become a little wiser? Maybe three years could do that. Wait and see. Angela's change was that she was now, finally, genuinely happy for him, being what he is.

Here came the graduates filing out as the audience stood applauding.

Suddenly Miss Priss pushed past Angela and ran to throw her arms around Auntie Judith. The two exited the auditorium hand in hand.

"I'm so sorry," Maggie said afterward, yanking Miss Priss roughly to her side.

"Why, I'm not. She made me feel ten feet tall." Judith leaned over to drop a kiss on the little girl, who was growing so fast that she did not have to bend much at all.

And Angela thought to herself, *Judith, you are ten feet tall*.

As they so often did, the three sat inside looking out at the lake. Spring rain sluiced down the big windows. The fireplace crackled and reflected in the glass, making the room even more comforting. Homer snored at their feet, and Miss Minerva lay curled up right beside his chin.

"What a ride it has been." Lynn watched the fire. "We know Judith's triumph. What have the rest of us gained in these last few years?"

"Not just a degree." Judith smiled. "All my life I wanted sisters. Now I have two. Lynn, you didn't really need sisters. What have you gained?"

Lynn leaned her head back and stared up at the ceiling. "For me, a new life. I feel like with the two of you here, my new life has really begun; I'm no longer trying to hang on to the old one."

"You mean letting go of the past? And grief?" Angela got up and put another chunk of wood on the fire. Then, hands tucked in the rear pockets of her jeans, she studied the flames.

"Exactly. And finally making peace with a life without Paul, letting it soak into my heart as well as my head. One door closes, others open. What about you, Angela?"

"This is so hard, zeroing in on one thing. You sisters and my new life in the library are so integral now that I have a hard time thinking back to without you. But probably the highlight for me is freedom." She paused a moment. "I suspect some would say that Jack's demands that I change who I am were a subtle form of emotional abuse. Whatever, I am free of it, with the help of you two. And now that I'm me again, I feel much closer to my heavenly Father. I am so incredibly blessed."

Lynn was nodding. "That we all are. Interesting that we all feel so much the same way. We've been through a lot these last couple of years. And I have a feeling, this next one is going to bring even more adventures."

# Reading Group Guide
## Discussion Questions

1. Had you heard of shared housing before reading *Some-day Home*? How did you hear about it and from where?

2. Which of the three main characters did you relate to the most and why?

3. Lynn thought she went into this idea with her eyes wide open. What do you think was the hardest thing for her to work with?

4. Each of the main characters had to make some personality changes for them to become a kind of family. Whose challenges did you think were the most difficult, or the easiest, and why?

5. The need to make changes is a real challenge for most of us. What has happened in your life that caused you to make changes?

6. Looking back on the changes you have made, what is one you wish you had made earlier?

7. After writing this book, shared housing seems to make good sense to me and I might be willing to try it. What about you?

8. Since *Someday Home* is all about change, how has this novel encouraged you to make changes you might have been putting off?

9. While doing research for this book, some of those I interviewed were already friends before life brought them to shared housing. How do you think this existing relationship would make a difference in their new living arrangement?

10. What was your favorite part of the book and why?

# Contemporary novels that celebrate love and family by Lauraine Snelling

## *Heaven Sent Rain*

"Snelling's story has the potential to be a big hit."
—*RT Book Reviews*

Scientist Dinah Talyor's life becomes increasingly complicated when she meets seven-year-old Jonah Morgan and his dog. As their friendship grows and the child faces a series of trying events, Dinah must decide just how much responsibility she's capable of taking on.

## *Wake the Dawn*

"Snelling's description of events at the small clinic during the storm is not to be missed."
—*Publishers Weekly*

Physician's assistant Esther Hansen struggles to run an ill-equipped smalltown clinic during a devastating storm. But she is both tested and finds healing when a grieving border patrolman arrives with an abandoned baby.

# Reunion

"Inspired by events in Snelling's own life, *Reunion* is a beautiful story."

—*RT Book Reviews*

Kiera Johnston is shaken when she uncovers the fifty-year-old secret that she was adopted, and soon after her teenaged niece's pregnancy is revealed. Will love be enough to hold the Sorenson family together in spite of these challenging truths?

# On Hummingbird Wings

"Snelling can certainly charm."

—*Publishers Weekly*

Gillian Ormsby arrives in California to care for her ailing mother with plans to return to New York as quickly as possible. But as her friendship with her mother's neighbor develops into more, Gillian considers trading professional success for a renewed and rewarding sense of family.

# One Perfect Day

"[A] spiritually challenging and emotionally taut story. Fans of Christian women's fiction will enjoy this winning novel."

—*Publishers Weekly*

Only days before Christmas, the tragic loss of a child devastates one mother but offers another the miracle she's been praying for. The gift of second chances made bittersweet, can these mothers find hope in knowing that the spirit of each child lives on?

# Breaking Free

"Reminding us that love can spring forth from ashes, that life can emerge from death, Lauraine Snelling writes a gripping and powerful novel that will inspire and uplift you."

—Lynne Hinton, author of *The Last Odd Day*

Maggie Roberts gains a renewed sense of purpose through working to keep a horse from being discarded. But her reason for living is threatened when a local businessman offers the horse a permanent home.

*Available in trade paperback and ebook formats wherever books are sold.*